Some Hero

By the Same Author

The Blue Marauders is a young-adult novel about a travel soccer team overcoming long odds to compete with the league's traditional powers. The book, available on Amazon, or to order from local bookstores, is perfect for kids playing travel soccer and for the parents driving them to their games.

Some Hero

Ted MacVeagh

STONE POND PRESS

STONE POND PRESS
PO Box 183, Thetford, VT 05074

Text and Cover Design: Linnea Spelman

First Edition, 2024

For information, contact Stone Pond Press at
stonepondpress@gmail.com

City of Publication: Thetford, VT, USA

Publisher's Cataloging-in-Publication
(Provided by Cassidy Cataloguing Services, Inc.)

Title: Some hero / Ted MacVeagh.
Description: First edition. | Thetford, VT : Stone Pond Press, [2024]
Identifiers: ISBN: 978-0-9972236-2-0 (paperback) | 978-0-9972236-3-7
(E-book) | LCCN: 2024922655
Subjects: LCSH: Teachers--Fiction. | Superheroes--Fiction. | Love--
Humor. | Teaching--Fiction. | Superheroes in comics--Fiction. | Comic
books, strips, etc.--Social aspects--Fiction. | Self-actualization (Psy-
chology)--Fiction. | Black humor--Fiction. | Conduct of life--Fiction. |
Romance fiction. | BISAC: FICTION / Literary. | FICTION / Romance /
Romantic Comedy. | FICTION / Humorous / Dark Humor.
Classification: LCC: PS3613.A28338 S66 2024 | DDC: 813/.6--dc23

For Alex, Lily and Casey

 Flight

CHAPTER 1
First Flight

The place to begin, ordinarily, is with an origin story. So here goes.

It all happened in the year I was teaching English in Boston at the Raymond H. Flynn High School (better known as the "Flynn") while I was studying for my teacher certification. It wasn't really that I wanted to be a teacher. I wanted to go to business or law school, or maybe become an architect, or go into advertising. But I'd done two years at Teach For America after college, and I hadn't gotten around to taking the GMATs or LSATs yet, and no one else was hiring. So when this job came open, and my mentor at TFA said it was basically mine for the taking if I enrolled in a teaching cert. course, I thought *Why not?* I had nothing else to do. Besides, I sort of liked teaching. I liked the kids.

It was September, the cold part of the month, and I was at work late. I was just collecting my backpack in the tiny office with a single desk that I shared with two other first-year teachers when Ellen looked in to shoot the breeze. Ellen teaches biology. She was my age, but already had her teaching certification, and was in her second year at Flynn. I would have left as soon as Ellen shoved off, but as I was about to go, I heard Sylvia and Principal Snowe out in the hallway, two people I definitely wanted to avoid.

Sylvia is the head of the English department and my immediate boss. I have nothing against her, except that she sits too close to me and constantly pats my knee or shoulder while we talk. If she wasn't in her fifties or something, I would think she had a major crush on me. The kids are all pretty terrified of Principal Snowe, and I understand where they're coming from. She has sat in on a couple of my classes, and though she has been encouraging, I feel she is disappointed in me.

Anyway, instead of heading out, I decided to wait until the voices moved away. As I had time to kill, and as I had stupidly left my phone at home that morning, I figured I might as well do something useful. So I started grading a batch of quizzes.

When I finally emerged from the school, I was hurrying to catch the bus. The bus stop is about five blocks from the school, and the buses only come once an hour. It was raining, so I didn't want to miss it. I started running hard, because I was still half a block away as the bus pulled into the stop, when a stupid little dog ran across my path. I jumped to avoid tripping over the thing, and I just kept going. I cleared the dog and then sailed totally over the bus.

Okay, Hank points out that's not really an origin story. It's a how-did-I-discover-my-powers story. Origin stories say how you *got* your powers. Hank's my roommate, by the way, and I'll get to him later.

But it was weird. After clearing the bus, I just kept going. It felt like I was being pushed along by an invisible hand. After the initial shock wore off, I started screaming and flailing my hands and legs trying to stop my momentum. Instead, I went higher and faster. I finally leveled out at like five stories up and maybe forty miles an hour, judging by the cars below me.

At that point I was vertical, like I was walking, and the wind was an absolute bitch. But I was afraid to try to lay out, because I wanted my legs under me if and when I landed. I mean, that's like Flying 101: don't land on your head.

The worst part came when I realized the road I was flying above came to an end at an office tower, and that I was heading straight at it. At the last second, in desperation, I tried to jump again, though there was nothing to push off against. I soared almost straight upward, roughly to the height of the Hancock Tower, before I stopped climbing. Once I cleared the building, I was finally able to work myself to a more or less horizontal position.

My eyesight was amazing—I could see everything happening in the streets clear as day—so that must be a gimme with flying. It took me almost half an hour, and I was deep in the suburbs, before I got a rudimentary idea how to steer. It turned out, it's not like sailing or jet flying or anything, where you use wind resistance or whatever to change directions, putting flaps down and all that business. It was all in the mind. I had to think left, right, up, down, slow and fast. It isn't as easy as it sounds, because who knows how much thought is required for a hard left versus an easy left. It took some calibration.

For a while I was scared to think about slowing down, because I didn't want to hit a stall speed and drop from the sky. So I wanted to be close enough to the ground before I slowed down too much. But I was also nervous about the down commands. I didn't want to overdo it and go into a nose dive.

Also, I didn't want to land where there were a lot of people to see me. Whatever was happening, I didn't want some TikTok of me landing on my ass to go viral. I was pretty sure that no one had seen my takeoff, despite the flailing and the screaming, because the road had been empty, it had been dark and rainy, and I had gotten above eye level quickly. So I wanted to keep the landing quiet too.

I finally hit on a plan. After working on left and right commands for a while, I nudged myself around, so I was heading back into

Boston. Genentech, the pharmaceutical company, had a building along the Charles River with a long flat roof. If I could adjust my height to the right level, I could use it as a runway and land on top. I'd come in just a few feet above it, think *SLOW* as I came over it, then *DOWN* as I slowed and finally *STOP.*

So I made my way jerkily toward Genentech. I had to make three passes before I was at the right height. On the third try, I came in just where I wanted, maybe two feet over the roof. I am pretty sure that when I was flying my perception of height, speed, distance and direction were enhanced too. Another gimme.

At any rate, I thought *slow, down, stop* as planned, and it worked fine. I tumbled as I landed, but that was mostly at surprise at how smooth the landing was. I could have stuck it.

I didn't have my phone, so I didn't know the time, but I figured it must have been near eight o'clock. I'd been flying for at least an hour, I'd made it to the Boston suburbs and back, and I was barely winded. I hadn't been cold either, which was amazing considering it was September and I was soaked to the skin. So flying had some other freebies. It didn't seem to take any energy, and it made me almost impervious to cold and rain.

But the freebies only worked when I was flying. Once I landed, I was wet and freezing my ass off.

Now the problem was that I was stuck on the roof. I didn't know how to get down. I found two doors, but both were locked from the inside, like they were afraid some cat burglar might climb up and sneak in through the roof. Which seemed paranoid to me.

Even if I could have gotten in the building, I wasn't sure what sort of reception I'd get coming in from the roof. Security would take me for a bad guy for sure.

On the other hand, I was so cold and wet I didn't really care what happened. I just knew I didn't want to stay up on the roof for long.

Well, a voice in my head said, *there's one easy solution.*

What's that? said the voice in my head that was really more me.
Leave the way you came in.
You mean . . . ?
Yeah. Fly out of here.
Gulp.

I went as near the edge of the roof as I could bring myself. Nothing about jumping off the roof appealed to me. It was a long way down. I'm not really squeamish about heights, and I was okay with the flying before. But it's one thing to fly when you start on the ground. It's another when you start on top of a building. It raises the stakes, so to speak.

You look like a doofus when you fall after jumping up from the ground. You look much worse when you do the same thing from the top of a building.

I went to bang on each of the doors to the roof. No luck. I couldn't even get myself arrested. It looked like the only way off the roof, unless I wanted to spend the night, was . . . off the roof.

But I wasn't going to just jump off the ledge. My balls weren't that big. I figured if I'd used the roof as a runway to land, I could use it to take off too. I didn't know if I had to get to some velocity before I could start to fly, but I figured it wouldn't hurt. I went all the way to one end of the roof and started to run, intending to jump when I was just about halfway across, so I would still be on the roof if I fell on my face.

I'm sure I jumped before reaching the edge of the roof, but it was confusing. Because whenever it was I jumped, it was like the wind caught me and swept me along, so I couldn't stop. I careened off the building, not knowing if I was flying or falling. Once again, hear the screams, see the flailing.

I didn't fall. After clearing the roof and having several Wiley E. Coyote-like seconds, suspended in the air, waiting to fall, I swooshed upwards as high as I'd ever gone. I don't know how high, but through some thick rain clouds that were hanging over the city.

The first flight was nothing but a terrifying blur. On the second, I began to get my bearings. First, I worked myself into the more classic flight position, horizontal, with my arms out in front cutting through the air like a diver. I tried the fists clenched, like in some of the Superman movies, but in the end I liked the hands pointed, with the thumbs entwined. It felt elegant. I also began to get a better sense of controlling my turns, so they weren't so herky-jerky.

By the time I landed again, this time on the Cambridge Common near my apartment, I was feeling pretty good. I didn't stick the landing, but I stayed on my feet. So all I had to do was figure out how to take off without the arms and legs flailing and I'd be pretty smooth.

You might have thought I'd have flown all night, but that didn't occur to me then. First of all, I thought I'd be able to fly for the rest of my life. Second, even though flying didn't make me tired, I was really hungry. And, at that moment, the thought of heading back to my apartment and chowing down on some noodles and cheese sauce seemed even more attractive than another flight over Boston.

CHAPTER 2

Talking to Hank

So I still owe you the origin story. The thing is, I don't know it. I don't know how I got my powers.

You can't rule out some weird chemical mix, like the Flash without the lightning bolt. Like any kid growing up in the US in the aughts, I ate enough vitamins and junk food that I probably had every chemical known to man sloshing around my body at some point.

And you've got the potential of activation through radiation, like the Hulk, Spiderman, Daredevil and many others. I grew up near the Mount Kisco power plant, where my dad was a technician. I don't remember hearing about any power leaks, but who knows? They may have been hushed up.

My mom told me that on a trip to New York once I fell in the East River. It was only for a few seconds before she pulled me out, and nothing ever came of it, but they say the East River is a primordial soup of strange, mutated organisms and chemicals. Some of them could have gotten in my bloodstream.

I was bitten by a bat once and had to get antibiotic shots in case of rabies. I also got a tick bite and never received treatment for it. We thought we caught it before it attached, or engorged, or whatever the dangerous time is. But maybe I had some sort of delayed reaction. Unlikely, but I'm just saying.

And of course the ticks and the bats also grew up around the power plant, for what that's worth.

Maybe a magical explanation works better than a scientific one. I grew up reading comic books. I always wanted, really desperately wanted, to have superpowers. I am sure I wished for them lots of times, on first stars, on birthday candles, on wish bones, on random rings or stones found in the street. So maybe one of those wishes was answered. Maybe more than one, and that's why everything's so confusing.

Maybe it's fate or some sort of higher power. You'll see I did at least some good things with my power, although I did shitty things too. Maybe one of the people I helped was fated to be helped, and maybe I was just the instrument of that higher power.

A possibility I like better is that I tapped into something in the mind, like a yogi mystic. Everyone could have the powers I had if they released the restraints on their psyches. The trouble with this theory is, first, though I did some yoga in college, I didn't do much. Second, my powers were pretty much entirely out of my control, at least my conscious control.

There's the *Matrix* theory too. You know, we're all brains in vats and I'm like Neo, the chosen one who can manipulate the computer program that is the Matrix. But why should that be the case? Hank says that unless there is a reason I'm "the one," this isn't an explanation at all.

I realize that none of these ideas are the slightest bit likely, but it's all I've got. And are they more or less likely than my flying in the first place? Hank and I talked about it for hours. At first, Hank wouldn't let it drop. But I wasn't much interested. I realized origin stories are much more important to those who don't have a superpower than to those who do. Hank wanted to know how he could get my powers. I just wanted to know how I could use them.

That's it then. There's no origin story; there's just discovering what the powers were and how to use them. Which was kind of cool, and kind of scary, and really annoying. You'll see what I mean by annoying soon enough.

When I finished my first night of flying, I went back to my apartment and made myself, like, three bowls of spaghetti, drank six beers and downed two pints of ice cream before I even thought about what had happened. Hank was home and just sort of watched me eat, amazed.

When I was finally done, I pushed my chair back, belched, and said, "I can fly."

I didn't mean to say it. In fact, I swore all the time that I was flying, and all the time that I was eating, that I would never tell anyone. First of all, they'd think I was crazy. Second, if I became a superhero, it would like immediately compromise my secret identity. Third, they'd want me to do favors for them the whole time.

Hey, Jason, can you drop this package off in Worcester? That kind of thing. *Give me a ride to work today. The T's super crowded.* Like the way people say you need to move if you ever win the lottery.

But I just sort of came out with it, and there it was. I mean Hank and I talked about almost everything. It would have been unnatural not to tell him. And I guess I wanted to tell someone. If anyone would understand, it was Hank-of-the-ten-thousand-comics-collection Nichols. And I did it without really thinking about it.

What I said just sort of hung between us for a moment.

Then Hank said, "What did you say?"

"I can fly. I flew home."

I don't know what you would say if someone said this to you, but you probably aren't like Hank. He said, "Since when?"

"Since today, I think. I've never done it before."

"Literally or metaphorically? I mean is this a sex thing?"

I'm a nerd. But Hank is a much bigger nerd. So in our friendship, I'm the one who explains worldly stuff, like stuff about sex, to him. He's always afraid that he's not going to know the latest slang, and people will laugh at him 'cause he thinks they're talking about something regular, like cars or swimming, and actually they're talking about something dirty.

"No, literally," I said. "Like in a plane, but without the plane."

"Prove it."

"I'd hit my head. We're indoors."

"Can't you hover?"

"I don't know. I wouldn't know how."

"What, so you can only fly forwards?"

"Or up. I flew out to Needham after work. I landed on the Genentech roof when I came back."

"C'mon."

You see how it is with Hank. You might have been skeptical right away. It took Hank like two minutes to get skeptical, and only after I refused to hover for him. That's what's so cool about Hank. So I jumped up thinking *Hover.* Stupid. I whacked my head on the ceiling and fell back down, killing my back on the coffee table. But I must have stayed up for a few seconds, or gone up higher than I should have, because Hank was totally convinced.

"How come you can fly all of a sudden?"

I shrugged. We started going through all the potential reasons (see above) and drew a blank.

"You gotta show me the real thing tomorrow," he said. "Does anyone else know?"

"No, I don't think so."

"What do you mean you don't think so?"

"I haven't told anyone. I don't think anyone noticed me."

"Yeah, but what about FAA radar? We should check out some flight-freak blogs, see if anyone reported anything."

I shrugged.

"Well, what are you going to do with it?"

I shrugged again. I was doing a lot of shrugging. I was sort of annoyed I'd told Hank before I thought all of this through.

"I don't know," I said finally. "It just happened."

Hank, however, had ideas. "Okay, you can't show me in the morning. People would see you. You should only fly at night. We should see if you have any other powers. Because maybe that's not all." He looked at me still holding my back from where I landed on the coffee table. "I guess you're not invulnerable."

"More's the pity. I did think I saw better when I was flying. And I wasn't cold or tired."

"How fast could you go?"

"I think I averaged around fifty. It took me an hour or so out to Needham and back. But I don't know what my top speed is."

"Didn't you test it?"

"No, I didn't. It didn't occur to me. It was pretty damned terrifying."

"Geez. So you might have like superspeed as well for all we know. I never saw someone eat so fast." Suddenly he threw his bowl of chips at me. The bowl thumped into my chest and spilled chips over me and the couch.

"What the hell did you do that for?"

"You didn't see it coming? Like in any sort of slow motion?"

"No!"

"I guess that rules out superspeed. But maybe you have super-strength. Or, wait, you said you had better sight only when you were flying? Maybe you're invulnerable or have superspeed or other stuff just when you're flying."

"Maybe, but why should I? I just found out I could fly. Why should I also be super-strong?"

"Why should you be able to fly?"

"One unlikely event does not make another unlikely event more likely."

"One sufficiently unlikely event creates doubt about everything we think we know. Anyway, there's a narrative logic that if you have one power you might have another."

"Right, narrative logic." Hank studied physics. I was the one who was an English major.

"So, what'll you do for a costume?"

I knew what he was thinking. It was the first thing that had crossed my mind too. We'd often talked about becoming heroes. Once I'd read an article about a guy in some place like Portland or Phoenix who'd decided to dress in a costume and fight crime. We talked about the possibility of doing that too, except Hank was a shrimpy, little dork, and I was a more normal-sized dork, neither of whom liked conflict or physical pain. So it was just talk.

Except that now I could fly. And people who can fly have to become superheroes. They just have to.

"I don't know. What do you think? A mask, definitely, 'cause I want a secret identity. And something warm. I was so cold when I landed last night."

"Maybe you should wear long johns."

"Great, long johns. I don't think Hawkman wore long johns."

"Yeah, he went around bare-chested. But he didn't moan about the cold. What about weapons? Hawkman carried a mace."

"I'm not that good a flyer. I'd hurt myself trying to hit someone with a mace while I was flying. Probably if I wasn't flying too."

"Well, you'll get better. But maybe at first, something to drop on people. Like hand grenades."

"I can't drop grenades in Boston. Are they even legal?"

"Well, what about rocks."

"I can always phone in to the police for backup." Less heroic, but better than dropping bombs.

"You can't carry a phone, man?"

"Why not?"

"You'd compromise your secret identity. Anyone can hack in and get the GPS data. They track the phone whizzing around Boston and you're caught."

We talked late that night, and I was really ready for bed when Hank finally let me go to sleep. I wondered briefly whether I would still be able to fly when I woke up, but I was asleep before I got too worked up about it.

CHAPTER 3
Trivial Pursuit

Hank was filled with plans the next morning. I had agreed with him that I would just fly at night and that I would not carry my phone. I also agreed never to mention my powers in any emails or texts.

He wanted to meet after work and head out to the Lincoln Arboretum to practice. He wanted to perform a lot of experiments to test the exact nature and limits of my power. He also banged on about all the reasons it was physically impossible, until I told him to shut up about it.

Instead he started in again about how I really should learn to use a mace, for the coolness factor if nothing else. I pointed out that, if I got close enough to hit someone with a mace, I would have lost the whole advantage of being able to fly.

My priority was that I didn't want to get shot. Hawkman either couldn't get hurt by gunfire or avoided shots by some inexplicable comic-book logic. But we were in the real world, and I would be an easy target flying up to someone with a mace. Hank said he'd think about alternatives.

I also pointed out that I couldn't come over right after work because it was trivia night, and my team was meeting at the Three

Harps pub for the evening competition. Hank was outraged.

"Are you kidding me, man? You are maybe the first person in the history of the world to suddenly get the power to fly, and you're going go to trivia night?"

"I'll meet you after. I don't want to let the team down."

"Fuck. Penny's going to be there, right?"

That annoyed me. I left, saying I had to go to work. But Hank was right, of course. Penny was going to be there. I had checked yesterday. She wasn't on our trivia team, but she showed up occasionally as an observer. She was in the history department with Toby Markham and came with him.

Hank didn't like Penny. He didn't think she was good for me. But he was wrong. She was amazingly beautiful. And I knew that if we could ever go out, my life would be complete.

Penny, properly Penelope Waters, had arrived at the Flynn a couple of years before me, and taught American history to juniors, Asian history to sophomores, and also served as the librarian. She had long, straight, honey-colored hair and flawless skin. It wasn't porcelain, because it had some color, but it had the same sense of smoothness. Her eyes were grey, and she looked at you with an incredible openness, like she was staring through you. She liked unfussy clothes, solid colors, no ruffles. She often looked like she had just come in from milking the cows. Very "Little House on the Prairie."

It's true that nothing had happened between us yet. But that was, first of all, because it had taken me two weeks to get the courage up to even talk to her. Second, when I did, I was too tongue-tied to be at my most charming. Third, she seemed to have an active social life outside of work. But I wasn't going to give up the chance to see her at a social occasion, no matter what.

Also, it had occurred to me that a man who can fly may have some sexual cachet that an ordinary high-school English teacher might not. There could be a serious Superman-Lois Lane moment if I could somehow find an excuse to sweep her up in my arms and fly her somewhere.

The people actually on the trivia team were Toby, Sylvia, Ellen, Raffy and me. Toby and Sylvia organized the team every year. They had each taught at Flynn for over twenty years, and bickered like an old married couple.

Sylvia, who I mentioned was my supervisor, taught English and French and played fantasy sports. She was the go-to person for any sports statistics. Toby taught Latin and history, and might have known everything in the world if knowledge had stopped accumulating in 1890. He was red-faced, balding and in somewhat better shape than was fitting for a man of his age.

Ellen was a science geek who knew everything about chemistry and biology, and also had a good grip on popular culture.

Raffy worked at Flynn as a techie, and was another math and science geek. He was only at the school as a part-time gig while working on a series of start-ups.

My role was English and American literature. I also backed Sylvia up at sports and Ellen in pop culture. My strength was trivia about books and writers that had nothing to do with anything important. In fact, until I could fly, it was the closest thing to a superpower I had. I could tell you the publication date of just about any book. I also knew about writers' lives, when they were born, when they died, where they went to college, who they married, what pets they had. That sort of thing.

Together we were pretty good, and had hopes of going far in the annual Boston-wide pub trivia tournament, which started in October. Tonight was just a local quiz we were doing for practice and to show off. I might have skipped if I wanted, but, as I said, Penny was going to be there.

I walked over to the Three Harps with Ellen and Raffy. Ellen was telling a story about teaching reproduction to tenth graders that

I normally would have enjoyed. But that evening, I was trying to think if there was a way that I could casually introduce flying into a conversation with Penny. I also wondered what advice Raffy might have. I mean, he was a start-up guy, and a supposed computer genius, so maybe he'd have some idea about how this happened to me.

Hank, who was at MIT getting his PhD in mathematical physics, would have disputed the description of Raffy as a genius. But, then again, Hank didn't like Raffy much, and figured if any of my friends deserved to be called a genius it was Hank himself.

The way I figured it was that Hank was brilliant in traditional academic ways, and Raffy was brilliant in like a new-economy, tech start-up way. Hank was jealous because Raffy was likely to make a lot more money that he would. While Hank was my best friend, and I totally respected his opinions, I thought a new-economy take on my superpower might be just what the doctor ordered. I mean, Raffy might know how I could make money off it. Not that Raffy had any money. He scrounged beers from me and Ellen once again that night.

I didn't get to tell anyone about my new powers. I couldn't find a way to talk with Raffy alone, and I didn't want to say anything to Ellen, who was fond of mocking what she said were "my pretensions." And Penny was squeezed between Toby and Sylvia the whole night, so I barely got to speak to her at all.

We romped at the trivia, but it didn't make me happy. Particularly when, after Sylvia left, and I had just managed to change seats so I would be next to Penny, two classically handsome, square-jawed types came in, and Penny immediately got up and excused herself, saying, "Oh, my friends are here. I have to go."

I should explain that I am not a classically handsome, square-jawed type myself, but I'm not bad. I owe that, I suppose, to Zach Braff. One of my theories is that Hollywood occasionally makes a character actor into a leading man and, suddenly, all of us with the face and bearing of that actor are rescued from ugliness. That happened with me when *Scrubs* appeared. Suddenly the Zach Braff look was all the rage, and instead of a dopey best friend, I could be my own star. Girls thought I had adorable eyes and the cutest smile. When I'm rocking the Zach, I can be a hit.

Michael Cera did the same thing for curly-haired dorks, and Spike Lee for spunky, height-challenged Black guys. Hank did a creditable *She's Gotta Have It* Spike Lee. If Raffy is ever going to get the girl, it's because he's doing more of the Michael Cera thing, and less of the John Heder from *Napoleon Dynamite*.

Older guys can play on Hollywood doppelgangers too. I think Toby goes for a Tony Curtis look, with some of the same struggles as an aging Tony. Sylvia has a pretty sweet late Joan Collins thing going. I'm not sure about Ellen. I think she may still be waiting for someone. I mean she's got a good figure, but her hair is a frizzy mess. It's hard to think of frizzy leading ladies.

Hollywood actors are almost all tens of their particular look, and I was no ten. But I was a Zach Braff seven at the very least. Probably an eight. Eight for a Zach Braff is like a seven Brad Pitt, but still, you're in the game.

Anyway, Penny is one of the few real-life girls who's a ten. Maybe that's why I can't even come up with a movie star to describe her. Tens are *sui generis*. So she was definitely worth pursuing. But if she was going to be hanging out with Brad Pitt-y bankers, it was going to be a tough fight.

I left the bar in a foul mood. I would've flown home, but Ellen insisted on walking with me to the Green Line. I might have blown her off but the school and the bar are in a bit of a tough neighborhood, so I figured I should at least walk her to the station. Once we got there, we took the T in opposite directions.

I didn't get back to the apartment until nine. Hank was waiting for me impatiently. He had my car packed up and was raring to go.

"Christ, Jason, I've been waiting for an hour at least."

"Hey, we said 8:30."

"I know, but it's nine. I hope you boned Penny at least."

"Ha, ha!" I said, but I didn't really like hearing that kind of thing about Penny, even though I knew that nerd speak was meant to embrace crude sexual imagery mostly to hide the essential innocence of our experience and imaginations. I mean, I am not saying I never did it myself, but it seemed wrong for my pure and chivalrous love for Penny.

"She didn't give you the time of day, did she?"

"What do you know about it?"

"Look, I know she's not interested in you."

"You've only ever met her like once."

"Yeah, and that's enough to realize she's not into you."

Once we got into the car, Hank cheered up, and I guess I did too. His big surprise was that he had managed to secure a cop's riot shield. One of the MIT polymer labs was testing them. He figured it was a good way for me to protect myself from bullets while I was flying. He also had a series of things that looked like lawn darts with rounded points, which he had hooked up around a belt.

"See some bad guy," he said, "you fly over and drop one of these on 'em. Gravity does the rest."

As we drove, I got nervous that I wouldn't be able to fly again. I was anxious for myself, but even more anxious for Hank, who'd put his trust in me.

It turned out I had nothing to worry about. We went out to the big field at the center of the arboretum and waited a few moments to make sure it was empty. Hank asked me if I was ready. I took a deep breath and started running. After ten yards, I jumped and thought *UP.* And just like the previous night, I sailed up in a vertical position, although this time I kept the flailing to a minimum. I quickly righted myself to horizontal and, having cleared the last copse of trees on the far end of the field in just a few seconds, banked around to land. I lowered my path and slowed my flight by degrees. I would have made a perfect landing except I had a bit too much speed and ended up pitching into a forward roll. Which was pretty cool. I had flown again, and it felt good.

Hank came rushing up. "That was fantastic! Let's do it again. We need to see how fast you can go. How quick you can turn. How well you see. A ton of stuff."

For the rest of the night, he ran me through a battery of tests, estimating my speed, endurance and other qualities. He must have planned all day. He'd brought a whole bunch of equipment, including a heart monitor, wireless GPS and altimeter devices, walkie-talkies and cones. He fixed the monitors on me, gave me a wireless headset and then shouted instructions into my ear as he watched my progress on his computer. He had me fly as high and fast as I could. He had me turn in tight circles. He had me swoop and dive. He had me locate cones on the ground from the air. He had me run courses around the trees. He had me fly on my right side, left side and upside down.

I didn't mind his yelling in my ear, at first, because I could tell that the practice was making me better and more confident. But, finally, I'd had enough. I swooped over him, dropped the headset at his feet and then soared up and away. I was tempted to buzz away and see how far I could fly, but then realized I was still interested in some of his tests. I was curious if I could fly with the riot shield, and if I could hit targets with Hank's darts. I came back down.

I told Hank what I wanted. He said, sure. Then he said, "Hey, do you think you can carry someone?"

"I don't know. I don't see why not." I was thinking of Penny.

"Will you carry me?"

Ah. Hank. A far cry from Penny, although about the same size. He said it so shyly it almost broke my heart. We were best friends.

Now I had something he wanted so bad, that he was practically begging me to share it.

"Sure," I said.

I went over to him, but did not know how to pick him up. We were awkward for a moment. Finally, he got on me piggyback. He was a little guy, but he was heavy. I thought *UP*, but nothing happened. I tried to run and jump, but I could only take a few steps. Instead of making it off the ground, I stumbled, fell and then got crushed by Hank landing on top of me.

"I don't think it will work," I said, lying next to him on the ground. "I can't lift you. I can't get off the ground."

"Fine," he said, but I could tell he was bummed. He wanted to feel what I felt.

All I could think was what a relief I hadn't tried to fly with Penny. That would have been a colossal fuckup.

We packed up soon after that and went to get something to eat. I ate like ten Big Macs while Hank gave me my official stats. My top speed was about a hundred twenty miles an hour. I could go 5,000 feet in the air before it affected my breathing. My eyesight was incredible, something like 20/5 or 20/4. Basically like an eagle.

I had hoped that the gimmes would include some other cool powers, superstrength or invulnerability, that would work while I was flying at least. But no such luck.

"So now you just need a name and a costume," Hank said.

Neither of us ever thought to wonder if being able to fly qualified me for being a superhero.

CHAPTER 4

Boston Traffic

The next night I chose my costume. A balaclava, black jeans and a black leather jacket. The balaclava was useful to hide my face, but also to keep the hair out of my eyes. I mentioned I look a little like Zach Braff. Well, my hair is a little like Zach's as well, pretty thick and worn longish and messy. Like I spent no time worrying about it. When I tweaked it just right, which was harder than you might think, I thought it looked pretty damn good. The rest of the time, though, it was a pain in the ass. I noticed on my first couple of flights that I was constantly blowing hair out of my eyes, or reaching up to try to smooth it back.

I also wore a belt that Hank had devised to carry the lawn darts, and a backpack, to stow the belt when I landed. Hank wanted me to wear a helmet, and offered me his bike helmet. I refused it.

"Hey, it'll protect you."

"I'm not going to crash."

"What if you hit a tree branch?"

"It's dorky."

"It's aerodynamic."

"Look, I'm not wearing it."

"What about the shield?"

"I can't fly with it."

"What you really need is a bulletproof vest."

"Yeah, what do they cost? Like a thousand bucks?"

"You need a sponsor."

"That'd be cool. Then I could quit my job. What's the pay rate for superheroes? I bet it beats first-year teachers."

"Phone?"

"Got it."

"No. No phone, remember." Hank stuck his hand out. "Give it over."

Damn, I had forgotten. I handed it over reluctantly.

"And you have the radio headset?" Hank asked.

"Yeah, but can't that be tracked as easily as the phone?"

"Nah, it's point to point. No network."

"The GPS you gave me has to link up with a satellite."

"Right, but unlike your phone, it doesn't have any identifying information on it. And the information it sends to my computer will be encrypted. You have it, right? The GPS tracker?"

"Sure. I'm all set. No worries."

But I was happy about his worry. I was nervous myself. The plan was that I would fly around the city looking for crime. When I saw it, I'd swoop down and stop it. Anything left over, I'd report to Hank over the headset, and he'd call the police. He'd also be tracking my movements via the GPS, so if anything happened, he could come and get me.

I know, I know. The plan's a net. More holes than string. But the point was I could fly, so we had to do something. And because I could fly, we figured we could get away with anything.

The main trouble was getting in the air safely. I wanted to find a place where I could take off without attracting too much attention. I was lucky the first night because it was raining, but the night of my first heroing was clear.

In the end, we decided that I should take off from the roof of our building. There was only a short flat area, but I was more confident about getting in the air now. We snuck up there around eleven, putting a stick in the door so it wouldn't lock.

Hank watched me take off. I waved and then soared away. He headed inside to track me on his computer. We knew that people looking up might see a dark shadow, but we figured that they'd think I was a bird or a bat or a drone. You could say we were naïve. I think we were just optimistic.

I figured that I would concentrate around Flynn. I kind of liked the idea of me being the neighborhood's guardian angel. I'd be the one to save the neighborhood. Mild-mannered teacher by day. By night, the Flynn Avenger. Not that that was my name. I hadn't yet decided on one.

I went high and circled the neighborhood, watching what was going on in the streets. The answer was: pretty much nothing. I practiced my turns and swoops in the air and I got bored. Every twenty minutes, Hank would ask how it was going over the headphones and I would respond, "All's well."

I had a pretty good view of the whole neighborhood surrounding Flynn, but it seemed like everyone was home watching television. What good was flying if all the bad-guy stuff was happening inside?

A couple of times I saw people looking up and pointing and I'd sweep upwards, far enough that I was pretty sure they wouldn't be able to make me out in the night sky.

It was only a little more than an hour before I had company. I had come down pretty low (maybe 500 feet) to check out an argument between a couple of kids when I heard a whirr above me. It was one of those television traffic helicopters and some guy was pointing a camera at me. I swept up and away at full speed, but the damn thing came chasing after me.

I soon realized I couldn't lose it going high and fast, because it could go just as high and fast. So I came back down, thinking I'd lose it in the city. I could fly lower than it, fit through tighter spaces and turn faster. But as I began to descend, I noticed two other copters headed toward us from the direction of Charlestown. Police copters, for Christ's sake. Either I'd tripped some radar, or the TV guys had reported me in. Or maybe the cops had simply been watching Channel Five. I was in trouble, and I had to get out of there fast.

"How are things?" Hank asked.

"Lousy," I shouted back. "I'm being followed by three copters. Two police and one television. I think I'm on TV."

"Fuck! Get out of there."

"That's what I'm doing."

I flew in a pretzel to get out of the sight of the television helicopter, then cut down low over the Fenway, heading east. The two police copters had lost me for the moment. They moved high, shining search lights down on the city, trying to pick me up. I wasn't sure where the traffic copter was. Maybe it had lost interest.

I cut into an alley formed between two skyscrapers where they'd have to be right on top of me to see me and slowed my speed way down. I couldn't land there because the street was too crowded. So I just hovered in the shadow of the building.

Hank's voice came over the headset. "I've got you on television. They think you may be a terrorist."

"Fuck!"

"But the weather guys have lost you, and it looks like the cops haven't locked onto you yet. Are you landed? You aren't moving."

"No. Everywhere below is pretty packed. I'm on some side street off Tremont. I'd guess about ten stories up."

"Yeah, you're on the GPS now. You're on Dedham. Jesus, the TV guys are headed back your way. Hey, head south down Dedham, then cut northeast. Cathedral Square is there, and you may be able to land. It's always pretty empty."

With nothing better to do, I followed Hank's advice. The buildings were low, three- and four-story apartments, and two-story single-family homes. I ducked down as far as I dared, but still above the street lights. I was moving fast too, maybe seventy.

I saw the cathedral and headed toward it. With nothing in front of me, I risked taking the time to look back. Two of the choppers were up nearer to the Charles, a third, one of the cop copters, was above me but spinning around like it was unsure which direction to go. I sped up and banked a sharp turn, hoping to get behind the cathedral's spire before any of the police search lights strafed me. I hovered within arm's reach of the far side of the spire for several seconds waiting to see how the chopper moved next. It purred away from me, and I finally looked down. As Hank said, the square was empty except for some bums huddled by a heating grate on Randolph. But they were more interested in their paper bags than the sky above them. I let myself down gently.

As soon as I landed, I pulled off the balaclava and took off the leather jacket, the lawn dart belt and the headset. I stuffed these in the backpack. Underneath the jacket, I wore a Red Sox sweatshirt. Hank and I had not expected that I'd be spotted so quickly, but we had at least figured I should be able to blend in case of emergencies. I ran my fingers through my hair and breathed. Unless someone looked in my backpack, there was nothing to connect me with the flyer, and I made it home without incident.

My first words to Hank were, "That SUCKED!"

"Yeah."

"What is the FUCKING point of being able to fly if you can't do it without being branded a terrorist?" When Hank didn't answer, I added, "And flying is not even a fucking superpower. It's doesn't let you do anything! Fuck, I'm hungry."

I ate a bowl of cereal while Hank made both of us grilled cheeses. I ate four of them. While I ate, Hank tried to have a conversation about what went wrong, and to "reexamine the assumptions" we had made about how I should use my powers.

Maybe we'd rushed the superhero thing, he said. Not that he was against it; we just had to plan more.

Plan for months, knowing him. I made it clear to him that I was in no mood.

"Maybe we should focus on how you got your powers. It might be interesting to take some tissue sample and get them analyzed at one of the MIT labs. I'd be curious about your red blood cell count."

I understood what he was doing. He still wanted the origin story. He wanted to fly too. I just wanted to be a hero.

"Fine," Hank said at some point, his tone indicating that I was being a jerk. "You want to fight crime. Go to the police or the military, show 'em what you can do and get deputized. They may even give you a bulletproof vest and some cool weapons. Maybe that invisibility cloak they're working on."

"You think I should do that?" I asked. I knew he was annoyed, but the suggestion had possibilities, even if we had previously agreed I should keep my powers secret.

"Of course not," Hank said. "If the Feds ever get their hands on you, they'll do worse than take tissue samples. They'll stick you in a government lab, and you'll be nothing but a lab rat for the rest of your life. But you say you want to fly around and be a hero, and won't take my advice to lay low while we figure out how it can work. And, right now, I can't see how you won't get caught."

CHAPTER 5
Heroics

The Boston press had a field day the next two weeks, demon-strating that our instinct to keep my identity secret was right. There were pictures on the front pages of all the papers, and the television and radio could talk of nothing else. It took a day for the national press to catch up, I guess because some remaining editorial standard-setters somewhere still felt that the whole thing might be a hoax.

We trended on Facebook, Snapchat and Instagram in a mega way, and I sort of wondered if that might not be the path to riches. Flying could make me a TikTok sensation. I could take cool videos from the air and get a million followers.

Unfortunately, the initial press speculation settled on a terrorist act. Folks from the Boston Police, the FBI and Homeland Security were interviewed, and made it seem like the mere act of flying around the city broke eight jillion laws and, if he was ever caught, the guy would be buried in Guantanamo for the rest of his life. The whole idea of a flying person seemed to drive authorities crazy.

It scared the hell out of both Hank and me, and we laid low. I kept telling Hank how much I owed him for making me leave my phone behind. He agreed.

A few days later, however, with no more evidence coming out about the great terrorist attack, the media focus shifted to a college prank, although the authorities did not seem any more amused. Hank said that half the students at MIT had been "interviewed" by the police. A host of experts appeared on television explaining what minor technological improvements would allow the creation of an individual flying suit.

Other experts insisted it was drone technology, and that the seemingly human flyer could have been a humanoid-shaped drone.

Another few days and the theories shifted again. People started to speculate that the flying man was a secret military project, like that Boston Robotics dog, never meant to become public. The whole talk about it being a terrorist attack was ginned up to cover the military's tracks. This theory had the advantage that, the less evidence that emerged for it, the more likely it was. This was when Hank and I began to breathe a sigh of relief.

By the end of the second week, the story began to drop from the news. First, literally nothing new had happened or been uncovered since the first night. Second, some people began to raise doubts about whether the incident ever happened at all. Sure, there was the Channel Five copter take, but maybe the footage was fake. Maybe the reporters were in on the gag.

Also, the internet helped put things to bed. As time went on, the deluge of flying-object posts and memes began to get nuttier and nuttier. UFO pictures from all across the world—lights and spheres and "unexplained distortions in the visual field"—proliferated, until anyone who wanted to follow the Boston story was put in the same category as the folks claiming to have been abducted by aliens.

I mostly kept my head down and focused on my classes. When the subject of the flying man came up, I shook my head and said things like, "It's a real mystery."

But I didn't give up flying, not after the first week anyway. I just waited for overcast nights, left my phone and went out to Concord. And I flew west, over the lakes and forests of Western Massachusetts, where there were few lights, no traffic helicopters, and no one to see me.

I didn't talk about it with Hank, because he didn't want to know. He figured he could get busted as an accessory-after-the-fact just for not turning me in.

Still, he can't claim complete ignorance. He knew I went out most nights after ten and rarely came home until well after midnight. So he must have known something was up.

Once I got in a fight with an owl, who took me for a new kind of prey, or perhaps a competitor. We had spotted each other over the Estabrook Woods. I thought nothing of it until I heard a *whooosh* above me and turned to see the creature diving at me. I swerved right, making the turn at absolute top speed, and just avoided getting the full force of the bird's talons in the back of the head.

I probably could have just flown off at that point, but my dander was up and I turned on the owl and flew straight at him—or her, it's hard to tell with owls—fists out, ready to fight. It was pretty satisfying when it ducked out of the way and fled. Take that, owls!

That night I stayed out later than usual, full of the blood lust from my fight with the owl. Sometime after midnight, I was flying around near Emerson Hospital and saw an old guy with a cane tumbling along near the edge of the Great Meadows wetlands. I knew there were several nursing homes in the area, because Ellen's grandfather lived in one of them, and I had volunteered to give her a lift out there one time. I figured maybe this guy was from one of them. His own business, of course, but I didn't think he wanted to be walking around in the wetlands after dark. I came lower, slowed my speed down and landed behind him.

I guess "landed" is the word. "Fell" maybe would work too. Look,

I'd gotten pretty good at the whole business of getting to ground. But that night I somehow missed seeing a branch stretching across the path—maybe I was close enough to the ground that my enhanced eyesight had turned off—and it slashed me across the face just before I touched down. It hurt like hell and it ruined what would have been a soft landing. I grabbed for my face, throwing off my balance, and tumbled forward on the path behind the old man, knocking the wind out of myself, and scratching my face further in the process.

I looked up, expecting to see the old man standing over me, but he seemed not to have noticed the commotion at all. Maybe he was deaf.

I stood up slowly and checked my injuries. Without a mirror it was hard to tell, but other than a welt and some scratches, I seemed basically okay.

Cursing, I ran to catch up with the man. I caught his arm and asked where he was headed.

"Home, young man. I'm going home." He didn't seem to notice my messed-up face.

"Where's home?"

"Garden Street."

"Oh, yeah? Where's that?"

"Everett. Nice place to live. Nice people."

Everett was like 30 miles away. Clearly this guy was a whack job.

"Sure, Everett's great," I lied. "But it's a long way. We need to find you a taxi."

"A taxi?"

"Sure. I saw a stand back a little ways."

"Okay."

The old man turned back with me, and we retraced his steps. As we walked, I kept up the chatter to see if he would give me any clues about where he was living. He told me about his family: mother, father, wife, children.

He didn't tell me which nursing home was his, but it turned out it wasn't necessary. As we got to the end of the path, there was a pedestrian bridge over a four-lane road. On the far side there was a large brick building with a sign outside, "Wind Haven." It had to be where we were headed.

I asked the man what he did. He said he was an electrician, and worked on the Garden. I was about to follow up when he became suspicious.

"This isn't the way," he said.

"Sure. We can call for a taxi just up ahead. It's not much further."

He shrugged and followed me. I led him right up to the door of Wind Haven. I told him to wait outside while I went in to see about the taxi. He did so, looking around as if he'd never been there before. I went into a dingy reception area where a woman with an angry face sat at a desk behind a glass screen, as if management was afraid of shoot-outs in their lobby. I didn't like the atmosphere.

I tapped on the glass and the woman looked up, annoyed to be taken from her word search.

"You missing someone?" I asked the woman.

She looked at me skeptically, taking in my dirty, bloody face.

"Look, I fell. Are you missing anyone?"

The woman rolled her eyes. "Maybe, maybe not."

"I came across a guy out in the wetlands. He's outside."

The woman looked at some screen that must have linked to a camera at the door. She pushed some sort of red button at her desk, got up and came out to the reception area. "That's Mr. Butler. Always trying to get away."

Two male nurses emerged from a door. They followed the woman out to grab Mr. Butler. I watched as they took either arm and brought him inside. I wouldn't say they were rough, but they weren't too friendly either. Mostly they looked like they had better things to do.

As he passed me, Mr. Butler turned momentarily from his guards and said, "Thank you, boy. They'll take care of me now." But his look said something else entirely. It said, "Help! Why did you betray me? Get me out of here!"

As the orderlies left the room, I turned to the receptionist, still out of her booth, and asked if Mr. Butler's family knew about his wandering.

"He doesn't have any family left. He's all alone."

"He told me about a wife and four kids. Grandchildren too."

"Wife's dead. Never seen a kid or a grandkid here."

I walked back to the wetland. On a path sheltered from the road, I took off and flew back to my car.

So not exactly crime fighting, but super-social-work at least. I felt pretty good heading home, despite the fact I'd only get a couple of hours sleep that night and I was getting further and further behind on my class prep.

CHAPTER 6

Confessions

I managed to drag myself into school the next day. I was not in bad shape physically, except for a red welt under my left eye, and some little scratches on my forehead. I figured I could have gotten the same injuries slipping while jogging, which is what I told everyone. I'm enough of a klutz that people seemed to believe it easily enough.

Worse, I had three classes in a row after morning meeting, and was not ready for any of them. I used a simple ploy, assigning in-class essays, for the first two classes. I sat at my desk, drinking my coffee and pretending to grade, although mostly what I did was close my eyes.

I was all set to use the same ploy in the third class, juniors reading *The Grapes of Wrath*, except the principal snuck into the class just after the bell rang, and I chickened out. I would have been better off just assigning the essay. Instead, I tried to bluff my way through a class I had not prepared, about a book I had not read for at least four years. Not a good idea, as I forgot the protagonist's name (it's Tom) and kept calling him Tim. Ugh.

As the class filed out, the principal asked me to stay behind. And then proceeded to give me a real dressing down. She started with all the bullshit about how much promise I had, and how she hoped to keep me. But pretty quickly it shifted into slipping standards, the importance of being prepared for class, setting a good example for the students, etc. Actually, it was a relief to get to that part, as all the talk about what a good job I had been doing just made me feel guilty for sucking so bad. And made me think she was going to fire me.

Then she asked me if I had been having any problems I would like to talk about.

"I don't think so," I said.

"You look terrible."

"I fell while I was out running," I explained.

"Maybe," she said. "But it's not uncommon for teachers to turn to . . . let's say artificial methods to help them deal with the stress and anxiety. I've seen it before."

"No, that's not me."

"Well, in case it would be useful, we have an employee counselor hotline for any sort of problems." She pressed a card into my hand. "Including abusive relationships."

"I don't need this," I said.

"I hope not. But you need something." Suddenly she turned back into disciplinarian. "I *will* fire you if you don't shape up, and soon. I can find someone to teach your English courses in two hours if I need to. If I hear about you showing up unprepared again, I will."

"It won't happen again."

"It better not. Now, go home and take care of yourself."

Whew! I had never gotten so bawled out at a job before. It almost made me forget how tired I was. Almost. I went into the teacher's lounge just to get a coffee to see me through the commute home, but ended up lying down on the sofa and falling asleep.

Ellen came over and woke me.

"What the hell are you doing?"

"Whaa?" I said, trying to wake up.

"The story's all over the school. You couldn't even remember the main characters. You know, once you lose a class, you lose it."

I looked at Ellen trying to figure what business it was of hers.

"You'll get fired," she said.

I was still groggy, and I told her that I hadn't been fired, just sent home for the day. "I'll see you tomorrow."

"Tomorrow? You mean tonight."

"Tonight?"

"Yes. Honestly, Jason. It's the opening match against the Bankers' Arms. You can't have forgotten that."

Oh hell. I *did* remember now. This was our first game in the Boston-wide pub trivia league. The Bankers' Arms was a downtown bar, whose trivia team was made up largely of people working at Fidelity. They had beaten us in a practice tournament, and we considered them our archrivals. I couldn't miss it. But my head hurt.

"I'll be there," I said, pushing myself off the couch. "But I've got to go home and sleep first." I just hoped Principal Snowe would not be in attendance. She might think that spending the night in the pub, after being sent home early from school to rest up, was not a good use of my time.

"And remember that you promised to bring Hank as backup."

She was right about that too. We had Ellen and Raffy, but you can never have too many science nerds. And Hank was killer at any math or astronomy stuff. So we had signed him up for the team, though he said he wasn't sure he could make all the matches. I hoped I'd reminded him about the match so he hadn't filled his schedule with some stupid MIT grad student networking event.

"Yeah, sure," I said to Ellen, waving goodbye and stumbling toward the door.

I set the alarm when I got home, so that I wouldn't miss the trivia game if I fell asleep, but I would have slept through it if Hank hadn't woken me.

"It's trivia time," he said. "You look terrible."

"You're going?"

"Yeah, I said I would ages ago. Are you feeling better?"

I said yes, which was not quite true. I still hadn't told him about my night flights, but he knew I was doing them, and I guess he was waiting for me to tell him about it.

I figured this was as good a time as any. After all, it'd be nice to get credit for the good deed I'd done the night before, and I had to explain my injuries somehow.

"I thought you were going to lie low."

"I like to fly."

"Yeah, I get that. It seems like you helped that guy out last night."

"You think maybe this superhero thing can work after all?"

"I don't know. It's hard to see. What you did last night . . . It wasn't really hero stuff, was it?"

What could I say? He was right.

As we walked to the T to get to the trivia match, we stopped talking about flying. Instead, I reminded him of the trivia games rules. Four rounds, ten questions each round, first to buzz answers. The only thing to remember was that you lost four points for every wrong answer, and only got two points for a right answer. Therefore, you had to wait to buzz until you were pretty sure. And in the last round all the points, plus and minus, doubled.

The game was from 7 p.m. to 8 p.m., clearing us out of the bar by the time the heavy drinkers arrived. I was glad to see both that Principal Snowe was not there, and that Penny was there. She was sitting demurely—she did everything demurely—who knew demure was so damn sexy?—next to Toby. I have no idea what she saw in Toby.

She asked me about my eye, and I told her I fell when I was running, but I didn't have a chance to follow up on the conversation because the game was starting. The Fidelity folk had a lot of fans there, cheering them on. We only had Penny and a couple of the school staff.

The Fidelity group jumped out to an early lead on recent politics and world geography. But Sylvia fought two of the Fidelity guys to a draw on sports questions, and we came roaring back with Hank, Raffy and Ellen cleaning up on a row of science questions. I held my own on a couple of questions on American literature, and we edged ahead on pop culture questions. Ellen answered most of them, but I helped out here with some deep knowledge of sixties and seventies television (yes, I can name all of the actors who had recurring roles on *F Troop*).

Fortunately for us, and unfortunately for the Fidelity guys, the last question was on Victorian mourning customs, and those guys had no chance against Toby. His answer gave us the win.

We were delighted, and it must be said that the Fidelity guys were gracious in defeat, buying us all a round of beers. Toby predicted that the Three Harps (that was the Flynn team—all teams were known by the name of their "home bar") would win the tournament this year, and he made Hank promise to make the second-round game in a month.

That's when the conversation turned to the flying man rumors from a couple of weeks back, and I made what may have been a big mistake. Sylvia, it turned out, was a believer. She was sure it was a person, and that he would turn out to be a hero. Toby was a skeptic, who thought it was a hoax. Raffy thought it was one of the Route 128 military companies testing tech. If not, the guy was an idiot. Flying around was stupid, when he could be marketing whatever gave him his power and making a mint.

Then Penny leaned in and gave her opinion that she thought it was wonderful the way he had escaped the helicopters, and that, if it really was a person, he must be very smart. And I swear she looked right at me as she said it, and I responded without thinking. Or thinking, but about other things.

I said, "It's me."

I saw Hank look at me in alarm, but that just made me go on. "The guy who flew is me. I can fly."

I knew I was going in circles, so I shut up.

The others looked at me like I was going batshit insane. Ellen said to Hank, "How hard did he hit his head when he fell?"

"Pretty hard, I guess," Hank said. "C'mon boyo, it's time to go home. You are drunk and delirious." He shrugged at the others apologetically.

But Penny was still looking at me. "I'll show you. C'mon. Let's go outside."

"I need to take him home," Hank said.

"No," Raffy said, with a horrible little sneer, "I want to see this."

"So do I," said Toby, holding back a laugh.

"Don't be mean," Ellen said. "He's obviously unwell."

"Not obviously," Sylvia said. "Someone flew. Why shouldn't it be Jason?"

"Yeah, why not?" I said, smiling at Penny.

Ellen was hardly able to speak as she seemed so overwhelmed by the millions of reasons why not. Finally she said, "Fine, let's go outside and have him show us."

Hank was furious, but I thought: *Why not? These are my best friends, aren't they? Maybe they can help me figure out how to use my power for good.*

I said, "I'm game," and got up. I held a hand out for Penny.

She took it and stood up too. Everyone, except Hank, followed.

"Aren't you coming, Hank?" Ellen asked.

"No. Someone has to keep the table." He practically snarled.

We piled outside. I said we had to find an empty street, because I still wanted to keep my power secret. Fortunately, that's easy in downtown Boston at night. The Bankers' Arms itself was on Custom House Road, a pretty quiet place. And several smaller streets, even less busy, intersected it.

We stopped on a little road called Well Street and waited around until a couple walking on the far side cleared out. Sylvia asked me if there was anything I needed. A runway, something to jump off, or some such.

"An umbrella?" Ellen asked.

"Feathers?" Raffy said. "A helicopter?"

"I certainly am looking forward to this," Toby said, and smiled at Penny in an infuriating manner.

I didn't let them bother me. Penny hadn't said anything, and I'd show them soon enough. I kept a dignified silence until the other pedestrians turned the corner.

"Ready?" I asked.

The others didn't say anything, but I could see their eyes shining with anticipation, mostly of my failure, I'm sure. I jumped in the air, thinking *UP* and *FAST,* and soared away over their heads. The wide eyes and open mouths were priceless.

I swooped down and hovered above them. Still they didn't say anything. They were literally speechless. I looked at Penny. She was staring at me with what I had to assume were adoring eyes. Suddenly I had a thought. *Leave on a high note; that's what people said.* If I left now, there would be tomorrow and tomorrow and tomorrow for Penny and the others to seek me out and tell me how awesome I was.

I soared away home.

I managed to make it back to my apartment without incident, landing unobserved in a nearby playground. I was definitely getting better at flying.

When I got home, I tried to prepare my classes, but my nerves were still buzzing when Hank walked in an hour later.

"Well," I asked, "how'd it go?"

"I made them promise to keep your identity secret."

"Yeah? Good. Were they impressed?"

"Christ, Jason, what are you thinking? Any one of them could go to the cops. In fact, it's probably a crime if they don't. We went all through this. What do you think the authorities will do? Give you a medal. No, they'll lock you away for the next fifty years studying your DNA, and you will *never ever* see the light of day. And now they'll probably take me too. Great!"

"Hey, they're my friends. They won't give me away."

"You're so fucking trustful."

"C'mon, though. Were they impressed?"

"They were stunned, of course. They had no idea what to think. And then you made it worse by flying off. It was all I could do when they came back inside to stop them telling everyone in the bar."

"So . . . ?"

"I know what you want me to say. God didn't give you the power to fly just so you could get laid."

"No, that's why he gave me my . . ."

"Well, stop thinking with it!"

Eventually, Hank relented and told me what had happened. Toby, Sylvia, Raffy, Ellen and Penny had gone back in the bar in a sort of daze. Hank collected them and told them, confidentially, the story of what had been happening the last few weeks. About how we didn't know where the power came from, about our struggle to figure out how I should use it, about the need to keep my identity secret. He told them that we needed their help with everything. That was Hank's ploy. To draw them in and make them part of the conspiracy. It seemed pretty brilliant to me.

Anyway, Hank said Sylvia was totally starry-eyed, sure that I could be the superhero Boston needed. Toby thought I should go into track and field, like high jump, long jump and pole vault, and set a bunch of records.

"Track and field?" I asked. Toby was the track coach at the school and cared about that shit. But still.

"Raffy thought the whole fighting crime idea was stupid. He wanted to form a start-up, of course. Sell energy drinks or something. He thought that was where the real money was."

"Not very heroic."

"Raffy's not about being a hero. He said a billionaire can do a lot more good than a hero. Build schools, give money away. All that stuff."

"Are you going to tell me about Penny or not?"

First, of course, he told me about Ellen. Ellen seemed to think the whole thing was a curse, and I should forget about it. Then, in the middle of the discussion, she picked up her things and ran out.

"Man, do you think she'll go to the police?"

"No, she won't."

"I thought you were the suspicious one. Trust nobody and all that. Why make an exception for Ellen?"

"You are such an idiot."

"I'm just being cautious."

"Yeah, by showing everyone in downtown Boston you can fly just so you can show off to god-damn Penny."

"Well, what did she say? Are you going to tell me or not."

"She just wanted to suck your dick."

"Really?"

"No, not really." Hank sighed. "She did say that she thought flying was 'supercool,' but I think what really turned her on were Raffy's money-making ideas. In fact, she knew a couple of the Fidelity guys at the bar who she bet would finance a start-up. I had to grab her to stop her from going to tell them all about it right away."

"Supercool, huh?"

"Jesus, Jason."

But I went to sleep happy. If I couldn't be a hero, at least I could get a girlfriend.

 Invulnerability

CHAPTER 7
Falling

Iwoke up pretty happy too. My courses were prepared, Penny thought I was *supercool,* and I could fly. I wasn't going to let Hank's negativity get me down.

I felt so good about the world, I figured I'd risk an early morning flight. It was overcast, and I was up early enough that there would hardly be anyone around. And I wouldn't fly far—just a quick buzz around the neighborhood. I went up to the roof, pulled on my balaclava and jumped off the roof. I was feeling confident now, so none of this chickenshit hopping, starting and stopping. Just a perfect swan dive off the roof, like Daredevil does before he ropes some flagpole and swings to safety.

As I did so I thought *UP, UP and AWAY.* And then *Oh Shit!*

I never got beyond *oh, shit* before slamming into the apartment courtyard. I hit hard, dislodging a couple of the granite paving stones below, and shattering one of them with my elbow. I only had time to think about life and death after I landed, and then I assumed I must be dead. If I was alive, it would hurt more.

Hank was the first out of the building, followed by several others. Apparently, no one had seen me fall, but some had heard the impact. Hank was pale as a ghost, while the others looked merely curious to have their morning interrupted.

"Just tripped," I said, whipping off my balaclava. "I'm fine. Really."

Hank insisted I come back up to the apartment. I let myself be led away, somewhat shaken by the fall. Physically I felt fine—more than fine, amazing—but I was confused by what had happened, and wondered if maybe my brain had been shaken. I even wondered if I was really bleeding to death down where I had landed, and Hank would be revealed as St. Peter leading me to the Pearly Gates. I wondered how my life would balance out. I hadn't done much harm, but I wasn't sure I'd done much good either.

Once we got inside the apartment, Hank slammed the door. "OK, what happened?"

"I'm all right, right?" I asked. "I don't have bits of brain hanging out, do I?"

"Yeah, you look okay. But what happened?"

"I jumped off the roof. And I just went straight down. I thought I'd be dead. But I feel great." It was true. No hangover, and all the cuts and scrapes from my adventure two nights ago were gone. I realized even the welt across my cheek had cleared up. I felt like a million bucks, maybe more.

Hank did some mental arithmetic. "The fall was over fifty feet, so you would have reached terminal velocity. Hitting granite and stopping dead. I mean the fall is technically survivable, but you shouldn't be walking. Your bones should be jelly."

"Hank, I couldn't fly. I tried. The whole *UP, UP* thing. But I didn't go up. I just fell."

"Try again now."

"In the house?"

"Yeah, just like you did before."

"Man, I don't want to hit my head on the ceiling again."

"You won't if you can't fly."

So I did what he suggested, and no go.

"See, it's useless," I said. "I've lost it. I've lost my superpower before ever really using it."

"Maybe," Hank said, "but I've got a theory. Put out your arm."

He had grabbed a kitchen knife and was walking toward me. I backed away. "What are you doing?"

"Christ, don't be such a baby. You just survived a six-story fall. Let me cut you."

"What? No!"

Hank rolled his eyes like I was being really dense. "You lost the power to fly. But I think you may be invulnerable."

I looked at him like he was crazy. "What? Why? That makes no sense."

"It doesn't make sense being able to fly in the first place. Now come on."

He advanced and I retreated.

"Don't be a wuss."

I took a deep breath and stopped retreating. I rolled up my sleeve and closed my eyes. I didn't really know what he intended. I had visions of the headlines the next day: KNIFE-WIELD-ING MAN MURDERS ROOMMATE. I wondered if this was how those things happened. I felt the coolness of steel on my forearm. I opened my eyes.

Hank was sawing away but not breaking the skin. He tried to cut a finger. Nothing. He turned the knife and, without warning, slammed it into my palm. Jesus! Can I just say that invulnerability is the suckiest power to test for?

Anyway, the knife skittered out of Hank's hand, the blade bent back and blood splattered over the kitchen counter and floor. But it wasn't mine, it was Hank's. He had a gash across a finger. I rushed to get some paper towels. Then I applied bacitracin and two Band-Aids.

As I did so, Hank looked at me marveling. "You've got a new power. You're invulnerable."

"Whoa, I don't know," I said. "I mean, the knife slipped."

"It bent," he said. "And you survived a 60-foot fall onto granite. You're invulnerable."

I tried to get used to the idea. Okay, not flying was a drag, but this might be cool. "Hey," I said, "You think if I'm invulnerable, I'm super-strong too? I mean, in comics they're never separate, right?"

"Maybe."

"Superman, Wonder Woman, Namor, Thor. Hulk. One implies the other."

"I don't know about Wonder Woman. She blocked bullets with her bracelets. Why bother if they'd bounce off her anyway?"

"Style," I said.

"And what about Achilles?"

"Come on, that's mythology, not comic books."

"Why should comic books be the only evidence? Anyway, I bet there's a comic-book Achilles somewhere."

"And I bet he's superstrong. Let's test it."

"That's easy. Lift the couch."

I had in mind a more awesome comic-booky sort of test, like juggling cars, but what the hell. I went over and tried. I lifted one end up easily. But when I found a grip and managed to get the whole thing off the floor, my muscles protested and I let it drop with a thud.

"So, no superstrength." Hank said after watching me struggle.

"God, no," I said, flopping down on the couch myself.

"We still need to figure out how invulnerable you are."

"Right, but not now," I said, catching a glimpse of the clock in the kitchen. "I can't be late for school today."

I felt great as I went into school. Flying was fun, but it was sucky as a superpower. Invulnerability, even without superstrength, had to be better. Hank was right, of course. I had to know how invulnerable I was. I didn't want to go try to break up a gunfight if I was only invulnerable to knives. And what about grenades? And flame throwers? Lasers? Radiation? Where were the limits?

What about sickness? I felt then like I could never get sick. But could I get, like, the Ebola virus? Or AIDS? Maybe my superpower was to have sex without a condom. That wouldn't be so bad.

But, of course, that raised an issue. I was never going to have sex again. I had just told all my friends that I could fly. And now I couldn't. They would think I was lying to them. Or playing some sort of elaborate trick. Would Penny think invulnerability was supercool too? Not as cool as flying, I bet.

Honestly, I couldn't really think of any way to impress anybody with invulnerability, except possibly jumping off cliffs for their amusement. Which sounded so desperate. Like trying to get attention by going over Niagara Falls in a barrel.

I just about managed to avoid Penny and the others when I got to school, waving vaguely to Ellen and Sylvia in the faculty lounge before I went into my first class. Which went okay.

But I ran into Toby after third period.

"Well, now, how is our most unusual specimen today?"

It took me a minute to realize he meant me. It was often hard to follow Toby's thoughts, and I suppose the fact that he didn't want to be understood by other Flynn faculty and staff made his sentences more convoluted than usual.

"Fine," I said.

"Excellent. I believe your next class is not until 1 p.m. No reason not to lunch with me. Your friend Hank started to fill us in yesterday, but nothing like the horse's mouth."

"I have to check the study hall duty list," I said, both because it was true, and because lunch with Toby was not what I had in mind.

"I checked. You're good."

"I haven't prepped my one o'clock."

"*Romeo and Juliet* for Freshmen English? Hardly needs prep, does it? Let them read to you. Anyway, I've asked the girls, and you don't want to disappoint them."

"The girls?"

We had reached the faculty lounge, and Toby gestured for me to enter first instead of answering. As I did so, I saw Penny and Ellen chatting at the coffee machine.

Toby followed behind and said, "Ah, there they are. Ready to go?"

They nodded, and I gave in. I'd assign the freshmen roles, and they could read from the play. Learning to act, I told myself, had a role in the Language Arts curriculum.

As we approached the main doors of the school, we ran into Sylvia, emerging from the copy room off of the receptionist's office. She saw the four of us together and said, "Oh, and where are the four of you off to?"

"Just a little lunch," Toby said.

"Hold on then. As it happens, I have a break right now. I'll get my coat and join you."

Toby grimaced, but didn't say anything. We went out of the school building together and headed for Lou's. No discussion was needed. Lou's was a small deli around the corner from Flynn where the faculty always ate their lunches when they could escape the school.

I was happy, as I ended up squeezed in a booth between Sylvia and Penny. I was acutely conscious of the feel of Penny's thigh rubbing against my chinos. She was wearing a tan skirt that had a slit that went almost mid-thigh. I discreetly adjusted how I was sitting a couple of times hoping that if I moved just right, her skirt would naturally split open so that my trouser leg would be in direct contact with her stockings.

I told them the main points of the story of my flying, leaving out the fact that I couldn't fly any more, and also most of the klutzier bits. In fact, I generally tried to make whole thing sound as studly as possible.

Which wasn't hard, to be honest. I mean, I was jumping off buildings after all. I *was* a stud.

Trust Ellen not to see it. Did she start with "Oh, Jason, you are so amazing?" which would have been normal and true. No, she treated it as a damn science problem.

"I still don't get it," Ellen said. "Hank said that you couldn't figure out how it happened. But there must be a reason. There's always a reason. If not, the headline story isn't *Man Flies* but *Rationality Overturned*."

"Come on," I said. "Maybe it's a quantum effect."

"A quantum effect of what?" Ellen said with a sneer. She was great to talk to, until she saw a weakness in your argument. Then she went in for the kill.

"I just mean that causality is not always so obvious." She sat back with a smug look on her face, as much as saying that I didn't know what I was talking about, which was right, but infuriating. And it wasn't like she knew what she was talking about. She didn't know my power had switched suddenly from flying to invulnerability, which really did make causality seem a bit of a stretch.

Instead of pointing that out, I said, "The important question that you, and Hank too, seem to miss, is what am I going to do with my power?"

Toby jumped in with his track and field obsession. He said he had done high jump and pole vault back in high school, and he considered competitors in those events the kings and queens of athletic accomplishment. He could teach me the Fosbury Flop and I could easily beat the current records. He said I should beat it by just a little at first, but then maybe go up a half inch a year. By the end of my career, my records would be untouchable.

Whatever. We listened politely until Sylvia finally interrupted him. "Toby, you're showing your age. People Jason's age don't care about that. They like things like skateboarding and the funny tricks they can do with bikes. Besides, Jason has already said that he wants to be a hero, not engage in tawdry trickery."

Toby sat back with a look of hurt dignity. But I couldn't worry about that, as I was facing a much more alarming situation. As Sylvia spoke, she placed her hand on my thigh, then left it there, hot and heavy. "I think Jason should tell us what he wants, and we should all be ready to do anything that we can to help."

I felt her hot breath on my cheek and smelled the slight bitter tang from the pickle she had eaten with her sandwich. The hand on my leg—I'm sure of it; I was sure at the time—was not the hand of a concerned colleague. It was not the comradely hand of a mentor comforting a mentee. I felt like Martin Luther King would have if Bull Connor had had pheromones in his fire hose instead of water. And it had about the same effect on my libido, leaving it a damp squib.

I took her hand off my leg gently and gave it a pat. "Thanks for the support, Sylv," I said, keeping my voice light. "I'm just trying to figure out how flying helps me be a hero."

Okay, I lost my moment then. That was when I should have said, "The thing is, I can't fly anymore." But I didn't. Maybe it was something about Sylvia's pheromones. They weren't sexy, but still it was kind of awesome to create that kind of reaction in someone. It made me feel like Keith Richards. Maybe I didn't want to sleep with every groupie, but I sure wanted them to want to sleep with me.

Besides, I was still waiting to hear from Penny how cool my flying was. And I was still aggravated by how unimpressed Ellen seemed. She didn't have to come on as strong as Sylvia, but she could at least acknowledge that I was a little bit awesome.

Anyway, instead of telling the truth, I turned to Penny and said, "What do you think?"

"Raffy says we need to analyze your cellular function. If we can bottle what you do, it'd be the greatest product in history. Who wants to play video games when they can fly?"

Where did Raffy come into it? When had Penny had all these long, detailed conversations with him anyway? Come on, I was an eight Zach Braff. He was no more than a six Michael Cera. And Zach Braffs start from a higher base.

I know, not everything is about looks. But Raffy was a major dork. All he talked about was programming, and even that he talked about in business-ese. I don't think he'd read a novel since high school. He couldn't cook (okay, I was guessing on that one, but he seemed to eat all his meals at Subway), and his favorite music was emo. Besides which, he was a Rand Paul-type libertarian. I mean, what was there in that mix to attract a woman? Precisely nothing.

"I don't want to be a research subject," I said. "Hank said that everyone would want to dissect me. I just want to fly."

"Well, it would be better to control the process than to have someone impose it on you," Ellen said. "And the point isn't just the money. Think of the carbon savings if everyone could fly."

"That's why we need to get on top of this," Toby said, conspiratorially. "Maybe Raffy and Penny have the right idea."

The conversation was not heading in the direction I wanted. No one except Sylvia saw me as a hero. They saw me as a lab rat. And every time I opened my mouth, I was lying by omission, leaving them the impression that I could still fly. Fortunately, it was almost one o'clock.

I pointed this out, and we paid and headed back to school. I spent the next hour listening to 14-year-olds mangle Shakespeare, and the hour after that supervising study hall. I found myself hoping for a fight to break out.

The bell rang, the kids left, and I made a decision. No one maximized their powers by being cautious. The school bordered several of the "no-go" neighborhoods in Boston. But they weren't no-go for me. I'd make a statement. All of Boston belonged to anyone. And if anyone tried to stop me, well, too bad for them.

I was about to get up and head out when I heard a dreaded sound, the distinctive clicking of Sylvia's high heels on the school's linoleum floors. I was trapped. The only exit led out into the hall, straight into her clutches. But the desk in the study room offered salvation. It was solid metal down to the floor, with plenty of leg room under the top drawer. Acting as quickly and quietly as I could, I swept my books and papers into my bag and crawled under the desk, pulling my legs in just as I heard Sylvia's voice call out from the doorway.

"Jason, are you there? Jason? Jason? I could have sworn you were still here." There was a pause as I imagined her surveying the room. I held my breath. A few seconds later, I heard her footsteps retreating back down the corridor.

I stayed under the desk another minute, terrified that it was a feint, and she'd be waiting at the door as I emerged. Finally, I had to risk it. I took a breath and crawled out from under the desk, banging my head as I stood up.

"Shit!" I said, automatically, because, of course, it didn't hurt.

"What are you doing?" said another voice from the doorway. "Why are you under the desk?"

Jesus, it was Ellen. "Uh, just lost something," I said.

"Right," she said, disbelieving.

I made a split-second decision to come clean. I needed advice about women, and Ellen, who was a woman, might be able to give it to me. "Look, okay, I was hiding from Sylvia."

"Ah."

"Did you see her at lunch? I swear she was practically salivating over me."

"The objectifier becomes the objectified."

"Yeah, yeah. But, what should I do?"

"I think she'll understand that no means no."

"Oh, that helps."

"Well, what do you want? For a lot of people flying is incredibly attractive. A symbol of liberation. You wanted to impress us, I guess, and you sure impressed Sylvia. You have a fan. Deal with it. Sleep with her, or tell her you don't want to."

"I don't know why it has to be Sylvia. You and Penny aren't throwing yourselves at me?"

"You want me to throw myself at you?"

"Uh, I just mean, people my own age. Sylvia could be my mother, for God's sake."

"Well, maybe others of us have better options."

"Right, thanks for pointing that out! The funny thing is, I can't even fly now."

"What?"

"I woke up this morning and the ability was just gone. I almost killed myself throwing myself off the roof of my apartment."

"What?"

"I would have too, except now I'm invulnerable."

"Come on, Jason."

"No, I'm serious. Hank and I tested it this morning. I mean I don't know how it happened. But I can't be hurt. Hank couldn't cut me with a knife."

"Jesus, I don't have time for this. I have to meet my mother in half an hour. Look, I bought into the whole flying thing, because I saw you do it. But there's no way you could fly yesterday, and can't fly today. And there is no way you're invulnerable now. That makes no sense."

"But I am. Do you have anything sharp on you?"

"I'll see you tomorrow. I can't deal with this nonsense now."

"It's true," I said. But I said it to Ellen's back, as she had already turned around and walked out of the classroom.

CHAPTER 8
Fighting

Well, that was it. I was going to do some fighting that night. It wasn't dark yet, so I went to a Starbucks near the school, had a snack and prepped my class for the next morning. I figured I owed the freshmen a real class on *Romeo and Juliet*. I put together some ideas about the crazy things love makes us do.

By six it was dark, and I headed out to look for trouble. I know it was stupid. I didn't know the extent of my invulnerability yet, so it might be dangerous. But I guess I was feeling reckless.

In retrospect, I think being invulnerable may have affected my judgment, maybe like flying changed my eyesight. I don't know if this was really a physical change in the brain chemistry, or just pure psychology. Invulnerability just made life seem a lot less risky. I had no idea if I could've survived being hit by a train, but I know I wouldn't have hesitated to jump down on the tracks of an oncoming train to save someone. The risk calculus had changed.

You might wonder how I knew I was still invulnerable. It's a little hard to describe, but I just felt so good. Like nothing hurt in my body. Like there was not a single viral cell bringing it down. Like my immune system could have felled an ox.

Now, I'm a young guy, and it's not like my body had all that many aches and pains to begin with. Not like old folk who you always hear kvetching away about their knees and backs. But until *nothing* hurts, nothing at all, you don't really even notice all the little sore spots that nag subconsciously at even a super-healthy person. Man, it felt good.

By paying attention to my body, I also knew that I still couldn't fly. I was missing some internal sense of lightness, some sense of the contingency of my tethering to the planet that I had felt before. If I'd been paying attention, I probably would have realized it before I jumped off the roof that morning. But it never occurred to me that my powers would come and go.

Anyway, as dark fell, I got up from the coffee shop and headed out into the mean streets of West Roxbury and Dorchester. I know there are worse places in the world, but not so much in Boston. There were plenty of streets with everything you expected of a slum: crumbling old houses, scary empty lots covered in weeds and razor wire, poor lighting, graffiti, store fronts closed and locked behind solid steel shutters. I was sure I'd been told that White guys like me were taking their lives in their hands to wander around after dark.

I didn't have any particular plan other than to walk around, be attacked by bad guys and show them what was what. I didn't have my flying duds, so I didn't have my balaclava. But I figured that hiding my identity was not so crucial when I wasn't flying. Being invulnerable is a less flamboyant talent.

I stalked around, trying to keep my anger high so I'd be ready for a fight. It was cold out, but my invulnerability meant, among other things, that I didn't get cold. The streets were oddly quiet. Actually, I don't know if it was odd or not. I'd never hung out much in West Roxbury before. But I didn't see many people, and those that I did see ignored me.

I saw a bar, a seedy one-story affair with two neon signs in the window. One was a Budweiser sign that looked of 1980s vintage. The other said, "Blue Hill Bar" in blinking blue neon, except that the "u" and the "H" were out. I stuck my head in, hoping to provoke someone, I guess. But all I saw were a couple of old men, nursing their drinks. So I went back into the streets.

I passed a group of kids laughing. I saw a man and woman making out on a street corner. *Jesus, how do you get attacked around here,* I thought.

Two hours I walked around. I hardly saw anyone, and the people I did see weren't breaking the law, and didn't seem much interested in me. I started walking in circles, trying to stay in the areas that looked the most dangerous. What good was invulnerability if life was so damn safe?

I was passing the Blue Hill Bar again when someone yelled out to me. "Son! Come here."

Here we go, I thought. I stopped and looked at the man calling me from the door of the bar. He was an old guy with a big pot belly. Maybe he was an ex-fighter, or maybe he had a weapon, but he didn't look like a likely combatant. I walked over to him.

"Yeah?" I asked.

"What are you doing here?"

"What business is that of yours?"

"I saw you walking around earlier. This ain't a good place to just hang out."

"It's a free country."

"Or maybe you're looking for trouble." When I didn't say anything, he continued. "Sometimes boys like you come looking for trouble. Hoping to get in a fight. Maybe they want to try out their new black belt. Or maybe they just bought themselves a gun. I don't see your gun so maybe you think you're Bruce Lee. You think you're Bruce Lee?"

"No," I said. "I'm just going for a walk."

"Well, that's good, 'cause this ain't no hunting gallery. And it does no good when hotshot White boys come down trying to stir up trouble. Maybe some angry kid will take a pop at you, and what will you do? Beat him to a pulp? Call the police and have him taken away. Get him six months in jail for rising to your goddamn bait? Make you feel like a bit of a hero?"

I didn't say anything, but I realized I was acting like a fool. The old man must have seen my face fall.

"Feeling stupid, hunh?" I nodded. "Well, you should. Go home and leave these kids alone."

There was nothing more to say. I walked home reflecting on what an idiot I had been. More supervillain than a superhero. And a racist bastard to boot. God, Hank was going to be on my case for six months. I walked all the way back to Cambridge, wrapped in self-loathing and frustrated at the uselessness of my power.

I was cutting across Harvard Yard, still in a funk, when I bumped into some drunken college kid in a lacrosse shirt, spilling the beer he was carrying in a red cup.

"Sorry," I said, and tried to keep walking.

The kid blocked my way and pushed me backwards. I looked up and saw that beer had spilled on his shirt and trousers. I also saw he was pretty angry.

I realized this was the chance for me to use my power. I could play the innocent, but get the guy riled up, ready to fight. After he started things, I'd show how cool I was. How invulnerable. I wouldn't be a racist asshole. The guy was a preppy, overprivileged Harvard jock. Who'd complain if he got a beatdown? Maybe he deserved it.

I imagined the old guy in Blue Hill Bar. He'd see right through my justifications. He'd know it would never come to a fight if I wasn't itching for it. That I was desperate to hurt someone just to show my power. And, man, what did I know about the galoot in front of me? Even Harvard jocks can have hard, difficult days. God damn it!

"I really am sorry," I said again, backing away.

The guy saw me retreat, and looked at me like I was nothing but a little worm he could crush. But it was enough that he had scared me. "Fuck you!" he said, turned around and stormed off.

I was ashamed of how I had acted earlier in the night, but this hardly felt better. Before I had superpowers, I would have been terrified of the lacrosse bro and backed away. Now, I was literally invulnerable, and I still ended up retreating and apologizing. If nothing had changed, what good were my stupid powers?

By the time I got home I was tired from self-recrimination. As usual, Hank was waiting for me.

"Man, where have you been?" Hank said. "I've got good news."

I didn't feel like being grilled and roasted by Hank about my misadventures in West Roxbury just yet. "Just working."

"I've managed to score some Super-Vac lab time tomorrow night. That will let us test your power without getting you killed."

"What's the Super-Vac lab?"

"It manages airflow using vacuums. It's usually used to measure air resistance on small scales. But we can create air pellets with exact forces that we can ratchet up incrementally so we don't blow you away while we're experimenting."

"Sure, that'll be great," I said. I wasn't really that interested in testing my invulnerability at that point; I just wanted to know how to use it. But Hank was excited by it, so I didn't argue.

CHAPTER 9
Hurting

The next morning, I confessed my prior night's adventures to Hank. He told me what an idiot I was, and I asked him how he thought I should use my invulnerability.

The problem was that daily life was structured so you didn't need to be invulnerable. Which only made sense, of course. But, for me, it meant I had to do something out of the ordinary to make use of my power. The question was: what?

Hank said that I was setting the cart before the horse. First, we needed to determine the exact nature of my invulnerability.

"I was thinking about it last night. I'm pretty sure I can't get hurt by bullets," I said. "I feel it."

"Very scientific. What about uranium-tipped bullets?"

I hadn't thought about that. The truth was I had no special insight on the subject. But I was annoyed. "Sure," I said.

"What about your eyeballs?"

"What do you mean?"

"Is everything equally invulnerable? What if you get a bullet right through your pupil?"

I didn't really like to think about it.

"Or the groin. Is your dick invulnerable too?"

"C'mon man." I had visions of testing myself each morning by letting Hank kick me in the balls. The idea made my coccyx wince.

"What about something that finds its way into your body, through your nose or ears? Are you invulnerable inside? Also, do you need to breathe? If it turns out that fire doesn't hurt you, you could run into a burning building and still die of asphyxiation. What's got into you anyway? These things are obvious. I'd have thought you'd be all over them."

He was right. They were obvious questions. But I didn't want to think about them. I had never heard the invulnerability of Superman's eyeballs explicitly discussed, although, of course, he regularly flew into suns and things. I hated to think that I could survive an explosion only to find my eyeballs melted away.

"Okay," I said, at last. "You've made your point. We'll test tonight." And then maybe we could figure out how I could use my power.

At school, Sylvia met me at the door of the teachers' lounge. She was leaving as I came in, and I couldn't avoid her.

"Hi, Jason," she said. It looks innocuous enough on the page, but let me tell you, her words sent shivers down my spine. I know you're not meant to use adverbs—I *was* an English major—but unless you know she said the words sultrily, lustfully perhaps, hungrily, you have no idea how freaked out I was.

"Hi, Sylvia," I said. And I didn't just say them. I squeaked them. I felt like a mouse cornered by a cat.

"Have you done any flying recently?" And not content just to speak throatily, she extended her arms over her head in a rough approximation of the classic Superman movie pose. Except that the effect was to thrust her breasts out toward me, and her hands crossed so she looked more like she was being crucified, or perhaps tied to a bed, than flying.

I looked around and shrugged my shoulders, nervously. "I need to grab some coffee. Still working on my second-period class," I overexplained, and tried to push around her.

As Sylvia didn't move, I made to squeeze past her. As I did, she whispered, in a manner chock-full of adverbs, "We should meet later to talk over how your classes are going."

I couldn't say anything. Far from feeling invulnerable, a spasm of fear wrenched at my bowels. Sylvia was my official mentor at the school. She was the person who approved my lesson plans, and whom I was meant to approach with any problems. I had a sudden insight into the dangers of workplace harassment.

I managed a nervous titter as I pushed past her and strode over to the coffee machine as if it was the only thing that mattered in the world. My only thought was that Hank was right. I was a fool to tell anyone about my powers.

I didn't turn around to confirm that Sylvia had left as I poured my coffee. So when I felt a hand on my back, I jumped, spilling hot coffee on myself and on the floor. It didn't hurt—it probably wouldn't have even if I hadn't been invulnerable—but it made a mess.

Still, when I turned and saw Penny, rather than Sylvia, a wave of relief shot through my body, and I realized that my shirt was soaked through with sweat as well as coffee.

"Jesus, Penny, you startled me." I grabbed some paper towels to wipe up the mess.

As I dabbed at my shirt and trousers, Penny got some more paper towels and started wiping the floor. Visions of domestic bliss danced in my head. Her blond hair hung down to the floor as she worked. I'd never seen her hair out of place before. I thought of the feel of her hand on my back. Had she ever touched me like that before? I couldn't remember. Did she do it because I told her I could fly? I remembered now why it seemed like a good idea to tell my friends. If Sylvia was hot for me, maybe Penny was a little too. And we were the same age. Clearly a better match.

"You seem jumpy," she said.

"It was just . . ." I had told Ellen about Sylvia, I should be able to tell Penny. After all, we were destined to be soulmates. To share everything. But perhaps the teachers' lounge was not the place to do it. "I didn't realize anyone was here."

"That was pretty neat, what you did the other night."

"Thanks."

"Have you talked to Raffy yet?"

"No, not yet."

"I bet. If I could fly, I'd never want to do anything else."

Ha! Sylvia and Penny.

"No, look," I said. "I can't fly anymore, but something really cool has happened. Look." I thrust my hand on the coffee burner.

"What do you mean you can't fly?"

"Watch. The coffee burner's hot."

"Stop touching it then."

"No, look. This is cool."

"You said it was hot."

"No, look, I'm invulnerable. It's my new power, I can't get hurt."

But she looked at me, uncomprehending. Look, in some ways invulnerability is as awesome as flying, but it sucks to show off. What I wouldn't have given for someone to come in and spray the room with bullets. I'd thrust Penny behind me, and she would watch the bullets fall harmlessly around me. That would be impressive. Better still if there were other people around, spouting blood and dying, otherwise she might think the gunman was shooting blanks.

Someone did come in then, but unfortunately, no one likely to let loose a barrage of gun fire. It was Jack Sprague, a long-time Flynn teacher, who taught chemistry to eleventh and twelfth graders.

"Howdy, kids!" he said. "No coffee left, eh? If you finish the pot, you make another, Jason. Am I right, Penny?" As he said this he leered at Penny and put an arm around her shoulder in a paternalistic manner. What is it about old teachers in this school harassing younger staff members?

I removed my hand from the burner and said, "Sure, Jack." It was a struggle not to say "Mr. Sprague." He was that old.

Penny, in the meantime, extricated herself from Sprague's embrace, and said, "I'm due in the library," giving me a look that said she was both disappointed in and worried about me.

Jack watched her leave and then turned to me and said, "That sure is one fine-looking lady."

"Jack, she's a colleague," I said, and picked up my things and walked out toward my first class without making more coffee.

It wasn't until after lunch that I finally got to clear things up with at least one of my friends. I hijacked Ellen during fourth period and made her walk around the block with me. I complained to her about how hard it was to explain the change in my powers to the others. I also told her of my encounters with Sylvia and Penny that morning.

"I guess Sylvia has it bad. Maybe she'll get over it when you tell her you can't fly."

"Why is that so much cooler than being invulnerable?"

"Well, what do you mean by invulnerable anyway?"

"I can't be hurt?"

"Subjectively hurt? You mean you don't feel pain? Or objectively? Like you can't be damaged?"

I paused, muddling through the question, and Ellen continued. "Not feeling pain is just sort of creepy. Like a deficiency somehow. Like those yogis who hang upside down from meat hooks. What's so great about that?"

"No, I don't think that's it. I mean objectively. I can't—what you said—get damaged."

"From anything?"

"Well, I survived a six-story fall unscathed."

"Yeah, but so do cats. Maybe you were just relaxed."

"I wasn't. I dented the pavement. And I can't cut myself with a knife."

"I'm not sure I could cut *myself* with a knife."

"Yeah, but I tried."

"Ick. I get the point, but it's sort of gross. So how invulnerable are you?"

"That's Hank's point. He wants to test me tonight. But I'm pretty sure he won't be able to hurt me."

"Baseless confidence. Is that part of your power?"

"Ha, ha. Look, will you tell the others? I mean, you see how hard it is to explain."

"I'll meet you and Hank at the lab tonight. If it pans out, I'll help you explain to the others."

"Thanks."

"But if it pans out, you need to start thinking about why it's happening. That is a lot more interesting than what you can or can't do."

"Thanks a lot."

"But you know what I mean, right?"

"Yeah, maybe. But *I'm* more interested in what I can do. And we don't know if there *is* any explanation. You jumped all over me the other day when I said it might be a quantum effect, but I just meant that maybe it's inexplicable."

"Inexplicable is interesting too." Then she reached up and tousled my hair, saying. "I have to get ready for fifth-period Bio for the Brainless. Try not to hurt yourself before tonight."

I watched as she walked away. Smart and mouthy. Maybe a touch of *Seinfeld*'s Elaine in one of her frizzier moments. I figured that maybe Hank's idea of testing my powers in the lab was not such a bad idea. At least I could tell people what I meant when I said I was invulnerable.

I grabbed a pizza and a beer before heading to Hank's lab that evening. I really wanted several beers, as the idea of being a guinea pig still didn't appeal that much. By the time I arrived, Hank and Ellen were already there, and so, to my surprise, was Raffy. Hank was walking around checking on his plans, while Raffy followed him, offering suggestions and criticisms. I could tell he was driving Hank crazy.

"Hey, Raffy," I said. "What are you doing here?"

"I heard from Ms. Waters that you couldn't fly anymore, and a little bird told me you'd be testing a new power."

I turned and stared at Ellen. She shrugged. "Hey, you wanted me to tell people."

"I guess so. What's the plan?"

Raffy spoke before Hank had a chance. "To start, you stand at the wall over there and Hank's going to shoot air pellets at you with progressively higher force. We'll see when they hurt."

Well, that did not seem so bad. And it wasn't. As I expected, nothing hurt or damaged me, and Hank and Raffy were suitably impressed. "The force of that last blast was equivalent to a .44 bullet," Hank said.

"So that's it," I said, feeling pleased with myself.

It was not. They had started shooting air pellets at my chest. Now Hank wanted to aim the pellets. At my face, knees, eyes, ears, etc. Hank amped up the power slowly, but it turned out that there was nothing to worry about. Even on the highest level nothing hurt anywhere.

Then they wanted to test me against fire. I started simply, holding my hand over a Bunsen burner, and ended up having them blowtorch my face. It was fun. My eyes did not melt. It felt like nothing, and I could see the awe in their faces. I was pretty much in awe of myself.

"What about harder projectiles?" Raffy asked.

"Well, I gave some thought to it," Hank said, "but I never thought we'd get this far. I don't have a gun, but I have some arrows. What do you think, Jason?"

"Bring it on."

They began with steel-tipped arrows, shot from a machine, aimed carefully at my arm. Then they tried several titanium-tipped arrows. Even the solid hits just tickled. Finally, we were all feeling somewhat giddy, and I invited them to shoot at will. They took turns, aiming wherever they wanted. Nothing hurt, nothing penetrated my skin. The arrows fell at my feet, broken and bent. I was like Saint Sebastian, only better, because the arrows actually skewered him.

An arrow Ellen shot, although she swears it was an accident, headed straight to my groin. It made no difference. I had a dick of steel. We collapsed in laughter.

There were two last tests. The first was a poison test, which I passed with flying colors. Hank had procured/stolen enough arsenic, and enough of some poison gas, that they should have left me curled up in a ball on the floor vomiting my guts out. I took each in turn, and they had no effect.

The second was the underwater test. Did I need to breathe? The answer, as it turned out, after I was essentially waterboarded, was that I did. Or at least that I could not convince my body otherwise, because thankfully, Hank, Ellen and Raffy didn't insist on actually killing me in the course of the test.

Then we went out and got rip-roaring drunk. I, for one, had earned it. (I know, I know—how did I get drunk if poison didn't affect me?—another mystery, but trust me, I was drunk.) Now that my awesome invulnerability had been confirmed in spades, the guys really started taking seriously what I should do with it.

Assuming I could avoid asphyxiation, firefighting was the one option that really made sense. But it was hard to know how to get into that. You couldn't just show up at the station and say "Hey, I can't be hurt by fire. Call me if you need someone to go into a burning building." They would expect you to go through channels, take civil service tests, work your way up from cleaning out fire hoses. All the usual crap. None of us could think of a good way around this.

Sitting next to me, Ellen kept feeling the skin on my arm, saying that it *had* to have something to do with a change in skin density. Then she would rub my arm and say, "But it feels so normal." She was pretty drunk too.

Meanwhile, it became clearer why Raffy only thought about making money. It turned out that he had never read a comic book in his life. He'd never even watched a Marvel movie.

"Wait a sec," I said. "You're a tech geek, aren't you? How can you have grown up without reading comics?"

"Wasn't interested," he said. "Why should I waste my time on stuff that isn't true?"

Jesus! It turned out, as far as I could tell, that he had spent his youth reading biographies of Jack Welch and Mark Zuckerberg.

I felt I had to defend comics and went on a rant about how all of Western literature was essentially about superheroes. The very first narratives—the epic of Gilgamesh, Homer's *Odyssey*, the Old Testament, *Beowulf*—all stories of guys with superpowers. Then medieval literature was all about saints, like Sebastian, and knights, like Lancelot and Galahad. More superheroes. So by the time the very first novel in the Western World came along it was already passé. Instead of writing a superhero tale, Cervantes wrote a mockumentary of the comic-book form, with Don Quixote as a wannabe Superman, seeing himself surrounded by supervillains (the windmill he thinks is a giant).

So-called realistic novels—Dickens, Tolstoy, Balzac and all that crap—are derivative works: superhero stories where the superpowers get left out.

But they don't always get left out completely. The relationship of Elizabeth and Darcy in *Pride and Prejudice* is total Lois Lane and Clark Kent. Darcy's secret identity is not milksop, it's arrogant SOB, but it's still a secret identity. And when Elizabeth's sister gets in trouble, what does Darcy do? He does the whole Superman thing. He drops his secret identity, whips on his cape and flies to the rescue, just like any regular comic-book hero. And mouthy, independent Lizzy is a dead ringer for Lois Lane. She has no time for arrogant Darcy, just as Lois has no time for milksop Clark. She only falls for him when she realizes he is, in fact, Superman and not Clark/Darcy.

Hank knew my rant and appreciated it. I saw Ellen staring at me wide-eyed, but I didn't know whether that was because she was really impressed, or because she thought I was full of shit.

Raffy was definitely unimpressed. He said it just went to show that literature was crap. Bill Gates and Warren Buffet did a lot more for people than Superman ever did.

The bad thing that happened that night was that Ellen slept over. Maybe it was inevitable. Watching me get shot at and incinerated over and over again seemed to stir all her female protectiveness. She confused the relief at my coming through unscathed with lust. I was drunk enough I hardly remember if anything happened, all I know was we woke up next to each other with no clothes on.

I realized it could be seen as a step backwards in my efforts to woo Penny. The last thing I needed was for Penny and my other friends, including Ellen herself, to think I was already taken.

On the other hand, I finally felt some of the awesomeness of invulnerability. If Penny, or anyone else for that matter, could see me emerge unharmed from genuine life-threatening danger, I could be in like Flynn. The Flynn Avenger.

CHAPTER 10

Tough Guy

So I had been drunk, I swear. But the next day I awoke with no trace of a hangover. I had a get-out-of-jail-free card. Still, I pretended to be asleep when Ellen woke up, slipped out of bed, picked up her clothes and left. I wasn't sure what to say.

She must have felt the same way, because we avoided each other at school for the next two weeks. She did her job telling people about my new power, though. By that afternoon, Toby, Sylvia and Penny all knew the score.

Penny was super sweet, in fact, I'd have to say, all over me. It made me think that maybe chicks dug invulnerability as much as flying. She wanted to know what I was going to do with it. I mentioned firefighting, and she offered to come along if I ever went looking for a fire, which cemented my plans to do just that. She also thought I should get Raffy working on a business opportunity, pointing out that if my invulnerability went away, I would regret not seizing the opportunity. She said I was like a star football player in college, one injury away from losing out on the big payday. It might have been the longest conversation we had had.

Sylvia had her hormones under control, rather too firmly, I thought. She said she wanted to review my lesson plans, to make sure my classes were keeping up with the curriculum. I said that would be okay and asked if Ellen had talked with her. She was rather prim about it. Yes, she had heard, thank you.

I had to remind myself that this new attitude was an improvement.

Toby, on the contrary, seemed enamored of my invulnerability. He kept beckoning me into his homeroom when no one was around and regaling me with new scenarios in which a single invulnerable warrior or spy might have turned the tide of history. Horatio at the bridge was mentioned more than once. One day, as he was talking, he paused and said, "You know my brother was in Vietnam, right?"

"Yes," I said. Everyone knew that. It featured in many of Toby's stories.

Then he opened his jacket and removed a big knife. It must have been ten inches long.

"This is his bowie. Left it to me when he died. You don't mind if I see how it works."

"Uh," I said, cleverly. "How did you get that in here?"

The school has a no-weapons policy, and every student and teacher has to pass through a metal detector on the way into school.

"They don't check on Saturdays," Toby said. "Now, come on. The others have seen you in action."

"Okay," I said. "What do you want . . ." I didn't get anything else out before he'd thrust the knife directly at my stomach. It turned in his hand and clattered to the floor, but not before ripping a gash in my shirt.

"I'll pay for the shirt, of course," Toby said. "Once more?"

"Uhhh, I'm good."

Raffy, meanwhile, had worked up a business plan, a powerpoint, incorporation papers, and a host of other documents, trying to get a business off the ground. He'd take me aside and walk me through them, showing me what he called the "value proposition." It all seemed to be about selling nutritional supplements that would give other people my powers. I pointed out that we had no idea how to do that.

"That's why we need to sequence your DNA, analyze your blood chemistry, your bone structure. Find out what makes you tick."

"What if we find nothing?"

That's where Raffy grinned, looking a whole lot less loveable than Michael Cera. "We'll find something to sell. I'm not saying everyone will be a superhero. But with what you can do, it's the mother of all marketing opportunities. People don't have to think that bullets will bounce off. All they have to believe is that they have a slightly lower chance to catch the flu. And with you out there flaunting your stuff, I guarantee you they'll give it a try."

I wavered. I didn't know what to think, but I did know that Raffy's plans had me going public with my powers. I wasn't ready for that. Raffy claimed that it was the safest route to go. I was certain to be discovered at some point. The only way to prevent some super-secret government agency disappearing me was to get rich and famous first.

All I had to do, Raffy said, was sign the papers. He'd do everything else.

It sounded like free money, and who was I to turn down free money? Anyway, hadn't Hank and I agreed that I needed money if I was to become a full-time hero? I said I'd think about it, but needed to talk it over with Hank.

Hank, of course, being Hank, wanted nothing to do with it. Even though he was named as the chief science officer in Raffy's documents, and got a pretty good chunk of stock. The funny thing is he wanted to sequence my DNA, and run batteries of other tests, just like Raffy. But, he said, that it was for science, not commerce.

Hank's purity-of-science arguments didn't really do it for me, but his other arguments were more persuasive. What, he asked, would

Peter Parker do? Hal Jordan? Matt Murdoch? Barry Allen? And I had to admit he was right. None of them would sell supplements.

Penny took Raffy's side of the argument, and you might think that I was enough of an idiot that I would let that sway me. And I'm not saying it didn't. But I still wasn't quite ready to sign anything. I read each new business plan Raffy came up with, but kept telling him that I needed more time.

Raffy might have been exasperated, but Penny did not seem to hold it against me. In fact, she began to accompany me after school when I sat around listening in on Boston Fire Department feeds.

The truth was that there was more hanging out than chasing fires. Do you know how many fire-related deaths there were in Boston last year? Five. I know that because I looked it up on the internet. Thirty-five in the whole of Massachusetts. So the chance of listening in on a feed where the difference between life and death would be a man who was invulnerable to fire was miniscule.

Still, Penny would sit with me in a café, sharing my earbuds, listening to the radio over the internet, and try to convince me to start a business, and life was good.

Sometimes we abandoned the fire department feeds and listened to eighties bands. We both loved the eighties arena pop that our parents had forced on us as kids. She was a Foreigner fan; I loved Styx. Or we talked about pop stars' memoirs, which we both consumed like candy. We loved Marianne Faithfull's autobiography, Debbie Harry's *Face It* and Rick James's *Glow*. She introduced me to Kim Gordon's *Girl in a Band*, and I told her about David Lee Roth's *Crazy from the Heat*. All of which showed that Hank was talking shit when he said we had nothing in common.

Not to mention, the number of people who checked me out when they saw Penny was significant. Who was the lucky schlub with a girl like that? Sure, I sometimes saw the shock of surprise— what's she doing with a middling Zach Braff? But what they didn't know, and what I really wanted to tell them, was: "Listen, bro, I'm fucking invulnerable." I almost signed up with Raffy just so I could let everyone know what was what.

On weekends, I did a bunch of stuff that I had been too chicken to do when I was not invulnerable, like bungee jumping and parasailing. It turned out this stuff was all expensive, and I wouldn't have been able to afford it at all on the measly salary that Flynn High paid for starting teachers. I was already using Mr. MasterCard to help me balance rent and groceries, and had worked up a nice fifteen-hundred-dollar balance since September. But my grandparents had given me some money the previous Christmas, and I used that. A single attempt at each activity, and the money was already gone, but I didn't mind. They didn't compare to actual flying.

One weekend, driving back through Concord, I saw the Wind Haven nursing home. I thought it would be good to check in with Mr. Butler again. He didn't seem to have anyone else to visit him. The receptionist quizzed me about how I knew Mr. Butler, but when I claimed to be his grandson, she reluctantly buzzed me through the security doors.

Mr. Butler, lying in bed with a thin blanket around him, looked grey, but otherwise okay. He looked unsurprised to see me. "Oh, it's you," he said. "Come in."

I wasn't sure he really recognized me. "Jason," I said, pointing to myself. "I walked you back here together the other day."

The room was a disaster. There must have been trays from four or five meals lying around, flies buzzing around the uneaten food. Clothes and medicines were strewn about all over. The floor and walls were filthy. And there was a stench in the room like a bathroom had not been flushed for weeks. I fought down bile in my throat, before getting the idea that I should document the mess. I took out my phone and began to take pictures.

"You don't mind, do you, Mr. Butler?"

"No, go ahead." The old man watched me calmly.

As I was taking pictures, a man in a poorly fitting grey suit came in followed by two orderlies.

"So sorry for the interruption, Mr. Butler," the administrator said. "This young man got through our security claiming to be your grandson, but we'll have him out in a second."

The administrator was really talking to me, not Mr. Butler, but it was Mr. Butler who responded. He seemed oblivious to the intent of the two goons circling me. "No bother at all. I'm glad to see the young 'un. Helped me out the other day. Should we go for another walk, Jason?"

I was touched that he somehow remembered me through whatever fog muddied the rest of his brain, and it made me that much angrier to see the condition of his room.

I turned to the administrator. "I'm going for a walk with Mr. Butler. This room better be clean when we get back, or, so help me God, I will call a lawyer and sue the hell out of you." I waved my phone. "And I will send these pictures to every paper in Massachusetts."

I felt like the kind of self-important fraud who says to the cops, "Do you know who I am?" But an odd thing happened. The man took me seriously. The administrator and I stared at each other for a while, but eventually he looked away.

"Dinner's at six," he said. "And the patient is due for his medicine after that."

Mr. Butler, whose name it turned out was Joe, and I went for a walk and talked about fire deaths. It turned out that Joe knew a lot about how fires worked. First, he had worked as an electrician, and he said that about 30 percent of all fires were due to faulty wiring in the electric system. He said that flaws in the arc-fault circuit breaker, whatever that was, were the leading cause of fire in the United

States. Second, he had been a member of the volunteer fire brigade in Everett for twenty years.

I also discovered that he was an encyclopedia of old Boston prejudices. He said he didn't trust the West African orderlies, believing they were always going to steal his stuff. I know that old guys can't always help what they believe, but it pissed me off, and I told him he was full of shit. I thought he might go off on me, but instead he just nodded and said that I was probably right.

When we returned, I insisted on examining his room, and it looked much better. Joe and I said our goodbyes, and I promised to visit again soon.

A couple of days later Ellen and I began talking again. Not about sleeping together, of course, but I had to ask her about a kid I was having trouble with. And after the ice was broken, I told her my story about Mr. Butler. She said that she had heard that kind of story before. Residents who didn't have family visiting them received poor services and bad care. Sometimes the nursing homes robbed them blind.

Hearing that, I decided to visit Joe whenever I could. Sometimes I accompanied Ellen on her weekly visits to her grandfather, who was in a different (nicer) nursing home in the Concord area. Sometimes I went alone. Sometimes Joe and I would sit in his room and listen to the fire department radio feeds together on my computer. Joe explained to me what the various codes meant. I never went to try to save someone, and I never explained to Joe why I had started to listen to the radio feeds in the first place. But I did notice that his room was a little cleaner the next time I visited.

About two weeks later I finally got a chance to use my powers again, or at least almost. I was sitting in the lunchroom, at a table with a bunch of ninth graders telling booger jokes, when Ellen rushed in and ran over to me.

"There's a fight in the gym. Jason, come quick!"

I loved that. "Jason, come quick!" All the ninth graders turned and looked at each other, and I knew what they were thinking. Why did Ms. Rinaldi (that's Ellen's working name) ask for Mr. Smithka (that's my working name)? Shouldn't she be looking for Mr. Ducksworth, the gym teacher, or the hulking Mr. Mason? Even scary Mr. Jones (that's Toby) or Ms. Lewis would surely do better than the nebbish, unthreatening Mr. Smithka.

But it was me she called, and it was I who responded. I pushed back my chair, jumped up and ran after Ellen to the gym. There I saw the school's worst nightmare, two over-sized teens facing each other with knives in their hands, surrounded by a bunch of idiots egging them on. Maybe they had brought their knives in on Saturday like Toby.

The White guy, his name was Chad Gregg, was a senior, and was rumored to be a member of a group that called themselves the Westies. The name was meant to honor some bygone gang, but Toby said the kids were more a gaggle of delinquents than an organized gang. The Black guy, Jonas Dunbar, had been in my English class before he was bumped down to another track. He was a junior who had connections to an actual gang the name of which I couldn't remember. I was no expert on gangs, but we all received the basics as part of our new teacher orientation, so I could guess what some of the tattoos meant. Both of the kids outweighed me by over fifty pounds and, as I mentioned, they were surrounded by their scary friends.

At orientation they told us to never intervene in a gang fight. Call the police and move the other kids out of harm's way. But they didn't expect a teacher to be invulnerable.

Even so I was nervous. I hadn't been involved in a fight since third grade, and now I had everyone, including Ellen, watching me. At least I had the element of surprise on my side. I stepped out between the two boys.

"Put them down," I said.

"Stay out of this, Mr. S.," Jonas said, without looking at me.

"We're not having a knife fight here," I said.

The kids on the sideline were whooping in derision and disbelief. What did Mr. Smithka think he was doing?

"You're gonna get hurt," Chad said.

"I don't think so. You had better give me your knives." I reached out my hands to the two boys.

"Get away!" Chad yelled, and swung his knife, more like you might scare off a mosquito, than to really hurt me. But I didn't scare these days. I just stood there, and the boys didn't know what to do with the crazy teacher between them. They were confused, and I was convinced I had the situation in hand.

Except, even as I thought that, one of the Chad's overgrown crew grabbed me from behind, wrapped me in a bearhug and pulled me away. I kicked out and shouted, but I couldn't free my arms. What a stupid power, I thought. I was invulnerable and useless. How could superstrength not be a gimme with invulnerability? It was ridiculous to separate them.

Slowly, Chad and Jonas returned their attention to each other and began circling again. But maybe the delay I'd caused hadn't been totally useless, because very shortly after the kids had pulled me away, the cops arrived. They burst in and mopped up the scene before anyone got hurt.

Chad and some of his friends stared balefully at me as the cops handcuffed them and moved them out. I knew they'd be back at school soon. After all, the most anyone had on them was violating the no-weapons policy. Chad and Jonas would cooperate and deny that there was even any fight. Probably they'd make like best buds at the police station.

Ellen came up to me and said, "You were great."

"I did nothing," I said, disgusted.

"You stopped the fight."

"Not really."

"I think you did. You want to get a drink after work?"

I hesitated, and she clarified. "Just a drink. I'm pretty on edge."

"Sure," I said, and then I realized I couldn't. "Uh, actually, can we take a rain check? I'm meant to . . . meet Hank and . . . we had plans."

I felt like an idiot. I was meeting Penny at the café to listen to fire department feeds. Why couldn't I just tell Ellen that? Invite her along? I was living in a cheap sitcom. But the thing was, Penny was warming to me. I was sure she was. She was sitting closer, playing with her hair as I talked. Last time we met, she said I looked tense and gave me a backrub. And somehow I didn't think Ellen would appreciate it.

And it turned out that I didn't have to even make that excuse, because I wasn't going out with anyone that evening. One of the police officers came up and asked, "Are you the teacher who tried to stop things?"

It turned out the police needed me to come down to the station to make a statement. This took almost three hours. At first, they were all congratulating me for stepping between the boys, but quickly it turned into a different message. I shouldn't get involved in a fight like that. I'm not equipped, and I might get hurt. The last thing the police need when they arrive is an injured civilian, or maybe a hostage. The principal came down to the station a little after that and repeated what the police said almost word for word.

"Congratulations, you're a hero. Never let me see you do that again. Insurance, reckless, blah, blah, blah."

I wanted desperately to explain that I was not some schlub. I was a hero. I was invulnerable. I was fucking invulnerable. But a fat lot of good it did me.

 Stretchiness

CHAPTER 11
Flexing

After the incident in the school gym, Raffy redoubled his efforts to get me to sign his papers.

"You gotta strike while the market's hot," he said.

But I had what I wanted now. I was a hero. That's how people treated me, despite my having done nothing but get pulled out of the way.

So, of course, I kept giving Raffy the cold shoulder. It wasn't about money, man. It was the glory. I was hungry for it.

Three days later I woke up and I wasn't invulnerable anymore. I realized almost as soon as I woke up because I stubbed my toe.

Hank heard me yelp and came running. It turned out he had been charting my powers.

"You flew for 37 days. You were invulnerable for 32. Now what?"

"Now when I get jumped by the Westies after school, I can bleed my life away. At least Raffy will leave me alone." I was oddly unconcerned about losing my invulnerability.

"Are you feeling okay otherwise? You look a little pale." He reached out and felt my brow. "And you're cold."

I looked at my arms. Maybe he was right. They did look a little pasty. Clammy. The pores looked too big, sort of like the skin on a dead chicken. But I felt terrific.

"I feel fine," I said. "Really good. I just need some sun."

"Maybe you have another power."

"You think so?" The powers had sort of sucked, but I didn't want to have no power.

"Look, when you stopped flying, you became invulnerable. After about the same amount of time, give or take a few days, you stop being invulnerable. Maybe it's time you get another power. Maybe you're super-strong?"

I looked skeptical. "I don't know how logical that is."

"Try to bend the spoon." He handed me a teaspoon.

I tried. It bent. But we have sucky cutlery.

"Well, it must be something else."

"It might be something else," I corrected.

"What other superpowers are there?"

"Speed, laser eyes, spider sense, teleportation, telekinesis, cold breath, ability to grow and shrink, invisibility, phantom powers, weather control, fire bolts, molecule manipulation. There's a million of them."

"So how can we test them?"

"I have to get to school. I have a first-period class."

"Go. I'll figure out something for the afternoon."

"Fine," I said. And I went off to school, no longer invulnerable, but feeling rather chill about it.

My classes went well. My students had decided I was a cool guy based on my stopping the fight, and I told some good jokes that kept the kids engaged. Then after lunch, Penny caught me in the hall and proposed dinner on Friday.

I must have looked really surprised because she laughed and said, "Don't be a goof. You're a very special person."

I was walking on air by the time I headed back home. We had another pub trivia match on Thursday. I had a date with Penny for

Friday, and, I thought, a good chance of ending up with a weekend in bed.

The only real negative on the horizon was whatever power-testing Hank had planned for that night. Finding the limits of my invulnerability was awful enough, even knowing my power. What Hank might dream up to see if I could shoot flames or create force fields hardly bore thinking about. Great! Just so long as my gonads were intact for Friday.

In fact, I was so busy thinking about the horrendous possibilities that I was not paying attention. At least, not the kind of attention you have to pay when you come out of the Harvard Square T station and are confronted with the explosive traffic patterns formed by mixing arrogant Harvard dickhead pedestrians and angry Boston drivers who fight like Ben Hur to get an edge on each other.

I had followed a crowd of students crossing Mass Ave, assuming a certain safety in numbers. But, contemplative and chillin' as I was, I may have dawdled. Whatever the case, when I looked up, I realized that the herd had moved sharply on, and I was standing alone in the path of the cream-colored Nissan Altima, the driver of which was definitely not watching where the fuck he was going.

Torn between leaping back (yes, into the path of a Volvo), leaping forward (I'd never make it) and leaping up (the *Jackass* version of the story—my memory was the car had to be traveling at least 90 miles an hour for someone to leap over it), I did all of them. My back foot went back, my front foot went forward and the rest of me went up. And, basically, the car went under my legs.

There I was standing like a fool in the middle of the road, twenty feet high, straddling half the road on stilt-like legs. I was confused as hell, but nowhere near as confused as everyone else. A large crowd was staring at me, and most of the traffic had stopped. (Not the Altima, though. It sped on.) With a will, I snapped back down to normal Jason shape and sprinted away before anyone could stop me.

It took me half a block to work out what had happened. I'd stretched. That was my new superpower. Elasticity. Stretchiness. What a stupid power. I just hoped that everyone who saw it wrote off what happened as impossible.

What about surveillance cameras around the area? People said they were everywhere. I had no idea, but—God!—probably. What sort of resolution did they have. Terrible, right? And maybe they never caught my face.

I was almost home before realizing that either I had lost any pursuers or that no one had followed me in the first place. I slowed to a walk and tried to calm down. Stretchiness, of course, has a long comic tradition. Mr. Fantastic, the Elongated Man, Elastic Lad, Plastic Man, Metamorpho, Elastigirl. Even Bart Simpson as Stretch Lad.

But that doesn't mean that it's a power mankind has always yearned for. It's not flying. It's not invulnerability. It's not strength. There's a reason why Plastic Man is more of a joke than a superhero. It's goofy to be stretchy.

Mr. Fantastic was cool, but he mostly used his stretchiness to reach a long way for coffee while performing experiments. There was a reason they made him the scientific genius of the bunch. He wasn't a natural fighter.

And you've probably forgotten about the Elongated Man and Elastic Lad. In the end, DC stopped producing these comics. And you know why? While fun to draw, no person has ever really sat around thinking: ooh, I wish I was stretchy.

Now that I knew what my power was, I realized that I had been using it all day in little ways. When I was surprised that Penny asked me out, my eyes may have bugged out, or my face contorted in some way. Or when I told jokes to my students.

Hank wasn't home when I arrived. I got a glass of water and went to sit on the couch.

Okay, maybe elasticity wasn't the coolest power in the world, but I wanted to see what I could do. I held the water glass and stretched out my arm. At first nothing, and then, presto, it worked. My arm snaked out until I could put the glass in the sink, at least twenty feet away.

The thing is, my arm thinned out as I stretched, but it never got as thin as you would expect. And I could still hold the glass to set it down. The fact that my arm was attenuated didn't seem to affect my strength. Of course, that's how it was in comics, but it made no sense in the real world. Ellen wouldn't like this at all.

I could telescope the arm back smoothly or snap it back into place. The snap created a force like a rubber band that knocked me back a little. I tried to see how far I could stretch just my pinkie. Six feet at its longest, about as thin as a pencil, and I could still pick up a teacup with it. If my two-inch pinkie could get to six feet, then my 71-inch frame should be able to stretch to . . . 213 feet. Wow!

I wondered if I could turn my whole body into a ball. Plastic Man does that a lot, and then rolls down hills. I imagined myself as Violet Beauregard in *Charlie and the Chocolate Factory*, blowing myself up like a blueberry. I felt my sides and insides stretch. It wasn't an entirely comfortable feeling. It didn't hurt, but it prickled. I ended up more like a lumpy sack of potatoes than a beach ball. But I filled almost the whole living room.

One thing I should mention quickly. In the comics, heroes have clothes that stretch with them. My clothes did not. There was a point as I blew up where my clothes ripped and burst off. The shirt provided a little resistance; the pants a little more. But in the end, the power of stretch was stronger than the seams on the clothes. I realized that I was just incredibly fortunate not to have lost my pants when I shot up to let the car go through my legs.

I snapped back into my normal form. I could have done this slowly, a bit at a time, but I liked the sensation of snapping. Also, I suddenly thought about the thing your mother tells you when you're making faces as a kid—you'll be stuck that way if the wind changes. I definitely did not want to be stuck as a gigantic sack of potatoes.

I tried to make my hands into tools, like scissors or hammers. Plastic Man did this regularly, so did Metamorpho. Other stretch characters less so. It turns out there's a reason for that. It's hard. Really hard. I made a sort of vague hammer shape with my fist, but I never got close to scissors. Stretching your body into a particular shape is like modeling something out of clay when you can't even touch the clay. Not to mention which, you have all these fiddly bits, like ears, knuckles and fingers, so it's hard to get a smooth block of clay to work with.

I went into the bathroom and admired myself in the full-length mirror. My skin was not good. Pale and rubbery, as Hank had noticed that morning. I'd have to make sure Penny and I went to a dark restaurant for our date on Friday.

But there were compensations. I made myself a little taller, narrowed my waist, broadened my shoulders, buffed up my abs, squared my jaw, raised my cheekbones. I was devastating. More like a buff Errol Flynn than Zach Braff. I liked it. And I was hung. In fact, I could be as hung as I wanted.

To me that sounded like a rap album. *Hung as I Wanna Be.* I should ask Hank, whose knowledge of hip hop was, oddly, as broad as his knowledge of comics.

Friday was going to be good. I looked in the mirror. Okay, maybe there could be too much of a good thing. Dial back just a little.

(Yeah–dear reader and crap–Hank has already made the point that folks don't want to read about my junk. So I won't tell you anymore. Just keep in mind: I was a single guy in my twenties, and I could do some amazing things.)

I heard steps on the stairs and realized Hank was home. I quickly ran into my room and pulled some clothes on. There had to be some excellent practical joke I could play on him. By the time he came in the apartment, I was sitting on the sofa.

"Hello, Jason," he said.

"Hey, Hank," I said. "We've got problems."

"What's wrong?"

"I think there's a rat in the kitchen," I said. "Or something, anyway. I just saw a flash of fur. It scared the bejesus out of me, and I got the hell out of there."

"Well, we have to get it out."

"I'm not going in there."

"Great, some hero! Aren't you supposed to be fucking invulnerable?"

"That was yesterday."

"Well, maybe this is your new power," Hank said. "You attract unusually large rodents."

"Ha!"

Hank rolled his eyes, fetched a hockey stick from our front hall closet, and turned grimly to the kitchen.

"Wait, what's that . . ."

Something brown and fuzzy flew at his face. Hank swung his hockey stick wildly, missed, smashed a hole in the front of one of the cabinets, and fell down. The brown, furry thing danced up and down on his face.

"Help! Get it off me! Get it off me? Jason!" Hank was screaming like a banshee.

I snapped my arm back, hid my monkey finger-puppet in the couch and rushed over. "What's wrong, Hank? Where did the creature go?"

Hank was breathless. He started to explain to me what had happened and then smelled a figurative rat. "Okay, what was it?"

"I don't know," I said. "I just saw something fly at you."

"No way! You're doing this! Where is it?"

He looked so angry that I almost laughed. I stretched my arm out to the couch and brought out my old puppet. Hank watched with eyes wide.

"You bastard," he said. And he punched me as hard as he could, which, admittedly, is not very hard. Somewhat to both of our surprise, his hand just sunk into my arm, leaving a fist-sized impression, but not hurting me at all.

"Sorry," I said, "I just couldn't resist."

Hank said nothing. I realized he was torn between being a good sport and being upset with the trick I played. He wanted to ask me about my new power, but was still too mad.

"I really *am* sorry. I know it was a mean trick. But it's just so cool being stretchy. Go sit, and I'll order some Chinese food."

"Elasticity," Hank said, relenting, as I went to find the phone. "I didn't expect that."

Then we got down to real conversation. I showed Hank my stuff (being careful to demonstrate my powers in a way that left me fully clothed).

"Wow!" Hank kept saying, every time I did something new. "Wow."

"What do you mean 'wow'?" I asked.

"Well, it's pretty amazing."

"More amazing than my other powers?"

"In a way, I guess. Weirder, for sure."

"You just don't sound so impressed." His envy of my flying and my invulnerability had been palpable. But now, let's just say his enthusiasm was constrained.

"Not unimpressed. Not at all. Freaked out maybe. It's pretty uncanny seeing you do some of this stuff. It's, I don't know, off-putting."

"Not macho, you mean?"

"I don't want to hurt your feelings."

"Yeah, well come on! Say it."

"It's kind of gross."

We didn't say much more that night. I cleaned up and we went to bed.

I knew what Hank meant, of course. Stretching one's body like I could was pretty disgustoid.

But, man, was it fun!

CHAPTER 12

Lassitude

As we made our breakfast the next day, we were like strangers, talking in overly polite phrases.

"Would you mind passing the milk?"

"Not at all. Are you ready for coffee?"

Finally, I couldn't stand it any longer. I said, "Look, I'm sorry. My prank yesterday sucked wind. I shouldn't have done it."

"Forget it," Hank said. "I get that stretching is pretty cool. I may still be kinda jealous of your powers."

"Yeah, but less so now, right?"

"Maybe, I don't know. I mean it's better than invulnerability, right? You've got some invulnerability built in, at least to blunt attacks. Also, you have an attack weapon."

"Not much of one."

"Well, you can't just be held down like the kids in the gym did to you. And elasticity puts some power in your punches."

"Yeah," I said. But we both knew the truth. On the scale of armaments invented by humanity, my offensive capabilities were more like those of the yo-yo than those of the flame-thrower.

"I just wish we could figure out a pattern. Where your powers come from and how they change."

"You and Ellen are a pair. There's more to life than science."

"It's dangerous to have no idea what's happening. If your power is going to keep changing, you could get hurt. Like when you jumped out the window thinking you could fly. It was lucky you were invulnerable."

"You know, I think I could jump out the window like this too. I'd just bounce. Maybe all my powers are throw-yourself-out-the-window-and-you'll-be-okay powers. That's the connection."

"Yeah, next time your power will be invisibility. It'll make it impossible to pick up the pieces. And what if Toby had tried to knife you again. Just for kicks. Your power wouldn't save you from that."

"Maybe I'll stick at elasticity."

I saw, or imagined, Hank shudder at that idea. "Or they'll just go away."

"Jesus, I still haven't really done anything with them."

"What do you want to do?"

"Save a city. Stop a war. Foil an alien invasion. You know. The usual stuff."

"You still want to be a hero?"

"Of course."

"Your powers changing every five seconds makes it hard."

"I'm not sure I could have done anything with flying and invulnerability even if I'd had 'em for years."

"You know, we never tested if you were affected by radiation. If not, you would have been great at helping out in nuclear disasters. Like at Fukushima."

"Right. I'd just have to be able to afford to toss my job aside and fly to places like Japan at the drop of a hat."

"Yeah. You need access to resources."

"That's what Raffy wants me to do. Make money. Maybe he's right."

"He *only* wants you to make money."

"So what do I do?"

"What if we find a sponsor? Some rich guy who can fly you around to do good deeds."

"Like Charlie with his Angels. I don't want to be the tool of some billionaire!"

"What's the alternative?"

"I don't know. The powers all seem kind of useless." I stretched my arm into the bathroom to find my comb. "At least this one's fun."

At the time Hank and I had the conversation, we had not seen the papers. On my way to the T, I did. *The Boston Globe* had a picture of me, from the waist down, with legs straddling most of Mass Ave. The headline said:

CITYWIDE MANHUNT ON FOR RUBBER MAN.

The *Herald* had its own photo spread, first of me at a stretch, and then me running away. Thankfully my face was turned away in all the pictures. I bought the paper and discovered that the police were asking anyone else who might have pictures to come forward. They thought that the "suspect"—suspect in what, I wanted to know, what had I done?—was a college student living in Cambridge. They even dug up some sources who claimed "on good authority" that the FBI considered the incident linked to earlier stories of a flying man in Boston.

Jesus Christ! Hank would freak when he saw this. I was sort of freaking out myself. I was just crossing the street. Now everyone—the newspapers, the Feds, the State—was out to get me.

I guess it didn't really surprise me. I was a millennial after all. I'd grown up in the digital age. I had committed the sin of being interesting. Anyone, or anything, interesting is going be hounded until properly pinned down for study and analysis by every single person with an internet account. Suddenly I knew how Justin Bieber felt.

Of course, in this case the masses would be disappointed. If I was found, the federal government would disappear me before the keyboard commandos learned a thing. Hank and I had talked this one to death. The military would want to make sure they could counteract my powers before anyone else had a chance to get a good look at them. The same way, according to Hank, the government quarantines quantum computing advances until it's sure that they won't break their cryptographic codes.

Or maybe they'd want to replicate my powers for brainwashed super-soldiers. Either way, I was screwed.

Now some of you dear readers may think that this attitude is unnecessarily untrusting of our good governmental servants, but that just means you are probably over thirty. For the rest of us, we grew up during the years of the Department of Homeland Security, indefinite detention, Guantanamo Bay and not being able to take toothpaste through airport security. We know better.

I should have been more worried than I was, but the truth was, I felt pretty good. Being elastic was just so awesome that it was hard to get too down. Anyway, I liked the idea of being a national security risk. If I did end up getting arrested, maybe I could find some cool accommodation with the Feds, and they could put me to use saving the world.

But in the meantime, there was a bounce in my step, literally. I couldn't help lengthening my stride and snapping my fingers. I found that if I grew my fingers just a tad I could make a snap like a firecracker.

I tried hard to control myself, but I knew that by the afternoon there was an undercurrent of talk about me. What was wrong? Why was I so happy? Was I always this expressive? Etc., etc. Principal Snowe came up to chat with me at the end of the day. She wanted to revisit the scene with the gang members. Tell me that I was a valuable asset to the school. That they just wanted to ensure

I didn't get hurt. But she watched me closely as she spoke, to see what all the talk was about, I assume. I kept my face absolutely still.

I had decided not to tell Ellen, Penny and the others because, hey, I was still pretty much invulnerable, and it was all too complicated. I forgot that they would figure it out for themselves as soon as they saw the headlines.

Raffy had popped his head in my room after my 9 a.m. English I class and said, "Hey, Stretch. Time's running out." He waved some papers. "Get in at the ground floor." He left before I could ask what he meant. There was no company without me.

Toby had come up during lunch and greeted me like there had been a death in the family. "Too bad, Jason." He patted me on the shoulder. "A definite downgrade." There were too many people around to explain to him that I didn't see it that way at all.

At any rate, I figured the game was up. So when I saw Penny in the faculty office I went right up to her and asked her if she wanted to see my new powers after school.

"Uh, it's a quiz night, right?"

Damn, I'd forgot.

"Well, you want to walk over together?"

She hesitated, looking more pale and beautiful than ever. "Oh, Jason, I have some errands to run. But I'll definitely see you there."

I was momentarily disappointed, then she reached out and touched my forearm. "But we're on for dinner tomorrow. You can show me what you can do then."

She smiled and I felt great.

Sylvia seemed as uninterested in elasticity as she was in invulnerability. She had observed one of my classes and we met after school to go over her notes. She was all business and only referred to my stretching at the end as part of her critique: "When you pointed your arm overextended a bit, and when you turned to face someone your ears and nose turned before the rest of your body.

You need to watch that."

The only person I didn't see that day was Ellen. This was weird enough that I wondered if she was avoiding me again. After meeting with Sylvia, I went to seek Ellen out in her office. On trivia nights, she and I usually ate an early supper at Nakamura, a hole-in-the-wall Chinatown deli that happened to serve cheap sushi. We treated ourselves to sushi on the theory that it was brain food.

But she was not around by the time I was through with Sylvia, so I guessed I was on my own that night.

I headed to catch the T to Chinatown—I was going to have sushi with or without Ellen—when I noticed that there was a cluster of Westies standing at the street corner. They weren't kids from the school—so no one I could identify to police—but they were wearing the gang colors we had been shown at orientation.

I was about to turn around and head the other way when they saw me, and my pride wouldn't let me. Superheroes couldn't go ducking bad guys.

Out of the corners of my eyes, I saw them move to block the road, and my heart started racing.

As I walked toward them, I began to get more mad and less frightened. Why were they bugging me? All I had done was stop Chad from getting killed by Jonas. Fuck 'em! Why should they stop me walking where I wanted?

Just before I would have bumped into them, I stopped and looked up. My anger boiled over, and I blew up in their faces.

And I mean blew up. I screeched and my face flattened and stretched sideways and up. My eyes popped out of their sockets, my mouth opened impossibly wide. My teeth lengthened and my tongue, huge and flat, stuck unnaturally far out of my mouth.

I'm not sure what else changed, because I snapped back immediately. It was just a momentary expression of rage. But it served its purpose. Even as I was snapping back, the Westies had turned their backs and were sprinting away from me as fast as they could. I didn't think they'd bother me again.

Scared straight. It was a shame in a way. I'd sort of wanted more of a fight. But, man, was elasticity a freaky power.

I felt self-satisfied as I headed to the deli. All we had to do was win that night, and we would be headed to the trivia Sweet Sixteen. If we won the tournament, we would get $1,200 to split. I sure hoped we would win because I had already spent my $200 several times over in my mind. I was going to take Penny to Vermont for the weekend, buy the slick pair of cowboy boots that I walked past every morning in Harvard Square, and get dad the Mizuno graphic wedge that he kept going on about.

I thought I might see Ellen at Nakamura, but I didn't. I had a combo platter (just $11.99) and an iced tea.

I needed to talk with someone other than Hank about my powers. I mean, he was brilliant and all, and we shared a comic-book sensibility, but I never quite trusted his common sense. I felt that something obvious might be escaping his notice.

Also, it wasn't just about superpowers. It was everything. Hank was my best friend, but I couldn't talk to him about choosing between law school and business school. He thought everyone should get a PhD and teach at MIT.

And Hank was just a guy. When you teach in a high school, with all the definitely unavailable, definitely-exploring-their-sexuality high school girls batting their eyelashes at you, you feel a lack of female company. Thank God, I had Penny to occupy my erotic fantasy life.

But it wasn't like I could talk to her. I couldn't ask her what tie went with what shirt, or whether I should look for a job in advertising. She was the reason I cared about the tie and shirt matching in the first place. The whole point was I wanted her to see me as a self-confident go-getter who could do everything effortlessly. I couldn't tell her that I had no idea what to do with myself.

So that left Ellen. I wasn't sure that Ellen was always right about ties and shirts, but she sure had opinions.

After supper, I headed over to the bar in the financial district hosting the trivia event, the Acorn. It was one of those bars that could not decide what to be. It had a trendy wine bar and too-dark red lighting like it was going to be an upscale, ferny kind of thing, but the rest of the space, with cheap tables, lots of standing room and the sort of solid wood floor that wipes up fast after a night of spillage and pukage, suggested it was a pack-'em-in-and-get-'em-drunk sort of place. The menu had wings and rings for the latter crowd, and some Spanish tapas for the former. It would not have been my first choice as a place to spend the evening.

We were battling a team from Citizens' Bank. I thought they would be the usual Masters-of-the-Universe type bankers, who assume that they are smarter than anyone, and whom we specialized in knocking off, but when we saw them sitting in their goofy purple team shirts, it was clear they were the other type of banking team. Underpaid back-office nerds and tech personnel. The type of team that could go toe-to-toe with us on the science and technology, which would mean we had to rely on Toby's erudition to beat them on questions covering things like Latin and Medieval France.

When I arrived Toby and Sylvia were already there. I joined them.

As I was sitting down, Raffy came in with Penny. "Yo, my brothers. What is happening?"

"It's a tech team. We should be fine, if you can hold your own in the science," Toby said.

"No problem," Raffy said.

"Who wants a beer?" Sylvia asked, standing up. "I'm buying."

As Sylvia made her way over to the bar to order for us, Raffy started talking about his damned start-up.

"So I've reserved time on the Genentech sequencer. All I need is your John Hancock and your DNA. I've located a pharma manufacturer in Western Mass that can start churning out made-to-order supplements within a month."

"We aren't sure it's genetic," Penny said.

"It doesn't matter. Everyone has some DNA anomalies. We figure out Jason's, create a product that reflects 'em and market the shit out of it. No one will take a chance that they miss out on superpowers."

"Recent developments notwithstanding?" Toby asked, returning with the first two beers. "I mean, it's more like a child's toy than a superpower."

"It'll do. Anything'll do. You see the way the papers went apeshit over that picture." Raffy turned to me.

"Yeah, but I haven't agreed to any of this," I protested. "The whole thing sounds like a scam."

Sylvia came back with our beers, and Raffy took a long draught before responding. "Jason, you haven't listened. We don't guarantee anything. We try to emulate your body chemistry. That's what we tell people. We don't promise it'll work."

"Oh, come on!" I protested. "It would be more honest just to rob a bank."

Penny came and took my arm.

"Raffy, stop pushing him. It must be very disconcerting. None of us know what he's going through." She slipped her hand around my back and gave me a smile. I felt calmer at once. "I mean, of course, Raffy is only trying to do what's best for everyone, but we all realize we have to move at your pace, Jason."

"Right!" I said as Penny massaged my neck.

"Well, I agree," Raffy said. "Can't do it without you."

But there was no more time for conversation. Hank and Ellen arrived together, and the quiz master announced from the bar that it was time for the teams to register. That just meant that we had to sign in and show our IDs to prove we were the people we were meant to be. There was no bringing in ringers.

But before registering, I was stopped by Ellen and Hank.

"We need to talk," Hank said.

I pointed to the bar to indicate that we had other things to do, but they shook their heads.

"We think you're being followed," Ellen said.

"There was someone outside the apartment all day," Hank said. "Plain white truck. Driver in a suit."

"Uh oh," I said, and molded my face into a somewhat exaggerated "we're in trouble" expression as I spoke.

"Look, this is serious," Hank said. "You saw the papers. They're looking for you. Maybe they found you. It's not like you've been discreet."

"Look, a white van. A guy in a suit. You guys are jumping to conclusions."

"We're not," Ellen said.

"Even so, we can't do anything about it now. The quiz is about to begin."

That stopped them. Hank nodded and he and Ellen went over with me to register. When we came back, I made sure to reclaim my seat next to Penny. I was not thinking about Feds in white vans. I was thinking porno thoughts about how my power might come in useful tomorrow night. And then the quiz began.

It went pretty much as expected. With Hank to supplement Raffy and Ellen, we held our own on science. Toby rocked on history, and I came through with some awesome displays of literary trivia. The pen name Nabokov used for his early novels? Vladimir Sirin. Where did Edgar Allen Poe go to college? He attended both the University of Virginia and West Point, but didn't graduate from either.

At any rate, we actually stomped the Citizens' Bank guys pretty good. In the round of 16, we'd meet the winner of a match between Akamai Technologies, who had reached the final last year, and Boston Pharma.

I wanted to stay out late and drink to celebrate, but Sylvia and Toby, being old, left right after the quiz, and Penny left soon thereafter saying she was tired and wanted to be fresh the next day. Which reminded me that we were going out to dinner, and I wanted to be fresh too. So I suggested to Hank we leave also.

Ellen said, "What about the van?"

Hank looked at me, but I just shrugged. "What can we do tonight?" I asked. "I just won't stretch in front of them. They'll soon get bored."

I knew Ellen and Hank were unconvinced by my brilliant strategy, but they didn't have any better ideas so they didn't argue.

What I didn't tell them was this: I wasn't sure I could stop stretching. I mean, looking back, I realized I had been using my power in public, off and on, all day. I hadn't really meant to, but it was just so much fun and so easy that I stretched without thinking about it.

It may not have helped that, in my elastic state, I felt so relaxed that it was hard to take anything too seriously. The Feds? The Westies? Preparing for class? Yawn! Nothing to worry about.

We had won our trivia game, I had a date with Penny the next night and I could twist myself like a pretzel. Life was good.

CHAPTER 13
I'm Rubber and You're Glue

Okay, let me spare you the tension. You are no doubt wondering: did I get it on with Penny? Yes, indeedy.

And then you'll want to know: how incredibly hot was it having sex with a 10? Super amazing, of course. Be jealous. Unless you are, yourself, a movie star, it will probably never happen to you.

So, if you can't be a hero, at least you got the girl, right? Doesn't that make up for everything? Darn right. Who cares about glory when you've got a girl like Penny? And if you're around next June, consider dropping in for our wedding. A big do in the Hamptons (I imagined her parents were loaded).

Hank, believing most people to have his almost nonexistent sense of humor, has recommended I delete the first three paragraphs of this chapter. "But the first paragraph is true," I argue. To which he replies that it is not relevant to the story, and that a gentleman does not discuss what he does on his dates, although he doesn't put it quite in those terms. I think he says, "You aren't some fucking rapper," but the point is the same. (I guessed he must have gotten bored and skimmed chapter 9.)

Maybe he has a point, but it is hard to tell the story of this year without some mention of sex. First of all, I was 24, immensely powerful and constantly horny. Second, and Hank knows this as well as anyone, you can't separate superpowers and sex. I know comics seem pretty devoid of sex, but come on, man. That whole "truth, justice and the American way" thing, all the crimefighting and baddie-punching? It's about nerdy teenagers sublimating their sex drives. At least, I'm pretty sure that was true in my case. And I am trying to tell the truth, mostly.

So here's the truth. Getting off with Penny was not the super awesome experience I imagined. First of all, I was drunk off my ass. I had tried to move quickly from dinner (for two at Figs in Beacon Hill—a month's rent down the drain) to bed, but she wanted to go out to a bar instead.

I suggested a karaoke bar I knew in Cambridge, and she was into that. We had a couple of beers and discussed what we would sing when our turns came around. I went first and poured my heart and soul into a version of Styx's *Babe*. It was good, drawing a smattering of applause from the bar and a standing ovation from Penny. As I put down the mike, I could almost hear the bar patrons thinking: Ah, that's why she's with him—he's a budding rock star.

Then Penny did a performance of Foreigner's *Juke Box Hero* that put me to shame. She belted it out like the second coming of Joan Jett. By the time she was done, she had the whole bar rocking, swaying and joining in the choruses. It might have withered my self-confidence, except for the knowledge that this beautiful rock star would walk out of the bar with me.

I never really wondered how I got so lucky as to go out with someone as talented as Penny, any more than I wondered why I, of all people, deserved superpowers. If asked I might have responded like Maria when she finally hooked up with Captain Trapp: "Somewhere in my youth or childhood, I must have done something good." (In the movie, she earned her good fortune by teaching seven pliable Austrian kids to sing—so think how much more good luck I deserved for teaching over 60 delinquent American teens to read Shakespeare!)

After her star turn, I suggested to Penny that maybe it was time to head back to my place, but Penny had other ideas. She wanted to hit a nearby hotel bar for a "nightcap." As we drank, Penny snuggled up to me and talked about how sexy it would be to have a whole company dedicated just to studying me. She ran her nails along my thigh and cupped my cheek with her hand as she imagined our traveling around France and making love (her words) on secluded beaches along the Riviera.

Finally, I got more concerned about "making love" that night. My vision was blurring, my bank account was getting thin (the scotches we ordered were $22 a round), her left breast was pressed against my arm, and I was impatient. So I agreed with pretty much everything she said, trying to move the conversation along. And when she pulled out the papers Raffy wanted me to sign, I signed them as fast as I could and suggested we move on to my apartment.

We did so pretty quickly, and, once we got out of the bar, things went pretty well. Or so I thought at the time. In retrospect, I'm not so sure. First, I kept trying to rearrange my face into the devastating Errol Flynn type I had created before. Unfortunately, being smashed, I think my jowls kept losing control, and I looked more circus freak than Hollywood. At any rate, she flinched a couple of times when I tried to kiss her, so I stopped trying.

When I stretched my arm a little unnaturally far to reach a nipple as we were riding back in the taxi, I was met with a slap and a, "Jason, come on! That's not sexy."

As for the rest, it was pretty much over before it started. I got undressed first, then I tried to undress her. But she wouldn't let me. She slapped a condom on me, tore off her clothes, jumped on top of me, and ba-da-boom, ba-da-bing, it was over. She got up, tore off my condom, went in the bathroom, changed, came out, kissed me on the cheek, said, "Later, big boy," and was gone.

I was left staring at a swirling ceiling trying to remember her naked body. But not for long, because I passed out almost at once. I kept saying to myself, "You had sex with a 10." Like a talisman.

Not to say that it wasn't amazing. It was. It must have been. Okay, so she didn't get down and dirty. She didn't lie in my bed for hours cuddling and exploring. You have to make allowances for someone as goddamned beautiful as Penny Waters. I mean, there was plenty of compensation for the bad sex. Getting to fantasize about the person you're having sex with, for one. Watching everyone's head turn when you are out at dinner, for another. It's a fair trade, and one I was willing to make.

Except I was never really given the chance. I didn't see Penny again for almost 10 days, and, when we did get a chance to talk, I felt a certain distance.

I mean not totally. She was all, "Let's get coffee," kiss cheek, etc. But it wasn't: hello man with whom I plan to spend the rest of my life. It was: hello old chum with whom I remember once having had a fling in the past.

But what could I do? Throw a fit and insist she had promised me her body for life? Was I that desperate? Of course not. Not at first, anyway.

Besides which, I didn't really know how grown-up affairs were meant to go. I mean, reading this you might reasonably have mistaken me for a debonaire man of the world. But it wasn't really the case. I'd had a girlfriend senior year of high school, but we never spent a lot of time together. Looking back, I think we dated because we were both desperate to avoid going to prom alone. I had a more serious girlfriend junior year at college. We spent all our time together, and thought we were in love. But really, we were just pretending. She was mega-political, and I pretended to be to please her. And she pretended she cared about books to please me. Just before summer vacation, we had a fight that ended things, which was a relief for both of us. So, for all I knew, Penny's on again, off again attention to me was just the sign of a mature, adult relationship.

As I say, I didn't see her for a little while. First of all, it was the weekend. I texted on Saturday, of course: "I had a really good time last night. Super hungover this morning." Then I waited for her to call or text back.

Which she didn't. Okay, fine. All I wanted to do that weekend was drink water and sleep anyway. My head hurt and I was sweating alcohol. Man, I wanted a little of that invulnerability back. On ordinary days, my stretching power made me feel so good. But it made hangovers worse. The sort of slippery, sloshing you feel in your stomach seemed to become literally true. I felt my innards sliding around like I had just swallowed a family of live eels.

Hank wasn't around that weekend at all. He sometimes did this, staying several nights in a row in his MIT lab working on a big project. But I was pretty sure the real reason was that he was pissed that I had made it with Penny. He was also mad because I wasn't doing anything about his "white van" theory. Which was ridiculous because we hadn't seen it since he and Ellen thought they'd spotted it Thursday night.

I texted again on Sunday, cool, not pressing. "On my way out to visit Joe at the nursing home. Call if you want in."

The subtext of my text was: "See, I have a life. Maybe it'll intersect with yours. No pressure."

I didn't hear from her and figured I should go out to Concord anyway. Just to back up my story. And because it wasn't like I had anything else to do. I wondered if I should call Ellen. She usually visited her grandfather on Sundays. But no one answered when I rang her apartment.

So I went to see Joe alone. The receptionist at the desk recognized me this time and waved me in with nothing worse than an unfriendly glare. Joe was watching football pregame shows when I got there. The breakfast tray hadn't been cleared, but otherwise his room was cleaner that it had been.

I suggested to Joe that we go for a walk. His room could get kind of stale after a while. He agreed and we walked down to Mill Pond. We didn't always talk a lot, and when we did we mostly talked about Joe's life back in Everett. But today we somehow got onto me. If I planned to stay a teacher, if I had a "lady" in my life, and why I was spending time with Joe.

I stumbled through my usual answers to the question of career, but Joe wasn't that interested in the GMAT or LSAT debate.

"It's a great thing to be a teacher," he said. "I still remember Mrs. Pignatelli in fourth grade. She was ugly as sin, and the first person who was kind to me for no reason at all. Of course, everyone called her Mrs. Pig. I did too, but I felt bad about it. I think I loved her more than my own mother."

I said I was not sure I was a good teacher. I didn't inspire kids. I could hardly keep them from throwing things at each other.

"You'll do fine. You'll learn what the kids need. Hardest job in the world."

"Not the best-paying one," I said.

"Maybe, maybe. Could be it's better to want things you can't have than have things you don't want."

Joe was also interested in my love life. I don't think I led him there, although obviously it was at the top of my mind too. I told him I'd had a date on Friday.

"Pretty?"

"Beautiful!"

"Smart?"

"Yeah."

"You love her?"

"I think so." I blushed as I said it. Joe was so direct.

"She loves you?"

"Well, it's early."

"Marry a girl who loves you," he said, "I married a girl I loved. Red hair, smart as a whip. I was sure she'd learn to love me. Never did. We lasted. That's what you did those days. But it wasn't fun. By the end, ooh boy, we hated each other."

I didn't know what to say. Penny was the sort of girl who tolerated you, not the sort who loved you. But her tolerance was a pretty darn splendid thing. I wasn't sure how to convey this to Joe. And he was ready to move on to another subject.

"Why you hanging out with an old fart like me?"

Because he was alone. Because even his family had deserted him. Because he needed me. I didn't want to say these things, but Joe said them for me.

"You feel sorry for me? Because my kids don't visit?"

"Why don't they come, if you don't mind my asking?"

"They're selfish bastards. Well, no that's not the whole truth. Me and their mother didn't get on very well for a long time. The kids were forced to choose. And they chose their mother. She knew how to win their sympathy. I never did."

"I'm sorry."

"Don't be."

"Could I talk to them?"

"They're older than you. They have to make their own minds up. Anyway, I've got you now. Even if you're just a teacher."

I looked over at him and saw the smile that just touched his eyes.

When we were back in his room, and the Pats game was on, I said, "Hey, Joe, can I show you something?"

"Sure."

I stretched up my hand and turned the television channel.

"Hey!"

I switched it back.

"Okay, leave it on the Pats. Now what was that you did?"

I did some more tricks, and finally told him the whole story. He sat there, listening I think, but his eyes fixed on the television. When I was done he didn't say anything for a few minutes. The Patriots were in the red zone.

When they scored he said, "That's a pretty strange story."

"I know. I can't explain it. But what should I do?"

"You asking me? A retired electrician with goddamn senile dementia?"

I looked around the room. "No, I am asking Tom Brady."

He laughed. "You'd be a heck of a receiver."

"Right, now. But my power changes all the time."

Joe snorted, probably imagining me facing a hit from an NFL linebacker just after realizing that my new superpower was archery skills.

"I want to use my power to do some good in the world, but I can't figure out how."

"Well, don't look at me. This whole superpower stuff isn't my generation."

"Yeah . . ."

"We had Superman, maybe, and Batman, but no one read those comic books. Nowadays every movie has some guy who can chuck a car across a city block."

"Yeah . . ."

"The problem is you don't really have superpowers."

"What?"

"You've got good powers, but they aren't super. They're meh."

I reached over, a good six feet, and turned the television off. "What do you mean?"

He grabbed his remote and turned it back on. "Look, you told me about your friend. The smart kid. What's his name?"

"Hank."

"Yeah. I understand he's got a brain that's gonna help him do great stuff."

"Sure."

"So nothing you got compares, right?" I didn't know what to say. "His powers are better than yours. And this dame you talked about."

"Penny."

"Yeah. You say she's a real babe. Sex appeal that can open doors and get crazy guys like you and me to do just about anything. She's got more superpowers than you. I mean, what can you do?"

I would have answered, but he wasn't done.

"You can change the television channel without getting up. So can I." He waved his remote. "And that rat you're talking about."

"What rat?"

"The guy who's trying to start a business. What's his name?"

"Raffy?"

"Yeah. He's got powers too. Energy. Salesmanship. Balls. You don't have that power."

"You are officially crazy," I said.

"No, but you gotta see your limitations. You can't be a superhero 'cause you can reach a long way. But maybe you can be a regular old hero."

"What do you mean?"

"You know who my hero was?"

"No. Who?"

"I told you. Mrs. Pignatelli."

It took me a second. "You mean, you're saying I should just be a teacher?" He sat back, not saying anything. "Jesus, Joe, that's stupid. I mean I just told you about the amazing things I could do. It would be a fucking waste to sit around and teach grammar."

"Dammit," Joe said. "They gotta cut Mac already."

I looked at the screen, now wholly absorbing Joe's attention. It showed a replay of a Patriot's quarterback getting swallowed in a sack. Joe was going to pretend now like we never had this talk, and go all dementia on me.

I picked up my coat and walked out without saying goodbye. Then I thought better, went back, poked my head around the door and said, "See ya, Joe."

He waved a hand without looking from the television. The senile bastard. All the way back to Cambridge I stewed over how short-sighted he was. How he'd undersold my abilities. Eventually, I tried to be charitable. He'd had a narrow upbringing. He was not, after all, a very educated man.

Still, I was just generally pissed when I got home. I wanted to be alone.

But, wouldn't you know it, I opened the door and saw Ellen was on the couch. With Hank nowhere in sight. Just what I needed— some of her tender nagging with a side of total lack of sympathy.

Well, actually, it wasn't all that bad. She had her hair pulled back and this intense look that mitigated her usual fuzziness. It emphasized her neck, and a long neck is a way underrated piece of female anatomy. Anyway, she was rocking an Ally Sheedy vibe, which was no bad thing. (Okay: Hank says that people whose parents did not force them to view the complete John Hughes oeuvre will have no idea who Ally Sheedy was. She was the bad girl in *The Homework Club* and the yuppie in *St. Elmo's Fire*. She was also Matthew Broderick's girlfriend in *War Games*.)

A thought flashed through my mind. She was hanging around my apartment without Hank even being there. The other day, she met Hank at his lab. And, Thursday, they had arrived at trivia night together. Had I missed something? Did my roommate and Ellen have something going on? Had they bonded over some science-dork question? Was I meant to feel happy for them? Somehow I wasn't.

But there was no time to analyze these feelings because as soon as Ellen heard me come in, she turned toward me and I could see she had been crying. "Oh, Jason," she said, "They've taken Hank."

CHAPTER 14

Taking the Blame

She was pretty worked up, and the whole story was sort of crazy elaborate, so it took a little time to understand what was going on.

Some guys, presumably the people in the white van, had abducted Hank. She was sure they were FBI because Hank had somehow found time to send a text message to her.

I hadn't taken the white van seriously, but Ellen and Hank had. And they had been working feverishly since Thursday to gin up a strategy to cover my missteps. The first part of that strategy was to hack into traffic cameras all over Boston and insert a program that distorted the digital images they took. The second part was to hack into MIT's computers—according to Ellen, the easiest part of the whole thing – to make it look like Hank had a history of experimenting with jetpacks and drones.

I didn't get it. What were they trying to do? It's like they wanted to get Hank arrested.

"Yes, that was the plan," Ellen said.

"First, that's crazy," I said. "Second, why are you so upset if that was the plan to begin with?"

"It wasn't the plan."

"You just said it was."

"Don't be an idiot," she said. "It was a fallback. But we hoped it would never happen."

My head hurt. I wanted Ellen to go away. I wanted Hank to be safe in his room. And I wanted to go into my bedroom and sleep for 24 hours straight.

"Please," I said, "explain it to me like I *am* an idiot."

"The idea was to protect you. Eyewitnesses aren't reliable, but if there's actually photographic evidence, that's different. Your stretch was caught on a traffic cam. We figured that, until that was explained, the authorities would never leave it alone. So we came up with a technological explanation for the photographs. We created an app that made everyone look stretched."

"Like the ones that make people look like they're crying, or they're cats?"

"Yeah. It wasn't too complicated. The software distorts the camera images so everyone has long, thin legs and looks 15 feet tall. We figured the cops would decide it was all an MIT prank and go off and do something else."

"They also have pictures, video, of me flying around."

"Yeah, but flying can be explained. Jet packs and the like. That's why we wanted Hank to have a history with that stuff. All we had to do was figure out how to attach one of those department-store dummies to a standard drone, and we figured we were golden. It wasn't a perfect match, but in your jacket and jeans it did look a lot like you flying around."

"Wait, are you saying Hank took my leather jacket?"

"Yeah. You look a little more lifelike maybe, but, come on, a drone carrying a mannequin has to be easier to accept than some guy flapping his arms."

"That was my favorite jacket. When can I get it back?"

"From the FBI? Probably never."

Shit!

"Don't you think you and Hank may have gone overboard on all of this?"

"Jesus, Jason, are you even paying attention? The FBI was watching this apartment building so they must have traced the flyer, or the stretch guy, here. But we couldn't let them find you. It had to be someone with the technological know-how to manipulate cameras and to modify drones. And it was best that it was someone from MIT. People are used to the idea of MIT pranks. And they can't make Hank reveal his superpowers because he doesn't have any."

"So Hank was meant to get taken?"

"We wanted to hide your tracks. Of course, we hoped they wouldn't find Hank either. We just wanted them to find Hank before they found you."

"And now they've got him. What do we do? Do we know where he is? I can't bust him out without knowing where he is."

"We don't bust him out, idiot."

I winced. It may have been an accurate description of how quick on the uptake I was being, but it hurt to hear Ellen repeat the insult with such conviction.

"We leave him there. The whole point is *not* to let the world know about your powers. He's taking the blame for you."

"What will happen to him?"

Ellen took a deep breath. "Look, he's a brilliant MIT grad student. People forgive them all sorts of crazy shit. They get a slap on the wrist and then a ton of job offers. Anyone that nutty has to be a genius. That's what we're hoping, at least."

"And if not?"

"I don't know. It's scary and upsetting."

I began to get scared and upset too. And feel really, really guilty.

"Shit!" I said and sat down on the couch next to Ellen. We didn't say anything for a while.

"I feel so stupid," I said.

"It wasn't your fault," she says.

"But what you guys did, what Hank's doing for me. It's not fair."

"He'll be okay. All he cares about is studying physics. And no one's going to stop him doing that."

"And we don't know where he is?"

"No. I don't think we'll find out. He'll just be disappeared until they decide he's okay. That's how it works these days."

"I feel awful."

"They may come to talk to you. You know nothing. He did everything in the lab. You had no idea what he was up to, right?"

"Right. I know nothing."

We sat in silence again.

"How'd you get into the apartment?"

"Hank gave me a key. For emergencies."

"Is there something going on between you two?"

Ellen looked at me. If she had looked upset and bereft before, it was nothing compared to the empty, devastated bleakness of her face now.

"It's okay," I said. "You guys would make a great couple."

"You are an idiot," she said, with even more vehemence than before, then stormed out of the apartment, slamming the door.

"What?" I asked to the empty space where Ellen had been. "What did I say?"

Then I leaned back on the sofa and covered my face with a pillow. Was it possible, I wondered, to feel bad in so many different ways as I did then?

I didn't get much sleep that night. But when I woke up, the pain I felt about Joe and Ellen and Penny and everything else had faded to background status, dwarfed by the enormous guilt and concern I felt about Hank.

Of course, I had not prepared my classes, so I tried to do it while I ate breakfast. But I was unsuccessful. All I could think of was fastidious Hank waking up in some dank rat-infested cell being fed grey mush for breakfast. I imagined pictures from Abu Ghraib, with smiling young women holding up latex-gloved fingers. I tried to control my imagination.

At any rate, I couldn't concentrate. It looked like the ninth-graders would be practicing their reading again today. God knows what the juniors would do. I couldn't even remember where in *The Grapes of Wrath* we were.

I reached out to get a second cup of coffee to see me through the day.

I reached out to get a second cup of coffee.

I reached out.

Reached.

But I didn't.

Or I did. Like you would, or any normal person. What I didn't do was stretch. My arm was five feet short of the coffee carafe and stubbornly stayed that way.

Damn, damn, damn! Just what I needed today. To lose my power. That may help explain why I was feeling so awful. It was like I had a hangover from the joy and release of stretching.

I tried to calm myself down by taking a deep breath and making some vague Eastern-y meditation-like gesture.

"Everything will be okay. Everything will be okay," I repeated.

"Sure," I responded, grabbed my bag and headed out.

No new power manifested itself on the way to school. My eyes did not shoot lasers. I couldn't turn into a rhinoceros (or needed more practice at it, if I could). I couldn't manipulate magnetic forces. I didn't have telekinesis. And I wasn't able to perform little magic spells, either by saying what I wanted to happen backwards, or by using a sort of pidgin Latin.

I considered the idea that my impossible powers had deserted me entirely and, all things considered, it seemed likely. Just at the moment of maximum suckitude. Hank arrested, Penny distant and Ellen furious. Most likely, given my utter lack of preparation, Sylvia or Principal Snowe would choose today to monitor my classes. Fuck!

I had *Romeo and Juliet* with the freshmen first period. I got lucky—no monitor. I guess God figured sending my roomie to Guantanamo was sufficient punishment for whatever I had done, so I could go ahead and have the kids read the damn play. I could spend the time figuring out where we were in *The Grapes of Wrath*.

In the end, though, I couldn't do it. I watched the kids file in, filled with all their pointless kid energy, good nature and optimism, and I imagined it all slowly draining out of them as they were forced to sit silently for an hour while their classmates read lines made utterly undecipherable by butchered pronunciations and rhythms. An image popped into my head like one of those overannotated Civil War-era cartoons: the kids, labeled the "Future of America" or "Hope" or something like that, being slowly strangled by a huge snake with my face, labeled "education" or "bad instruction." Christ, what would Mrs. Pignatelli do?

I had a brainstorm. "Okay, kids, today is trivia day!" I had each kid write three or four questions about the text. I added several more of my own. We divided into four teams and then played the game by Boston Pub Trivia rules. I told the winners I would buy them ice cream bars from Lou's and bring 'em to the next class.

We started with basic text questions, interspersed with general trivia about Shakespeare's life and times. Then we moved onto some of the more difficult questions I had inserted: "Name an example of someone in Romeo's situation in contemporary film," "Use three adjectives to describe the Nurse's motivations in the book." That kind of thing. These were questions that would have normally produced a resounding silence as the kids listened to the ticking of the clock, waiting for me to call on Malia or Scott (the two eager kids) to get an answer. But in the context of the trivia game, the kids were shouting over each other to get their answers out, many of them dead-on. My hardest job was to figure out who had buzzed or yelled their answer first.

The energy was so crazy that the teacher in the classroom next to me, Mr. Huling, came in and complained. "Sorry," I said. "They're just overenthusiastic."

"Well, I wish they could share some of their energy with my group," he said and went back to his classroom.

In the end, the Dragon's Head—I had named the teams after bars in our pub competition—won the day and I took their ice cream bar orders. The others made me promise to hold another trivia day in two weeks.

I was exhausted at the end of class. One thing people don't get about teaching is how tiring it is. Teaching, at least teaching well, is like an actor doing improv. Your mind races a million miles an hour, you emote, you mug for the class. Every time the kids say something, it's like a new cue. You have to hit your mark, retain their interest and win their hearts. All the while without being able to swear or talk about sex or race, and while communicating a lesson about fucking grammar. Come to think of it, it's way harder than improv.

It was one good class, but how could one possibly do that day after day, year after year? I could never be Mrs. Pignatelli. Meanwhile, I had lunch duty and the juniors. I hoped Hank, wherever he was, was having a better day than I was.

CHAPTER 15
Frustration

Okay, you guys can read the section heading so you know what my new power is. And I know you are asking how I could not have known? How could I have not tested strength when I was testing my ability to control weather?

It's a fair question, but look, I just forgot. I didn't feel stronger than usual. I just felt normal. And I guess I figured that, if I was super-strong, it would be obvious. But it wasn't, so it took losing my temper and slamming my fist through my kitchen counter to reveal my strength. It happened like this.

When I arrived home after work, I was greeted by a phone call from Hank's mom. I answered it right away, hoping she could tell me something.

"Hey, Mrs. Nichols, what have you heard about Hank?" I asked before she could say anything.

"Hello, Jason. Actually, I was calling to talk with him."

"Oh, I'm sorry. I mean, he's not here."

"Is there something I should have heard about him?"

"No, no. I was just . . . joking."

There was a silence that embarrassed me. She liked me, and I liked her, but I knew she thought that Hank could find a more accomplished roommate. I felt her judging me through the phone.

"Please tell him to call me. We want to know if he's getting in Wednesday evening or Thursday morning?"

"Getting in where?"

"Buffalo, of course."

Hank's family was from Buffalo, but my mind raced to figure out why he was going there. Were the feds releasing him? Some sort of house arrest?

I started to ask when suddenly I remembered. Thanksgiving! How had I forgotten? Maybe because my life was so crazy. Maybe because my parents were going out to visit my sister and her new baby in California, so I was on my own this year. At any rate, it took me a minute to process. I'd been to Hank's for Thanksgiving before. His mother took it mega-seriously. They had more than 50 people from his extended family every year, and his mother prepared dinner for at least four times that number. On Friday, the whole family served the vast quantities of extra food at their local homeless shelter.

Hank and I had not discussed whether I would join his family this year. Of course, now Hank himself might not join his family this year. I racked my brain to figure out how to break this to Mrs. Nichols.

"Uh, Wednesday. I'm not sure Hank . . . well . . ."

"Jason, what are you going on about?"

"Hank mentioned he had some big projects at school. I'm not sure he was intending to go home."

"Don't be ridiculous. He always comes home."

I was silent, unsure what to say. But her mom-dar was working overtime.

"Is something wrong, Jason? Has something happened to Hank?"

"No," I said. "Of course not." I gave a little laugh, failing to convince even myself.

"Jason, don't lie to me."

"He's fine," I said. "I'll tell him to call as soon as he gets in."

"Jason, ..."

"Bye now, Mrs. Nichols." I hung up while I still could.

That's when I put my hand through the kitchen counter.

It took a minute or two to understand what had happened. The counter had just disintegrated beneath me. I thought, at first, that someone had played a practical joke—replacing my furniture with a hollow movie-set version.

It dawned on me that this was unlikely.

Not that our kitchen counter was anything like solid oak. More like plywood and linoleum. It wouldn't have surprised me that I could damage it. But I did more than that. I demolished it.

I'm strong, I thought. I'm super-strong. Finally, a real superpower. The king of all superpowers. The *sine qua non* of superpowers. I mean, we'd seen that already. Flying, invulnerability and stretchiness were nothing without superstrength. Every hero, almost every hero, has superstrength. I wondered how strong I was and how long it would last, hoping this was the endpoint. The final evolution. Man, I would break Hank out of wherever he was in no time flat.

Obviously, my initial thoughts were less cogent than they might have been. I heard Ellen's voice in my head: "First, we don't even know where Hank is. Second, the whole point of what Hank is doing is to stop the Feds from realizing you have superpowers."

Yeah, yeah, yeah! I get it.

But how strong was I? No doubt Hank would have some cool way to measure it. Me, I just wanted to go break some stuff. It took some self-control not to start destroying the apartment.

I remembered there was a tool kit under the sink. I took it out and looked at it. It had a hammer, a screwdriver, and a wrench, each of which seemed fairly sturdy. I tied the screwdriver in a knot.

I pulled the wrench apart like it was taffy. I squeezed the head of the hammer, deforming its flat hitting surface into a scrunched-up blob. I remembered they were Hank's tools.

But, Jesus, I was strong. I wondered what I could do with cars and trains, the comic gold standard of strength. Then, thinking about it, I put my hand flat on a remaining part of the counter and hit it with the hammer. I didn't hit it too hard, but I hit it harder than I would have if I hadn't suddenly become convinced I must be invulnerable.

It hurt like hell and a nasty bruise rose up on the back of my hand.

But how can strength work without invulnerability? I'd throw my back out trying to lift a car. Thinking about it, why didn't I break my hand smashing the kitchen counter? The best I could come up with was limited invulnerability while I was using my superstrength. When I was hitting, but not when I was getting hit. Without some sort of gimme like that, I'd end up squashing myself under the rock I lifted. Sort of like a not-all-powerful god, who can lift a rock his skeleton can't support.

I took a long drive out to western Massachusetts, found some deserted woods around a neglected pond and started hurling rocks and pulling out trees. I know Hank would have had some precise way to measure what my feats meant. I just reveled in the comic-book impossibility of what I could do.

I also discovered some more that invulnerability was a limited gimme. Using my strength I could smash my hand into a tree and not get hurt. If the same tree had a trailing branch that happened to catch my chin after I threw it, it would hurt like a motherfucker.

As I drove back to the city, I heard Ellen nagging me again: "Satisfied, now that you've almost killed yourself?"

"Yeah," I said aloud. "Satisfied." But wondering if my chin would need medical attention.

"And if someone had seen you?"

"They didn't." And I *had* been careful. That's why I was in the middle of nowhere in the middle of the night.

When I got back in my apartment, I realized that I could hardly open my mouth, and I had a gash across my forehead. I couldn't think what else to do, so I called Ellen and asked her to come over and take care of me.

It was past midnight when I called, so it took some convincing. But I think the fact that I could hardly speak did more to convince her than any of my arguments. She came over and we repeated many of the same discussions and arguments I had already imagined us having.

I'm not sure what all Ellen did for me. Gave me ibuprofen and ice and tucked me into bed, I know. Swabbed my cuts, I guess, and washed them out. Whatever it was, I didn't feel any better when I woke up the next day.

She was gone and had left a note. She had called the school and told them I was sick. She would be by in the evening to check on me. Keep up with my medicine: three ibuprofen every four hours. Also, she had gone to the local convenience store and brought plenty of ice. It was in the freezer.

I took some more pills. Tried to drink something and went back to bed. The day was painful and boring. I waited for Ellen to come back and fantasized about Penny.

When I did get out of bed, I checked myself out in the mirror. The left side of my face and my shoulder were bruised and swollen. It looked pretty ugly, but other than when I tried to open my mouth, it had mostly stopped hurting.

I looked at the rest of my body. It looked . . . ordinary.

It's not like I have a horrible bod. I worked out when I could get to the gym. Maybe I could do more, but I wasn't like Hank, at least, who had given up exercise entirely as soon as he had gotten out of mandatory gym class. Although, he remained rail thin anyway, probably because of the calories his brain used up.

But as for me: you could see my biceps when I flexed. My pecs had some definition. At the right angle, you could see some ripples in my abs. Overall, totally acceptable, if not outstanding.

But I hoped for more. Like every male, I had spent countless hours staring at myself in the mirror, yearning for the perfect mesomorph torso of a Calvin Klein underwear model. Fine, I hadn't done anything to achieve it, but that didn't mean I didn't lust after it. Now, at least for the moment, I was the strongest person on the fucking planet. Would it have been so hard for my body to give some hint of the fact?

Honestly, given a choice between superstrength and a super-hot body, I might prefer the body. It'd do me more good. Think about it. The world showered rewards on good looks. If I had suddenly acquired a perfect body, all I would have to do is take my shirt off and I'd get a lucrative modeling contract and a raft of women throwing themselves at me.

What did being the strongest man in the world get me by comparison? Not much. The world was not designed for people to need superstrength. True, if I happened to be around when the support on some railroad trestle bridge collapsed, I could jump into action, hold up a rail and save a bunch of lives. But, first, how often does that happen? And second, even if it did, would I get to sleep with a bunch of supermodels? I doubt it. Uncle Sam would want to talk to me for about a hundred years to make sure I wouldn't decide to throw an SUV in the direction of the Oval Office.

If I couldn't find a use for my strength, it would be particularly depressing because it was the power I'd been waiting for. I'd thought it was the king of superpowers. Was it actually the three-legged cur of superpowers?

Predictably, Ellen was not sympathetic. My jaw was beginning to work again by the time she came to the apartment, although not so well that I could compete with her in an argument.

"Well, what should I do?" I asked as she ordered Thai food—soup for me and Pad Thai for her.

"I don't know. But not whining about having special powers is high on the list."

"Do you still think there's a scientific explanation?"

"No, I've given up on that."

"You? Ms. Science-explains-everything? Never?"

I thought I'd tweak her. But I was wrong. She looked at me. "I think you don't have any powers."

"What?" I said. I looked around for something to show my strength on. A coffee cup? No. My phone. No. I settled for, "But you've seen them."

"They make no sense. Hank and I discussed this. Our best explanation is a mass delusion of some sort."

"I'm just a delusion?"

"Your powers are. I'm not sure what's happening or why. But I think it's all some sort of mass hysteria. Sort of like the papers said about everyone seeing you flying."

I was surprisingly hurt.

"It's why you can't change anything. Not really."

I stood up, walked into the kitchen and picked up one of the cast-iron skillets my mother had given me. I squeezed and twisted the handle. "What's that?"

"I can't explain it."

"It didn't really happen?"

"All I know is that it is much more likely, based on the totality of my beliefs, that it did not happen than that it did."

"Even though you just saw it?"

"Even though I just saw it."

I went back in the living room and sat down on the couch. I

thought I couldn't feel worse, but now I did. My so-called superpowers were not only useless. They were actually the sign of a diseased mind. Not only would I not be celebrated, I'd end up drooling in a padded room.

"Seems rough for Hank to be taken away to preserve a delusion," I said.

"Yeah, I'm beginning to worry. We haven't heard anything for two days."

"And I have to call his mother and explain that he won't be at Thanksgiving."

I could have used another day at home, but Ellen had mentioned to me that Principal Snowe was complaining about how many teachers got conveniently sick so they could leave for Thanksgiving early. I didn't want her thinking that was me, so I was determined to drag myself in to school the next day.

Ellen didn't think I was well enough. "Your face is still a mess."

"Yeah, I'll have to explain that," I said.

"No worries there. I said you slipped in the shower."

"Are you kidding?"

"It's believable. Lots of people do it."

"Couldn't you have gone with 'fell while rock climbing' or something?"

She just looked at me and smiled. I could have killed her.

CHAPTER 16

Heavy Lifting

I had other reasons to go into school besides proving my dedication to Principal Snowe. I wanted to see my juniors one more time. They would have papers due on *The Grapes of Wrath* shortly after Thanksgiving, and I wanted to hand out the assignment early enough to let the eager beavers get started over the break. And I realized the freshmen needed a reminder about MLA quotation style before they started their papers on *Romeo and Juliet*.

Also, I needed to talk to my peeps. Look, I knew Ellen thought I shouldn't tell anyone else about my new power. She thought I owed it to Hank to basically never use my powers again. That wasn't how I saw it. Hank had sacrificed himself so that I *could* use my powers. His point was that I couldn't figure out how to be a superhero if the government threw me in some cell. I needed to be a hero for Hank.

But I was all out of ideas on how to do it. Raffy and Toby, at least, were guys, and might understand the need to occasionally just punch someone in the mouth. I knew Sylvia was on board with the whole hero thing. As for Penny—besides being my girlfriend, as far as I was concerned at least—the fact that she had come and hung out with me while I was listening in to fire department feeds showed she was pretty supportive of the hero idea.

Even if she wasn't supportive, she was still my inspiration. She was part of the whole reason I wanted to be a hero in the first place.

Yeah, and I don't mean to get laid. Look, she represented everything I was fighting for. Truth, beauty and everything good with the world. Yeah, fuck you, Hank. Creamy thighs and perky nipples too. But they were all related.

I felt bad sneaking out to Lou's without Ellen, but I had to do it. I overcompensated by giving Ellen a starring role in my story, emphasizing how awesome she'd been. Which was at cross-purposes with my other goal of reassuring Penny that Ellen and I were in no way involved. (Or was it? Halfway through lunch, I suddenly had an idea that lighting a little fire of jealousy under Penny wouldn't be the worst thing in the world. She seemed remarkably nonobsessed about how I spent my time.)

At any rate, if I was waiting for the collective wisdom of my team to reveal how I should use my strength, I was disappointed. Sylvia suggested that maybe I could meet the people who had taken Hank and offer them my services. But Toby took as dark a view of federal power as me and Hank, although he expressed it in the most unclear and overly historical way possible.

"Even if you were to volunteer for the armed forces, could you morally serve their violent ends from a state of historical ignorance? Should you kill Caesar at the behest of the Senate? The resulting civil wars between Augustine and Antony were exceedingly vicious and destroyed the last remnant of the democratic tradition the Senate was hoping to restore. On the other hand, the result was, arguably, another 500 years of stability."

We looked at him like dull students.

"The military may ask you to kill people. But how would you determine if this were an ethical use of your unique power? In retrospect, killing Hitler or Stalin seems like the right course, but even in these most compelling cases, the evidence was less clear at the time. If you were asked to assassinate, say, the Syrian leader, would you do it? Should you?"

"He couldn't do it anyway," Raffy said. "He'd be mowed down before he got to Assad."

"I could lob a car at him," I said.

"We can lob cruise missiles at him now," Raffy said. "The point is getting close to him."

"My point is philosophical," Toby said. "Is it a proper use of his power?"

I thought about it. I wasn't sure I wanted to be ordered to kill people. I had watched enough movies and read enough spy novels to know there were always factions within the US security apparatus. How would I know that I hadn't fallen into the hands of the bad guys? The guys promoting African civil wars and making a mint off arms contracts?

Raffy brought us back to reality. "Look, it's a moot point. He can't do it, and he's not going to join the army anyway. What we need to do is get our marketing plan working."

"What marketing plan?"

"For our company, man. Remember you signed the papers."

Penny reached out and put a hand on my thigh.

"Right, I remember," I said.

"Anyway, superstrength is the killer app. We have to strike while the iron's hot."

"What do you mean?"

"Are you around this weekend? You're not going away for Thanksgiving, are you?"

"No, I'm here."

"Great, we should meet Saturday morning. Beacon Athletic Club. Say 10:00. I have a guest pass you can use."

"What's the plan?"

"We're going to show people what you can do."

"But that's just what we can't do," I said.

"Come on, man. It'll be subtle. We need to tease. Not give the game away."

I still wasn't sure what Raffy meant, but Penny broke in. "I can pick you up and take you. My yoga class is at 11:00. I really want to see you lift." Her arm moved to my bicep. Fair to say, the thought of Penny in yoga pants drove any objection from my mind.

It wasn't until late in the day, when I had gotten through my classes, dealt with Principal Snowe's suspicions of an abusive relationship, and my head was beginning to throb again, that I ran into Ellen. Of course, she'd heard about my meeting with the others.

"You did just exactly what you shouldn't have, didn't you?"

"What?" I asked, innocent, or at least innocent-like.

"You told them about your new power. Widened the circle. Increased the chance that word would get out. That Hank would have taken all the risk for nothing."

"Have you heard from Hank?"

"You're his roommate. I think you'd hear before me."

"But you're his girlfriend."

She looked at me again and sighed. There was suddenly a thing going on that reminded me of Sigourney Weaver in *Gorillas in the Mist*; beautiful, just a little intense.

"I guess you caught me. When I slept with you less than five fucking weeks ago, it was just a ploy to get to Hank!"

Her voice dripped with sarcasm, and I knew a response was called for, but I didn't know what. Nothing that involved super-strength, unfortunately. I tried misdirection instead.

"Don't they have to contact his family at least?"

"Who knows what they have to do? None of the rules we learned in civics seem to apply anymore."

"I have to call his mother," I said, suddenly full of dread. "She's expecting him for Thanksgiving. Jesus, what should I tell her? I can't say he's been arrested. She'd have a heart attack."

"I'm sure you'll think of something." She picked up my copy of *Romeo and Juliet* from the table and wrote something. "This is my parents' number. Call me if you hear anything. And Jason, don't fuck up."

I thought that was it. I was staring down at the number, assuming that she had turned away and was striding out the door, when I felt her hand on my arm and she reached up and kissed my cheek. I was too surprised to react. Then she gave a half smile and walked away. I was left holding my book and staring after her. I figured I was lucky I didn't have to answer any questions on the category of "women" for our pub trivia. I would suck.

Walking home after I got out of the T, I realized I hadn't used my superstrength at all that day. I mean, I suppose I did walking to and from school. I didn't get tired and my backpack felt like a feather. But my commute wasn't so strenuous even with regular old strength.

On my way home, I imagined the lies I would tell Hank's mother. A sudden cruise? A research project in Chile? Why didn't he call her before he left? I couldn't think of a reason. I reminded myself that it didn't have to be a good lie. Just something plausible enough that she wouldn't get hysterical (and start thinking crazy things, like that he'd been abducted by the FBI).

I had the best surprise of my life waiting for me when I got home. I walked in and there was Hank, packing for Thanksgiving.

"Hank!" I yelled, rushing up to give him a hug, reminding myself not to squish his insides out.

"Hi," he said.

As I drove him to the bus station, I told him about getting superstrength and he told me about being arrested. As it turned out, his ordeal had not been so bad after all. He was held in some office building, and had to sleep on a cot, but they ordered anything he wanted for meals. During several days of questioning, he stuck to his story and acted amazed when his interrogators tried to convince him that there might be an actual flying or stretching man. By the end, Hank said, they fell all over themselves to make it clear they never believed those things anyway.

They checked his lab records, discovered he was a hot-shit grad student doing groundbreaking work in mathematical physics and, eventually, they let him go. Well, almost anyway. They did some sort of secret, suspended indictment that ensured he wouldn't leave the country without their say so, and that they could call him in for "services" occasionally. And they charged him a $10,000 "investigation fee."

"You have to fucking pay to be investigated?" I yelled.

"Nowadays, I guess."

"How are we going to pay that?"

Hank shrugged. "I'll borrow it and add it to my Stafford. I'm like $150,000 in debt already. Another $10,000 won't matter."

"You can't pay it," I said, or really shouted. "You did that for me. I need to pay it."

"How can you pay it?"

I couldn't. I couldn't pay my bills as it was. "I'll put it on my credit card."

"With like a 24 percent interest rate? Anyway, what's your limit?"

"Five thousand," I admitted. "Look, I'll steal it if I have to."

"I'm doing this to keep you out of trouble," he said. "Look, I'll be back Sunday. I want to see your power then, assuming you don't lose it. But don't go and do anything stupid between now and then."

He and Ellen were even talking alike these days, I thought, as he headed into the terminal. And that, too late, made me think I should have asked him about what was happening between those two. Whatever it was, it seemed to make Ellen really tense.

Ellen! I should call her. I pulled over, dialed her home number and got her parents' message machine. I asked her parents to let her know that Hank had arrived home, unhurt, and everything was okay.

Driving home, I felt empty and happy. Hank was back. I was going to see Penny on Saturday. And the Feds were off my back. And I was free. The next four days I could sit in front of the television, order in pizza, drink beer and pig out on ice cream. A perfect Thanksgiving vacation.

The next morning I felt lonely and abandoned. Thanksgiving Day and I was all alone. Abandoned by my parents, by Hank, by Penny and by Ellen.

I let myself get good and depressed. Two years out of college, I had no job prospects but to become a teacher. I'd probably end up like Toby, single, bitter, impoverished and clinging to the delusion that force-feeding morsels of culture to apathetic teens somehow makes for a better world. Or, worse, no longer even believing the delusion.

Who cared if I had superpowers if I was too timid to ever use them? I thought of my high school classmates, the ones who got drunk before school and had lost their virginity in tenth grade—the bad boys, the cool kids, the guys I disdained and envied. I thought of Kenny Ransom. He would have buzzed the State House the first day of class and landed on top of the Washington Monument the next day. He wouldn't have cared if he was thrown in prison. He would have turned invulnerable and then demolished anyone who had looked at him cross-eyed. As Mr. Elastic, he would have slipped out of jail, headed to Latin America, made a bundle selling drugs and giving interviews to Kimmel. He'd have scored a reality TV show and juggled cars for a rating bonanza. He'd have left a trail of jilted lovers and bruised rivals in his wake. The one thing he wouldn't have done is waited around like a scared jackrabbit, hoping to be a drippy superhero and terrified to reveal himself.

God knows I didn't want to be Kenny. I just wanted some of his chutzpah. Some of his willingness to cut loose and not give a shit.

I did not cut loose. Instead, I picked up a pizza and headed out to Concord to see Joe. He'd probably be watching the Thanksgiving football games, and he might like company. It seemed fitting somehow that we two losers would end up together. Me and some senile old geezer locked up in a nursing home.

CHAPTER 17

Marketing

On Friday morning, I headed to Harvard Square to get a haircut and browse the comic stores. I would read about my peers as I sat with a latte in Starbucks. The event was almost as good as the anticipation. The hairdresser at Supercuts flirted with me, and I got an excellent cut. I bought a couple of X-Men comics, an Avengers and some Justice League because they all included superhero groups, and I wanted to think about what powers might be coming next. I also bought a couple of Hulks because I figured Hulk's power was most like my current one.

Reading them as I drank my coffee was made just more awesome by my secret. I imagined people looking at me disdainfully. *A man his age wasting time on comics.* But, in this case, they didn't know what they were talking about. Comics were real and this was research. I felt liberated from self-consciousness by my special knowledge of how the world worked. Other people just saw shadows on a wall. I saw the things themselves.

Around 4:00, I texted Penny. "You back? Catch some supper?" See that? A marvel of self-control.

She texted back: "Back late. Can't wait to see you lift."

On the one hand, I was disappointed. On the other, thrilled.

"Can't wait," she had said. Hank had said that Penny would never sleep with me. That she was only interested in fashion and money. That we had nothing in common. But it just went to show that no one should let their hopes be crushed by the unreasonable crankiness of their friends. We *had* slept together. We shared a love of eighties rock. And now she "couldn't wait" to see me. What we had was a mature relationship between two busy people.

I headed home and prepared my classes for the next week. I spent some time thinking about how to teach *The Diary of Anne Frank*. The kids were going to hate it at first, but they'd love it by the end. That's just how it was with Anne. She was such a cool customer. I thought quite a bit about how I might have used my power during World War II, slagging Nazis. In fact, I wondered if there might be an assignment in it. Choose one superpower and say how you would have used it to help prevent—mitigate?—the Holocaust. Probably not, but I would keep thinking.

Raffy's plan was fairly simple. We would show up at the Beacon Athletic Club, one of the places in Boston where the serious weightlifters congregate and work out together. We'd do a couple of normal warm-up rounds and then take a break and drink some of Raffy's special formula. We'd be pretty public about it, but Raffy said we didn't have to oversell. All the lifters watched each other obsessively. Once everyone began noticing me, I'd take another swig of Raffy's vitamin juice and do a killer round, impressing the hell out of everyone. Then clear out before anyone asked too many questions.

Raffy would find a way to let everyone know what my drink was, and that was all there was to it. He bet we'd sell a hundred cases of bug juice within the week. I couldn't believe that weightlifters were that suggestible.

"It's the culture," Raffy had said. "They eye each other like hawks. No one wants anyone else to get an edge. They'll try anything."

"What about the whole 'body-a-temple' thing. They'll just throw any old shit in their gut?"

"This isn't any old shit." Raffy looked hurt, or more accurately, like an elementary school kid trying to act out what someone who was hurt would look like. "I've worked on this a long time. It's a carefully calibrated mix of fruit juices, herbal supplements, electrolytes and vitamins. This shit's good."

I didn't know what to say. It was so clearly crap, but he was pretending to believe it. I looked at Penny, but she seemed on board. "Raffy and I have been using it for a week, and it's great."

Nevertheless, I was a little nervous when I showed up at the gym. It was one of those free-weight places for guys with ginormous, freakazoid muscles. And those guys intimidated the hell out of me.

First, there was the whole steroid thing. I imagined them in the locker room, all shrunken testicles and large heads, shooting each other up. Then there was the rage thing, also steroid-related, I guess. They might be the nicest guys in the world, but who knew when they would snap. Finally, there were the impenetrable rules of free-weight etiquette. Was that large, angry dude panting on the bench done with the barbell? Or just resting between sets? If he was resting, how long did he maintain his right to the equipment? What if I could I get my reps in while he rested? The whole thing was an Emily Post minefield.

As it turned out, Raffy was a perfect guide to this particular underworld. He showed up with Penny in tow, which would have bummed me out until Penny kissed me good morning. Walking into the gym with her at my side, I figured, gave me street cred for when I didn't know what to do with the weights.

Raffy and I headed to the locker room to change. Raffy looked ridiculous in his workout clothes. His shorts were too short, his socks too long, and his T-shirt, advertising VM Ware or some such geeky company, was cut off to reveal his abs. But, to my surprise, it turned out that he knew what he was doing. His skinny arms and chest bulged with muscles when he began lifting. When he did his bicep curls, his arms just blew up like on a Popeye cartoon. It gave me a whole new perspective on the guy.

Anyway, since he knew what he was doing, it was easy enough for me to follow him around and imitate him. If I was lifting wrong, he would whisper a correction.

We went through the weights, and I lifted just what Raffy did. Curls, bench press, shoulder press, break for ab work, lat pull-down, glute press, break, squat. We stopped and drank some of his vitamin drink, which tasted awful. Raffy said that was a feature, not a bug.

The bottle was small and squat, with intimations of Western medicine and Eastern magic at the same time. The label was pretty well done. Raffy had called it JME for "Jason's Miracle Elixir," and somehow had photoshopped a picture of Penny holding up the Earth, like Atlas. I never thought to criticize him for using Penny rather than me on the label. I'd buy something with her pic on it.

Penny came up to us, slipping her hand under my shirt onto my back as she did. "You aren't even sweating," she said.

I glowed.

"Okay," Raffy said. "We have their attention. Let's go for the deadlift."

We went over to the area where a lot of large dudes were hanging out. There was five hundred pounds on the bar.

"That good?" Raffy asked.

"Maybe add fifty," I said, hoping it was the right answer.

After Raffy added the weight, I went and stood over the bar. I breathed and made some faces. "Method acting," I told myself.

Raffy, I noticed, had taken out another bottle of our JME and was prepping it for me after my lift.

I cricked my neck and bent over and grabbed the bar. Making a show of effort, I jerked it up to standing the way Raffy had shown me. There were literal gasps in the gym.

At that point, I almost decided just to curl the damn thing up and lift it over my head one-handed. The reaction would have been priceless. Based on the account so far, I realize you may have come to the conclusion that I have poor impulse control and are expecting this is just what I'd do.

But I didn't. I stuck to the plan and let the weight drop. The thing is that I don't have poor self-control. I would have aced that test for two-year-olds where you get more candy if you can sit without eating the M&M in front of you. If I didn't make good choices about how to use my superpowers, it wasn't because of bad character. It was because the choices were so goddamn new and different, it was hard to know what choices you were meant to make. My point is, I'd like to see *you* exercise impulse control if you could suddenly fly.

I looked up and saw the faces of the other weightlifters around me, filled with a combination of curiosity and envy. I suddenly dreaded being bombarded with questions about how I did it, when I started training, what my routine was. All of the questions I didn't know how to answer. I turned to Raffy for moral support, and he handed me a bottle of JME.

I downed it and told him I had to head to the showers.

"You gotta stretch," a voice called out. But I ignored it and headed quickly for the locker room. I saw the crowd turning to Raffy instead of following me, and was relieved. I decided not to shower. If I was quick enough, maybe I could slip out while everyone was still talking with Raffy. He was a slick customer. Maybe he'd make use of my shyness in whatever huckster story he made up.

"Penny," I thought. Of course, I wanted to find her and not leave her in Raffy's evil clutches. But she had her yoga class coming up at eleven, and I definitely wasn't hanging out until it was done. I'd just have to call her later.

I picked up my bag from the locker room and left the gym as quickly as I could. Raffy would let me know how things went.

I thought about Penny, feeling less sure about the state of our relationship than I had the day before. I could barely remember our night together, and we'd hardly touched each other since. Hank thought she was cold and calculating, I knew, but I couldn't see her that way. She wasn't cold. She was just a lock I hadn't yet found the right key for.

Right about then, the phone rang again, and it was Penny herself, suggesting we meet for "brunch" the next morning at some café near her place. I usually hated brunch—either I ate beforehand and wasn't hungry, or I didn't and was starving. As it turned out, my dislike of brunch wouldn't be a problem because she wanted to meet early, at seven, which made me wonder why she called it brunch. Maybe "breakfast" seemed a little too forward. Maybe she wanted to see what it would be like to wake up together.

She had chosen a place near her, up one of those narrow, steep Beacon Hill streets. The morning was cold and grey, and the street was empty. I was surprised the café was even open as none of its potential customers looked to be awake. I speculated that Penny may have had things other than brunch in mind. A warm bed, intertwined bodies, seemed a better start to the day than "brunch" in the freezing rain. I started to calculate the odds that she would meet me and lead me right back to her place. One hundred percent, if she was me. Ten percent, said my head, probably still overweighting my own preference.

What happened next happened pretty fast.

A man cried out, "My car!" I looked up. A Volkswagen Jetta had picked up speed and was rolling down the hill fast. A girl in a shawl in the middle of the road shrieked and seemed to freeze. The car was headed right at her.

I heard another voice, across the street, "Stop the car! Save her!"

I reacted, jumping between the car and the girl. The car was a split second away from plowing into me when I lowered my shoulders and reached out my arms, desperate to stop its momentum before it crushed the girl.

The car hit me and I dug in my feet and pushed back hard. My hands punched through the bumper and, purely by luck, found some sort of metal rods in the engine block to grip. I grunted and heaved and found myself sunk almost an inch into the tarmac with the car over my head.

The girl, taking off her cape, materialized into Penny. The man across the street was Raffy. He had something on his face.

Penny said, "Oh, Jason. Be careful, Toby's in there."

I suppose I looked around stupidly. "In the car," she said. She came up and kissed me on the cheek as I stood with the car in the air. "My hero."

I was confused, but I put down the car carefully. Penny led me, dazed, to the sidewalk. Toby emerged from the car. Then I realized Raffy was holding a camera. He had been filming the whole time.

Penny, still holding my arm, handed me something. A bottle of JME. She turned it around in my hand so the label faced Raffy.

"Drink," Raffy said.

I did so automatically. Then I put down the bottle and said, "What the fuck is going on?"

Raffy lowered the camera, laughing and clapping. "That was awesome. And I totally got it."

"I feared for my life for a moment," Toby said. "I thought you were going to chuck me down the street."

"Look what he's done to the car," Raffy laughed. "Thank God I got the damage waiver."

Penny squeezed my arm and held me close. "Amazing," she said.

I wished she would shut up. She was distracting me from working up some righteous anger. "What the hell just happened?"

Raffy held up his camera. "YouTube, man. We have the best viral advertisement in the history of marketing here."

Penny ran one awesome hand down my chest. "I had no idea you were so strong."

I wanted to ask her what part of superstrength she didn't get. I wanted to lean over and kiss her. But I was trying to focus on Raffy. And Toby.

"Let's eat, then we can explain everything," Penny said.

I let myself be led away while Toby excused himself to get the car towed back to the rental office. Raffy and Penny refused to explain anything until we got food and coffee. Then, finally, they let me in on what had happened.

The gym thing had worked beautifully. The lifters all wanted to know my workout routine. Raffy was coy, but let it be assumed that JME was part of it. Everyone wanted to know where to get it, but Raffy wouldn't tell them.

"This is the next stage. A viral video. The muscle heads are for sure burning up Google looking for JME. They'll find the video and totally fall in love. We'll give them a couple of weeks to badger their local supplement stores to find some. We'll drop a site with an address and get flooded by calls. We tell the stores we're still tinkering with the formula and won't sell. The 'roid crowd redoubles their efforts. The nutrition companies beg us for product. Reluctantly we agree to sell early, lock the stores into long-term supply contracts. And—boom!—we've got the pay out."

Raffy leaned back, completely self-satisfied. Penny, sitting next to me, hand on my thigh, looked into my eyes seeking approval.

God, I wanted to give it. But . . . I couldn't.

"Penny could have been killed," I said.

"No way, man. That's why Toby was in the car. Crouched down so the camera couldn't see him. He'd brake before he hit Penny.

And she could have jumped out of the way anyway. It was a setup. Perfectly safe. Like a movie stunt."

"What about Toby?" I asked.

"We didn't see that coming," Raffy admitted. "You actually hoisting the car over your head. That was neat."

"Neat?" I said. The adjective seemed so wrong, but I tried not to let it distract me. "Look, the point is . . . ." I waited trying to figure out the point. "The point is, why didn't you tell me if it was just a movie stunt?"

"Realism, man. It's what's going to make the video go viral."

"I think it will work," Penny said. "You were a real superhero."

"One big trouble," I said, hating myself for disagreeing with Penny. "I have a secret identity. My roomie just spent three days with the Feds to throw them off my scent. Even if no one saw this happen, anyone seeing this video will know my powers are real."

Raffy looked at me with pity. It was left to Penny to explain. "Jason, no one will believe you really did this. It's on video. It could have been faked."

"Well, why the fuck didn't we fake it? And how do you know no one saw me?"

"It's seven in the morning, partner," Raffy said. "No one will have seen it. And I told you why we didn't fake it. Realism, man. That's the key."

I knew something was wrong with his logic. You can't claim realism was the selling point and then say no one would believe the video. It made no sense. But I tried to focus on what was important. "It'll blow my secret identity."

"Be serious, man. Your secret identity?"

God, I hated Raffy at that moment. I hated him because I knew—some part of me knew—he was right. I was being a child. But I wasn't going to admit it then. I would stand on my outrage.

"Don't you care what Hank went through? You want to just

throw that all away?"

"You signed the marketing agreement. That was part of your contribution for your stock. Besides, we'll pixelate your face. The mystery will make it realer to the lifter crowd."

"What marketing agreement?"

"The one you signed when we fucking formed the company. Jesus!" Raffy stood up and put some cash, not enough, on the table. "Penny, make him see reason. This is a chance to use your talents instead of skulking around doing fuck-all. We have a chance for a serious payday here if you don't blow it."

He was gone while I was still trying to formulate my comeback. It didn't help that Penny was nibbling on my ear. "Raffy thinks your best protection is getting rich and famous. And he's trying to help you get there." She curled up against me and gave me a long kiss. "We all are."

After we left the restaurant, she led. me back to her apartment and sat me down on her couch. She flashed me a smile and then removed her top and bra. Several minutes of necking, led, step by glorious step, to just the consummation I had been fantasizing about as I made my way over to brunch that morning.

Then, all too quickly, the moment was over. Before I had quite recovered from the postcoital bliss, I found myself bundled out of her apartment on my way back home. Sitting on the T to Harvard Square, I thought about what I could do with the payday Raffy was promising. Pay off Hank's FBI fine for a start. Pay off my Visa bill for a second thing.

It wasn't until I got home, and saw lights on in our second-floor apartment, that I realized the shit I was in. Hank was home. Ellen was probably somewhere in the city too. How could I explain to either of them what I had just done? What Raffy had done? Why there was a video of me lifting a car overhead careening around the internet when I had promised to keep my powers under wraps.

I decided that I couldn't make Hank understand, and I didn't have to. It was just a video. It was just for weightlifters. No one would know it was me. Hank would have no contact with it. Ellen would have no contact. They'd never know about it. And it was probably best to leave it that way.

I went in and greeted Hank. We exchanged stories of what we'd done during Thanksgiving, me leaving out all the bits I told you here.

Including that, contrary to his doubts, Penelope Waters, the most beautiful girl I had ever met, had just that morning reconfirmed her love for me.

CHAPTER 18

Christmas

So I was trapped between loyalty to Hank, my roommate, and to Penny, my girlfriend. It might have been manageable except that with Ellen playing the role of Scylla on Hank's side, and Raffy as Charybdis on Penny's side, I didn't have much room to negotiate.

I dealt with the situation by throwing myself into my teaching. When someone asked me for lunch, or even just came up to talk, I pretended I had a grading deadline, or a meeting with a student.

Cornered and forced to converse about something, I talked about how the ninth-graders had taken to Anne Frank, or how the eleventh-graders had done in their exams on *The Grapes of Wrath*. I didn't use, or even think much, about my superpower. Why should I? It was useless.

Raffy started forwarding emails he had received looking for JME. I ignored them. Ellen came by to tell me what a terrific job I had been doing keeping my power under wraps, and I told her that we might need an intervention with one of her advisees who was getting a D in English. Same with Toby when all he wanted to discuss was how far I might possibly be able to throw a discus.

I couldn't avoid Hank, but I was uncommunicative, and he figured out I needed my space. He spent time in his lab.

I didn't mean to avoid Penny, but she was never around. Just about the only times I did see her, she was with Raffy.

The only person I talked to was Sylvia. She was conducting my mid-year review and sat in on a bunch of my classes. At a meeting with her and Principal Snowe, she told me that my teaching had come a long way. That the ninth-graders really seemed to have made a connection with Anne Frank, and she was hoping to share some of my syllabus ideas with the other teachers.

Chuffed, I turned to Principal Snowe, hoping for some more praise. Which was not forthcoming. She shuffled her papers and said to Sylvia, "No more manifestation of personal issues?"

Sylvia said no and Principal Snowe turned to me, "Well keep up the good work. Don't let me keep the two of you."

It was only when Sylvia stood up and nodded to me that I understood that I was being dismissed. As the two of us walked out I said, "Is she always so abrupt?"

Sylvia nodded. "That's teaching. Doing a great job under impossible circumstances just means you aren't criticized. Anything less you get crucified, fired or sued, depending on the state of the school's finances at that point. Do you want to get lunch?"

I looked at her carefully for signs of lascivious intent. I mean, surely strength was more on the flying side of sexy than the stretchy side. I saw nothing, but she saw what I was doing.

"Oh, for heaven's sake, Jason, I'm old enough to be your mother."

"You were before, too."

"Look, I can admit some of my behavior toward you was careless, and subject to misunderstanding. But I think you may have overinterpreted some gestures that were only intended to convey my fondness and support."

"You didn't lust after me?" I was unsure whether to be disappointed.

"Perhaps I was somewhat infatuated by the idea of meeting a superhero. Like I was infatuated with Mick Jagger and Robert Plant when I was twelve. But they were so much older than me that I never thought about sleeping with them. Now, you're too young for me to really lust after. The whole idea is ridiculous."

We did not go to Lou's, hitting a falafel stand near a playground instead. I think Sylvia knew that I didn't want to run into the others.

When we had gotten our lunches and were sitting down to eat, Sylvia said, "Honestly, Jason, I am not sure you are right for the whole hero thing."

"What do you mean?"

"I don't know much about comics. I never read them growing up. But it seems to me that their portrayal of heroes is, well, let's say somewhat unrealistic."

"Thanks for the newsflash, Sylvia." I grinned liked I had never taken them seriously in my life.

"I mean, when you say you want to be a superhero, I take it that means someone who puts criminals away. That sort of thing."

"Yeah. And saves the world from alien invasions and stray asteroids."

"Well, that may be. But think about reality. The sort of people drawn to that in real life. Policemen or soldiers. Of course, many of them are noble, even heroic people. But they tend to be of a certain personality type. Doers rather than thinkers, maybe. People comfortable with confrontation."

"Okay."

"You don't seem the type to wade into arguments and break them up with your fists. It's not your personality."

"I never had the physical tools before. I broke up the fight in the gym." I sounded defensive, but I didn't mean to. I knew her point was deeper than that.

"Certainly, Jason. I'm not saying you can't do it. The question is: do you really want to be a policeman? God knows we need policemen, but they think the worst of people. They meet violence with violence. Is that you?"

"I just want to help people."

"You are helping people. The freshmen seem really energized by your class. But I did want to ask you about the juniors."

It turned out she was concerned that I had not yet finished the unit on *The Grapes of Wrath*. I explained that we were reading an essay in *The Atlantic* about a person who had followed Steinbeck's footsteps in light of the 2009 financial crisis, detailing the lives of contemporary economic immigrants.

"The kids are really identifying with it. A lot of them have personal stories. I want to let them get their stories out before we move on."

Sylvia considered and then said, "Well, you may have to rush through *The Great Gatsby*. We have to get the students through it for the Common Core."

"I know. It's going to be a great follow-on. The flip side of the poverty in Steinbeck. The kids will eat it up."

So Sylvia was okay. We met occasionally and talked about teacher-student types of things. I caught one of the juniors cheating on a test, and I didn't know how hard to come down. We decided on a warning, which was definitely not school policy.

Otherwise, the only time I saw the group together before Christmas was our home trivia match against Akamai. Hank didn't come, but the rest of the team, and Penny, were there. The Akamai guys came in way overconfident, even making disparaging remarks about the Three Harps. Trouncing them was incredibly satisfying.

My main goal during the evening was to make sure that we didn't get into a conversation about me. Particularly, Raffy and Penny's plan to build a nutritional supplement empire around my power. But it turned out I didn't need to worry. One of the sophomore girls had been harassed by a group of boys after drama class, and that took up all the conversational air.

So I was able to mostly avoid difficult conversations as the semester wound up. I even found time to buy some Christmas presents. Soap for my mother and the Mizuno wedge for my dad. Not very imaginative, but the soap, at least, was in my budget.

Also, my sister was coming out with her new baby, and without her husband, who couldn't get time off work. I bought her a Big Papi shirt. We had grown up Yankee fans, but she had married a guy who had gone to college in Boston and switched alliances.

I didn't know what to get for the kid. I had never shopped for a baby before. It would have been cool if he had been ready to read comics or play games, but he was still only four months old. What do you get for a kid that age?

As it turned out, the answer became obvious when I was shopping for my sister. A matching Big Papi onesie—who knew there was such a thing in the world? It said for 10 to 12 months, but I guessed that would give the kid room to grow.

I don't want you to get the impression I was looking forward to Christmas. I wasn't. Four days with my parents and my sister in the house where I grew up was definitely not what you might think of as "fun." My sister and I slept in our respective childhood bedrooms, embarrassingly still decorated as we had left them in high school. A sop to her getting married, my sister, at least, had a double bed, and a crib for the baby.

My father seemed still unclear on the idea of adulthood, and there was a fixed expectation that we would join our parents in watching television after dinner and go to bed when my parents did. Meanwhile, my sister and I reverted to our traditional roles. As the elder, less disappointing child, my sister sat in the den with my father and discussed career prospects at her software firm. As the younger sibling, who had chosen to major in English, I tended to help my mother in the kitchen, fending off worried queries about my love life.

Not that we didn't love each other. Mostly we did. But we loved each other best from a distance. When I was around, mom and dad's concern manifested itself as criticism. In order to not disappoint my parents, I ended up making up stories that exaggerated my meager accomplishments, sometimes fabricating small but important details while my sister rolled her eyes or made snide comments. Thus, for example, my parents still believed that I was captain of the chess club in high school, and that I had gone on a date with Laurie Gabler, homecoming queen and class valedictorian.

We lived in Kingsport, a little outside Mount Kisco. As I drove down, I realized that my parents would want to know how the LSATs had gone. I had made a big deal about teaching as a step to something else, and that I would be taking the law school entrance exams as soon as I had the chance. But I hadn't. Part of this was just normal procrastination, but my sudden acquisition of superpowers was also to blame. It had been hard to focus on the regular tasks of daily life while trying to figure out how to be a superhero.

I thought about telling them about my superpowers. I mean, surely becoming a superhero would be an excuse enough for not being a lawyer. But it was hard to imagine Dad agreeing. I could just imagine how they'd react to the news that I could throw a bus across a football field.

My mom would say something like, "That's nice, dear."

My dad would say, "Is there a paycheck in that? Because I never heard of anyone paying for that kind of thing."

And my sister would smirk and say, "Oh, that must be what Laurie loved about you. Your manly strength."

I tried to think if there was anything concrete and useful I could do for my parents with my superstrength. If they had a farm, maybe I could clear a field or something. But their yard was about a quarter acre and pretty manicured. Even in summer, there was not much to do in it. In winter, the best I could hope for was a snow dump. Shoveling was something I'd be really good at.

It didn't snow during my four days at home, but thanks to the baby, it turned out that was okay. First of all, the fact my sister had a baby seemed to finally convince the 'rents that she was an adult. And, much to my surprise, they conceded the same status to me. There was no more talk about lights out, early to bed, house rules. Instead it was, "Will you be here for dinner?" "Are you likely to go out afterwards?" "Help yourself to the liquor cabinet." The last was not a direct quote. But one night, as he was going up to bed, Dad told me that there was more beer in the garage if I was looking for it.

Also, the kid had something my sister called colic, which meant, as far as I understood, that he cried all the time for no reason. As a result, the normal pattern of life was completely disrupted. First of all, my sister was a wreck, with dark circles under her eyes and subject to crying jags. Second, normal conversation was impossible with this hideously squalling infant around. Third, Mum didn't cook, but spent most of the time sitting on the sofa with my sister. Mostly we ordered supper in and ate leftovers at lunch.

Meanwhile, I was excused from every task but one: holder of the baby for most of the time that it was not feeding. There were a couple of reasons for this. First, as a teacher and young person, I seemed less affected than everyone else by the kid's constant screaming. Sure, it was loud and annoying, but I was used to loud and annoying. Second, as my sister claimed, not having kids myself, the crying baby didn't awaken any sense of being an inadequate caregiver. I just blamed the baby.

More importantly, maybe, I was good at quieting the thing. I discovered that it calmed down if I twirled him in a circle in his car seat. I could do this well and—duh, superstrength—I could do it pretty much forever without getting tired. Second, if it got really bad, I'd strap it in the snuggly and go for a walk. That gave me a chance to get out of the house, and the kid really seemed to love it. I mean, he might cry for a while, but outside it wasn't so noticeable. I'd let him bawl himself to sleep and then keep walking. It felt good to have my nephew nestled against my chest, and I thought about down the road a bit when he would come visit me in Boston without his parents and I could spoil him rotten.

Hey, I even changed his diapers, which is not something I was planning to do. But Mom and Sis were so overwhelmed, and I found I didn't mind too much. Baby poop is plenty disgusting, but it's a hell of a lot better than the adult stuff. Also, once cleaned, the kid's butt was cute as shit.

So, really, the only time I had to give the kid up was when my sister was feeding him. At first, it was amazing to me that my sister kept whipping out her tits right there in the living room. But, honestly, it wasn't a biggie. Growing up as a younger brother I used to have a scientific interest in her breasts, as examples of the sort of things other girls I knew might have. Detached, as you might think of it, from my sister. Now, however, her breasts didn't even hold that interest. They were so obviously just tools for a job, the exposure of which had no more lustful potential than her whipping out her smart phone. Well, maybe not her phone—she had the new 5G thingy and I really wanted one—but like a hammer or a screwdriver. You get the idea.

The upshot, at any rate, was that I had a really nice four days and my family, particularly my sister, appreciated my pitching in. At the end of the weekend, she hugged me and thanked me for all the help I'd been. "I think he really likes you," she said. "You were so sweet with him."

"Yes, Jason," my mom said, "you were the hero of Christmas." And my dad stood there nodding like he agreed.

And it made me think, as I drove home, that heroes are always super-strong or super-tough or super-dangerous. They're never super-gentle or super-kind. Why was that?

Of course, maybe I was able to be more gentle *because* I was super-strong. I certainly was able to spin the kid in his car seat for longer. Maybe it's like Frank Perdue always said: "It takes a tough man to make a tender chicken."

Or whatever. I could be a hero to my family, but I had made no progress on being a superhero.

CHAPTER 19
Exhaling

I discovered the end of my superstrength, essentially unused for any earthly good (other than swinging my nephew), a week after school had started. I was busy because the frosh were writing their first papers on Anne Frank and needed a good deal of hand-holding, and I was giving the juniors a pop quiz on *The Great Gatsby*, basically to remind them that they were still in school. I had also made the mistake of volunteering to lead not one, but two extra-curricular activities.

The first was easy enough, a kids' Magic: The Gathering session. We met after school and hung out for a while. I would play a game or two and occasionally be called in as a referee to stop a nerd fight breaking out. Otherwise, I drank coffee and listened to problems that the students would usually never have told me during the school day.

The other club was a mistake. Toby, claiming he was getting too old, asked me to take over the debate club. It turns out I know shit about debate. I had some vision that because I taught English, I would at least be ahead of the kids in forming coherent arguments. I was wrong. These kids speed-talked circles around me. They hoped I could critique their arguments and help them get better, but it was quickly apparent that they were out of my league. On the rare occasion I noticed and pointed out a specious argument, the kids acted like I was some sort of awesome debate guru, but I'm pretty sure they were just taking pity on me—like the way you overpraise a klutz on a baseball team who finally doesn't blow the easy catch.

I knew the kids deserved better than me—Toby had really known what he was doing—but no one else volunteered and Principal Snowe was on the verge on cancelling the team. If I couldn't coach debate, at least I could stay after school to make sure the team had rooms to practice in, contests to compete in, working email lists, buses to get them where they were going, etc.

The point was, I was busy being King of the Dorks at Flynn, so I hadn't had much time to think about superheroing. When I woke up two weeks into the semester, as a dreary January was about to turn into a frigid February, and blew on my morning coffee to cool it down, I didn't consider superpowers when the coffee froze over and ice formed around my glass.

Hank realized at once what was going on.

"It's your new power. Cold breath."

"Ugh. Not a trade-up."

"Hey, don't prejudge. Let's see what you can do."

I could do a bunch of cool things. I could make impenetrable ice walls and ice suits. I could freeze a person or a car in its tracks. I never got cold (although I never really got warm either). Over small areas, under standard pressure, I could bring the ambient temperature down to about minus 160 degrees, low enough to freeze carbon dioxide, xenon, and argon.

What I couldn't do was get a hot cup of coffee in me. Every time I brought the coffee up to my mouth a thin layer of frost formed on the surface, no matter how careful I was not to breathe. I was doomed to drink iced coffee for the rest of the winter.

At the end of the week, with my classes and clubs all under control, and a new power to explore, I tried to reengage with the world. I looked for Penny to see if she wanted to go out that weekend, but when I finally caught up to her she was on the phone and made discouraging "Let's schedule something" gestures.

I ran into Ellen but before I could tell her about my new power, she showed me Raffy's video of me lifting the car and yelled at me for being so selfish that I would "put Hank at risk after all he'd done for me." I tried to explain that they hadn't told me they were planning to make the video until after it happened, then went off to find Raffy to channel some of Ellen's outrage toward him.

I ran into him in the teachers' lounge. Before I said anything, he handed me a $5,000 check. "The first JME proceeds, and that is just the beginning," he said.

It was hard to thank him and bawl him out at the same time, so in the end I didn't really do either. Instead, I told him about my change in power, which he seemed to take personally.

"It's hard to build anything if I can't count on you," he said.

But before I could protest, he had moved on. "I guess we'll have to use digital techniques for the next video. We're established and that's the main thing. And there might be some fast cash in this other thing. Can you freeze nitrogen?"

"No," I said. Nitrogen froze at minus 185. I had never managed that in Hank's tests.

"Well, that's where the big money is, but I'll see what I can do."

And he left me before I had a chance to ask any more questions. He was one seriously weird dude, I thought, looking at the check in my hand. But not bad, not bad at all. One more check and I'd have enough to pay Hank's fine.

On the ride home I made a list of what my power was good for. I really racked my brains. I mean, I had read about Bobby Drake, Captain Cold and Mr. Freeze. And freezing breath was one of Superman's powers. They were all totally badass. My list was not:

1. If I ever saw a robbery or a mugging (which I never did), I could coat the robbers/muggers in ice and prevent them from getting away;
2. If someone tried to shoot or stab me (which also never happened), I could stop the attack by
   i.   creating an ice wall,
   ii. freezing the weapon, or
   iii. freezing the attacker in place;
3. I might be able to put out a fire by blowing on it (time to start listening to fire department radio feeds again);
4. I could help kids who wanted to skate get ice time.

Hank said I had to take number 3 off the list. First, my blowing might spread the flames before it put them out. Second, if there was a fire, there might not be enough moisture in the air for me to freeze. Third, before freezing a whole building to put out a fire, I'd have to make sure it was empty. Otherwise the people I was trying to save from the fire might die from the cold.

But Hank thought there were some things I missed. He said I could stop traffic, bring planes down, freeze ships in the sea. "It's really a war power," Hank said. "You could really help a country facing an enemy with superior air and naval power."

"Great. Our friends in the US government will take really kindly to that."

"But there's so much we don't know. How much of an area could you affect? All you've done so far is a few quick puffs. What if you really worked at it for an hour or two? Could you freeze Boston harbor? The whole city? What sort of an area could you cool? And how quickly? I mean there don't seem to be any entropic costs, so who knows, maybe your power is infinite."

"None of my other powers have been."

"The best-case scenario is that it makes a measurable difference on a global scale. Since, as far as I can tell, there's no one-for-one match between the BTUs you consume and the amount you cool things down, you might be able to combat global warming."

"Really?"

"Well, most likely not. Unless you can make a pretty fucking big area a fuck of a lot colder, it's probably a drop in the bucket."

But I was excited. "We should definitely test it. I mean maybe this is my real purpose. Ending global warming. That's even better than fighting crime."

That weekend, Hank, Ellen and I headed to Maine to test what I could do. Why Ellen? Well, Hank said she really knew her meteorology. Which . . . fine, but he was at MIT, and surely there were seven world experts on the stuff that he could have dug up. He also said there was no reason to extend the circle of people who knew about my powers, which made more sense. But they were spending an awful lot of time together, and I was sure there was more to it.

It turned out that it was good to have Ellen along for another reason. She had been one of those outing club/wilderness types in college. She knew a lot about the Maine coast and tucked-away places where no one would notice what we were up to. I guessed hiking was what she did in college instead of dating. Or, since she mentioned visiting Quoddy Head with some guy named Dana, maybe it was what she did *for* dating.

I did consider what it would have been like; a college-age Ellen in a cozy tent for two with Dana, no doubt bearded and vegetarian. I tried to remember what Ellen's body had been like the night we had slept together, but I had been pretty drunk and could only conjure masses of hair falling over my face. I also remembered being surprised at how strong she was. Probably from all that hiking.

"Hank," I reminded myself. Also, I had a 10 on the line so I could afford to be generous. Although I wondered if Penny would agree to kiss me while I had this stupid cold breath. It'd be like sucking on an ice cube. Which can be nice in summer, but I doubted that Penny was an ice cube type of girl. And one false move, a sneeze say, and I could accidentally freeze her insides. Suddenly I pictured Penny's frozen, dead body, naked, gorgeous and blue, being wheeled out of her apartment on a gurney on its way to the morgue. My libido deflated like a popped balloon. I wasn't going to have sex for some time.

At any rate, Ellen led us to some secluded bay, involving a long hike through a trackless wilderness. The lack of people freaked me out.

"What's the wolf situation out here?" I asked Ellen as we made our way farther from the car than I really wanted. "Or bears?"

"For Christ's sake, Jason," Ellen said. "You're a fucking superhero. If a bear tries to chomp on you, freeze him in a block of ice. And while you're at it, stop worrying about dying of exposure. Best we can tell, in case you'd forgotten, you're immune to cold."

I looked at Hank, who was more of a city kid than me, but, bundled in a grey anorak and over-the-top hat and gloves, he seemed happy as a lark. Which made sense, he was playacting he was on some groundbreaking exploration of the Artic, with a potential booty call to boot.

Once at the bay, I started to work. Which, in this case, consisted of exhaling as much cold air as I could for as long as I could. Hank advised me to go slow and not lose my wind. So, while Hank and Ellen built a fire in a ring of rocks, I blew cold air at the sea. The temperature began to drop. Ellen broke out artic gear like Hank's from her backpack, and I realized they were pretty smart. It was getting seriously cold. Not for me, of course. I was in shirt sleeves and was my usual just-too-cold-to-be-comfortable self that wouldn't go away even if was practically standing in a fire.

Hank was taking measurements and announced each ten-degree

drop in temperature. Then he and Ellen broke out walkie-talkies and coordinated taking temperatures in an increasing radius to where I was located. It must have been pretty substantial, because practically the entire cove began to ice over and some pretty serious winds were whipping up.

I had visions of freezing the entire Atlantic. This would, I was pretty sure, cause untold death and destruction, so I couldn't get too carried away. But, man, what raw fucking power! It made my superstrength look piddly in comparison. Maybe my superherodom wasn't about crime-fighting, which was, after all, pretty stupid, but about saving the world from global catastrophes. Maybe my powers would get more progressively awesome until I was practically godlike.

I took my shirt off. There may have been some element of showing off here, but mostly I just felt in love with the cold I was creating. I wanted to be one with it. I wanted to get totally naked but restrained myself, knowing Hank and Ellen would be back from their measurements soon.

When Ellen came back before Hank. I noticed that she was now wearing goggles and a face mask, so no part of her skin was exposed. A few minutes later, Hank emerged from the woods, also in the full artic. "It's amazing. A twenty-degree temperature drop for about half a mile. After that, as best I can tell, it dissipates a several degrees every hundred yards or so. And I am fucking freezing."

A heavy snow began to fall, and Ellen shouted to Hank, "I think we maybe should seek shelter."

"Let me," I said, feeling limitless power course through me. And quickly, without too much thought as to what I was doing, I directed my breath to cause a crude igloo-type structure to emerge out of the air in one corner of the cove.

I swear that I could see their shining, admiring glances even behind their goggles and balaclavas. Then I turned back to the sea and wondered if I could emulate Iceman and lift myself high on a tower of ice to survey the changes I was creating. When I was done, again like Bobby Drake, I could create an ice track to surf gracefully back down to my frozen sea.

This was a mistake. First, my tower was a shambolic, leaning mess. Second, once I got up in the air, my normal fear of heights kicked in, and all I wanted to do was get down as soon as possible. But my ice track was as rickety as my tower, and I found myself as excited about sliding down the ice as I had been about skateboarding down the ramp in the skate park that my friend Joey Belson had taken me to in sixth grade.

That moment in sixth grade was when I had decided to give up skateboarding for good. Now, on the Maine coast I gave up emulating Iceman. I made a wider ice ramp and scooted down on my rear. Look, my power was cold, not cool.

Not long after that humiliation, I was done. I was out of breath and exhausted, and Hank's measurements said that the temperature had begun to warm back up. I got dressed and we hiked out of there.

"So, did we do it?" I asked as we walked back to civilization. "Can we combat global warming?"

"Not even remotely," Hank said. "The amount of cooling was still very local, about a 10-mile radius. You might be able to change local weather patterns, but it won't do anything on a global scale."

And that was that. We went back home. Another useless power. Ellen and I went to school the next day, and Hank went back to the lab. I snuck out at lunchtime during school that week and made sure that the ice at the local Boston ponds was perfect for skaters. It was the least I could do. (And the most.)

CHAPTER 20
Going Nowhere Fast

You know the drill. I wake up one day and the old power's gone just as I was getting used to it.

Of course, the old power deserted me in the usual annoying way. I was late to school because we had stayed up late the night before kicking the ass of a team of BU grad students in the trivia tournament. This put us in the semifinals, and we stayed out a while to celebrate. The next morning, as I was running around getting ready, I grabbed the cup of coffee Hank had poured for me and tried to slug it down, expecting the same unsatisfying, lukewarm sludge I had been forced to get used to since the advent of my cold breath.

Instead it came in hot and burned my lips and tongue like a mother before I spit it out all over the kitchen counter. Hank laughed watching me, and I realized at once that it meant I'd lost my cold power.

"I wonder what my new power is?" I said, after confirming that I could no longer ice up the room with a breath.

"Superspeed," Hank said.

"Why do you say that?" I asked.

"You should have seen how fast you cleaned up."

On reflection, I realized that I had seen the coffee spray out of my mouth in slow motion, like I could have caught the droplets before they dropped. I hadn't tried, though. I'd figured that was a hangover effect. Instead, it was my new superpower.

"Cool," I said, because speed is obviously the best superpower. You don't need anything else.

"Are you going to test it?" Hank's eyes glowed. He knew that speed was the best power too. But the particular version of super-speed made a big difference.

Was I Flash, who was the most powerful superhero ever, except when Superman's writers got jealous and pretended that Super-man is as fast as Flash? If so, I could move invisibly fast, vibrate through walls, run over water and up buildings. I could run faster than light and even go backwards in time, whatever that means. The point is, I really could change the world. I could run in, search Iran and carry out their nuclear weapons before anyone even no-ticed. I could disarm North Korea. There were no limits.

And let me be quite clear: Flash could totally take Superman and Green Lantern in a fight, because it would be over before Supes or GL really knew it had started. Flash could search the world for a pile of kryptonite and drop it in Superman's shorts while Supes was still warming up. He could take GL's ring off before the fight even started. In either case, he could get close, and vibrate his hand through their chests and remove their hearts.

Unless, of course, you think that Supes is as fast as Flash, which makes no sense, or that GL's ring could operate automatically as fast as Flash, which is less idiotic but still wrong. Or unless you think Flash is not really as fast as Flash is often depicted, which is a whole lot more arguable. I mean, the writers always make Flash way slower in fight scenes—like his opponent can raise a wand or whatever and get off a blast before Flash lands a punch—than in the rest of his life. So maybe the battle speed is the real speed, and the regular-Joe speed is just poetic license. (Yeah, whatever. Assuming, *arguendo*, that there was an underlying truth to the matter. Or poetry.)

Or maybe I was just Quicksilver or the Flash of Earth 2, Jason Garrick. They could go about the speed of sound, or several times the speed of sound when comic logic required it, but nothing approaching the speed of light.

Also, what would the "gimmes" be? Probably not superstrength, because my history tended to only let me have one power at a time, even if it didn't make sense. Force equals mass times acceleration. If I could up my acceleration a jillion times, I should be able to up my force, right?

I should have some sort of speed-related invulnerability, if only so that I didn't kill *myself* when I hit something at speed. Or get burns on my feet or serious static electrical shocks or the like.

What about sonic booms? Comic fans, or maybe ex-fans, were always going on about the real physical problems that superspeed would cause, including the fact that you would leave sonic booms in your wake.

I didn't really understand sonic booms. What was booming? Hank was always amazed by my lack of scientific knowledge. "How did you get to be a geek and know so little about how the world works?" he would ask me. I told him that I was more of a humanities-type geek, and that just because you read fantasy books, played D&D and had no social life didn't mean you had to be interested in math and science or be on the spectrum.

I was always pretty depressed after those conversations. It meant I was the kind of geek who got neither the girl nor the high-paying job at Google.

In the end it turned out I was more Quicksilver than Flash, which was disappointing. I know I shouldn't complain. I could do some wicked cool things. My maximum speed was about three times the speed of sound. I could reach that speed from a standing start in about five seconds. My reactions were enhanced while I was running so I could run through city streets without crashing into things. I could turn and stop just like I was running at normal speeds. When I paid attention, everything in the world around me looked like it was moving in slow motion.

It was all immensely cool, but it wasn't world-changing, like Flash's power. And I couldn't do things fast enough to be invisible. If I could be seen, I was still vulnerable.

There were the expected freebies. I did not set off sonic booms. Friction did not burn me to a crisp. Other than being hungry afterwards, I did not deplete my energy in any noticeable way. And the rapid pounding did not destroy my joints. In other words, my powers were, once again, according to the best analysis of Hank and Ellen, completely impossible.

Which didn't mean that I didn't have to listen to Hank, Ellen and Raffy spend hours debating the hypothetical physics of superspeed, even after we determined that none of it applied to me.

"Uh, who cares?" I asked while we were sitting around drinking a beer after Hank's latest round of testing. The whole crew had come, Toby, and Sylvia and Penny as well. Speed was a sexy superpower. "I thought you said we're all just delusional."

"We're talking about what the physics *would* be if they were real," Hank said.

I suddenly saw why pretty girls weren't attracted to geeks. I mean here I was, sexy as hell and able to move at supersonic speeds, and all these people wanted to talk about was pretend science. What did a guy have to do to get a little attention?

None of us could think up particularly useful ways for me to use my power. Toby risked mockery again by returning to the subject of track and field, but this time I sort of agreed with him. That really seemed to be what most of my powers were about. Not helping the world. But offering athletic wish fulfillment.

If you think about it, that is probably the real point of superpowers anyway. I mean, consider who invented comic books. Major dorks from the '20s, '30s, '40s and '50s. They grew up in the shadow of football, baseball and basketball players who were more popular and more beloved than they were. So what did they do? Did they imagine a future in which artists and brains were more respected than athletes? No, they imbibed and endorsed the culture that granted the jocks first-class status, and wrote self-hating, wish-fulfillment fantasies in which they could suddenly out-jock the jock.

And just for a bonus insight into the self-hating nature of comics, look at the villains. They're all the super-smart scientist types. Luther, Brainiac, Doc Octopus, the Red Skull, etc. and so on forever. And they're usually short, misshapen and ugly compared to the superheroes as well. Far from challenging the stereotype of the handsome jock as the moral force for good, and the less perfectly symmetrical brainy kid as someone only a mother could love, they reinforced them. Comics: not a good guide to life.

But if I couldn't use superspeed for heroing, what could I use it for? I did a couple of gym appearances for Raffy. He figured a couple of cool stunts on a treadmill could help sell more vitamin drink just like my free-weight feats. Not as well, of course, because who wants to watch someone run on a treadmill? Also, because lifters are amazingly, uniquely gullible when it comes to this sort of thing. The cardio crowd not so much, at least if the product can't claim to be organic and vegan.

I almost refused Raffy's request because I still was conscious of Ellen and Hank's worries that I keep my secret ID in place. But Raffy gave me another check—for a lot less this time, apparently the novelty had worn off—and I felt obligated. I figured I wouldn't do anything impossible, anyway. Just something cool enough to sell our vitamin drink.

With the vitamin racket slowing, Raffy thought we might be able to make some money by doing due diligence in complex litigation where lawyers have to go through millions of documents to check if they are relevant. Raffy wasn't sure he could break into the market before my power deserted me, but we did some test runs to see what I could do. It turned out that, although I could flip through the documents with full superspeed, my brain turned to Wheatena after ten minutes or so and I had no idea what I was reading. Which was a relief in a way. Sitting in a basement in Quincy looking through mortgages was not how I wanted to use my superspeed.

It also meant that I could not use my power to read all the books in the Boston Public Library, or maybe get fluent in six or seven languages. Which was a shame.

Still, I was so determined not to let it go unused that I started searching on the internet for amateur UFC fights. It turned out there was a league you could join just by signing up. So I did, and registered for a fight in some gym in Revere for that weekend. Easy as that.

I headed out, with Hank reluctantly in tow, to compete in a UFC amateur tourney in the 160-pound weight category. What I really wanted was to win a big check, but that wasn't the way it worked at amateur tourneys. You just fought for points. When you had enough, you could qualify to enter pro fights. Maybe there were underground fight clubs somewhere in Boston where I could have fought for money, but I had no idea how to find them.

I asked Penny if she wanted to come along. I figured I could get her in bed at the end of the night if she saw me smashing up major hardos all day. But somehow she didn't think that spending the day in a smelly gym watching amateurs beat the pulp out of each other was for her.

I said, "Well, are you around Saturday night? We could get dinner to celebrate my win."

"I'd love to, Jason," she said. "But I'm hosting a party for the alumnae of my sorority that night."

"I can come by," I said. "Meet your sisters." I imagined a room full of girls of Penny-like hotness swooning before descriptions of my physical prowess. I swallowed.

"Girls only," Penny said.

So it was just me and Hank that day. We arrived to register in the morning. The gym was in an almost abandoned strip mall, with potholes in the parking lot. It stank of sour sweat and had plastic milk jugs put about for collecting drips when it rained. It was not five-star quality. I was glad Penny hadn't come.

They did a quick physical, took my medical history and assigned me a fight number. That was when one of the guys organizing the tourney came up and asked me to confirm my fight history.

I should tell you that I had to talk about my martial arts and fighting background in my initial registration. Rather than say "None," which would likely have gotten me a fight with some doughy beginner like myself, and would have been totally unfair given what I could do, I made up a whole history. Black belts in Tae Kwan Do and Judo, wrestler at a national level in college and 10 previous fights. All won by knockout.

"You, Jason Smithka?"

"Yeah," I said.

"Where'd you train?"

"New York. Upstate," I said, forgetting the name of the gym I made up.

"We have you as the last fight, but I'm not sure about the weight category," he said. "I mean you look a little . . . . You still 160?"

"Yeah," I said.

"I don't want you to get hurt."

"Worry about the other guy." I was enjoying this. Trying to think what Vin or Arnie might say in my place.

"Look, we have you against one of our regulars. One of our best. Jose Changa. He's won some regional tourneys. I'm not sure . . ."

"Don't worry about me," I said. "I'll try not to hurt him too bad."

I could see the guy look at me, take a dislike to me and figure, "What the hell. Let Jose take him apart."

Once the fights got started, I saw what he meant. I'm pretty slim, but I'm just a regular guy. Which means I have my share of body fat. I'd say I carry it well. It doesn't detract from my Zach Braff good looks in any way. In fact, I may have been skinnier than Zach himself, who always seemed a little on the pudgy side to me.

It turns out that for fighters, with like zero body fat, 160 pounds is like a regular guy's 200 pounds. If it wasn't for superspeed, I'd have been quaking in my boots. It didn't help that I kept thinking of Ellen saying my powers were the result of a delusion. I hoped Jose Changa was in on the delusion.

The truth is, I wasn't too worried. The fighters may have seemed fast in the real world, but when I clicked in my superspeed vision they seemed incredibly, agonizingly slow. I haven't really explained how my eyesight worked. I had discovered that, while I mostly went around seeing and reacting at normal speeds, I could sort of snap my body into superspeed mode where everything slowed down to a crawl. I tried not to do it too often, mostly because watching some kid raise his hand or someone hand you a cup of coffee in superspeed mode was incredibly frustrating. Everything took so long and got so boring, that it was almost impossible not to jump in and take the coffee or call on the kid, almost before they'd begun their actions. Which, of course, freaked the person out.

In fact, I watched most of the fights in regular mode so I could enjoy them. In speed mode, they were like endless, bad, super-slow-mo Tai Chi. So I knew my fight would be a piece of cake. The guy could never touch me, and I could hit him whenever I wanted. Unless he had superspeed too. Okay, that thought threw me for a second. But just for a second, because, come on, how likely was that? If the guy had superspeed, he'd have found something better to do with it by now.

Rather than anticipate my fight, I was already bored by it. We had to wait like two hours for the other fights to finish up, and when I saw my opponent, looking big and in shape and psyching himself up to tear me apart, I didn't feel scared or angry. I just felt sorry for him. What had he done to have to face me? It was like I had been allowed to play in some kindergarten soccer tournament. Or a trivia game against toddlers. Of course I'd win, but where was the glory in it? It wasn't a fair fight. It didn't really reflect well on my skills, my willpower or anything else. I had superspeed and he didn't. Big whoop that I could beat this guy.

I started to explain to Hank, but I had taken too long agonizing over the whole state of affairs internally, that just as I had begun my explanation, one of the event organizers tapped me on the shoulder and said it was time to get ready. I went in the dressing room and changed.

When we came out, Jose bounced up and down on his toes and stared at me in the aggressive manner they seem to teach fighters. I stood flat-footed and looked back at him.

After going over the rules, the ref whispered to me, "Tap out if you need to. There's no disgrace."

Jose said, "Yeah, let's make this quick. No point getting hurt."

I was touched how worried they all were about me. I guess Jose was feeling the same thing I felt: there was no glory in beating me.

If you read this far, you might be expecting my power to desert me just as the fight begins. And I'd get beaten to a pulp. But it wasn't like that at all. It was way worse.

I switched into superspeed mode and watched Jose throw jabs that looked like they were moving through molasses and kicks that were being delivered parcel post. I moved out of the way easily, not feeling awesome or proud, but stupid that I thought this was a worthwhile use of my talent.

I could tell he was getting frustrated, but it just didn't seem fair to hit him. I was mostly concentrating on moving slowly enough as I dodged his efforts to hit or grapple me that I didn't give away my powers.

Finally, I realized that dragging things out would humiliate him more than knocking him out, so I moved in (still trying to move slowly enough to make it plausible) and hit him gently in the sternum. I didn't want to put a hand through his chest. I didn't have anything like superstrength, but the speed still added a lot of oomph to my punches.

He staggered back, falling down and gagging for breath. You might think I would have hurt my hand, and I did a bit, but no more so than I might have with an ordinary punch. I had a freebie protection from injury when I used my superspeed.

Jose was on his knees groaning. When he did catch his breath, it was just to say, "I think he broke my fucking ribs." Then he fell down on the canvas.

The ref jumped in then and waved me off, which was unnecessary because I had already walked over to my corner. Looking down at Jose, he raised his arms, calling off the fight and calling in the medics.

There was a smattering of applause as he took my hand, raised it and announced me the winner. But not much, because my win was obviously weird and unexpected and stupid, and Jose was a crowd favorite, and they could see no reason he lost to me. I worried I'd caused Jose permanent injury for no reason but to show off. I felt like a putz.

I went to change. A couple of guys, including the event organizer who had quizzed me about my experience, came up to tell me I was a great fighter. But you could tell in their eyes that what they really thought was that I was a freak.

Thankfully, Hank came in, understood my mood, and got rid of anyone who tried to talk to me. We left the locker room and we sat in a dark corner of the gym waiting to hear news that Jose was all right. As it turned out, Jose had a broken rib but was going to be okay. He was able to walk and was heading to a nearby hospital to get it checked out.

I didn't go see Penny that night. I didn't feel like it. Instead, Hank and I got bibimbap and headed home to watch television. The cool thing was Hank basically understood how I was feeling so I didn't have to explain it.

I guess there was something of the Spiderman thing in it: With great power comes great responsibility. Or, at least, it sucks to use power irresponsibly.

CHAPTER 21

Stumbling on Water

I couldn't stop thinking about my fight with Changa. Why couldn't I just enjoy my supreme physical prowess? Wasn't it what I'd yearned for all my life? Isn't it the dream of every slightly klutzy kid dominated and oppressed through high school by the jock oligarchy? Surely, that's the whole point of superheroes and their origin stories. All we comic obsessives really care about is the moment when dorky little Peter turns the table on his jock tormentors.

Part of the problem was that my superpowers didn't feel much like me. They were not permanent, as far as I could tell, and felt like a borrowed cloak draped over my real self. Think of it like this: If my power was to project a holographic image of myself as Brad Pitt, everyone would say how handsome I was. But the more people said how handsome Brad Pitt was, the more I would know they were thinking that the real me—the Zach Braff me—wasn't handsome. That's Mystique's problem, right? She can take on the look of anyone, but she wants to be loved for her blue reptilian self.

There was also a problem of scale. My powers were too great. My advantages were too overwhelming. No one cares if a man outraces a turtle. It takes no courage. No effort. No dedication.

No smarts. No moral superiority. No nothing. I wanted to show my worth. I wanted glory. Relying on my powers to beat Changa nullified all of that.

People who write comics know that you eventually have to move on from that first cathartic standing up to bullies. It's stupid and boring for Spiderman to beat up high-school students or Superman to chase muggers the whole time. The power imbalance is so great that there's no suspense. Which is why comic books always end up introducing supervillains whose powers are almost identical to those of the hero.

So Superman meets General Zod, another Kryptonian with the exact same powers (or Flash fights the Reverse Flash, or Green Lantern fights Sinestro, or Daredevil fights Bullseye, or Spiderman fights Venom, or Iron Man fights Iron Monger, or Hulk fights the Thing, or Dr. Strange fights the Scarlet Witch, etc., etc.). Now the hero can't rely on his (or, rarely, her) powers alone. They have to rely on grit and determination. On moral superiority. On intrinsic goodness.

When Superman fights Zod, superpowers are irrelevant. They are just two equally matched schmoes. And Supes has to "earn" his victory. But, of course, these storylines end up being tedious in their own way. We read superhero comics to fantasize about what we could do with extraordinary powers. If everyone has the same power, what's so super about them? They're irrelevant. You might as well read *Crime and Punishment*.

On the other hand, I had two experiences using my powers in the week after my MMA fight that I didn't feel so bad about. Or, maybe, one I felt good about and another that was ambiguous.

First, on Tuesday, I realized that clicking into superspeed mode, I could actually follow the arguments of my debate students. Not only that, but for the first time, I was able to respond in kind, talking as fast as they did. What happened was that one of the stars of the club, a girl named Chantelle, was arguing in speed-talk mode against physician-assisted suicide, claiming there was nothing in its favor. I would ordinarily have missed the argument, but in fast mode, I had a chance to see what she was skipping over, so I interrupted and laid out like seven arguments in favor of it in about three seconds. The kids were stunned by my sudden display of competence, and it felt good to surprise them.

"Hey, Mr. S., where'd you learn that?"

"You were holding out on us."

"No, just learning from you guys. Just learning," I said. "But, remember, speed isn't everything. My main point was that Chantelle's argument was weak. She was saying that there were no reasons for physician-assisted suicide, and I named several. You can't just ignore the other side like she was doing. You have to acknowledge it and respond. So, go on, Chantelle, let's hear what you have to say in response."

I sat back and smirked. It felt good to get the kids' respect, even though I realized I was only using the same not-really-me power I had used to knock out Jose Changa.

Then, on Thursday, we had another trivia match, this time the semifinals against one of the really good teams from Boston Semiconductor. They had been in the finals the previous year and were expected to beat us. But they didn't. In fact, we won handily, and mostly because of my superspeed.

You see, one of the things in a trivia contest, at least at the higher level, is winning the race to the buzzer. Thanks to me, we won the race to buzz every time. As a result, we beat the other team going away.

Once again, I used my power to get an unfair advantage. And it didn't feel bad. Well, the first couple of times, Ellen looked at me funny, but when the others realized what I was doing, they were totally supportive. Toby and Raffy laughed and clapped.

Sylvia said, "That'll show 'em."

Penny whispered something in my ear that I didn't catch, but seemed as sexy as hell. Only Ellen seemed a little peeved, which she explained as I walked her back to the T.

(I had thought I was going home with Penny, but maybe what she had whispered was something about a change of plans, because when I looked around at the end of the night, she wasn't there. And when I asked if anyone had seen her, Raffy said, "Sure, she was meeting her sister, who just came into town. Didn't she tell you?" Maybe she had. But I was mad anyway.)

"We could have beaten them without you using superspeed," Ellen said.

"Yeah, but it was sweet seeing the expression on their faces, wasn't it? They just couldn't buzz in."

"It felt like cheating to me."

"It wasn't," I said. "I just used my natural abilities."

"Come on," Ellen said.

"Come on yourself," I said. "What did you want me to do? Besides, we still had to get the questions right."

She gave me one of those looks like she wanted to be sure that I realized she didn't agree with me, before she changed the subject. "I talked to Chantelle the other day. She's one of my advisees. She thinks you're doing a great job with the debate team."

"Thanks." I still felt a little sour.

"Have you gone out to see Joe recently?"

"No." Something else to feel bad about.

"How about this weekend? I'm going out to see my grandfather. We can go together."

"Okay," I said.

"Great, see you then," Ellen said as she headed down into the T, leaving me scratching my head. She went from attack to praise to proposing an outing. What was going on?

I just focused on the attack. I didn't feel bad using my power to win the trivia game, even though I could sort of see Ellen's point that it was cheating. So what made it different from the Jose Changa situation? Maybe because it was a team sport. Because my team (most of them) were supportive. Maybe because it didn't involve breaking the ribs of the semiconductor guys.

I *did* feel lousy as I headed home, but I figured that wasn't because of Ellen accusing me of cheating. It was Penny, blowing me off again. We had slept together—well, had sex—like two times. But I could never get an angle on her. She didn't want to sit and talk. If we met, it was only because I chased and chased. She was always running away. Always having something else scheduled.

But if Hank was right and I meant nothing to her, why did she have sex with me? It didn't make sense. Was it just because of my powers? Was I, like, a notch in her belt, like some girls sleep with basketball stars? Maybe Penny just wanted to say she slept with someone who could fly or stretch or whatever? I was angry and frustrated. What was I to her? I was through with her playing around. She should be a proper girlfriend or maybe she shouldn't be my girlfriend at all.

Part of me wanted to head over to her apartment and have it out with her. But it was late, and I had to be at school by 7:30 the next day, meeting with a student who was lost in *The Great Gatsby*. And a train was arriving, headed my direction. An uncertain confrontation lost out to the guarantee of getting to sleep in thirty minutes.

The upshot was that I headed to Concord that weekend with Ellen.

We didn't talk about powers and heroing. We talked about school.

"How long do you expect to stay at Flynn?" I asked.

She looked at me in surprise. "As long as I can. It's a great place to be. You really feel like you're making a difference."

I knew what she meant. Many of the kids were from tough situations, but there was some sense of hope at the school. Maybe you couldn't save everyone, but at the end of the day, most of the kids would be okay. And, if you were lucky, some would take off.

Still, I was shocked by what Ellen had said. There was so much to do in life. Money to earn. Places to go. People to meet. To stick at Flynn and slowly turn into the single Toby, or the divorced Sylvia? Teaching the same class year after year, returning at the end of every day to dismal one-bedroom apartments? To grow old, while the students remained always the same age, so that you slowly lost touch, until, finally, you become a school joke for something inconsequential like mimeographing your handouts, or failing to understand the difference between Snapchat and Instagram? Wasn't that a nightmare rather than a career ambition?

I put the case to Ellen, and she was silent for a while. I felt like I had treaded on difficult ground. But I wanted to know what she saw in teaching. She was so smart. She could go back to school, be a scientist. Be a lawyer. Or a manager. Didn't she have ambitions?

"Sylvia isn't a joke. Nor is Toby."

"Not yet," I conceded. "At least, Sylvia. The kids make fun of Toby. His red face. The fact he's stuck in the 19th century. I don't really know if he can connect with them at this point."

"You know he's not really single, right?"

I hesitated. I wasn't sure what she meant. I mean, a lot of people clearly thought Toby was gay. I didn't know either way, but I could see it might be the case. I hadn't really paid any attention. But I thought this might be what Ellen meant.

"He has a partner. He's just in the closet. So he doesn't advertise."

"I didn't think people were in the closet anymore."

"Guys his age. Especially teachers. You think he ever would have gotten hired in the '90s if people knew he was gay?"

"I guess not."

"He could come out now, I guess. But habits die hard. He'll talk about it if you ask him."

"I never have."

"Anyway, I think he's happy. He and his partner do historical re-enactment stuff. He's like an expert on Civil War buttons or something."

"I knew that. What a strange thing to be an expert in."

"It takes all types, I guess. Did you know that Sylvia has two kids?"

"I've heard her talk about it."

"One is studying computer science at Tufts. The other graduated like a year ago and is doing an internship at the Kennedy Center."

"An actor?"

"I don't know. I think he does something with sets. He's going to do graduate theater work at Emerson next year. It's one of the top-rated programs in the country."

"Your point is her kids are successful."

"No, my point is she's successful. She gave her kids a great life. They're smart. They seem happy. That's what you can do as a teach-er. Have a happy family."

"What about money? And respect? I mean, who respects teach-ers? No one. Who thinks we're good at anything? No one. That's the whole point of the joke: those who can, do; those who can't, teach."

"Do you buy that?"

"Sometimes."

"What the fuck, Jason? You want to be Raffy with his stupid start-ups? Whoring yourself to the highest bidder."

"I wouldn't mind the money."

"The question is what you'll do to get it. That's what I like about you. You might wish you had money, but you won't compromise yourself to get it."

"What do you mean?" I said, angry myself now. "If I go off and get my MBA, then I'm a sellout? Just like that? No way. You were the one who said it takes all types."

"I'm not saying that anyone who gets an MBA is a sellout. And you're right that Raffy isn't a sellout. He's just being true to himself. I'm just saying *you'd* be a sellout. Because you don't really believe in it."

"How do you know what I believe in?"

"I know you want to be a hero, don't I? That's pretty cool right there."

"Yeah, well as far as I can tell, it's impossible."

I'm not sure where that conversation would have led, but it was interrupted by our arriving at her grandad's nursing home. We picked up Mr. Rinaldi and then headed over to Joe's place.

The plan was that we were going to head to the deCordova Sculpture Park and grab a sandwich at the café there, but it turned out that the olds had other ideas. They knew a Red Lobster that had an early bird lunch special. All you could eat for five dollars. Ellen and I argued against this helplessly as Joe and Mr. Rinaldi ganged up on us. Red Lobster it was.

I ended up with a crab cake special that was really very good. I also finished Joe's surf and turf and was quite happy. Ellen hardly ate anything, explaining to me later that she grew up eating at Red Lobster and despised it.

At any rate, Joe and Mr. Rinaldi seemed to get on like a house on fire. Mr. Rinaldi, in his nineties, was tall and frail, but in pretty good shape mentally. He had been some sort of insurance salesman back in the day, and you could see him work the old salesmanship on Joe, trying to keep Joe talking until he would reveal how much insurance he could afford.

Joe had good and bad days. But on his good days, and this was one of them, he was a pretty fair storyteller. Today, he told stories about his days in the Everett fire department, which seemed to include rescuing a remarkable number of naked women. Listening to this stuff with Mr. Rinaldi and Ellen, stone sober in a Red Lobster, made me squirm. But when I glanced over at Ellen during one of the worst stories—about some girl he had to untie from a bed after her boyfriend set fire to the drapes with the candle he was using to drip hot wax—she was grinning.

When he was done with that series of stories, Joe starting banging on about what a death trap he thought the new Garden was.

"You mean the old Garden," I said. "You told me you worked on the old Garden."

"Yeah, I did mostly. But my company reviewed the plans for the new one. Worst design I ever saw. Electric explosion in the right place and the whole building will go up."

I nodded apologetically to Ellen and Mr. Rinaldi. "I think Joe's confused," I said.

"Nonsense," Mr. Rinaldi said. "He knows what he knows. Now, what sort of shop did you work Joe? Sole proprietorship? Partnership? Some sort of corporation?"

Before we could head further down this road—we'd already sat in the restaurant for almost two hours—Ellen and I intervened. "Wouldn't you two like to go to the museum?" Ellen asked.

"Yeah, we could go for a couple of hours and drop you back at your places by like three o'clock," I added.

But it turned out that the two of them had other ideas. Mr. Rinaldi's nursing home, just a few miles down the road from Joe's, had mini concerts on Saturday afternoon and Mr. Rinaldi wanted to attend. There was, he informed Joe, a devastatingly handsome woman who played clarinet.

"A touch of the Joan Crawford," he stage-whispered to Joe, who nodded as if that meant something.

It was not clear if Mr. Rinaldi was inviting Joe to join him at the concert, but having told his stories, Joe was done for the day. He mumbled something about wanting to watch a basketball game and started walking out, even before we had paid for the meal. I ran to catch up and left Ellen to foot the bill.

So in the end, we just dropped the oldsters off at their respective nursing homes—Ellen made it clear to me that she did not want to stay and watch her grandfather drool over the clarinet player—and we hit the sculpture garden by ourselves.

"Well, that was a fucking waste of time," I said, as we wandered through the park.

"Nah. Granddad and Joe got on really well. And Joe's stories . . ."

"Yeah, sorry about that."

"They were great. Classic old Boston. I hope you're more careful when you tie a girl up."

I was blushing and hating myself for it.

We walked together for a while, looking at some of the art. It was March and there was snow on the ground, but the sun was shining and it wasn't bad to be outside. If the old folk had been with us, of course, we would have stayed inside.

A few minutes later, Ellen said something I didn't quite catch. I asked her to repeat. She did, not looking at me.

"You still involved with Penny?" She was looking at a statue, hardly paying me any attention.

"Yeah, well," I said. "I don't know what's up with that. I mean, she never has any time."

"Busy, you think?" Ellen rubbed her hands carefully along the grain of a wooden horse.

"I don't think we're meant to touch," I said. She turned and stared at me for just a second and then went right back to it.

"I guess so," I said. Man, I hated this conversation. "What about you and Hank? Is anything happening there?"

"He's a great person," she said. But she said it just as she started rapidly walking over to the next statue.

"What?" I said, trying to catch up.

She stopped short and turned to me again. "He's a great person. That's what I said." She was practically yelling.

"Yeah," I said. "I just think . . . Well, I don't want him to get hurt. He hasn't had much experience with girls."

"Not like you and Joe?" Ellen was at the next sculpture. A marble ball. Maybe something symbolic of the earth. I couldn't tell.

"Who'll just fuck anything," she added.

It took a second or two for what she said to register. It was like a conversation over some bad phone line, so there was a disorienting delay between the person saying something and your being able to hear it. It felt like we were miles away, even though we were right next to each other.

Was Ellen joking? Was she just carrying on with Joe's salty humor from lunch? Was she angry? I remembered that Ellen and I had slept together. Was that the issue? Fuck! Can't casual sex ever just be casual? Anyway, she had Hank now, didn't she? Who was so obviously a better catch than me that she should be happy. Or relieved.

I wanted to ask her what she meant. Or maybe just to repeat what she'd said, in case I'd misunderstood. But I also didn't. And wouldn't it be better to move on? Laugh it off? Pretend I hadn't heard?

"Hey, look at the banana," I said, pointing to a huge yellow sculpture down the hill which I had, inexplicably, not noticed before. "You want to go down there?"

"No, Jason. I want to go home."

"Okay."

So we drove home. There was not much talk on the way. We flicked through some radio stations. When we found one we agreed on, Ellen turned the volume way up.

"That's pretty loud," I shouted.

"Yeah," she shouted back.

Instead of driving her all the way to her house, she asked that I just let her out at Alewife, where she could catch the T.

"I'll drive you," I shouted.

"Next time," she said.

"Fine."

She got out and that was it. I got home and it was still only four in the afternoon. The night was young. And so was I.

I knew Penny said something about her sister being in town. But I was going to surprise her. If we were going to go out, we should go the fuck out sometimes.

CHAPTER 22

Cut to the Quick

Now I did something you'll probably think I shouldn't have. Heck, I probably think I shouldn't have. But it was nothing compared to the stuff I did when my power changed again. That's when you'll really start to hate me. So you might as well hold your fire.

The problem was that, in order not to expose Hank, I hardly ever used my powers. Here I was, imbued with the most awesome abilities known to man, and I never had a chance to show them off. When I first started to fly, it seemed like a good idea to keep a secret identity. But that was mostly to protect myself. The idea wasn't that I would never fly, but that I would fly with a hood and a mask on. Now, keeping Hank safe seemed to mean never tapping into my powers at all.

I knew I owed him. He saved me the scrutiny of the very mean Federales, who, we all agreed, theoretically at least, would have locked me up for years. But it was one thing to hide my powers for my own selfish reasons, it was another to do so out of a moral obligation to Hank. I could ignore my own safety at will—it was my own damn business. But now, flaunting my power wouldn't just be foolish, it would be selfish.

The more I reflected on this, the more frustrated I became. I managed to convince myself that, more than unfair, it was intolerable. I couldn't be expected to rein myself in for the rest of my life entirely for Hank's convenience. And, look, it wasn't really Hank busting my balls over this. It was Ellen, if anyone, and my own overanxious imagination. For all I knew, I told myself, Hank would want me to use my powers more. We'd hardly talked about it at all since he had been released. But he had wanted me to be a superhero as much as I did, just about. And he didn't save me from the Feds so I could waste away as a schoolteacher for the rest of my life.

These ideas had been percolating around my head for some time. And when I arrived back in Cambridge after the uncomfortable afternoon with Ellen, and started to think about going over to see Penny, they seemed pretty convincing.

I decided, caution be damned, I would run over to Penny's and see what she was doing. Even better, I could cut down the Charles Embankment and run along the river (literally). I hadn't run on water yet, but Hank and I had discussed the theory, and it shouldn't be hard. I just had to keep my speed up.

I couldn't run fast enough to be invisible. People would definitely see me, but if I ran top speed they'd only see me for a few seconds and I'd be gone. They'd question what they saw, and they definitely would not recognize me. Even street cameras would only pick up a blur.

Anyway, there was no reason to connect my running with some earlier flying guy, or a guy who could stretch. They were totally different powers.

Were there counterarguments? Maybe, but one thing I learned in debate club is that you have to cut off debate somewhere. I chose to do so now and, given the arguments raised thus far, it was clear there was no reason not to run over to Penny's and plenty of reasons to do so.

I walked down through the Harvard campus, stretching out my neck and shaking my legs, for no particular reason—I didn't have to stretch to use my power—and finally began to jog. Cutting through a relatively secluded alley, I picked up my pace. My vision shot into superspeed mode and I accelerated at a rate that should have left the flesh on my cheeks flapping wildly against my cheekbones, popped my blood vessels and sent my brain and the rest of my internal organs into serious shock, but thanks to whatever (magical, delusional) changes my superspeed effected, my body did none of those things.

I ran (briefly) through the crowded streets of Cambridge, using my enormously heightened reflexes to easily swerve among and around other pedestrians, cars and bikes, at what I estimated would be roughly the speed of sound (but, as mentioned before, no booms). People would notice something. They'd be buffeted by the air in my wake. But no one would get hurt, and no one would recognize me. In fact, by the time anyone even registered me as a blur, I'd be long gone.

Hitting Memorial Drive, I ran back west, knowing I could access the Charles through the Cambridge Boat Club. I sped up as I shot down the boat ramp and hit the water.

I guess I had gone about a third of a mile before I hit the river, and it must have taken me like two seconds, so maybe I was going a little slower than the speed of sound, but I was also ducking around stuff, so who knows. Once I hit the water, where it was less crowded, and because I was somewhat worried about sinking despite Hank's theorizing, I increased my speed, making the roughly three-mile run down to the Charles River Esplanade in about ten seconds.

The thing about running on the water was that the footing was trickier than I had anticipated, and I almost fell flat on my face when I first hit the water. Only my lightning reflexes kept me up.

I slowed down again once off the water, taking another couple of seconds to pull up in front of Penny's apartment, a process that again should have subjected me to multiple-G deceleration that crushed my capillaries, but didn't. There was one old lady on the street when I suddenly emerged from superspeed mode to a light jog. She just looked annoyed that I was young and moving fast, no doubt the same way she would have looked at kids on scooters.

So, running like that. Awesome, right? Less than 20 seconds from Harvard to Beacon Hill. Running on water. The whole she-bang. I mean, I did feel good. I wasn't tired, I just was sort of glowing. I felt good just the way anyone feels good after a run. I felt healthy and powerful. Like I was ready for anything.

On the other hand, the whole thing was so quick that there wasn't much time to enjoy it. In superspeed mode, I could take more in than I otherwise would have been able to. Like read signs on buildings as I sped by them. Check out this one crazy girl who hadn't heard of skin cancer, trying to catch some rays sitting on the banks of the river holding a reflector up to her face in the middle of March. But 20 seconds was hardly enough time to luxuriate in my speed. What I really needed to do was run across the country or something.

I rang Penny's bell. There was no answer. Of course, there was no answer. What a stupid waste of time. She was out at some spa or something with her sister. She had a life. She wasn't waiting around for me. I didn't really know what I was doing there. Blowing off steam, I guess.

I wondered if I could find her. I could zoom around Beacon Hill, maybe Back Bay too, looking in coffee shops and beauty parlors. Where else would Penny hang? High-end clothing stores? A gym? It was funny. I swear she looked like she had just walked off the set of *Little House on the Prairie*, but it was impossible to imagine her anywhere except surrounded by the most expensive luxury. Or maybe that's why she looked like she came from *Little House on the Prairie*. The price of flawless skin is the complete absence of hardship.

And then, suddenly, there she was. Walking up the street. Arm in arm with some dude. And not just any dude. A big, handsome dude with a square jaw who was a dead ringer for Henry Cavill. He was carrying packages for her, including one from Agent Provocateur, just the most fucking expensive lingerie store in Boston.

The fact that she was hanging out with this guy now didn't mean her sister wasn't in town. They didn't have to spend every minute together. The fact that she had friends outside of Flynn didn't mean she didn't adore me.

But I wasn't deceived. At that moment, I realized that the whole thing with Penny was fake. Everything Hank had ever said about her came back to me. She had no interest in me. She would marry for money. She would marry someone who wasn't me for money. I was, at best, a distraction, at worst, an annoyance to her. I knew it. I really, really did. On some level at least.

Knowing it and acting cleverly on the knowledge are different, of course. Right then I almost decided to confront her. Insist that she declare her love for me and throw over this overgrown Biff. Then, at the last moment, some instinct, some instinct I wish I had been able to call on later, protected me, telling me I needed to think things over. Telling me to get the hell out of there before she saw me.

It took me less than 30 seconds to get home. When I walked in, Hank was heating up some macaroni and cheese.

"Do you want some?" Hank said.

"No," I said, heading into my room and trying not to slam the door, so that Hank wouldn't know how angry I felt.

Then I came out again. I was starving. "Okay," I said, "But cook three packets."

We sat down and ate in silence. That is one of Hank's many good points. He can deal with quiet. He doesn't have to have conversation all the time. It's not a good point I share, particularly. As far as I can tell, I'm always interrupting some gigantic scientific advance that would happen if I just let Hank think through an idea. But, heck, maybe that's what Hank likes in me. I can distract him from his ever-churning brain.

Anyway, this time we sat in silence, when finally I said, "I ran along the Charles today. To Beacon Hill and back."

"I thought you were out with Ellen in Concord."

"I was. We got back around 3:00."

"Oh." I could see he was figuring out why I ran to Beacon Hill, but I did not want to talk about Penny with him. Not now. I was still processing.

"Look," I said, when my guilt boiled over, "I've also been doing some ads for Raffy. You know he's selling that vitamin drink to weightlifters and stuff. We go to a gym. I do something a little more amazing than I should be able to and then claim it's all down to the drink."

The last confession came out in a rush. I think Ellen and Hank basically knew about this stuff, but I hadn't exactly talked about it with them. I mean, if you're going to get technical, I had avoided talking about it with them. But they must have known. Raffy, Penny and I did talk about it sometimes during quiz nights. Even Toby and Sylvia were in on it.

But the whole supplement business sounded so stupid and evil. I added, "I've made almost $10,000 so far. I think Raffy is holding about that much for you too. I'm going to use my share to pay off the FBI."

For a moment, I was afraid Hank was going to go super-geek on me and walk out of the room without a confrontation. I was relieved when he finally said, "I thought you were going to lay low?"

"I have," I said. "I've tried. But what do you want me to do? *Never* use my powers? I mean, isn't that unfair? I have the chance to . . . to do something no one has even done before and maybe will never do again. Do you just want me to sit and wait until they go away? I can't do that."

I waited on tenterhooks. If Hank told me I was being selfish and foolhardy, and yes he goddamn expected me to never use my power in public, I was sunk. I would be the most emasculated superhero in history.

But my roommate was bigger than that. He was the real superhero. After a brief pause, he scratched his chin, ate a bite of macaroni and said, "Yes, I see that."

Oh, thank you, thank you, thank you, Hank.

"So, what? You want to go public?"

I gulped. I had not gotten that far in my thinking, but even as Hank said it, I thought maybe I did.

"Yeah, maybe," I said, "or find like some Nick Fury type who would be my like protector."

"Your Charlie? We talked about this before."

"I guess so. But I thought I'd be able to do something on my own."

"So the question is whether you go super public. Like get a TV special and show your stuff. Or go small scale, and just find some whacked army colonel."

"I don't want to show off on TV and then have my powers go away. It'd be awful. I'd be like a famous child actor who grows up to have no talent. Everyone would revel in my being a poor schlub. I'd end up on some celebrity boxing circuit, getting my head pounded in for charity."

"But how do we find Nick?"

We decided we should ask the others. Maybe they had better contacts than we did, although it seemed unlikely. And I was reluctant to talk to the others now because Penny was part of our "group," and I really didn't want to see Penny.

Which didn't stop me, the next day, when I caught sight of her heading into the library, from tracking her down and doing just what I had told myself not to.

"Hello," I said, cornering her at the checkout desk.

"Hello," she said pleasantly.

"Did you have a nice weekend?" I asked.

"Yes, fine," she said, already sensing that something was up.

"Did you have a nice time with your sister?"

"As a matter of fact, she couldn't come. She had a cold and cancelled," she said.

"Shame you didn't let me know. So maybe we could have done something." My voice was rising.

"What's this all about, Jason?" she said.

"I saw you," I said. "With that fucking whatshisname and your packages from that store."

"You mean Leander? Look, this is not the place," Penny said, lowering her voice, to make the contrast with my increased volume clear.

"Well, where then? Where would you best like to tell me that you're cheating on me?"

Penny actually laughed at this. Which, I suppose, she was right to. I was making such an insane ass of myself. But what got to me then is how unconcerned her laughter was. Light and filled with an utter lack of concern that she might not be taking me seriously enough.

"You think it's funny?" was all I could manage.

"Yes, Jason." She stood up. "Walk with me and let me tell you some things." She grabbed my arm to lead me out of the library. I shook off her hand but trudged behind her like a truculent five-year-old. She didn't stop down the hall, but led me out of one of the fire escape doors (unalarmed) into an alleyway where teachers who smoked congregated at various breaks.

Once there she stopped and turned to face me. I closed my eyes. I knew they were wet and bloodshot. My face was probably red and splotchy. I was not at my best.

"We hung out, Jason. Maybe we had sex. So the fuck what? You were desperate. A little puppy following me around with a big sad face. The first time I couldn't help myself. You needed a pity fuck. The second time you were being a dick to Raffy, and you needed something to calm you down. But I don't think I ever said anything about us going out. I'm pretty sure I didn't, and you didn't ever ask me either. Frankly, Jason, you're not in my league."

"I'm a superhero," I said. Pathetic.

"And what's that gotten you? Fame? Money? Glory? No, you just hang out with your roomie and complain about the government."

I muttered something about privilege, and she actually looked angry for the first time.

"Fuck off, Jason! You never asked, but my dad's on disability. My mother's a secretary in a dentist's office. I'm the first person in my family to even go to college."

That news shocked me. "But your apartment . . ."

"Yeah, I work three jobs. I hostess four nights a week and work retail weekends so I can afford it. That and some nice clothes. I'm trying to make something of myself. Which is more than I can say of you. You don't even try. The only time you go to the gym is when Raffy and I drag you there. And your clothes? Have you bought anything since college? Your socks have holes in them. Your shirts have sweat stains. I mean, what the fuck do you think is meant to attract me to you?"

I looked down at myself. She was right. All my clothes were at least five years old.

"Oh, and you still haven't taken the LSAT have you? Or the

GMAT. Or whatever it is that you keep saying you're planning to do. Excuse me for living, but I am looking for someone who is willing to work at their dreams a little."

"You are a shallow bitch," I said.

"And what does that make you?" Penny said. "The only reason you wanted to stick your dick in me is because you think I'm beautiful. But it never occurred to you that I also might be attracted to someone who had a little going on in the hotness department. No, I should just fall over you because . . . because why, exactly?"

"Why did you sleep with me then?"

"I already told you. Look, I'm not trying to be cruel, Jason. But it's best for you to know it won't work out. And you can't 'talk me around,' right? I admit, I was kind of intrigued when you first got superpowers. Who wouldn't be? But you haven't used them really, have you? If you really think you have something to offer, tell someone about it. Put yourself out there in the marketplace. Make a difference. Don't sit around moaning."

"That's what we decided yesterday. I'm going to see if I can help the police."

"Well, there you go. You should talk to Raffy. He may be able to help."

I was spent, and Penny could see it. I was ready to walk away when she said, "Come on, Jason. Don't take it so hard. I do care about you. I think you're funny and sweet. You have great taste in music. It'll be better now we've gotten things off our chests. Let's be friends." She held out one perfect hand, leading to a perfect arm.

And I realized it would never be mine. I tried to take it. I tried to be a reasonable person. I tried to be rational. I tried, but I couldn't.

Instead, I looked at her hand and racked my brain for a stinging rebuke. Something to leave a mark as I walked away. "Save it for Raffy," was all I came up with. Perfect. Jealous, stupid and small-minded to a fault.

The thing about an unrequited love is that it turns us into just the horrible, unattractive person that our rejecting partner sees us as. My reaction to Penny's rejection made me into just the sort of person, if I wasn't that person already, who so richly deserved the rejection. And the more I turned into that person, the worse my reaction was, and the more loathsome I became. It was a vicious cycle that I really had to cut short in 10 minutes so I could teach the juniors a class on *The Great Gatsby*. And then lead the Magic: The Gathering club.

All with a weight on my chest so that I could barely talk. I didn't know what to do. I went and locked myself in one of the faculty bathrooms and sat on the toilet, trying to start breathing again.

I shouldn't have gone to my 2:30 class. Not in the state I was in. But I did. I came in and looked at the assembled kids. Kids from ragged homes, resentful of being in class. Kids who hadn't done the reading assignment. Kids who never would. Kids who maybe wouldn't read a whole book for the rest of their lives; not when there were gaming apps, TikToks and YouTube videos to fill out the holes of their existence.

I called for quiet and tried to start. "Is Jay Gatsby a fool to love Daisy when he can have anyone in the world? Does love always make us into fools?"

I hadn't meant to go there. But it was what was on my mind. Then I couldn't say more. I didn't have the heart. How could I talk about love among a group of sex-obsessed seventeen-year-olds, when I was such a failure myself? The old expression: those who can't, teach.

"Mr. Smithka." Grace Dietz, a large girl with a shrill voice who is like an unofficial class spokesman, raised her hand. "Mr. Smithka, it's just Chris Brown and Rihanna, ain't it. He loved her, I'm sure. But look at what he did to her."

"Beat her up, that what he did."

"It's more like Biebs and Selena, because he loves her, he just won't show it."

Neither of these analogies to Jay and Daisy, based on my store of knowledge, was particularly accurate, but the kids were off, mentioning celebrity couple after celebrity couple, trying to find parallels with the love affair in *Gatsby*.

This was not normal. They never did this shit. Just sit around having an intellectual discussion. Even on my best day, getting a series of three relevant comments in a row was an astronomical improbability. But here they were jamming, on subject, like a college seminar.

And I realized it was for me. They didn't care about this shit. But they knew something, something vague, about my scene with Penny. I hadn't been exactly subtle, and it's practically impossible to keep any excitement from becoming common school knowledge within seconds. Then I had come in with a red face and hardly able to talk, and they just took this on themselves. They didn't want me to break down and cry. So they took up the work of running the class on themselves. Mostly Grace, but the others too. As best they could, they were being solicitous of me. They were taking care of me.

I have to tell you, I almost started bawling again as I realized this, but just as I did, I realized that the conversation had turned personal. The kids were talking about how love turned them into fools. Mostly it was kids accusing each other of acting like buffoons, along the lines of, "Hey, Jaycee, remember when you skipped like two weeks of school because Carli moved to Philadelphia?"

But some of the kids, Jaycee for one, talked about themselves. "Yeah, man. That was fucking hard."

"Language," I said, my first contribution in like 20 minutes.

"I didn't think I'd ever get over it." Jaycee didn't say much and didn't do much work. I'd never had much of a read on him.

"What happened?" Grace asked.

"Time. man, time. And the fact I discovered the little bitch had banged Bill Habbard the week before she left."

Even I laughed at that one. When the bell rang, I didn't say anything. I was so grateful to the kids that I was afraid I would choke up. Thankfully, they ignored me as they barreled out of the classroom.

Grace Dietz was last. "See you Friday, Mr. S."

I turned quickly to the blackboard, pretending to go over it with an eraser.

After that, the Magic Club seemed a small price to pay to get to spend a little more time with the kids of Flynn, every single one of whom I decided I loved deeply.

I suppose I should be grateful to the Magic players for getting me over that crazed thought. For the most part, they were younger than the juniors, and less aware of what was going on in the community. So they didn't show me any particular kindness. Instead, they were unusually obtuse and quarrelsome. I had to break up two fights over accusations of cheating and yell them into silence more times than I could count.

After the club ended, I waited in the English office until I was pretty sure everyone but the cleaning staff was gone, then I snuck out and headed home. Thankfully, Hank was out, because I really couldn't stand another moment of human contact that day. I took a pint of ice cream and a six-pack into my bedroom and ate and drank while listening to break-up songs on Spotify. I fell asleep at like nine o'clock that evening.

Of course, I woke up in the morning and nothing had really changed. I felt just like people always tell you they feel: empty, dead inside. I could get up, get dressed, head to the kitchen and fix breakfast, say "Good morning" to Hank, and all the normal things. But it was like I had been replaced by an alien robot, which had been programmed to imitate all the normal human actions and reactions, but for whom the interior processes that normally give rise to the actions were absent.

Taking leave of roommate, raise hand and wave briefly, crinkle face to slight smile/grimace. Say, "See you later."

Enter school and see Sylvia. Place face in smile mode, state "Hello, Sylv."

She asks how I'm feeling.

Processing. Recommendation: Lift shoulders in shrug motion to suggest modest embarrassment. Adopt neutral tone and proceed. "Fine. Really fine." Change subject. "Can you cover my second-period study hall today. I have some freshmen papers I have to get graded by this afternoon."

Adjective "freshmen" may have been superfluous. Otherwise, went well. Proceed to school assembly. Etc., etc.

I really only had to make it to the end of the week, when I had a week off for spring break. I could be the Terminator until then. I had enough experience with being human that I didn't actually have to feel human emotions to be able to fake them.

With my automaton strategy working, I could make it until Friday. I was sure of it. As long as nothing got past my human mask. And I didn't see why anything should.

The juniors tried. Knowing in some unconscious way that they had saved me in the class on Monday, they seemed to regret and resent their previous kindness and became the class from Hell. They treated me that week like a substitute. They didn't do the reading, would not respond to questioning, got in fights and shouting matches and were almost impossible to quiet. But my mask was firmly in place, and I was equal to the task. I lectured four straight days and gave out a handful of detentions. We were ahead of schedule by the end of the week. One thing about being an automaton was that it was easier to be an authoritarian.

I even managed a lunch with Toby and Ellen, chatting with a great deal of superficial normality about potential police contacts to whom I could reveal my superpowers. The whole new plan to work for the government somehow was a good front, on which I could seem convincingly engaged in my own life. I think it even threw Ellen off.

I didn't use my superspeed that week. I didn't have the heart. At some level, running, any physical activity, is an act of joy and optimism. Joy in one's corporeal existence. Optimism about the perfectibility of man (via push-ups). And I felt no such joy. I felt no such optimism.

So for a week the fastest man that ever lived, possessing the absolute king of superpowers, moved in slow motion. Indifferent to the horrendous waste of ability.

All I wanted to do was make it to the break and disappear.

CHAPTER 23
Supervillainy

Okay, here's where we get to the place where you, dear Reader, are likely to stop liking me very much.

I suspect some of you are already sick of me. Maybe you think that my efforts to become a superhero have been pathetic and you've taken a dislike to me based on my general ineptitude. Maybe you think that I have taken Hank and Ellen's friendship for granted, and I should have been a little more appreciative of their efforts on my behalf. Maybe you think I have been unfair to Penny and to Raffy. Maybe you think I should have been more dedicated as a teacher. What can I say? You're right. But I hope that some of you believe that I was trying to be a decent person, all things considered. That, in the face of temptation, I was doing my best to make the world a better place, even if I hadn't had much success.

Now I enter a phase where I really didn't live up to my ideals. To anyone's ideals. Indeed, I was just a little bit creepy. A lot creepy. I hope nothing I did really hurt anyone in the end. Not badly, at least. But I was flirting with the Dark Side and I did a bunch of things I am ashamed of. I like to think that I stopped the flirtation before anything got too serious. I hope you'll agree.

The thing I don't think you should do is blame my mistakes

on my power to turn invisible. You may be tempted to conclude that my story backs up the idea from that old interview question—"Would you rather fly or be invisible?"—that people who choose flying are better human beings because the invisible folk want to skulk around and do bad stuff, whereas the flyers are joyous people who are unafraid of public opinion.

Sure, you have all the old myths of invisible bad guys. Gyges in *The Republic*; the guy in Wells's *Invisible Man*; Gollum; even Frodo in his way. And, sure, my turning bad coincided with being able to turn invisible. But as Ellen sometimes says: correlation is not causation.

(Okay, Hank wants me to admit that the last twenty-plus chapters contradict my argument here. He says that I claimed to be extra relaxed when I was stretchy and more of a daredevil when I was invulnerable. He also says that I was pretty darn cheerful when I could fly, and a little hyper on superspeed. Well, right. But you shouldn't read overmuch into that. Anyone would be less risk averse when they were invulnerable. The point is: don't blame my powers for what I did when I was invisible. Blame me.)

Getting back to the interview question, simply in terms of power, I'm here to tell you that anyone who chooses flying over invisibility is an idiot. Invisibility is a real superpower. It's up there with speed and strength, maybe better than both of them. Flying, all things considered, is pretty useless. It's fun, sure, but so are 'shrooms. And, like taking mushrooms, it doesn't accomplish anything. Anyone with an ounce of ambition would rather be invisible than fly.

The last thing I want to address before you start this chapter is a question that may nag you as you read it. Namely, why? Why am I writing this shit? Why should I tell you all this stuff? Sure, maybe mention the good parts. Not the spying on Penny stuff, the life-of-crime stuff, the sexual desperation. Just let it go.

Well, I'll tell you. The whole point of this exercise is to share some of the wisdom I have learned by having superpowers. If I were to focus exclusively on my good side—my devilish good looks, my commitment to teaching America's youth, my moral determination to make the world a better place—who would read that hooey? And what would it teach you?

Maybe you'd wish you were me. You'd wish you had superpowers. You'd think how hard it is to limp along in life just being of regular strength, not being able to stretch across a football field or shoot laser beams out of your eyes. In other words, you'd be where I was when I started this whole affair.

My whole goal is to tell the truth. I'm not DC Comics here. I'm not even Marvel. More like one of those independent labels that fat kids with greasy ponytails distribute direct to comic stores on the hope of selling one copy. I'm all about reality.

Anyway, my defense of my behavior, such as it is, was that it was a sort of sickness. A temporary madness. I didn't wake up thinking: let's spend March break as a criminal. But, then, I didn't wake up thinking I would be invisible.

I woke up late on Saturday and thought Hank had already left when I went into the kitchen. I poured myself a bowl of cereal, sat down at the dining table and thought that it would be nice to disappear for the week. I thought I might see how far I could run. Head down south; see if I could make it to Florida.

I was surprised when Hank emerged from his room as if he had just woken up himself. But I didn't say anything to him. I was in my world, he was in his. Roommates need space sometimes.

Except that he has this awful way, when he's preoccupied, of humming tunelessly through his nose. It is massively dorky and deeply offensive to any normal human, and we had talked about it before. I knew he tried not to do it when other people were around.

I didn't want to talk, so instead I tried to catch his eye with a baleful stare, so he'd remember I was in the room and shut up. But he completely ignored me.

I tried to return the favor, but he went on humming, getting louder and more discordant, and finally I broke.

"Shut up, Hank!"

Hank, who was pouring his own cereal, surprised me with his reaction. He freaked and dropped the cereal box on the floor.

"Jason?" he said, sounding confused.

"Yeah, doofus. I'm right here."

That's when he turned, looked right at me and said, "Where?"

"What the hell is wrong with you?" I said, and we stared at each other. Or rather, I stared at him, and I guess he stared through me. Our minds began to move along the same track.

"Jason?" he said, getting it. He started to move to where he thought I must be. He wanted to touch me. To confirm I was there.

But I too had gotten it. And, right then, I was not in the mood for our usual discussion of my new power. Hank's enthusiasm. His wanting to science me to see exactly what was going on. His general puppy-dog nice, tuneless-humming, perfect-best-friend-and-roomie act.

Okay, I was being a bastard. Normally, that was just what I liked about Hank. But I had had a bad week. I just wanted to be on my own. And my power was a gift from heaven. A gift to avoid everyone for a little while.

So while Hank edged toward me, I circled around him and snuck into my room. Without shutting my door, which would tell Hank where I was, I dressed and grabbed my wallet and keys.

"Come on, Jason. This isn't funny. Where are you?" Hank was standing in the middle of the living room, when I came out of my room, cut to the front door, opened it and slammed it behind me.

The last thing I heard was Hank yelling out the window, "Jason, don't be an idiot."

That good advice was ignored. The first thing I did was head to Cambridge Common and sit on a swing and think. I needed to see if I could control my power. Was I just invisible? Or could I blink in and out of visibility at will? To be a superpower, it should be the latter.

I noticed a little girl—maybe five? I was no good with little kid's ages—who seemed to be staring at me. But I realized she was watching the weird middle swing that went back and forth by itself. I willed myself to be visible. In my experience, most of my powers could be controlled by some sort of mental exercise.

The girl started, and I said, "Can you see me?"

She nodded.

I willed myself invisible and asked, "Can you see me now?"

She shook her head.

"Thanks," I said.

Great—I just had to will myself visible or invisible. No taking off clothes or any of that ridiculous stuff. It was clear that I could still make noise. And that actions I took, like swinging a swing and slamming a door, could be noticed. But as I practiced, I learned that a "gimme" power muffled much of my sound. Sure, a door I opened might creak, but it was unlikely anyone would hear my footsteps or my breathing. My power offered a sort of blanket undetectability that went beyond sight.

But what if I picked something up? Would it become part of the invisible me like my clothes? A little more experimentation revealed that things became invisible as long as I held them off the ground.

I also learned, sadly, that I couldn't go immaterial like Phantom Girl or "phase" through material objects like Kitty Pryde. I also couldn't project force fields or make other things invisible, like Sue Storm from the Fantastic Four.

As I walked into Harvard Square, I pretended to myself that I was thinking about grabbing a coffee at Tatte. That maybe I'd read the paper and contemplate what to do afterwards. But the truth is I was fooling myself. I was heading to spy on Penny.

Yeah, spy. I wasn't going over with any thought of winning her back. I had no illusion that I would show her my new power and her heart would melt with love and admiration.

Maybe you'll assume that I wanted to catch her coming out of the shower, naked and on display to an invisible audience. But, honestly, despite what you may have surmised from my previous confessions of lascivious intent, that was not the point. The humiliation of our bust-up had somehow broken her erotic thrall on me. The sight of her, even the thought of her, I guess, was too upsetting to be sexy.

Not that my intent was any more honorable. What I wanted was just to dig up the dirt on her so I could hurt her like she hurt me.

I really don't know what I thought I would find, but I know what I wasn't expecting. I wasn't expecting to find her in full fucking flagrante delicto with Raffy. The front door was unlocked, so I knew Penny was at home, but I didn't hear anyone as I made my way to the living room.

A grunt made me turn my head toward the bedroom. And there, through the bedroom door, I saw them, in all of their spread-eagle glories. Whatever I said earlier about a girl like Penny not getting down or dirty I have to take back, or at least amend to add, "with me."

Hank tells me that when he said readers did not want to hear about my junk, he didn't mean they wanted to read about other people's junk. So I will spare both you and myself the pain of reporting on the glorious perfection of every line of Penny's exposed torso, undiminished even by the proximity of Raffy's pale, gangling, lugubrious, weirdly muscled, impressively tumescent presence.

Yes, I knew I should turn away and leave. Any gentleman, any vaguely ethical human, would recognize that this was a moment that demanded privacy. But I stared, unable to move, each image reaching my eyes like a knife in the gut.

At some point, my eyes strayed to Penny's bedside table, where I saw a copy of David Lee Roth's memoir, and I realized that not everything about our relationship had been fake. She had taken my book recommendation. Our connection on music, at least, was real. Somehow, seeing the book allowed me to turn away from the bedroom at last, just as Raffy and Penny headed to the conclusion of their coupling.

Again, I should have left. I did not. Instead, I wandered around Penny's living room. Her bookcase contained all the rock memoirs we had discussed, highly notated with yellow sticky notes. She also had an extensive collection of books about the history of the American West, and I remembered that was the subject of her college thesis. There was a picture with her parents outside a modest bungalow. Her father was standing with the aid of two forearm crutches. A picture of her, from college maybe, holding an electric guitar and dressed as a goth. In a basket in the kitchen, I found her Flynn ID card and two other work IDs. One identified her as a salesperson at Agent Provocateur. Another as an employee of the Capital Grille.

While I was busy discovering how much of Penny's life I had been unaware of, Raffy emerged from the bedroom, fully dressed and in a hurry.

"Catch you later, babe," he yelled to Penny as he picked up his backpack and swept out of the apartment. It hardly surprised me that Raffy was a love-'em-and-leave-'em type. I'm sure he thought that hanging out and talking after making love was an inefficient use of time.

I thought of following him. I thought again of leaving the apartment. I did neither. I had come to find a way to hurt Penny; instead she had just found another way to hurt me. And now, sitting at the kitchen table, feeling shattered, I didn't even have the energy to get up to leave.

As I was sitting there the landline rang, and Penny came out of the bedroom in a bathrobe to answer it. Her mother, maybe. I wasn't sure, but the conversation was eye-opening; some serious next-level Mrs. Bennet shit. She wanted the skinny on the financial implications of Penny's love life, and Penny was more than happy to oblige. Which meant that I got to hear a detailed ranking of the net worth of the men she was dating.

I learned that Raffy was well on his way to making a boatload from at least one of his start-ups—he was CIO for some company that was negotiating a first round of VC financing at a seven-million-dollar valuation. Which meant, among other things, that he should be spotting the rest of us for drinks rather than the other way around. However, Penny and her interlocutor had concerns. Raffy's share of the financing wasn't good enough, or sure enough, or something. I wasn't clear.

And Penny had several other promising irons in the fire, including that Leander guy that I saw, a banker at some place called Brown Brothers, and some consultant with access to a private jet.

I realized then that, whatever our connection, I had never had a chance. Christ! Maybe Penny's family needed the money desperately and she was heroically sacrificing herself for them. I can't say that wasn't the case. But I wasn't going to give her the benefit of the doubt. I felt dirty just listening to Penny's Machiavellian gossip, and I knew I had to leave. The only silver lining was that Raffy was likely to be left as far out in the cold as I was. Or, if he won the day, his prize is that he would be stuck with her.

[I slammed the door on my way out. Probably, Penny jumped. I hoped so anyway. I was so pissed off with humanity. Penny and Raffy just proved that most people were selfish bastards for whom the only point of life was to get as much as you could while the getting was good! And I was the sucker, wasting my powers trying to help people and make the world a better place.]

I headed down Beacon Street feeling like the world owed me and I was going to collect. I didn't have a destination in mind until I ended up outside Boston's Ritz Carlton, and saw the limousines lined up outside. Dirty, rich fuckers!

I headed into the hotel, again with the worst of motives. I sat down at the bar, ordered a gin cocktail ($23) and shrimp rolls ($22), and thought about how I could hurt these lousy one-per-centers. But as Sylvia said, I'm not really very good at conflict. As I sat there my anger changed to self-hatred, misery and jealousy. Someone near me had ordered black-garlic pork belly, and the smell made my stomach rumble with desire. Also, I wanted another cocktail. The whole shebang would be $100 before tip. Which I couldn't afford, even on my poor, abused credit card.

I had taken out my wallet to pay when I had a sudden realization. I could turn invisible. I didn't have to pay. At least not with my own money. I guess I could have just run out on the check, but that seemed classless. Better to pay with someone else's money. I went to the bathroom, blinked invisible and walked back out into the bar. As luck would have it, the bartender was just depositing a cash tip into the large old-fashioned register as I emerged. Distracted as he talked with the patron who had offered it, he left the cash drawer open long enough for me to sneak my hand in the till and draw out a wad of 20-dollar bills.

This was more like it. I went back to the bathroom and came back out to my barstool visible. Why hurt the rich when I could join them? And the great thing was, I didn't have to feel any guilt. All around the bar, there were wallets and purses waiting to be emptied. Every single person here could afford to lose a thousand bucks without batting an eye. I would spend my vacation as a guest of the Ritz. Kindly sponsored by the other guests.

Even as I sat back down at my seat and ordered a second cocktail and the pork belly, I began to think bigger. Why go for petty cash? Maybe this was the time I could really set myself up. The world owed me, after all. I was teaching its children to be good, solid citizens, to think critically and to become productive members of society. And it paid me shit. Perhaps it was time to renegotiate my salary.

I started planning. All I needed to do was crack a bank vault, lift a bag of cash (say a hundred thousand dollars) and I'd be set.

CHAPTER 24

Taking Candy from a Baby

Over the next five days, I stole everything I could. I started with banks. At first, I went to small banks. I discovered that it was relatively easy to follow a teller into the cashier's area and swipe a few hundred bucks while his or her back was turned. I had some close calls—almost bumping into one guy, having one woman turn around too quickly and see money disappearing into thin air—but for the most part it was easy-peasy.

Easy but not terribly lucrative. The most I ever got from these walk-bys at small banks was a thousand dollars. My initial successes, however, made me want to try some bigger banks. Banks with large safes and safe-deposit boxes filled, no doubt, with ill-gotten gains.

But it also worried me. I wasn't sure how the safes worked. What if I got caught in one and it didn't open for weeks? Would I run out of air? Would some bank clerk come and trip across my invisible skeleton? I assumed that I'd turn visible when I died. I realized I had no idea if I turned visible when I slept. I would have to watch that.

I spent some time hanging out in the financial district, trying to figure out what I needed to know. Did the big downtown bank buildings have richer customers and big safes with lots of gold? Or just lots of guys in suits with Bloomberg terminals?

I also had some idea about grabbing untraceable stock certificates or commercial paper worth millions, but I had no idea what either of these things really were, or what they would look like. In this day and age, did people even have stock certificates?

I learned that a building near South Station was the headquarters of the Boston Federal Reserve. I did some quick googling on my phone (not too much, I didn't want anyone to trace the robbery back to me by my internet use) to see if it had a gold reserve. First, I couldn't tell. And, second, I realized it would be stupid to steal heavy gold when I could steal cash. I doubted I could pay for my meals at the Ritz with gold anyway.

Didn't they print money at the Federal Reserve? Again, I couldn't tell. But I had another thought. Didn't the Federal Reserve keep the serial numbers of all their notes? If I stole a batch of bills, wouldn't they be able to trace my usage of those bills back to me? All in all, I thought, best to stay away from the Fed.

But that gave way to another paranoid thought. Or maybe not so paranoid. Did all the banks keep track of the serial numbers on their bills? While I was hanging out at the Ritz, I was paying for all my extremely expensive meals with cash. But I had handed over an ID and a credit card to get a room, figuring I would deposit the money I stole to pay my credit bill. That meant the Ritz had my name and address, and if the police discovered that all of the bills stolen from local banks were being spent there, they'd eventually be able to trace it back to the lonely young man sitting around eating lobster and paying cash.

That scared the bejesus out of me, and I made up my mind to stop my walk-bys altogether. That wasn't to say I gave up stealing. Instead, I just started stealing from high-end clothing stores, jewelry stores and the like, particularly along Beacon Street.

The cash in these places was not as good—I rarely got much more than a couple hundred bucks. On the other hand, I got some stuff I cared about more than cash. At one jewelry store, a proprietor with a demanding customer left the watch case open and I was able to pick up a really nice-looking Cartier watch. Did I need it? No. I wasn't much of a watch guy. But, then again, I had never had a Cartier watch, and it was a thing of beauty.

Stealing from clothing and department stores was easier. I picked several leather jackets (I was *definitely* owed a jacket to replace the one the FBI had taken), like ten pairs of John Lobb and Jimmy Choo shoes, a couple of excellent shoulder bags and a bunch of other stuff I could never have afforded in a million years.

You might think that the descent from grand criminal who was going to pull off a big heist at the Boston Fed to sneak-thief grabbing shoes at Macy's would feel like quite a comedown. And maybe I was scraping the bottom of the barrel, but the life did have compensations. I was staying at the Ritz, I was dressing like a boss, and I was eating lavish meals. I always ordered an expensive bottle of wine at dinner (there weren't cheap bottles at the hotel) and left a massive tip for the waitstaff.

One of the cute bartenders at the Ritz Carlton restaurant started flirting with me. A chick called Miranda. She had an English accent and would normally have been totally out of my league. Usually. But with my new expensive wardrobe and seemingly endless supply of cash, well, maybe I appeared a bit more of a catch than usual. By Friday night, I figured she would make her move and I would be ready.

Except that just before dinnertime I realized that my hotel room was littered with all the loot I had stolen. And that if I wanted to bring her back to my room, I should get it out of there. I mean, it had all the labels and stuff still on. It looked stolen. So I decided to run it back to my apartment and stash it in my bedroom closet.

I figured I could get in and out of Cambridge before six o'clock, so I wouldn't see Hank. He almost always stayed late in his lab on Fridays.

As a result, I was surprised when I almost ran into Hank and Ellen in the courtyard outside the building, walking close together and talking in a very animated way. I was in invisible mode, so they couldn't see me, but I almost said hello to them before I caught myself. I could swear Hank looked up as I passed, like he had caught wind of my scent or something. I stood very quietly, waiting for the moment to pass.

Fortunately, they were heading out, rather than in, so the apartment was mine if I wanted it.

I did. More than I even knew. In fact, I spent too much time there. After stashing my loot, I sat down in the kitchen and had a couple bowls of cereal. Honestly, they tasted better than all of the fancy meals I had had at the Ritz over the last few days.

As I was sitting in the kitchen, willing time to stop flowing so that I wouldn't have to get up and head back into Boston, I noticed a note on the cork board over the telephone, which is how Hank and I generally left each other urgent messages. Of course, I hadn't thought to look because, after all, Hank didn't even know if I was still in the city.

It said, "Jason, I know you are going to come back and read this. You aren't a supervillain."

But I couldn't stay. If for no other reason than Miranda was waiting for me. Under Hank's note, I scrawled my own: "Back soon."

In half an hour I was back at the Ritz, sitting in the bar, trying to turn on the charm. I ordered the most expensive thing on the menu, but I was too full to eat more than a few bites, then started on shots of their 17-year old Special Reserve Glenmorangie. My flirting was under par, so I had to compensate by flashing bills.

Miranda didn't seem to mind too much. She laughed at my lame jokes and happily accepted when I bought her drinks. I learned something about her, too. She had graduated from Leeds University last year and came over to America when she couldn't get a job in architecture.

"Hey," I said, "I've considered going into architecture."

"What do you do?"

"I teach."

"Must be a pretty lucrative gig."

Whoops! I was getting too drunk. I hadn't meant to tell her I was a teacher. "What time do you get off work?"

"Eleven thirty. I was wondering when you were going to ask."

"Well, can I see you?"

"Yeah, that'd be great. My friends and I are meeting up and going clubbing. You should definitely come along."

"We can walk over together?"

"Silly, I have to go home and change."

"You look great," I said.

"Hee. These are work clothes."

"I'll come with you to your apartment."

"Hee. You don't want to do that. It's out of your way. We'll meet at half past twelve. I bet you can live that long without me. Then I won't leave your side."

"Promise?"

"Cross my heart."

But, when it came time, I couldn't face it. It was late, I was drunk, and I didn't want to spend the night lying to Miranda and her friends pretending to be someone I was not. My alarm rang at 11:30, telling me it was time to shower and head to the Royale. I snoozed it. I snoozed it again at 11:39, 11:48, 11:57, 12:06. At 12:15, I turned it off and went to sleep.

Maybe Penny would marry a billionaire. Maybe she'd become a rock star. Maybe Raffy would become a captain of industry. Maybe he would sleep with a series of supermodels. But it wouldn't stop them from being pricks.

My life, my ambition, such as it was, was about not being a prick. And, lately, I was doing a really shitty job of it. This last week, I'd fallen into a hole of superprickdom. Spying and stealing, of course, were part of it. But so was trying to trick Miranda into dating me, as well as sitting around hating on Penny and Raffy just because I was jealous of them. (I tried to remember Ellen's point. Something about Raffy not being a sellout because he was being true to his essential self. I wished my essence justified a little more grasping at material success!)

I'd been a prick, but I didn't have to stay one. I needed to get back to my life. My dingy little apartment that I shared with Hank. My unimpressive job teaching unmotivated teenagers. My history of being rejected by any girl I fell for.

When I woke up the next morning, I checked out ($2,500 on my credit card, and I was still too scared to deposit the money I had stolen) and went home.

Hank was out, probably at his lab. I slept for another six hours, and Hank was still not home. But I checked the message board when I got up and saw that he had written under my scrawl, "Welcome back."

Before my roomie came home, I headed to the supermarket to buy the ingredients for tuna melts, two four-packs of Guinness and a tub of Ben & Jerry's Phish Food, all Hank's favorites. Then I went home to make dinner for my roomie.

CHAPTER 25

Being Visible

Hank didn't ask me to explain anything, but after dinner, as we sat with our beers, I told him everything that had happened.

As I started, he interrupted, "You don't have to tell me anything. It's like it was your private affair, right?"

"Yeah, but I think I want to tell you. To confess. To somebody at least."

"All right, but if you tell me what happened, I'm going to tell you that you have to return all the stuff you stole."

I thought about this. "I've spent almost all the money."

"Well, whatever you have. At least the jackets and jewelry and shoes."

"I can do it invisible, right?"

"Of course."

"Okay. Now can I tell you what happened?"

"Yeah."

So I told him about Penny, about Raffy, about all the stuff in this story. At the end, he said, "Wow, that was really pathetic."

What could I say? I agreed. And we went to bed. With school starting up again, I had to get up early the next day. As I fell asleep, I tried to remember where I was in my classes.

It was weird to return to normal life. As if all my calluses from the grating elements of being a poor working stiff had been torn off, and I had to get used to the whole routine—the boredom, the crowds on the subway, the rudeness of the students, the noise in the hallways, the insipid conversations in the faculty lounge, the depressing certainty that you are not being listened to, and that you wouldn't know what to say if you were listened to—all over again.

Worse, there were my friends. Toby was okay. The first time he saw me he just said, "New power yet? Or same old, same old?"

"Invisibility," I said. I didn't really want to tell people, but I felt like pretending I was still super-fast would end up being worse.

"Really? Let me see!" He chuckled. "That was a joke. Found a use yet?"

"Not a good one."

"Hmm, I'll think about it. Let you know if I come up with anything. Not track and field, though."

Sylvia didn't ask me about my break at all, or my powers. She wanted to know where I was in the curriculum. I told her.

"Not bad, Jason. Looks like you'll make it through. That can be hard first year."

Ellen was not so easy because she knew I'd gone missing. And I didn't know what Hank may have shared with her. She caught me at lunch.

"Where did you disappear to last week? Hank was very worried about you."

"I know. I told him I was sorry."

"But where were you?"

We were in the lunchroom. There were people all around us.

"I'll tell you later," I said.

She caught me at two o'clock, the first period we both had off. She came into the English office, shut the door and said, "Okay, now spill the beans."

"I got a new power. Invisibility." I winked out of sight.

"Wow," she said. "So where did you go? And why didn't you tell us?"

"I was dealing with some stuff."

"Yeah, I'm not totally deaf and blind. I heard you and Penny had a fight the Friday before break."

"It wasn't much of a fight. I just got dumped on."

"Hank says you were asking for it."

"Hank says that?" Wasn't he supposed to be on my side?

But before we explored that, Ellen's eyes lit up with inspiration. "You were stalking her, right? I bet you were."

"What did Hank tell you?" I asked.

"He didn't tell me anything. I just figured it out. God, men are hateful creatures."

"I didn't stalk her, exactly. Sure, I went to her apartment. But I was only there for half an hour tops. I told you, I was working things out."

But Ellen just nodded like she thought she had it all figured out.

And, of course, there was Penny too. The hard part of losing your shit is the number of people you have to look in the eye afterwards and pretend that it just didn't happen. Or, at least, won't happen again.

I first saw her from a distance walking down the hallway at around 10:54. (Yes, as soon as I saw her, my whole body tensed and went into hyper-alert mode. I noticed every detail around me, including the exact position of the hands on the hallway clock). I didn't call out to her. But I ran into her in the library—she was at the check-out desk—at 2:22.

I could have gotten the books I needed later. I could have turned invisible. But I didn't. I said, "Hey, Penny," as I walked in.

She smiled back in a manner anyone else might have mistaken for genuine. "Oh, hello, Jason."

As I walked out, I stopped with two books I needed and said, "Could you check these out for me?"

She smiled again. "Of course."

There was a brief silence until she handed me the books, and I said, "Thanks. See ya."

She replied, "See ya."

As you can see, totally normal. No tension at all.

Finally, there was Raffy, the person I least wanted to talk to.

I didn't see him on Monday at all—his hours were a little hit or miss. We ran into each other in the hall on Tuesday, and he looked like he would stop and talk. But I was in the middle of a conversation with two students in my freshmen class, and I made sure that conversation was long and intense.

He cornered me after the second section of my eleventh-grade class on Thursday, and I had no place to hide.

"Hey, I found your man."

"What?" I asked.

"You know what you and Hank were talking about before break? Finding some senior guy you could show your power to. Who could use what you could do for law enforcement or whatever."

"Right," I said, remembering now that we had talked about that.

"Invisibility now, right?"

He must have talked to Toby or Ellen.

"Yeah." I wished I had never told anyone about my powers.

"It's perfect. So you want to meet?"

"Who?"

"The guy I know. The guy who can use you. Make you a real hero."

"Who is he?" I asked. I was stalling for time because, although I remembered my conversation with Hank now, and I remembered making the decision to work with someone official, I wasn't sure how I felt about that decision now.

"Head of the Mass Police Special Investigations unit. Gerry Whoriskey. The title doesn't say much, but he's basically responsible for all the state's antiterrorism efforts. I know his son. Anyway, I emailed this Gerry guy and I said we had something he might be interested in, something like a new crime-fighting technology. He said he was interested in meeting. So what say you? Are we a go?"

"I have to think about it."

"What's to think? We've been over this. Without someone like him, you'll waste your talents."

"I'll tell you tomorrow," I said.

The next day, after talking with Hank, I agreed to meet with Whoriskey. The guy who would make me into a hero. Raffy arranged the meeting for the following Wednesday.

For some reason, I was nervous. I made Ellen promise to accompany Raffy and me. I felt like I was going to the principal's office. Like I had done something wrong. Of course, I had done something wrong. Lots of things recently. But this meeting was not about my petty thefts. This was about my helping Boston's finest. This was about me being a hero.

It didn't feel that way as Ellen, Raffy and I waited outside his office in a totally nondescript building near the Natick Mall. A guard at the entrance sent us up to the fourth floor. The elevator opened to a reception area where a secretary sat at a desk talking to a tall man wearing short sleeves with a shoulder holster.

He motioned us to a row of seats, where we sat and waited while he disappeared behind one of the doors. The guy with the gun had said Gerry would just be a few minutes. But it was almost half an hour before the door opened and a big guy with pale skin, grey hair and a walrus moustache entered. He was followed by the tall man with the gun.

"Who's Raffy?" the man with the moustache asked.

Raffy stood up.

"Okay, and the other guy?"

We looked at each other. Ellen indicated that he meant me, and I should stand. I did.

"Fine. And who are you?" the man said to Ellen.

"She's a friend," I said, my voice almost giving way.

"Okay. I'm Gerry and this," he turned to the tall man, "is Tom." He turned to Raffy and said, "My son said you were worth listening to. I'm a busy man. What you got?"

I went invisible. No one seemed to notice.

I said, "I can turn invisible."

Gerry turned to my voice and I blinked in again. He didn't say anything, just waiting for me to continue.

"So, uh, we thought that it might be useful for you to have someone who can do that. As, like, an option."

A look passed between Gerry and Tom. "Okay, neat trick. How's it work?"

"No trick," I said.

"What's the angle? A tech thing? My kid said you were some sort of entrepreneur," Gerry said, turning to Raffy. "You looking for funding?"

"No," Raffy said. "It's just Jason. He can do strange things."

"Fuck off."

I went invisible again, this time causing a reaction. Tom pulled his gun and pointed it right at Ellen.

"Jesus," I said, turning visible again. "I'm just showing you what I can do."

"Stay the fuck where we can see you," Gerry said.

"So can you use me?"

"Tell me how it works," Gerry said, nodding to Tom to lower his gun.

"There's nothing to tell. It's just something I can do. I woke up like this, like, five days ago." I had warned Raffy and Ellen that I intended to lie about this in advance.

"And you woke up with this amazing gift and the first thing you said to yourself is, how can I help my fellow humanity?"

"Yeah, just about."

"You didn't think, first, maybe that you could steal a boatload of cash and spend the rest of your life fishing in Miami?"

"No," I said. Which was not quite a lie. And I'd never thought about stealing so much that I could move to Florida and retire. Maybe because I was so much younger than Gerry.

"And these," he waved to the others, "these are your friends? Or can they do something too?"

"They're just friends."

"How old are you?"

"Twenty-four."

"What do you do?"

"I'm a teacher."

"So what do you think I can use you for?"

I stared, confused. I could tell Ellen and Raffy were as confused as I was. Wasn't it obvious?

"Like if you wanted to get information on someone? I can go in and listen to conversations. Wear a wire if you want."

"You mean like if I know where a terrorist cell is going to meet?"

"Yeah, like then."

"And, I gotta have probable cause, right? Because you're a walking illegal search. Am I right, Tom?"

Tom just nodded.

"But if I know when they're meeting and I got a probable, what's to stop me from a judicial wiretap? Ain't too many places in this state I can't tap."

This wasn't going the way I wanted. I swallowed. "Well, what if you wanted to steal something?"

"Kid, I'm the cops, not the robbers. I don't steal. I bust in, show my IDs and confiscate."

"Maybe you don't want to give yourself away," Ellen said.

"Maybe I don't," Gerry said. "But maybe you're a bunch of kids who confuse movies with real life. Because I gotta say, I don't really see how a kid with precisely zero law-enforcement experience is going to help me out much."

We were silent. "I mean, let's suspend disbelief for a moment and let's just pretend that you can do what you're claiming, and this isn't all an elaborate trick. Fair enough, Tom?"

Tom nodded.

"And let's say that there's no evidence attaching you to a series of smash-and-grab thefts in Boston last week, that happened without anyone identifying a single suspicious person. With me so far?"

I stared ahead, not even daring to blink. I couldn't see Raffy and Ellen, so I don't know how they reacted.

"And we'll say, for the sake of argument, that Mr. so-called Invisible here had nothing to do with earlier mysterious 'superhero' sightings in the Boston area, even though I did a little digging and discovered his roommate is the hotshot MIT guy who confessed to the Feds that he was pranking the city. You may not have cottoned on yet, kids, but nothing happens in this state without me knowing about it.

"But let's make the tenuous assumption that this is not just another prank. And that the whole point of your visit here today is not a scheme by leftist college kids to trick some dumb old law enforcement officers into showing off their dirty tricks so that they can be posted all over some fucking Insta-book site. Got it?"

We nodded.

"Great. Well under this admittedly tenuous set of assumptions, might it be possible that I could occasionally use the help of a bored high-school English teacher, trying to get his jollies off by pretending to be a hero, who happens to be able to turn invisible? Tom, what do you think?"

"I think not," Tom said.

"Which is why you carry the gun. I think maybe."

Raffy, Ellen and I breathed out at the same time.

"I think a test is in order," Gerry said. "Come by here tomorrow afternoon and pick up an envelope."

"Tomorrow I have debate club," I said.

He looked at me like I was an insect. "I'm not running a fucking nursery here. Tomorrow at four o'clock. At that time, you'll also get an address. Your mission, your test let's say, to see if you can do what you say you can, will be to introduce this envelope, into a desk drawer at a certain address."

"What's in the envelope?" I asked.

"That's on a strictly need-to-know. As is, before you ask, any information about the address or the purpose of the mission. I'll tell you that we don't deal with kids who haven't done their home-work. We deal with people who are trying to commit mass murder. That means military discipline, and soldiers don't question their orders. Do you understand?"

I nodded.

"Now to put your mind at ease, I'll tell you this much. This is a real mission and, if it's successful, it may help us nullify a substan-tial threat to the city. Good enough?"

I nodded.

We left him shell-shocked. When we were outside the building, I asked Ellen if she could cover for me for debate the next day.

"You aren't going through with this, are you?" she asked. "I mean, you heard what he said, didn't you?"

"I'm not sure he's giving me a choice."

"Who do you think is the 'substantial threat to the city' he wants to nullify?"

"I don't know."

"Christ, don't you study literature? I thought you were good at words. It's you, isn't it? He's getting you to do something so he can blackmail you."

"But he can already do that. You heard him. He knows about . . . ." I realized Ellen didn't really know about it. "When I first went invisible, I stole a bunch of stuff."

"I figured that out, doofus. But, look, the point is he has no evidence of it. He said as much. There are no witnesses."

"Help me out, here, Raffy. I gotta do this, right?"

"If you want to be a hero," Raffy said. "So what if he's blackmailing you? It's like an initiation. You do this, and you're part of the club. Then you get the real assignments."

We kept arguing, but eventually Ellen gave in.

"Well, I think it's a stupid idea, but if it's really what you want, I guess I can cover debate."

So I picked up the envelope the next day. Gerry wasn't around, just Tom. Before he handed me a thin envelope colored with pink elephants, he made me put on latex gloves.

"No fingerprints," he said. "That's important."

I hoisted the envelope experimentally.

"Don't open it," Tom warned. "All you do is slip it into one of the bureau drawers. Master bedroom, remember."

"You can't tell me what's inside?"

"No." Tom handed me an iPhone. "Now, here is a secure phone. Call when you complete the assignment. My number is loaded on it."

"I get to keep this?" I asked. It was an iPhone 15; I had a six-year-old Samsung.

"For the time being," he said.

"And I can use it for other things, right?" I was eager to play with it.

"Fine. Now can you remember the address?"

"Sure."

"6 Woodchester Drive. Chestnut Hill. Got it?"

"Woodchester."

"That's it."

"Is there a deadline?"

"Tonight, if possible. Tomorrow if not."

After I left, I stuffed the envelope in my bag and played with the phone, starting out by downloading Kitty Death Room and Beach Buggy Racing 2. First things first.

Driving back toward Boston, I went right past Chestnut Hill, so I figured why wait. They were anxious to get the job done, and I could impress them at how easy it was for me. I located directions to Woodchester on the phone and drove over. I parked a few blocks away, found a dark corner and turned invisible.

It was child's play to find the house, sneak in, and place the envelope in the top drawer of a bureau. In fact, the hardest thing in the whole gig was figuring out which of the huge bedrooms would be considered the master.

In no time at all, I was back in my car, visible again and dialing Tom's number on my new phone. I didn't feel exactly like a superhero, but super-spy, sure. A superpowered James Bond. Maybe a Black Widow type. I envisioned myself as the head of a secret squad of elite agents, performing incredibly secret missions to avert catastrophes in the nick of time.

"Yo," Tom answered his phone.

"Done," I said.

"Done what?"

"I delivered the envelope."

"Okay. We'll call you on this line for future assignments."

"Right," I said.

The unhelpful conversation with Tom did something to bring me down off of my high. That, and the fact that I checked the papers and the internet for the next few days looking for the story of a big bust, but never saw anything.

I waited for a call back from Tom and Gerry. Once they saw what I could do, surely they'd want to take advantage of my unique talents all the time. But I didn't hear from them and didn't hear from them until I figured they must have forgotten about me. So much for my efforts to use my powers.

But it was hard to worry about it because school kept me busy. First, I was offered a new two-year contract, which was kind of flattering. Also a relief, because I had not yet gotten around to taking either the LSATs or the GMATs. So after a little heartache, I signed on, thinking that one good thing about teaching was that it gave me time to be a secret agent. If Gerry ever called me again.

The day I signed, Sylvia was particularly sweet. She took me out to lunch and told me how much it meant to her to have new young teachers join the profession. "Flynn needs people like you," she said. "Toby and I are getting old. The school needs new faculty leaders."

Which made it feel like it was not the right time to tell her that the main point of working at Flynn was the time it would afford me for crime-fighting.

Also, the kids in the Magic club had decided to hold a tournament at the end of April, and it turned out that I was in charge of the logistics. We were inviting three other local schools. And I was concerned because I had no idea what a Magic tournament even was.

Then the debate club entered a tournament to be held in Leominster, and I was also somehow the faculty member in charge of that. And the idea that becoming a teacher would leave me more time for spying began to feel really stupid.

Except for the fact that I didn't need any extra time for "missions" because, as I've said. I didn't get any calls.

Until, inconveniently, the night of the trivia semis. Tom called me at lunch and said he needed to see me urgently. "We need something done tonight."

"I can't," I said. "I have the trivia semifinals."

"What?" Tom said.

"We're in the pub trivia semis," I said. "Three Harps. That's the Flynn team. If we win, we'll be in the finals. Which is televised on Cable Access. And the winning team gets . . ."

"I don't give a flying fuck about your fucking trivia team," Tom said. "Who the fuck do you think we are?"

"I know who you are. But I'm a free agent."

"Like fuck you are."

There was some talking on the line as, I suppose, Tom was explaining things to Gerry. Because when someone next spoke to me, it was Gerry's voice on the line.

"Jason," he said, "I want you to come in right now. We have a task that has to be performed tonight. It really is very important, and you may be able to finish up early. You did so well with your first assignment."

"Just tell me what you need over the phone."

"No can do. Not secure."

"I'm on the secure phone you gave me."

"Not secure enough. Anyway, we have some tools you'll need."

What a pain in the fucking ass. I got Toby to cover Magic Club and Sylvia to teach my afternoon class, and off I went to Natick.

It turned out that they were doing an internal investigation of the deputy head of the Boston Police Department's Narcotics Division and wanted to get his laptop, which they knew he had left in or on his desk in his office at police headquarters in Schroeder Plaza.

"Wait," I said. "You want me to break into the police headquarters?"

"Sure," Tom said.

"Why don't you march in and take it?"

"We'd need a warrant," Gerry said. "There's a lot of red tape involved. And if we try to get one, our bogie may get tipped off and destroy the evidence. So be a good boy and get us the computer. You may even get back in time for your darts game."

"Trivia," I said.

"What?"

"Trivia, not darts."

"Whatever."

"So why did I have to come down here?" I was beginning to resign myself to my fate.

"We have keys for you. To his office and his desk."

I left feeling extremely disgruntled, trying to remind myself that I was a good guy. Despite the fact that I was breaking into the police building and stealing evidence. "Need to know." Fuck!

I explained my new assignment to Ellen, and warned her that I might be a little late for trivia.

"Christ, they want you to break into the police headquarters?"

"They say it avoids the red tape of getting a warrant."

"Some superhero," she said. "What a very superman-like use of powers."

"At least I can use my powers now," I said. "Sure, I'm a cog in the law-enforcement machine, but at least I'm a cog. What's wrong with being a cog?"

Ellen relented somewhat. "Maybe nothing, but I'd feel better if we knew what you were accomplishing."

What could I say? I agreed. And I resolved to press the issue next time I talked with Gerry. Meanwhile, I headed to Schroeder Plaza. It was crowded, but that didn't matter to me. I blinked invisible and walked in.

CHAPTER 26
The Long and the Short of It

At least, I thought I had blinked invisible as I walked into the station.

"Can I help you?" asked an old guy in a police uniform and a name tag reading "Corporal Goodhart" as soon as I walked in.

"Uh, can you see me?" I asked.

The man put up his arms in a placating manner. "Calm down, young fellow. You just need to dry out."

I thought "invisible" again and looked at myself. I was not invisible. I hadn't noticed before because, the thing was, I could see myself when I was invisible, I just looked a little more filmy than usual. I didn't look filmy now. I was my usual fleshy, Technicolor self.

While I was thinking, the cop had come up and put his arm around me. He led me over to some plastic seats in a waiting area.

"Easy now." He was friendly enough but had an iron grip.

"I'm okay," I said.

"You're hallucinating," he said.

I tried to remember if I had turned invisible earlier that day and guessed that I hadn't. So maybe my power had deserted me again. Right when I needed it, as usual.

"No, I'm fine," I said as he levered me down into one of the chairs.

I didn't resist. I had to think. Maybe I had another power that would be useful. But what? I needed some time alone.

"Thanks," I said.

Corporal Goodhart moved away from me and I took some deep breaths. Could this be it for my powers? Could I be back to being just normal Jason Smithka?

I tried to think of powers I hadn't had. I hadn't had a fire power, or a laser beam power, but, really, my cold power was just a different form of hot power, right? Wasn't it Robert Frost who said that it didn't matter if you killed someone with fire or ice or lasers?

I guessed I could have something like telekinesis or magnetism, which are still totally common comic-book stuff. But don't these powers just come down to superstrength in the end? If all you could do with your magic telekinesis powers was pick up a pen from a distance, big whoop. If the most you do with your magnetic powers is shuffle paper clips, so what? The thing that is super is not doing it with the mind or with magnetic fields. It is not even doing it from a distance. It's the fact that comic-book characters use these powers to lift cars and tear down bridges. It's basically the same power as the Hulk has.

At any rate, I'd been strong, fast, tough and stretchy. What if there wasn't anything else? What if I wasted my six months of superpowers accomplishing exactly zippo?

As I was worrying, the policeman who'd collared me decided it was time to check on me. I saw him look up from his computer, stand up and start to walk over. Not ready to deal with him, I tried to shrink into myself and disappear.

And I succeeded.

The experience was dizzying. From Corporal Goodhart's point of view, I suppose, it was a little unusual too. After all, he was looking right at me as I contracted.

But if the policeman was disoriented, for me it was much worse. Look, I didn't know what was happening. The seat around me started expanding and the walls around me shot up. I felt like I was falling. At some point, I must have slipped off the chair. I suppose this is because I shrank down toward my feet, rather than from both sides in toward my belt. The vertigo made me want to puke, but I had a bigger problem. The corporal, who had just seemed burly before, had taken on elephantine portions. He was running toward me and seemed certain to crush me.

My solution, to keep shrinking (although I didn't know that was what I was doing), hardly seemed likely to help as the policeman rapidly changed from a charging elephant to a careening redwood. Then—boom—darkness. I thought I was dead.

The light returned after a few seconds, blinding me. I was alive, but I had no idea where I was. I was surrounded by alien life-forms gyrating about me. At first, I thought I might have developed some sort of teleportation power. Or that I had fallen through a wormhole and landed in an alternate universe.

In my panic at the charging policeman, I must have gotten pretty much as small as I could, which, as per Hank's later measurements, was about the size of a human blood cell, or eight micrometers. Bigger than an atom or a molecule, or even most viruses, but still enough to change one's perspective. The floor of the police station, like almost any surface from the point of view of a blood cell, was a forest of horrific, pulsating plants and animals. It took some getting used to.

Oh, let's not be modest. It took some god-damn heroism not to totally freak out. When I first looked around, I was totally hedged in by flying, crawling, flailing creatures that made snakes and spiders seem cuddly by comparison. I didn't know they were standard-issue microbes, rather than alien life, and I also didn't know then that they were harmless to me. Eventually I learned that something about my presence, maybe the fact I didn't really belong in their world, made me too strange to even notice. But when I first changed you better believe that it took all of my co-jones (both of them?) not to panic.

Instead, the imperturbable Jason Smithka, in one of his proudest moments, sat down amid the horrifyingly strange and disturbing fauna and thought with clarity and insight. I am not sure when it came to me. It was like doing a crossword where you stare at a clue for hours not getting it, and then suddenly you do. I racked my brains about where I could be, then suddenly the Atom popped into my mind. Not a main DC character, but always one of my favorites—and then I got it. I was small. Very small.

After a passage of time, seeing that I had not been eaten or attacked, I gradually found the courage to look beyond the creatures in my immediate vicinity. I saw a series of vast mountains and occasional columns reaching far into space. Reasoning from the fact that I had shrunk, I theorized that the mountains might be the nodules in the police station's linoleum floor, and the columns might be chairs or pant legs or the like.

You might think that I would be too tiny to recognize or interact with the regular macroscopic world. But—you've got this already, right?—my powers came with the necessaries to make them work even when it made no sense. I could see the world on a micro scale, but I could also perceive and grasp macro features.

And that was hardly the weirdest thing. Even in microscopic form, my body looked just like my body. My clothes (even my wallet and phone) shrank with me, just like they had previously gotten invisible with me. (The difference was that my phone still had reception when it was invisible, but not when it shrank.) And if you want a conundrum to consider, try to figure out how big the cells in my own body had become when I was myself microbial. Face it:

you just can't science it out.

(Similarly, later, when I got big, there was none of this smarty-pants trouble with the square/cube law—the fact that if you double in size and remain in roughly the same proportion, you have four times the muscles but eight times the weight, which should leave you too relatively weak to move—that killjoy geeks use to critique the realism of comic books. I got bigger and stronger, and that was that.)

Anyway, once I realized what was happening and my vision sorted itself out, I could look around and see the police station and its denizens, rather than an unimaginably alien jungle. Seeing the macro world, it turned out, was mostly just a matter of knowing what to look for. In my moment of insight, I guessed that when everything had suddenly turned dark, I had been under Corporal Goodhart's shoe, safe between the treads.

I could hardly wait to get home and show my power to Hank. He would be filled with ideas for science experiments. I remembered that Atom often dialed a number, then leapt into the phone at atomic size, racing at the speed of light to the other end along with the electric current. (Hank, the spoilsport, later told me that, even if I could have gotten down to atom-sized, this wouldn't work. It isn't the individual atoms that move along the phone lines, but information waves. Science really is a downer.)

But I wasn't ready to go home yet. I had come to the station to do a little superheroing—or at least a little super-spy work – and I was going to do it. I was going to steal the computer of a corrupt cop. (At the direction of a couple of assholes, it must be said, but hopefully in a good cause.)

And there was no reason I couldn't pull it off. I wasn't invisible any longer, except that I really was. So far I hadn't had any repetitive powers, but shrinking seems a lot like a repetition of invisibility, doesn't it?

I know that you don't really care about the details, even if, in my own estimation, finding and smuggling the laptop out of the police station, all while learning to use my new power, was one of my finest moments as a superhero. What you want to know is that before long I was back out on the streets, computer in hand. Mission accomplished!

I found a quiet corner and grew back to normal size. But before I delivered the laptop to Gerry, I had trivia to play. I raced downtown to a bar called Yvonne's, and made it just minutes before the match started.

We won, thanks for asking, but I was off my game. I missed on Steinbeck's dog's name for God sakes (Charley—duh). It didn't help that Penny was there and I had to act normal the whole time, trying not to melt into a puddle of tears.

Still, Ellen and Raffy held their own in science, and Toby and Sylvia dominated history and sports. Leaving us, amazingly, in the final against SAP, the giant computer software company and last year's runner-up.

We celebrated and stayed out late, so, of course, I woke up late, had to rush to school, and then was running around all day to catch up and stay ahead of my hangover. So I did not even turn my iPhone back on until a free period at one that afternoon.

Lucky me! I got to listen to a string of abusive phone messages from Tom. And a somewhat less abusive one from Gerry, urging me to give them a call.

Really, I just wanted to be done with the whole thing. It didn't feel like I was doing any good. I was, as far as I could tell, a pawn in a game. Were Tom and Gerry good guys? I had no idea. In fact, I had no real evidence that they even worked for the government, beyond Raffy's say-so.

But what could I do? Working with Tom and Gerry was so far the only way I'd found to use my powers that might be semi-legit at all. And maybe I was doing good. Maybe I'd taken down a drug dealer and a corrupt Boston cop. Maybe my Medal of Freedom had already been secretly awarded (along with a good cash prize), and Gerry was just waiting for the right time to hand it over.

I called and arranged to drop off the laptop after school.

CHAPTER 27

Big Time

I didn't tell Tom and Gerry about my new power when I dropped off the laptop. I had another idea. I knew they would watch me depart on their video cameras, and then feel safe from my invisible snooping when the doors were shut and locked behind me. But they didn't know that I could now, effectively, both become invisible *and* slip under doors. So I did this, heading out, shrinking and then doubling back to hear what they were saying about me.

What I heard confirmed, maybe not my worst suspicions, but many bad suspicions. On the one hand, I guess they were honest enough cops. The narcotics cop whose laptop I had stolen seemed like he was, potentially, a really bad guy.

On the other hand, I freaked them way the fuck out. They didn't really believe in my powers. They figured I was using some trick. Whatever the case, though, they were going to keep an eye on me, and were convinced that they'd need to put me away sooner rather than later. A guy who did the things I could was not to be trusted. I was a bigger danger to the city than any corrupt cop.

Worse than that, they figured they could control me through my friends. When I got back, they weren't talking about me, but about Ellen, Hank and Raffy. Gerry was asking about their surveillance.

"Anything yet?" Gerry asked.

"Nah, not really. The Raffy's guy's a minor-league operator. Smart. The roommate and the girl are boring as fuck. A teacher and a grad student."

"Maybe. But I sense there's something going on. Could be the Black kid. Meant to be clever."

"He's a drone. Nothing but work. Does astrophysics or something. Abstract. Nothing weaponizable."

"So the girl?"

"I don't think so. Sleeps in the buff, though. Nice ass too. You want to see?"

Tom held up his smart phone running some sort of surveillance feed. Gerry glanced up and then said, "Nah, but keep 'em under observation. Don't know when we'll need them."

That is when I popped into view.

I didn't mean to. I thought I had pretty good control over my shrinking powers. But the conversation had gotten me so mad: spying on my friends, dismissing Hank, and then talking about Ellen so crudely. I couldn't help it. I filled up with rage and started to grow.

And before I knew what was happening, I was visible, right in front of Tom and Gerry.

Tom said, "What the fuck? Where did you come from?" and made to tackle me, like I was about to run.

But angry as I was, and as hopeless as it was for me to get in a scrape with someone like Tom, his move prompted a fight response in me. I puffed up ready to brawl. And to my surprise, by the time he tried to tackle me, it was like being tackled by a 10-year-old. His head was at my waist, and his body weight was negligible.

I might have kept growing but I hit my head on the ceiling, and was shocked into settling in at about 14 feet.

I pushed Tom away harder than I meant to and he slammed

against the wall. I was afraid I had killed him, until I saw him unbutton his coat, going for the gun in his shoulder holster. I quickly reached down and snapped off the holster, gun still in it, before he had a chance to draw.

My strength was not only sufficient to allow me to operate in my enormous body (take that, square/cube geeks!), but actually increased in a nice intuitive way with my size. My agility did not increase, but it was no worse than it had been before. At any rate, I think I only beat Tom to the gun because he was a little concussed and scared out of his wits.

Gerry seemed less unnerved than Tom. "So, what's this? Another trick?"

"Another power," I said. "If you mess with me, I'll fuck you up."

Tom, who had gotten up by this point, started on a tirade, "Look, you little dipshit . . ."

But Gerry waved him off with a laugh. "Big dipshit, I think we'd have to say." Tom shut up. "Seriously, Jason, are you threatening us?"

"Yeah," I said, with less conviction than I intended. "If you touch my friends . . ." I petered out.

"Look, kid, I've been at this job for a while." Gerry had a big smile on his face. "I've been threatened by 80-year-old guys in wheelchairs who scared the shit out of me. I've been threatened by 95-pound teens who made my blood run cold. You want to know why they frightened me?"

"Why?"

"Not because they had big muscles or could throw a fucking fireball or any of that shit. They scared me because they meant what they said. The wheelchair guy would have happily watched his dogs eat me fucking alive while he enjoyed the show. The kid, given half a chance, would have killed every living being in the state without a second thought."

I may have gulped. I was 14 feet tall, but I felt like a weakling.

"You don't scare me. For all your little tricks, you're a fucking schoolboy. You are never going to touch us."

"You hurt my friends and you'll see," I said.

"Hey, I don't mind you standing up for them. Tommy, we don't need the surveillance. We've got an understanding, Jason and us. Right?"

"We do?"

"Same as it was. You want a chance to use your little tricks without getting hassled. Feel like you're doing some good. And we sometimes may need some of the things you can do. That's fair, right?"

"You'll leave my friends alone?"

"We don't need 'em. We have you. You probably heard this, but make sure you fucking know it. We got your balls in a vice. And if you ever even give off a fucking whiff of threatening our city, or the state, or the country, we'll be down on you like a ton of fucking bricks."

I tried to look tough.

"Yeah, you do some freaky shit. Scare the piss out of some folk. But I'm thinking there are some pretty fucking severe limits. And if I decide to lock you away in a hole, you won't be able to do much about it. But, hey, if you cooperate and stay in line, you and I can be good friends. Good for each other. Right?"

"Okay," I said. "I think it's a deal."

I shrank down to normalish size. Gerry came around the desk and put his arm around my shoulder. "Thanks for the computer. That was good work."

He made a motion to Tom, and Tom nodded to me. I handed back his holster and walked out feeling as if I had blown my chance to renegotiate our deal. I still felt trapped into working for them.

If working for Gerry still sucked, it didn't mean I wasn't liking my new power. The shrinking had proved great at the police station, and I often replayed in my mind the act of knocking Tom over.

It also offered more mundane advantages. First of all, I went around an inch or so taller than usual. Nothing too outrageous, but it made a difference. I could tell people looked at me and reevaluated. I must have gotten a hundred comments from other teachers, staff members and students, asking me if I had done something with my hair, and assuring me that it looked really good. It's true: everyone loves a tall guy.

But it was useful to be small, too. When Ellen and I drove out to Concord in her Corolla to visit Joe and her grandfather, I slid down a few inches and the car felt roomy.

The thing I couldn't do, other than once busting up a scuffle between ninth-graders, which I probably could have managed even without the extra couple of inches I slung on to look menacing, was find any superheroing opportunities.

Hank and I really racked our brains over it. One obvious thing was being some sort of super-whistleblower/investigative reporter. Instead of going after Gerry's targets—bedraggled Muslim kids or old-news mobsters—I could dig the dirt about the rich and powerful. Find the corruption in the elite halls of powers, among presidents and CEOs. The trouble was, I didn't know where to look. I mean, sure, I could break into the mayor's office, or even the White House, but then what? Secrets aren't hanging around in plain sight. They're on password-protected computers. Maybe after months undercover, I could learn a password and find records on a shady deal or two. And become universally beloved like most whistleblowers (ha ha!—that's a joke). In any case, my power would likely go before I managed to find anything good.

Okay, if I was really lucky, I could find myself in the Oval Office with my tape recorder running when the president said something evil, maybe offering the Koch brothers free coal leases if they'd take down some senator, but—Jesus!—was that even illegal these days? Maybe I could record him ordering the arrest and torture of some shmoe. Then the attorney general would say, "You know he is a completely innocent American citizen." And the president would say, "Sure, but I don't care. He is a competitor to one of my major financiers, so I am ordering you to violate his constitutional rights for my own personal gain." Maybe that'd be clear-cut enough. If I had video to go with the audio.

But regular crime fighting. Bleh. You need to find the crime. And, as I'd discovered, it's hard to find crime to fight. That's what's good about organized crime. It's settled and stays in one place. But fighting organized crime was what I was doing with Tom and Gerry, and it hardly felt like superheroing. Mostly I was a shortcut around procedural rules for a couple of dickish cops.

Maybe the lesson was one that should be familiar to every teacher—it was repeated to us *ad nauseam* after all—policing doesn't effect social change. If you want to make the world a better place, etc., the most important task is to give disadvantaged youth better prospects, more hope and improved analytic tools. All that shit. And the best way to do that, of course, is teaching. Which was already my day job. And going around being Ant-Man didn't help fuck-all. In fact, to the extent it took time away from my preparing for classes, it may have hurt.

Eventually, Hank and I decided that the best use of my powers would be as an assassin. I could get in anywhere, get big and snap a neck as easy as pie. Then escape to tell the tale. But think about it. If you could assassinate anyone, who would it be?

I talked about it with my friends. Joe had a list of suggestions, which was fine enough when he started out with Kim Jong Il, Muammar Gaddafi and Saddam Hussein (unaware that they were all already dead). It began to seem overbroad when he included Elizabeth Warren, Julian Assange and "that French president who slept with all the underage girls". And a little unhinged when he added Peyton and Eli Manning, Barry Bonds, Alex Rodriguez and "every other scumbag ballplayer who ever took steroids," even when he added, "except Clemens—always liked him."

On the other hand, I was pretty convinced that Kim Jung Un, the alive guy, would be a legitimate target. I went so far this time as to try to get Ellen and Hank to help me work out the logistics. Hank was grudging, because he didn't believe superheroes should kill, period. Ellen was actively uncooperative, not only because she thought I had no moral right to do it, but because she thought I had no idea if I would be making the whole situation better or worse.

We got in a bit of an argument about it, but I could hardly dispute Ellen's basic point (even though I did at the time). I was completely fucking ignorant about North Korea, so maybe I should just stay the hell away.

As it turned out, the logistics of killing Kim Jung Un were surprisingly difficult, not to mention expensive. It would have been much easier if there were an evil dictator within the US, preferably within driving distance. At any rate, the project got shelved when Hank pointed out that, if I worried about Gerry violating police procedure, it didn't make much sense to engage in a series of extrajudicial killings instead.

It was the same old, same old. Other than for personal convenience, my power seemed kind of useless. Achieving anything heroic was frustrated by a combination of the complexity of the real world, my moral values, my ignorance of world affairs, and the need to keep a job.

I needed the job, first and foremost, because I needed money. I had blown most of the money Raffy had given me on staying at the Ritz, and I was deep in debt. I was only just managing to meet my monthly student debt payments. Every month my credit card balance increased alarmingly.

Still, I was working for more than just money. It sounds hokey, but teaching actually made me feel like I was making a difference. More than stealing stuff for Gerry. Not every day, of course. Most days I got home and just wanted a long hot shower and a beer.

But every so often there was something more. Like the Saturday after my adventure in the police station, when we went to the debate tourney in Leominster. We didn't win, but the kids were amazing, and we did come in fifth of 17 teams, which was pretty amazing in my book. I mean, if you talked to some of these kids in the hall, you would swear they couldn't put together a coherent sentence. But here they were out-arguing and outmaneuvering teams from all over suburban Massachusetts.

It's not like I had anything to do with it. I was the driver. I signed forms and pretended to be a grown-up. But that didn't stop me from taking compliments on behalf of the team.

We stopped on the way home from the tournament and I treated everyone to McDonald's. I couldn't really afford the 75 dollars that it cost, but it was worth every penny. The kids were in a mood to celebrate, and it was one of those magical shared moments where you feel like you're part of a group descended from the clouds to demonstrate happiness, humor and fellow-feeling to the rest of humanity.

Then there was walking to the T with Malia Sykes, one of the smart girls in my ninth-grade English class. She was one of those cute, underdeveloped girls who look and act younger than their age; she was more like a sixth-grader than a high-school student. Anyway, she spent the entire time telling me all the things she loved at the school and just before we got on the train she asked, "But you know what my absolute favorite is, Mr. Smithka?"

"No, Malia, I don't."

"Reading *Romeo and Juliet* in your class. Bye, see you tomorrow, Mr. Smithka."

I'm glad she was going the other way. I was practically bawling by the time I got to the subway.

Yeah, so it was all very mawkish, like living in an ABC After-school Special. But that's school for you. The kids lead these intense lives, their hearts racing like sparrows, reeling from triumph to disaster and back to triumph. But it's impossible for a young teacher not to get caught up in it.

The old hands like Toby and Sylvia stay on a more even keel, warning you not to get attached, that the kids will move on, that everything they seem to care about will change in the blink of an eye. But don't let them fool you; even they aren't immune to the second-hand adrenaline of high-school life. I've seen Sylvia come alive as she rushed down a hallway to comfort a girl sobbing over a breakup. I've seen Toby forget his arthritic knee and jump up and down like a madman celebrating one of his sophomores winning through to the regional decathlon finals. It's just what happens when you're a teacher. The kids are your last thought when you go to sleep at night, and the first thought when you wake up in the morning.

The disasters are just as sappy-novelistic as the successes, even when they are real. One of my eleventh-graders didn't show up for two classes. When I asked after him, I discovered he'd been arrested for beating up his girlfriend.

I found another girl, not in one of my classes, but friends with some of the debaters, crying in the hallway by her locker. I went up to try to comfort her and she showed me the text she had just received. Her grandmother, the principal caregiver for her and her brothers since her parents were in drug rehab, had just been informed that her breast cancer had spread through the rest of her body.

I had no idea what to do. I took her into the faculty lounge and got her a hot chocolate. We sat there for a little while, me not knowing what to say, and her crying, before I led her down to one of the school counselors. It felt cowardly to hand her off, but the counselors are trained to deal with these situations. With the number of kids in crisis at Flynn, I needed to be able to respond better than I did that day.

In the evening, I asked Hank whether there was any research I could do on cancer, or really any diseases, as the Atom. My extremely vague idea was that I would shrink down, pop in the bloodstream and be able to report on how well some experimental drug was working. Hank cocked a skeptical eyebrow at me, indicating that I had no idea what I was talking about, but said he'd think about it anyway. (And I know, I know, "Atom" is not the right name. I couldn't get down to atom-sized. But I didn't know what else to call myself. Ant-Man could control ants. The "Incredible Shrinking and Growing Man" seemed dumb, and "Blood Cell" just sounded wimpy. Maybe "Shifter" or something, but that sounded like I was a werewolf.)

Researchers, doctors, teachers, nurses. These were the people who made the difference in the world. Not cops or soldiers. Super or not.

After dinner, I signed up for a summer course in high-school counseling at Leslie College, where I had been taking my teacher certification courses. I'd be damned if I would be so tongue-tied with someone who needed me again. Then, because it sort of freaked me out that I had essentially zero money in my account to pay for the course, and because I had no intention of staying a teacher my whole life, I also signed up to take the LSATs.

CHAPTER 28
Thinking Out Loud

Everything went well for a while. Tom and Gerry didn't bother me with stupid jobs, and my classes were winding up to a big finish. The juniors were working on a five-page term paper; and the freshmen had divided into groups to present plays they had written themselves.

I spent most of my time outside of school pouring over research protocols with Hank, and studying for the trivia finals with Ellen, Toby and Sylvia. Raffy was meant to be with us, but he had flaked out, claiming to be super busy on some other project. Which I happened to know was his start-up that was about to get major funding. Penny stayed away from wherever I was, which was a relief.

Ellen and I went out to Concord a couple of times to see Joe and her grandfather. Joe was in a pretty bad phase, remembering very little of our conversations from week to week. But it didn't seem to bother Mr. Rinaldi, who had started dating the clarinet player in his nursing home and was talking about marriage. Have you ever noticed how old people seem sort of like young kids in their ability not to worry about what other people are doing, and instead focus entirely on their own needs?

Ellen didn't seem too shocked by her grandfather, in his eighties, starting to date again. Even when he mentioned over lunch that he and Lydia (that was the name of the clarinetist) had been sleeping together for three weeks, and that they had to be very careful because of her bad back and his hips.

I asked her on our way home if it didn't bother her.

"No, why should it?"

"Come on," I said. "Even when he started talking logistics?"

"You think old people don't want to have sex?"

"No, I just don't want to hear them talk about it. I mean, I would never tell him about sleeping with . . . ." I stumbled to a stop. I was going to say "you" but I realized that we weren't really talking about that. We never had. So I shut up.

"What?" Ellen asked. "Penny?"

"Sure," I said. "That's what I meant."

"Yeah, but you aren't. So there's nothing to tell, right?"

"Yeah. Ha, ha, ha!"

"Maybe you're just jealous."

"Of your granddad? Sorry. Toothless Lydia does nothing for me."

"I didn't know you were so picky."

"You know what I mean, right? Imagining them doing it?"

"Every time people mention sex, you don't have to imagine it."

"It's hard not to."

"If you do that, of course it's icky. But imagining anyone having sex is icky."

"Anyone?" I asked, somewhat meaningfully.

"Yeah, just about. Except yourself, maybe. If you insist on thinking about it too much, you'll want to stop any sex at all. I think that's the problem conservatives have."

"What?"

"Overactive imaginations."

I didn't tell Ellen what I was imaging right then, fairly sure that the term overactive might have been applied. I did see what she meant though. I hated imagining her and Hank going at it. But if I just subbed Hank with myself, the whole scenario seemed miraculously less icky.

That was Sunday, May 10. The Pub Trivia finals were on Friday, May 15. On Tuesday, I bugged Hank for still not having found a research protocol for me to help on.

"What's the delay?" I asked him.

"It's hard," he said. "I mean, no one's ever had to think through what an observer slipped into the bloodstream might be able to report back on. It's hard to figure out what would be useful."

"My power's going to go away soon."

"Then there are the logistics of sneaking you into the experiment. I mean, I seriously doubt it would be within the university's IRB."

But the next day, the issue became moot. I lost the power to shrink.

I hadn't realized yet when I walked into the kitchen after getting dressed, but I *could* tell something was preoccupying Hank.

"So you found a project for me."

"How did you know?"

"You must have mentioned it. In Professor Mielke's lab. One of his lab assistants will let me in. What's her name? Charlene, right?"

"I never told you about this."

"I didn't you know were into Charlene." I looked at Hank. We were both confused at this point. "You're planning to ask her out? How did I not know this? Stop what? Get out of what?"

"Get out!" Hank yelled and then starting singing "Onward Christian Soldiers" at the top of his lungs.

"Jesus, Hank. What's wrong with you? You'll wake up the fucking dead."

"Get out!"

"Okay," I said, backing out of the kitchen. "I'll go into my room, if that will make you feel better. Why would a wall between us help?"

But before I got to my room, I turned around.

"Wait, you think I'm reading your mind?"

"Stop this, Jason."

"What."

"*Stop, or you'll find things you don't want. I don't want you in my head.*"

I looked at Hank in astonishment. His lips had definitely not moved.

I looked down. Okay, Jesus! I could read minds. Hank was freaked the fuck out. I closed my eyes and realized—saw?—how nervous I was making Hank.

Well, there was an easy solution. "Don't look!" I told myself.

I spent the next 30 minutes learning not to read Hank's mind. It was hard. It was like not scratching an itch. I wanted to go in and look at everything. But every time I approached, the first thing I saw was a big ball of anger. A desperation to keep me out. I asked him what he was hiding. He said his soul.

"We're best friends," Hank said. "But if you read me, we won't be."

"Why?" I asked, resisting the temptation to get the answer non-verbally. "Don't you trust me?"

"Jesus, Jason. Don't be a prick. We all have internal lives. We think things. It doesn't mean anything. But if you start reading them, you might think it does. Get it?"

"I guess so."

"Well, get it better. I mean, I can think you were a total dick about Penny, right? And a total dick to Ellen, right?"

"Hey."

"I can think your understanding of science is awful. That you appreciate all the wrong things about science fiction, right? That you're way too obsessed about money and status."

"Hey, I thought you were trying to save my feelings."

"I'm trying to explain to you. When I say these things, you know where I'm coming from. That we're friends. That we're different. If you just read them off me, like I was trying to keep them secret, you'd go total paranoid on me."

"I wouldn't."

"You would. You're doing it now."

"I sense a lot of hostility," I said, trying to make a joke.

I only had moderate success trying to *not* read Hank's mind. The power to look directly into someone's mind was so wondrous that it was hard to resist. The philosophical implications alone were staggering. I was like one of Plato's philosophers, staggering out of the cave for the first time. Plato made a big impression on me because I took a film course with a professor where we did a whole unit on films inspired by the cave analogy. Anyway, for all I knew I was the first person to directly observe someone else's mind, rather than just having reports of it. I was the first person to disprove solipsism.

And sometimes it seemed that Hank was so leaky, it was like he wanted me to see what he was thinking. I complained to him that he was practically broadcasting his thoughts, and suggested he be more careful.

"I've never had to be careful before," he said, getting more and more agitated. "I don't even know what being 'careful' means. You're the one who has to be careful. You're the one who has to learn to stop it."

Okay, he was right. Reading my friends' minds, I might lose all my friends. But reading strangers was a different proposition. I was eager to get away from Hank and head off to work. Into the middle of a scrum of commuting strangers where I could really test my powers.

The ride to work on the T was intense. I picked up inchoate anger, desperation and lust all around me. But it was hard to pinpoint the precise locations. And when I tried to delve in to see what someone was thinking in more detail, all I got was boringness. A woman was wondering if she'd go to the gym first or head straight to her desk.

A guy was worried he wouldn't get his taxes done on time.

Another woman was wishing she wore different underwear, because the ones she had were itching her crotch. I moved on.

Another guy was worried about his son's grades. His son was at some private school and he thought he should pull him out. But he was afraid of having that argument with his wife.

One man was concerned about his armpits smelling. He had taken a shower that morning, but apparently he had a thing about it.

I missed my stop and had to walk back. I tried to catch the eye of a girl who looked cool and sexy to me, but I got a wave of hostility and a word—*Creep!*—covered by the cutest little smile. If I couldn't have read her mind, I might have spent two days fantasizing about how into me she was.

I wandered into school late and disoriented. I didn't know how I would manage it.

The receptionist greeted me, "Hi Jason. You missed morning meeting."

She was a nice woman. She liked me. But then she liked everyone and everything. Except that she was afraid of Principal Snowe. By some strange, convoluted logic, she was afraid that she would be blamed by Ms. Snowe for my being late. That was her scourge, thinking that everything that went wrong was her fault, when, in fact, very little of it ever was.

"I'll explain to Ms. Snowe why I was late," I said, "but I have to run to my first class now."

She gave me a grateful smile. *Nice boy. I hope he stays.*

I passed some people in the corridor on my way to my ninth-grade class. I kept my head down, trying not to read them. Trying, really, not even to recognize them.

I slipped into my class just as the bell rang. The kids, unsupervised, were jumping up and down, throwing things, and generally yelling at each other.

I was stunned. My students lay before me like an open book. I saw at once who hated me, who loved me, who resented me. The worst, maybe, were the kids who had no opinion of me at all. I was like the desks or the wallpaper. A part of the school machinery that in no way impinged on their lives.

"Mr. Smithka?" one of the boys who sat up front said.

I shook my head coming out of a dream. *"What is wrong with him?"* were the boy's thoughts. A girl next to him thought, *"He's on drugs!"*

I couldn't focus. "Okay, class. Oh, come on Pedro. No texting."

He looked up at me guiltily. "I wasn't."

True, he wasn't. But he was about to. He was going to let his girlfriend in tenth grade know that his teacher was stoned out of his mind.

"I'm not stoned, Pedro. Just a little disoriented. I had . . . a tough morning. The chalk, William."

William Alvarez had taken all the chalk and hidden it in his pocket. Kids did that sometimes. "Now, I am going to play a guessing game. I am going to guess who read the assignment last night."

I went through the classroom identifying people who had read the worksheet on writing dialogue I had handed out and who had not. It was depressing work. Only six had read it. Twenty-one had not. The ones who had not read it sometimes lied about reading it, but I made some shrewd "guesses" about what they might have done instead, making them laugh, sometimes embarrassing them, until they admitted the truth.

I omitted the most embarrassing facts. That Pedro had been fighting with his girlfriend. Two kids had been gangbanging. Another was shooting up. A fifth spent the night under his covers trying to stay out of the way of his mother's scary boyfriend. Another stayed up all night with a knife, intending to protect her mother from her father, if it came to that.

But what I did say made the kids laugh and admit skipping the homework. So we went through the worksheet, and I was able to force their attention, intervening when I sensed anyone's mind begin to wander. It was a good class.

Except for the fact that at the end, I felt awful. I had robbed their thoughts to bully them into listening to me. To listening about some stupid fact sheet about writing dialogue, when all that mattered was that these kids were dodging bullets on the streets, taking drugs, and being abused by the adults in their lives. The kids left energized. I felt rotten.

Here I had been given the greatest gift for teaching in the history of humanity, and all it showed was how worthless teaching could be. We had to strike at the core of the social problems facing these kids. We had to . . . I had no idea. Be Tom and Gerry, fighting crime and drugs? Hadn't I just decided that wasn't important? I had no idea.

I sat in the classroom for a while with my head on my desk. Then I remembered I had promised to see Principal Snowe. So I walked down to her office and knocked on the door.

"Enter."

I did.

"Ahh, Jason. You were late this morning."

"Yes, sorry about that."

"You've been doing so well recently. I hope you're not falling back into your beginning-of-the-year habits?"

I had been right to be afraid of this woman. She'd happily destroy anything that threatened the school. Fortunately, she seemed to have a soft spot for me. I had just signed a two-year extension contract, and she had decided I had a future here.

"Jason, are you listening?

Was I really going to stay long-term at the school? I thought about Raffy, about to make a kajillion dollars. I'd like to make a kajillion dollars too. Or maybe a kajillion and one, just to best Raffy.

On the other hand, Ellen had taken a job here. So it wasn't just for losers. She wasn't a loser. I was pretty sure of that. What had Joe said? Ellen was "one smart cookie." Something like that. It didn't sound like much. But from Joe it was high praise.

Like I cared what Joe thought. I was getting lost in my thoughts and I heard Ms. Snowe beginning to lose patience. Just before she said anything, I said, "Really, everything is okay. My alarm clock didn't go off."

"*He's an odd one,*" I heard her think.

"Well, you'd better get back to class. And get a second alarm so it doesn't happen again."

The rest of the day was a fog. I had two study halls. I was lunch proctor. And I had two sections of Junior English to teach. I was in complete information overload, and my verbal response function was working in super-slo-mo.

Fortunately, I had managed to avoid reading the minds of my close friends. Look, I had read all the same literature as Hank. I knew the dangers of ESP to personal relationships, to sanity. It was the classic plot. A person gets to read minds and then learns to hate everyone. I knew I had to avoid probing the thoughts of Toby, Sylvia and Ellen. Not to mention Penny. The last thing I needed was her insight into exactly what kind of worthless, pathetic little insect I was.

But I still wanted to take my power out for a proper spin.

So after school, I headed to one of the crowded cafés next to the Harvard T station. A chance to do some deep dumpster diving into the psyches of the nation's elite students. I was like a kid in a comic store. I wanted to read everything, and the hard part was figuring out which book to open first.

I ordered a hot cider and was lucky to find a seat in the window of the café. Instead of engaging any one person, I let my mind float on the mental hubbub that surrounded me. Like listening to the noise of a crowded cafeteria, capturing a word here or there, I surfed the din of thoughts, catching a feeling or an idea without a clear sense of where it came from.

My goal was to learn to control my power so I didn't go insane. But that isn't to say I didn't learn a thing or two about humanity in the course of eavesdropping on people's thoughts. Since I may be the only person who has ever had such a direct line into people's minds, I figure maybe I should share what I learned.

First of all, most people say what they're thinking, at least most of the time. It's boring, but that's just how it is. Talking takes enough brain power that it's easiest just to say what you are thinking.

Rather than outright lying, people add silent qualifications and intended caveats and cautions that they don't quite ever actually say. They just assume them to be read in their tone and general manner. So when everyone else finds out that they've "lied," they deny it. Their silent provisos ("I know I said I would come to your party, but the clear implication was that I'd do so only if there was nothing good on TV") turned what they said into nothing less than the truth.

Another thing is that people don't think about sex as often as people claim. I'm not saying people don't notice people's physical attributes. But thinking "She has a nice smile," or "He has great abs," is hardly imagining having sex with them. And these sorts of thoughts, take this for what you will, are as likely to happen between people who would deny being sexually attracted to each other as to people who admit to the attraction. (Okay, what do I know? Sexual identities are mutable, culturally established things etc., etc. Now we're above my pay grade. I'm just telling you that beautiful people attract attention irrespective of presumed gender or sexual orientation.)

On the other hand, when people suddenly do start thinking about sex, it's like alarms are blaring, red lights flashing and the volume on a person's thoughts is turned up to 11. It was one of my favorite things to see (or sense, I guess) when some girl, or some guy, was sitting around thinking about homework or coffee or the crisis in the Sudan, or whatever, and then suddenly—BAAAB, BAAAB, BAAAB—they'd be in full-scale sexual alert, and everything else would be forgotten in some strange sexual exigency. Often, there was no outward sign. People would act completely cool, pretending to keep reading or looking at their phones, as if their brains had not just exploded into a sexual swampland.

Mostly the alarm was just a general alert, unaccompanied by specifics. When a person's thoughts did dip into specifics—the body parts, the gyrations, the role-play, the dialogue—it was often more horrifying than erotic. Apart from the fact that many people have straight-out unpleasant fantasies, they also have terrible imaginations. Anyway, it's just an extension of what Ellen told me. Not only is it icky to imagine other people having sex, it's also icky watching them imagine it themselves.

I know this makes me sound like a worse voyeur than when I was invisible. But it really wasn't like that. First of all, I mostly didn't even see the people whose thoughts I read. So the information was deidentified, like in medical research databases. Second of all, I wasn't spying on friends, I was just trying to understand people around me. Pure research, man!

I could go on. But the main point is that if you want to know how people think, look at your own thoughts. That's mostly what other people's thoughts are like. We have irrational hatreds and prejudices. We are sentimentally attached to ridiculous things. We have secrets that we are ashamed of, often around acting like cowards. We have secrets that we *should* be ashamed of, mostly around acting like bullies.

I did learn you couldn't judge a person by their thoughts. Thoughts are amorphous and changing. Most people can *think* something one second, and then, with the exact same level of commitment, the opposite thing a second later.

Also, people spend a lot of time feeling misunderstood and unlucky. The particular stories are all different, and some circumstances are objectively more awful than others, but the attitudes are the same. So a little kindness never hurts.

I guess most of this is obvious. The sort of thing we've all already learned from Hallmark. But what can I do? If the truth is a greeting card, then the truth is a greeting card.

Except that Tuesday afternoon, while I was collating these deep thoughts, something else happened. I was sitting back, enjoying the coffee, scanning the thoughts of the crowd, and suddenly I heard, *"They'll die. They're all going to die."*

Now, I did hear that sort of thing occasionally, but this thought was particularly vivid. There was no "A curse on both your houses" lack of specificity. It imagined a time and a place. There was a clear image of the Boston Garden in flames. More, there was a picture of a bomb, recently laid in the ductwork. A big ugly thing with wires and plastic explosives and a timer. It looked just like a movie bomb. And the whole thing was happening soon—next week, maybe? The guy dripped with self-satisfaction. With mission-accomplished smugness. George Bush in a flight suit.

"Just a coffee. Hot, black."

What? Damn, I'd lost the thread. Was that the same guy, his thoughts about the bombing interrupted by needing to order? It sometimes happened that a person's mind went dead as they gave up a train of thought, and I slipped into the thoughts of someone nearby without even noticing. I stood up and looked around the checkout line.

But there was a crowd in the coffee shop and it was hard to see through the mass of people waiting in line. Reaching out with my mind, I received a barrage of thoughts, but it was hard to tell who was thinking what. Most people were thinking about their orders. Some were pissed about standing in line. Others were relieved to be off work. Suddenly one of those BAAAB BAAAB BAAAB red-alarm moments exploded as a guy was admiring the ass crack of a girl two places in front of him revealed by her low-cut jeans.

Then I had it for a moment. A gleeful picture of the Garden in rubble. A picture of shirts that said "Tinder" on them. "Thunder" maybe.

But where was the guy? I looked around and wasn't sure. Then a horn blew and suddenly everyone was rubbernecking, in thought and action. A hundred people thought in unison, *"Damn cabbies."* Who knew they evoked such hostility?

Had he left the café? I hurried outside, opening my mind to the crowds of Harvard Square. But it was too much. All I got was a large undifferentiated buzz. I went back into the café and focused my ESP net there. I picked through some individual thoughts. A book report. A party. A girl. A boy. Paying the rent. A dying parent. Supper. A harassing prof. A rude boss. Shoes that pinched. A possible lump in the breast. All the normal, tragic life of the world.

But I didn't see/hear/whatever my bomber. He—she?—had slipped away into the tumult of the world's thoughts.

CHAPTER 29
I Can't Hear You

So, the first serious bit of trouble I had run into since I had acquired superpowers and what did I do? I decided to ignore it.

That may seem not in keeping with the ideals of heroism I espouse, and I'm not going to disagree. But here was my thinking at the time. People had a lot of violent fantasies. That didn't mean they were going to act on them.

Okay, I agree the bomber was a little different. The thoughts were closer to the surface, more specific. More in the line of "plans" than "dreams." But I wasn't really experienced enough with my powers to know that at the time. I thought I might be imagining the difference. The distinction between memories, plans and dreams is tenuous enough in real life, that it seemed unlikely that I would be able to tell the difference in the strange medium of thoughts. And, remember, it was still the first day I'd used this power.

Maybe you already know I was fooling myself. And, as it turned out, I could tell the difference. That's what ESP was; that's what made it a superpower. The guy was planning on bombing the Garden. He'd already planted the bomb. I should have acted right away.

But I didn't. And the second reason I didn't is that I had decided to keep my new power secret. Hank didn't come home that night, or Wednesday or Thursday, until after I was asleep. And he'd left each morning before I was awake. I knew why. The idea of me waltzing around in his mind uninvited wigged him the fuck out.

I understood. I really did. When I went deep, I saw some seriously personal shit. Formative memories that no one wanted to share. Secret shames. Life attitudes that, fuck, I knew I would want to keep private.

If even Hank felt that way, and he was my best friend, how would other people feel? I'd be a leper. No one would want to interact with me at all.

I had learned to control my power somewhat. I could choose not to read someone. But it was hard, and my self-control still slipped, overwhelmed by my curiosity. And it didn't really matter if I actually read someone or not. It mattered that I could. That's what my friends (and everybody else) would object to. So I decided not tell anyone about what I could do.

And how could I tell anyone about a secret bomb plot without explaining how I knew about it? No, I decided. The plot was a passing fantasy of an angry young man, and nothing dangerous. I wasn't going to tell anyone about it.

Instead, I worried about my own problems. My classes would take care of themselves that week. The freshmen were doing their plays and the juniors . . . well, I think they were meant to be breaking into small groups and critiquing each other's papers. But the trivia finals were on Friday, and I was dreading them. How was I going to keep up the policy of avoiding reading my friends' minds there?

There was so much that I didn't want to learn from accidental mind-reading. I didn't want to see myself through Penny's jaundiced eyes. Or Raffy's.

And Ellen was even worse. I'd seen enough in Hank's mind to realize he and she weren't going out, but where did that leave us? I was aware of the fact Ellen and I sure hung out a lot, and I'm not a total idiot. I realized that there might be more to it than that. On her side, and maybe on mine too. But did I want to learn what was in her mind before I even knew what was in my mind? What if she lusted after me? What if she loved me? What if she didn't? The best I could manage after reading Ellen's mind would be to come out conflicted. The worst would be to have every nasty, scornful recrimination made by Penny validated in spades.

I had been looking forward to the final match. Now I was dreading it.

I woke up on Friday morning to find that Hank had never come home from his lab—still avoiding me, I guess, thanks, Hank. I could have used your advice. Instead, I was forced to think through my problems on my own.

Over breakfast, I wondered if I could search people's minds from afar. I had just assumed I had to be in the vicinity, maybe a sight line with someone whose mind I was reading. That was why I'd chased after the guy I thought was planning the bombing. But there was no real evidence that I needed proximity, and in fact, some evidence to the contrary. At the coffeehouse, I hadn't been able to see everyone whose thoughts I intercepted. Some of them were playing chess outside while I was in line ordering. One of them—thanks for asking—was in the bathroom with the door closed.

So maybe I could read minds from far away. Maybe, if I kept what I was looking for firmly in mind—bombing the Boston Garden—I could sift through the Cambridge/Boston area and find the person I'd "overheard."

I had tried to ignore what I'd heard and move on. But I suspected that guilt was one reason I had slept so badly the last couple of nights. And without Hank around, I had to be my own Hank. And I, as he, was saying to me, "Seriously, dude? You're just going to ignore the whole thing? You think that's what Batman would do?"

"I'm not Batman," I, as me, replied.

I, as he, said, "I'll say. And I'm sure you'll feel great when you wake up sometime next week to find a hundred people dead in an explosion at the Garden. Some hero!"

"Fuck you, Hank. Okay, I'll do some checking."

So I did. I sat in the kitchen over a nice bowl of Apple-Cinnamon Cheerios and tried to look for the bomber. Or, I guess I should say, the bomber-suspect.

I discovered squat. Well, that's not strictly true. I discovered that I could do some pretty cool things. I could definitely read minds from afar. I found I could do something like cast my ESP in a rough direction and distance. I didn't have any built-in GPS, so I didn't know where the minds I read were except by what they were thinking. But if I focused east and threw hard, I got kids thinking about physics and admiring MIT architecture. If I focused south and threw hard, I got people finishing up a night of drinking in Allston bars. I found that it took me no more than a few seconds to sift through someone's thoughts to see if they were thinking about placing a bomb.

I also discovered that there were limits. I mean, I tried to throw hard enough west to get a starlet or two. I ended up, best as I could tell, in Boxboro. I tried to go far enough south to get some insider trading tips from a New York banker. I was in Brookline.

What I did not discover was a needle in a haystack; namely a kid—or an adult, I guess—thinking about bombing the Boston Garden. I searched through a couple of hundred minds, but I had to stop at each one. I couldn't just sort of fly overhead and take in hundreds of people at once. If I tried to scan several people at once, I just got a dull buzz.

So no luck. I went to school trying, on the one hand, to forget my mad bomber, and on the other, madly scanning random people to see if they were the mad bomber.

It was a relief to get to school and safely into the classroom. I had made a promise to myself earlier that week not to scan the kids in class, both to practice my self-control, and to respect their privacy.

And I'd done a pretty good job. Kids were so easy to read that you didn't need ESP half of the time.

Then, that morning, Toby appeared at my classroom door inviting me to lunch to discuss strategy for that evening and, without hardly meaning to, I slipped into his mind.

Look, I don't know how mind-reading works. All superhero physics are pretty dubious; but the physics of mind-reading seem particularly dubious. What was I even reading, after all? I am no expert on brain science, but I am pretty sure that minds are not normally set up like library reading rooms.

Except Toby's mind really was, complete with card catalogue. Everything was dusted and spotless and perfectly in order. He had stopped by to make sure I would be ready for the trivia finals. He was concerned that my superpowers had made me act erratically, and the lunch invitation was just to make sure that I didn't go off and do anything crazy.

"So, I'll see you at Lou's?" he said.

I saw that he felt a fatherly concern for me. I reminded him of a much younger brother who had died years ago in a motorcycle accident. I found it neatly filed under "Smithka, Jason, resemblances to." His younger brother was a bit of a hellion and so, Toby thought, was I. Which was not true at all. I was a nerd of the highest order and quite risk-averse. The whole thing was ridiculous. But try telling that to Toby. He was so convinced of our psychological similarity that he had started to wonder if some of his younger brother's actions could be explained by his having gotten sudden superpowers. Toby was a sweetheart, and a total loon.

Oh, yes. The question of lunch. Toby wondered when I would answer. And if I was high.

"Jason?"

"Yes, Toby. I'm here. I'm not high. Just . . . distracted." I saw that I would not put him off. He was even thinking of reporting me to the principal to be sure I got treatment. "Of course, I'll meet you for lunch. Twelve at the diner, right?"

Finally, I was alone. So much for not reading people. It was so easy to slip in. I was very worried about how this lunch would go.

Until I decided to skip it. I mean, the whole thing with the potential bomber was still bugging me, and I realized—duh—that I could just report it to Tom and Gerry. They were in charge of antiterrorism for Boston. If there was anything there to worry about, they were the perfect people to take care of it. I could buzz up to them during lunch, give them the lowdown and get back for my first afternoon class.

I hated to initiate contact with them. They didn't exactly give me the warm fuzzies. I had no illusions what they thought of me. I was a dangerous tool that had some temporary usefulness. I was afraid of what would happen when I stopped being useful.

But finding a real live terrorist plot would surely be the definition of useful. And it was their job to stop things like that. So I blew off a meeting to discuss the paper one of my juniors was writing, went outside the school and rang them on the iPhone.

As usual, Tom picked up after the first ring. "Yeah?"

"We need to meet."

"Yeah?"

"I overheard a bombing plot."

"Right, sure."

"If I leave now, I could get to Natick at lunch."

"Tell me now."

"Okay." I had hoped to avoid this. I sort of knew how it would go. "I getting coffee in Harvard Square a couple of days ago and I heard this guy talking about blowing up the Boston Garden. I'm pretty sure it's going to happen sometime next week."

"What'd he look like?"

"I didn't see him."

"You didn't see him?"

"No."

"Okay. Good surveillance technique there. What'd the other guy say?"

"What other guy?"

"The guy he was talking to."

"There was no other guy."

"You mean he was talking to himself?"

"No," I lied quickly, "I guess he must have been talking to someone. But I didn't see them. And I didn't hear the other guy say anything."

"Funny. Guy tells me he's going to blow shit up, I might say something back to him."

"Look, this is serious. I could tell they were serious."

"From overhearing a single sentence?"

"I can explain. But we have to meet."

"Well . . . ."

"It's important."

"You got nothing."

"I can't explain over the phone."

"Give me a hint?"

I was going to have to tell them sooner or later. I put my hand over the phone and lowered my voice. "It's my new power. I can read minds."

"Yeah? What am I thinking?"

I knew he was thinking that I was a delusional twit. But that didn't take any special power. "I can't read your mind over the phone."

"Hold on."

I knew he was talking with Gerry. After a couple of minutes, Tom came back on the line.

"Come by in half an hour. We can hear your fairy story."

So I checked out of school, telling the secretary I had a doctor's appointment.

"Let Toby know," I said. "We were meant to meet for lunch. But I'll be ready for the trivia tonight."

"The finals," she said. "It's so exciting. Flynn's never made it this far. Me and my girlfriends are going to watch."

I smiled and nodded. Then I left to catch the T. It was going to be nip and tuck whether I got back in time for Junior English.

The trip out proved no problem, as a tram was pulling up just as I got to the station. I hopped on and considered how to sell my proposition to Tom and Gerry.

When I got out to their office, I headed up to the fourth floor and met the receptionist. Immediately, I knew something was wrong. She was not going to wave me into the office.

Instead she handed me the phone. "Tom says you have to talk with them over the phone."

"Why?"

She shrugged, of course. They weren't going to tell her that they were afraid I'd read their minds. But they had made a mistake. I told Tom that I couldn't read minds over the phone, and he thought I had to see them to read their minds. Really, I just had to be close enough and know roughly where they were. Now, it was easy enough to cast my mind through the walls and see their thoughts.

I got Tom's mind first. It turned out that, for all his tough talk, ever since the incident when I grew to giant size and shoved him, he was terrified of me. I guess it was a kind of bravery that he pretended it was no big deal.

I looked for Gerry's mind. He didn't fear me like Tom did. He thought I was weak and pliable. And he still didn't really believe in my so-called "powers."

Deeper down, I saw that he thought of himself as a good cop. He'd worked hard to keep Boston safe from terrorists and to keep gang violence down. Even if his relationship with Rory the Sparrow eventually came out, people, policemen at least, would understand that he was acting for the greater good. Maybe some of the compensation that flowed his way was a mistake, but that was how negotiations went.

It took me a moment to realize that Rory the Sparrow was the scary wheelchair-bound gangster Gerry had mentioned. Rory's brother was one of Gerry's father's best friends. Rory had been a source for and a mentor to Gerry for years. Rory kept order in return for Gerry keeping cop interference to a minimum. Rory was behind many of Gerry's greatest successes.

The secretary was trying to hand me the phone and talking. "Tom on the line for you," she said.

"So, what's the story," Tom said.

But I was distracted. Neither Tom nor Gerry gave a single fuck about the plot to blow up the Garden. I mean, they didn't want it blown up. That was the kind of thing they lived to stop. But they didn't believe I knew what I was talking about, and, frankly, they were way more concerned about my claim to read minds than about the Garden.

"Can you fucking hear me?" Tom shouted.

"Uh, sure."

"You said you could read minds, right? Tell me where Barbara went to school." Barbara was the receptionist.

"UMass-Dartmouth," I said before my strategic thinking caught up with my mouth. I didn't want to prove I could read minds. I wanted to prove I was bullshitting when I said I could read minds. "I mean, she has a mug. How would I know where she went to school?"

She didn't have a mug, at least not that I could see. But would Gerry and Tom remember that?

"Maybe you read her mind." That was Gerry on speaker.

"Look, I was just joshing with Tom because he didn't believe me. Like I said, I overhead the guy talking with someone. A bomb in the Garden. Next week, maybe."

But even as I said it, I knew it was useless. The message was lost in their concern with the messenger. They didn't believe I had discovered a bomb plot. I was just some jumped-up trickster with delusions of grandeur. I hadn't been trained as a policeman. I wouldn't be able to tell random chatter from real intelligence. Even if, by some chance, I had come across some angry young man expressing frustration with the world, it didn't mean anything.

On the other hand, they were worried by my claim to read minds. Here their thinking got a little convoluted. While they didn't believe I really could see people's thoughts, they still asked themselves, "What if he's telling the truth?" Unfortunately, that did not lead them to, "If he's telling the truth, then there might really be a terrorist plot," but rather to, "If he's telling the truth, he's a danger to have around."

"I asked who she's sleeping with." Gerry's voice sounded in my ear, impatient and angry. I must have missed a question while I was scanning their minds.

I looked at Barbara. She was married and sleeping with her husband. Duh! Oh, but she was having an affair. She had slept with Tom too. Although, "slept with" may not have been quite the right verb. It was in the bathroom. She was a little confused about the episode. She thought Tom was gorgeous, but she'd never consented to sex. At least, she hadn't meant to.

But I was on the clock. I needed to answer. I could say I didn't know and forget them ever believing me about the Garden plot. Or I could tell them that she had recently taken up with a man with a plumbing business in Natick. Hal Burgess.

I felt the tension building in Tom and Gerry too. Christ, suddenly I saw that Gerry had men blocking all the exits. They had no intention of letting me out, whatever I answered. Wrong. Or right. Or whatever.

I reached out, caught the mind of one of the policemen waiting at the top of the stairs. He had no idea what was happening, but he was armed with a Taser and jittery as hell.

The only other time I had won a concession from these guys was by a show of strength. I made a decision to go back to that well. I smiled apologetically at Barbara.

"Her current boyfriend is a plumber called Hal Burgess. She was raped about a year ago by Tom in the women's bathroom. Tom thinks it was consensual but he's wrong. You, by the way, have a deal with Rory. You let him run crime in exchange for tips every now and again. You worry that it's a bad deal, but can't find a way out."

I saw Tom's and Gerry's minds explode. Gerry pushed a button and said, "I want him unconscious now."

"Don't do that or . . ." I didn't even finish the sentence. Which was probably for the best. I couldn't think of a anything to threaten them with. Fifty thousand volts from a dart Taser flowed through me and I collapsed.

My last read was of Tom. He dearly wanted to kill me.

CHAPTER 30

The Greater the Obstacle

He didn't. I came to in a small concrete room. A small night-light kept the room from being totally dark. I was lying on a narrow cot with a thin mattress. My head hurt like a mother-fuck-er. My whole body ached and I felt like I needed to throw up.

Sitting up on the bed, I noticed that my pants were wet and I stank of piss. So I had wet myself somewhere along the line. Great! Life was just wonderful.

I looked around. There was a small wide-lens camera in one corner. I was being watched.

I put my head in my hands and rubbed my eyes. I was hungry and, despite having released my bladder earlier, I needed to piss again. Also, I dearly wanted a shower and a change of clothes. Tom and Gerry wouldn't have kept me alive if they were just going to starve me to death, would they?

I was about to gesture at the camera, when I had a realization. If someone was watching me, they might not be too far away. Before I motioned, I cast my mind out.

It took a couple of minutes until I found the someone. A low-level guard. He had no idea who I was or why I was here, but he had orders to turn on a tap flooding the cell with a sleeping gas if I disappeared from view. I guess Tom and Gerry were worried I could still turn invisible or shrink.

I looked a little bit more through the guard's mind. He knew nothing about me, little about Tom and Gerry, and nothing about their plans for me. But I did discover one thing: he was a Red Sox fan and he liked this gig because he was close to Fenway. He'd miss the game tonight, but he was close enough to hear the crowds when the Sox hit a home run.

That was interesting because it meant that I wasn't in Natick. In fact, I was not too far from Flynn. And just across the river from MIT. And what made that interesting was that it meant I might be able to reach out and read the minds of some of my friends.

But first I had to get cleaned up. I waved my hand at the guard. He came down and brought me towels and a change of clothes. The change was an orange prison jumpsuit, but it was better than nothing. He also brought me a bedpan and some leftover pizza. It was all encouraging. Tom and Gerry weren't going to kill me yet.

The guard, Pete was his name, worked for Tom and Gerry to earn a little overtime. I tried asking him when I would get out, where Tom and Gerry were, if I could call a lawyer, how long I would be held, and whether I could shower. Reading his mind, I saw he didn't know the answer to any of these questions, but he wouldn't talk to me anyway. He just unbolted a panel covering a slot in the door, slid a package through to me, rebolted the panel, and left.

He had done two tours in Afghanistan and sectioned out after an eye injury. He felt blessed to have passed his police exam on the first try. He had a young wife who was pregnant with, he hoped, a boy. He thought a lot about playing catch with his son.

I did learn something else from him. I hadn't been out for days. It was 4:30, just a few hours after I had stopped by Gerry's Natick office. At school, the sports teams would just be wrapping up practice.

I hated missing school. The juniors could muddle through critiquing their papers with a substitute, but I had been looking forward to hearing some of their ideas. And helping people improve their writing was one of the things I was pretty good at.

Oh, fuck! The trivia finals. They were going to start in less than four hours and, unless Tom and Gerry started moving things along pretty damn quickly, I was going to be stuck in a cell in Fenway. Who'd answer the literature questions? If we lost because of this . . . well, it'd be really annoying.

I zipped through Pete's mind again. He had no knowledge of when I'd be released, but I saw that he had been told to expect some overtime for the next month or so. The next month or so? Excuse me? I had a fucking life to lead. A trivia finals to win. Students to teach. Goddamn it!

I sat on my cot and felt sorry for myself. How was this fair?

I cast my mind out for Tom and Gerry. If they ran this joint, they had to come by some time. I didn't find them. I didn't find anyone I knew. I'll tell you what I did find. I found some other regular police dudes in the Fenway station. And I discovered that no one was out looking for a terrorist wanting to blow up the Boston Garden. If Tom and Gerry were taking me seriously at all, they had decided to go about their investigations in a quiet, "low-impact" way. But I suspected that they had ignored my warning altogether.

I looked into Pete's mind to keep track of time. Five o'clock. He was on for another three hours. In fact, he'd get off just as I was meant to be arriving at the Black Horse Tavern in Quincy Market, where the finals were being held.

Six o'clock. Christ, I don't understand how people stand prison. I'd only been here less than two hours and was going crazy.

I decided I needed to find Hank, and started casting toward MIT. Then I had a thought. The finals were being held in the Black Horse Tavern, a little east and north of MIT. It was way too early for Hank to get there, but I was going to need time to find the place. If I started now, then I might have found it by the time Hank arrived. Even if I didn't find him, lots of my other friends would be there, so I had a marginally better chance to find someone I knew there than at MIT.

It may seem like a hopeless prospect, finding one mind in a city of a million people via the inexact method of casting my thoughts in a vague direction. But I had a strategy. I would cast my thoughts, read someone—anyone—to figure out where I had gotten, and then adjust on my next cast. Also, I was desperate and had nothing but time.

I had another theory that encouraged me to keep going. I had been reflecting on how I'd gleaned information from people that they had no reason to be thinking about at the moment I read them. Like where Barbara went to college. One possibility was that I could somehow read memories and potential thoughts as well as actual, current thoughts. A second possibility, what I hoped was the case, was that somehow my probing of their minds caused them to think about the subjects I was looking for.

If that was the case, it meant that the whole ESP thing was not necessarily a one-way street. So far, I had only used it to listen in, but maybe I could use it to communicate too. This was the sort of thing Hank would have been all over if we had had a chance to explore my power before everything went kablooey, and if he hadn't been so freaked that he'd avoided me for four days.

So I looked for Hank. Or rather, I looked for the Black Horse, hoping that, once I found it, I might find Hank. I cast my mind out again and again and again. Found someone, figured out where I was and moved on. From the outside, for Pete, things must have been pretty boring. I was just sitting on my cot staring off into space as I moved from one street to the next. Not going far enough. Going too far. Veering north. Veering south.

Finally, I reached a point where I could reliably pick up someone in Quincy Market. There I found someone who actually knew where the Black Horse was, and I cast again trying to hit it spot on.

It took me twenty more casts, but suddenly there I was, back in the Black Horse, hearing the din of multiple people's thoughts. And then, all of a sudden, one stood out above the crowd because it was thinking about me. About Jason Smithka. I grabbed it and carefully worked my way back to the mind in which it resided.

I must say, the particular thought I ended up tracking was a little dispiriting. Because the full substance of it was something like: *"Jason Smithka—I can't believe that rat bastard abandoned us!"*

On the other hand, I had found Ellen. Other than a general condemnation of me, her current thoughts were all about trivia. The match had started a few moments ago and SAP was already ahead.

I was trying to get a read on how many questions had been asked when Ellen's mind filled with a question: *"What is the real name of the author of* Le Malade Imaginaire?*"*

It was a hard question. You had to know both that the play was by Moliere and his real name, which clearly Ellen didn't. Maybe Toby would, if he knew the play.

I waited, as breathless as Ellen seemed to be. One second, two seconds. Surely someone from the other side would buzz in and increase their lead. No one did.

Three more seconds and they'd move to the next question. But *I* knew the answer.

"Jean-Baptiste Poquelin," I yelled out loud in my little prison cell, and tried to yell in Ellen's mind.

Ellen touched her buzzer. I saw her reaction as the moderator turned to her and said, "Three Harps."

But Ellen just seemed confused. Why had she thought she'd known the answer? She'd never heard of the book. She should never have buzzed. Now she'd get it wrong and Three Harps would be even further behind.

"Jean-Baptiste Poquelin," I said again, madly trying to race around her brain and find some way to communicate.

"What," she murmured, half to herself. I didn't hear the murmur, but saw the slightly formed intention to speak.

"Jean-Baptiste Poquelin," I tried again.

"Two seconds," said the moderator.

I closed my eyes and concentrated. *"Jean-Baptiste Poquelin."*

"Answer please."

"Jean-Baptiste . . . what?"

"Poquelin," I thought

"Poquelin," she said.

"Correct," said the moderator.

"Ellen, it's me!"

"What the fuck?" That was what she aloud as she turned to try to find who was talking to her. Her thoughts were the same with more swears.

"Jason. I'm in your head. That's my new power. I read minds. I guess I can talk to you too."

I have to say, Ellen was amazing. She hadn't even heard of my power change, but she managed to absorb the new information without totally freaking. More than that, she managed to follow my explanation of what had happened to me, keep up in the game, answer questions in her own field, and relay each question to me. Even more, she was able to take answers I gave her, buzz in and reply as if she knew the responses herself. All while pretending to her teammates and the rest of the crowd that everything was normal.

It was an impressive juggling experience. As she described it later, having me talk in her head was sort of like the feeling you get when you get water in the ear—not necessarily painful, just a feeling like something is in the wrong place.

Despite my mediated presence at the quiz, we did not do as well on the literature questions as we might have because of the slight lag time between the questions being read and my reading them in Ellen's thoughts. There were several times when I was sure I would have beaten the guy from the SAP team to the answer if I had been in the room. But at least we were able to stop the bleeding.

And this disadvantage was more than made up for by my being able to access Ellen's deep memory banks much more efficiently than she could herself. I mean, we all have a vast store of knowledge that we sometimes forget. Particularly about pop culture. Ellen was good at that shit, but she knew a hell of a lot more than she could easily recall. We romped on those questions.

Nevertheless, the quiz was close. The fuckers at SAP were good. Amazingly, it came down to the last two questions. We were two points ahead, but now each question was worth four points. And each wrong answer was worth negative eight. If we got the second-to-last question right, or if SAP got it wrong, we would win.

The moderator read the question, "Who played Dobie Gillis?"

Ellen buzzed in fast and the moderator said, "Answer please."

She was about to say Bob Denver, who also played Gilligan in *Gilligan's Island*, which sounded like an okay guess. But I read some small doubt in her mind, just a smidgen, which was enough for me to yell *"Wait!"* in her mind. I think that was then she spilled her drink.

"Answer please."

"It wasn't Bob Denver," I said.

"Well, who was it?" she subvocalized at me. I was impressed watching her brain multitask. Keeping up with the game, interacting with her teammates, and communicating with me telepathically, all at the same time.

I searched madly.

"Dwayne Hickman," Ellen said.

"Correct. Four points. Three Harps 112, the Rolling Bear 106. Final question."

What the fuck? Where did that even come from? I had not seen it anywhere in her mind. I said as much.

"You must have been looking in the wrong place," she said to me.

But it didn't matter, we had won. All we needed to do was not buzz for the final question.

"What animator of *Mighty Mouse: The New Adventures* went on to create *The Ripping Friends*?"

I was sitting back basking in our victory when Ellen's panic struck me. I was not sure what had happened at first because I had not realized she had inadvertently buzzed in to answer the question.

"What were you thinking?" I asked.

"I don't know. I just sort of did it."

"Well do you know who it was?"

Ellen's brain was in full-on overload now, as she was trying to deal with me and her teammates bombarding her with questions, inside and outside her head. I let her deal with the team and focused on sifting through her brain. I figured that, if she buzzed in, she may unconsciously have realized she knew the answer, so all I had to do was find it.

That was when I noticed something I had overlooked before, which was essentially a large cluster of neurons labeled "Jason." Maybe it's surprising that I had not seen it earlier, as I've told you how quickly I could move through someone's thoughts. But there were a couple of reasons I may have overlooked it. First, we had both been very focused on the trivia game, so I never did a general survey of her mind. Second, reading people while I was talking to them—or I guess I should say communicating with them—was much harder than going through their thoughts when I was lurking in their brain. Sort of like the difference between reading a book while you're having a conversation, and reading a book when you're alone.

At any rate, I saw this huge set of neurons marked "Jason," and it took all my willpower not to jump in and find out why she had so many thoughts about me. I know we had spent a lot of time together, even slept together one drunken evening, but still.

"Answer please."

I didn't have time; we were up against the clock. Ellen buzzed, so I figured she must have the answer. I raced through her childhood viewing records, her college television days, her hanging out with friends. It was nowhere.

"*YOU'RE THE FUCKING COMICS WHIZ,*" Ellen subvocalized in all caps. "*Look in your own fucking brain.*"

Thanks, Ellen. I watched Mighty Mouse after Hank got me hooked on the *Animaniacs*. Ralph Bakshi's *Mighty Mouse* was a huge influence. But I knew it wasn't Bakshi. *The Ripping Friends* was a Canadian import done years after Bakshi had turned full time to painting.

"Answer please."

Canadian. That was the key. *Ren and Stimpy*. And the cartoonist . . . Nic something. Something weird. Nic Kricfalusi.

Then, simultaneously, Ellen and the moderator spoke. "Nic Kricfalusi/Time."

I saw Ellen think, "*We lost.*"

Then, "*He's nodding yes.*"

"*Who?*"

"*The referee. Moderator asked the referee. He's nodding. I don't know what it means.*"

"Correct," the moderator said, and then all I could see of Ellen's thoughts was a high-pitched scream of elation, which rang around my head like a fire alarm. I winced and tried to back off, but accidentally moved too far and broke our connection.

Fuck. I tried at once to cast back in. But I had lost my sense of where the Black Horse was. I got Boston's Back Bay.

Fuck, fuck, fuck. I'd lost her. Now, I was rotting in jail while my teammates were celebrating a historic victory. But why had I even wasted time on the stupid trivia? I needed Ellen's help to get out of here. She needed to go to the police. I had just given her the broad outlines of my story. Hardly enough for her to know what was going on. And now I had lost her. And I had no idea when or if I could ever get her back.

I lay down on the cot. My head hurt. I was scared and tired and I wanted to go home. I won't say I cried myself to sleep. That sounds overdramatic. But I was feeling pretty sorry for myself. And I did, eventually, go to sleep.

CHAPTER 31

The Boston Irregulars

I woke up discouraged. A different guard was watching me. His most pressing worry was whether his brother-in-law could get him tickets to the Celts-Thunder game Tuesday night.

He did, however, bring me food and a bedpan. I ate, filled the bedpan and waved for him to take it away. The bastard let it sit there for thirty minutes while the stench of my own excrement made my cozy little room stink to high heaven.

At least the stink gave me something to think about. The only other thing I had to do was stare at the walls. Stare. Stare. Stare. I guess I could have read minds, but I was feeling perverse. Some part of me wanted to experience the horrors of solitary.

You read about prisoners who get in great shape. Because instead of staring at the wall, they do push-ups and sit-ups. I did ten push-ups, then turned around and did one sit-up. Then stopped. My heart wasn't in it. I didn't want muscles. I wanted freedom.

The only good thing about it was that when I stopped doing sit-ups, I was staring at the ceiling instead of the wall. That made a difference.

I knew I had to reach out and find Ellen or Hank again, but it was hard to work up the concentration to start casting about the city again. What could they do for me anyway? Complain to someone maybe. Find me a lawyer. Reveal the secrets I'd learned about Tom and Gerry. It all seemed pretty hopeless.

Saturday afternoon, I noticed Tom was in the building. The guard had talked to him in the last hour. I cast my thoughts around the building and I found him. He wasn't here to see me, just to check in with my guards. He and Gerry were sweating me, making me think I had been abandoned for a few days. I'd be so thankful when they showed up again, that I'd give them anything they wanted.

It probably would have worked if I hadn't been able to read their minds. Tom and Gerry seemed confused about this. On the one hand, the whole reason they locked me up was that I could read minds. On the other hand, their whole strategy seemed to assume that I couldn't.

Whatever. The one thing I was sure of was that I had to keep my new trick—using ESP to communicate, rather than just eavesdrop—secret. The last thing I needed was for the two of them to know that I could tell someone about their misdeeds while rotting in this cell.

The other thing I found out was that they didn't want any of my friends contacting the police about me. To prevent this, Gerry had sent out an alert through the Massachusetts Police system to report directly to the Special Investigations unit (that would be Gerry) if Hank, Ellen or Raffy reported a missing person.

The only semi-good thing I learned was that Tom had looked into my claim about the bombing of the Boston Garden and had decided there was nothing to it. There was no "chatter" on the terrorist websites they monitored, and there was no other sign of enhanced activity from their various informers.

But that wasn't really a good thing at all. I mean, it would be if they were right. But I knew they weren't. I knew what I had seen.

It wasn't a dream or a hope or even a scheme to be worked out. The guy was reflecting with satisfaction on a job well done. A job already done. I'd *seen* the bomb. It was laid and waiting to go off. Thousands of people were going to die, whatever Tom and Gerry thought.

You may well wonder why, all of a sudden, I seemed so sure that the bombing plot was real, when earlier I said I only had the briefest glimpse of a thought, and didn't necessarily take it seriously. Well, look, I'd had more time with my ESP power since then, and I had begun to be able to discern the difference between airy hopes and dreams and actual actions and events. The bomber's thoughts, which were somewhat seared into my mind, had all the telltale signs of reality.

And reflecting on them, I suddenly knew when the bombing would take place. I had seen jerseys that said something like "Tinder" or "Thunder" on them. The Celts were playing the Oklahoma Thunder on Tuesday. The bombing was happening Tuesday. I had to do something fast. I had to find my friends.

If it was a weekday, I might have reached Ellen at Flynn. But it was the weekend, and I was a little unsure where her apartment was. So I decided to try Hank again, knowing that he'd be in his lab.

I cast and cast, but I couldn't find him. I had planned to stay up all night trying, but I think I ended up dozing off around two in the morning. When I woke up, I waved for my breakfast and bedpan and started again.

Around noon on Sunday, I began to get some folk who worked in the same lab complex. But the whole thing was a bit of a rabbit warren, and trying to locate Hank's lab from Fenway would require a bit of luck.

After a couple of hours, I thought I'd try an experiment. The next time I got someone in the same general lab vicinity, I was going to ask them to find Hank for me.

I cast and hit someone who seemed like a prof. Not who I was looking for. I tried again and got a custodian. Again, that didn't feel right. I wanted a grad student. Someone who might not freak.

I hit the jackpot with a young guy in a biocomputational lab that I remembered was somewhere near Hank. He was Vietnamese American and a virgin. Perfect.

"Hello," I said into his mind. *"Could you find Hank Nichols for me?"*

His mind, I saw, went into serious overdrive. He thought he was hallucinating. He pretended he didn't hear me.

"I said, would you mind if you could find Hank Nichols for me?"

"Hank?" I saw him think. Not to me, but just generally, as he was trying to figure out what was happening.

I considered strategy. He had grown up in a pretty conservative Vietnamese family, and there was a whole tradition of spirits in the folk religion of Vietnam. I could try that route. But, when it came right down to it, I decided that the kid was a grad student at MIT, so I chose a different tactic.

"Yeah, I'm Jason. I'm in the AI lab. We're just practicing a new tech called Thought Projection."

"This is so cool." I read in his thoughts that he said this out loud.

"It's very experimental."

"Can you hear me speak?" The guy, Giang, said. Out loud again. He seemed to assume that I could project my own thoughts, but not read his. That he had to talk for us to communicate. Mostly, I could see what he planned to say, but there was a possibility of confusion. Sometimes what someone *thought* they were going to say didn't match up with what they *did* say. Still, it was the best I could do.

"Yeah. Your lab has a preinstalled recording system that we use." I lied vaguely and hurried on. *"The thing is, we are doing an experi-*

ment and to get a result, I need Hank to get my message."

"Which Hank?"

"Nichols. Vaughn Lab 423(d). Astrophysics."

"Sure, what's the message? Wow, this is awesome. What sort of electronics are you using? Can I come by your lab? Where is it?"

I got a little confused at this point because I suspected he had not said all of those things, but he had thought about saying them all. I decided to ignore his comments.

"Tell Hank: Wait at St. Mary's T stop on the C line. Eight this evening. Think about Batman."

"That's sort of a weird message. Is it like a magnetic resonance tech?"

"Good guess, but that's still under wraps. Can you give him the message?"

"Sure."

I made him repeat the message and then broke contact. The address of the building where I was cooped up was 1300 Boylston. I figured that St. Mary's was close enough that I could get my thoughts there easily, but far enough away that Hank wouldn't run into Tom or Gerry. Also, the T stop was usually not crowded, so if I caught hold of a thought, it would be Hank.

I practiced casting to St. Mary's. I got a lot of doctors, commuting back home from the Boston hospitals. I kept track of the time by looking in my guard's mind.

He brought me supper and my bedpan at 6:00 p.m. I wasn't hungry. I was too nervous about whether I'd reach Hank.

A little before 8:00 p.m. I started casting for real. I was pretty accurate, getting one hit after another for St. Mary's, but finding only regular commuters. Then I cast and saw someone imagining a hunky Christian Bale in bat-bikini briefs and humming the theme from the '60s batman television show: "Da da da da da da da da BATMAN!"

I went in for a closer look, surprised that Hank had chosen this imagery. When I arrived I found Ellen, not Hank.

"What are you doing here?"

"Hank's here too," Ellen thought. *"He's just got a thing about getting his mind read."*

I was hurt. I'd let Hank read my mind. But I put that aside because we had more pressing issues.

I told Ellen the story of being taken prisoner from the beginning, and she relayed it to Hank. Then I told her my worries about the bombing at the Garden, including my big conclusion: *"I figured out when the bomb will go off. There's no game Monday. But Tuesday the Celtics play the Oklahoma Thunder. I saw Thunder jerseys in the guy's mind."*

"So we have to go to the police," Ellen said.

"It won't work. They'll take you to Tom and Gerry and nothing will happen."

"So you have another plan?"

"I don't think there's anything we can do."

"We can't just give up. We'll have to stop it ourselves."

"How?"

"Let me think," Ellen said.

I watched her neurons explode like fireworks while she talked the situation out with Hank. It was a beautiful sight. They were the two smartest people I knew, but there was nothing they could do. All those people were going to die, and it would be all my fault.

Ellen's thoughts snapped me out of reverie: *"Jesus, Jason, are you paying attention?"*

"What?"

"We're going to go to the Garden and disarm the bomb ourselves."

"I'm stuck in this cell."

"Not you. The rest of us.

"How will you find the bomb."

"*Joe. You said he knows the Garden. He had a bee in his bonnet about a design flaw where a small explosion would cause a whole lot of damage. I bet that's where the bomb is.*"

"*Okay. Then what?*"

"*That's where Hank comes in. He says he'll read up on bomb disposal this weekend.*"

Jesus, were they actually going to do this? "*How are you going to get into the building?*" I asked.

"*We could just buy tickets to Tuesday's game, but should we go in Monday? The bomb is in place already, right? If we wait until Tuesday, we may be too late. And if we screw up, the bomb will blow up in a building full of people.*"

"*So we need to get in the Garden on Monday?*" I said.

"*Sylvia has a friend who works at the Garden. Like, mid-level admin. She's said before she could get us tours.*"

Ellen and Hank started talking. I could see some of what Hank was saying in Ellen's mind, but I didn't want to interrupt. Finally, Ellen said to me that Hank thought it would be better to get a tour for a large party. It would be easier for some of the group to skulk off.

I smiled. This was really happening. We spent another hour talking, and by the time we were done we had a perfect Mission Impossible team. Ellen was the leader, who would keep in communication with me. Hank was the brains. Raffy and Toby were the muscle (okay, so we were working with what we had). Penny was the femme fatale. It was Ellen's idea to bring her in. Sylvia and Joe were . . . well, the analogy breaks down there. Sylvia was the woman with local knowledge. Joe was the old guy.

I love it when a plan comes together.

CHAPTER 32

Saving the Garden

There was just one thing missing from the plan. Me! I'd be the guy stuck in my cell while my friends became heroes. I said, *"I wish I could be with you guys,"* and maybe Ellen heard the self-pity behind my thoughts.

"Don't worry, Jason. First things first. We'll stop the bombing and then we'll figure how to get you free. Promise."

And after watching her in action, I almost believed her. And it's not like I had any better options than waiting to see what Ellen and Hank could come up with.

I stayed with Ellen while she and Hank headed back to our apartment in Cambridge to organize things for Monday. Their first call was to Sylvia, to see if her friend could get them a Garden tour the next day.

Flynn would be out of luck on Monday when four of its teachers and its part-time IT guy called in sick. Ellen would go pick up Joe early Monday morning and then meet the rest of the crew back at Toby's apartment, which was in the North End and fairly near the Garden.

Finally, Ellen said goodnight to Hank and caught a cab home. I stayed with her again in the cab and as she walked up to her apartment. I think she could tell I was lonely, and maybe a little scared, and that I didn't want to be left alone.

She paused at the door. *"You want to come in?"*

"Sure," I said. *"For a nightcap."*

We went up and Ellen poured herself a glass of wine.

"So I guess you know all my secrets now," she said.

"Not really," I said. *"I've been avoiding stuff that isn't my business."*

"Like what?"

"There's some stuff about a guy called Jason," I told her.

"Really? There are 'Jason' bits of my brain?"

"Yeah, there are."

"But you don't know what's in them?"

"I'm sort of afraid of what I might find," I said.

"What about the rest of it?"

"Well, I saw a lot of childhood memories trying to find answers to pop culture questions. You were happy? Your mom and dad seem great."

"They are, and I guess I was. Although I'm not sure who should be telling whom."

"You should tell me."

"High school was hard."

"Greg? I saw just a little about him."

"My first love."

"It seemed pretty intense."

"Isn't it weird? You knowing more about me than I do?"

"I don't really. Did you love him?"

"I did. I maybe still do, despite everything. A pregnancy and him walking away. Sometimes I think I'd still run off with him if he just called."

"You really love the people you love," I said.

"You mean everything's black and white. Love or hate."

"No, I just mean you commit yourself. Completely. It's cool. Beau-

tiful, really."

"Don't most people?" Ellen asked.

"No. Most people—me—are full of hedges and caveats. Provisional commitments."

"I admire it. People who can withhold judgment. I wish I did more of it."

"I wish I did less. Like the way you jumped into teaching and never looked back. Got a job at Flynn and decided that's where you wanted to retire," I said.

"It sounds stupid when you talk about it like that."

"No. God, I wish I could do that. I'm going to stumble through life, always dissatisfied."

"It's not wrong to keep an open mind."

We were silent for a while as she drank her wine.

"Are you going to look at the 'Jason' file?" she asked.

"Do you want me to?"

"I don't know."

"I'll wait."

"Are you going to go away now?"

"Do I have to? If I go away, I'll just be in my cell. And we'd have to figure out how I'd get you back again."

"Where are they keeping you?"

I told her what I knew about where I was locked up, as well as some of the compromising information I had learned about what Gerry was up to. Who knew if Ellen might need it.

"Are you scared?"

"That I'll never get out? That Tom and Gerry will figure out some way to lock me away forever?"

"Yeah."

"Yeah."

Ellen took another sip of wine. I watched her make a decision.

"Stay then. Stay in my mind. I'll try to sleep."

"I'll fight off any nightmares." I was mostly joking.

She went into the bedroom and lay down. I could see she was thinking about whether she would change into her pajamas. And if she could go to the bathroom.

"Pretend I'm not here."

"It's embarrassing."

"Like we're camping or something."

Eventually she went to the bathroom, shutting the door behind her, as if I was in the bedroom. She changed out of her clothes there too.

When she took her shirt off she saw her own breasts in the mirror. She thought her breasts were misshapen, and hated the way the left one was bigger than the right one.

"No," I said, as gently as possible, not wanting to ruin the mood. *"You're not seeing them right. They're nice."* I tried to convey the beauty I saw in them.

I don't know if it worked, but she gave me a cheeky thought and took her pants off then, too. She put her pajamas on and went over to her bed. In my little cell on Boylston Street, I was aroused. We could have had like, the greatest phone sex in the world.

But I also saw she was tired and still shy.

"Are you all right in there?" she asked, more formally, as if we had not been sharing naked pictures of her moments ago. Better than Snapchat.

"Yes," I said. *"I'm great."*

"Good night, Jason."

"Good night."

"It's nice to have you over."

"It's nice to be here."

I could tell that the very banality of our exchanges had put her close to sleep. I stayed quiet in a corner and watched, somewhat in awe, as she was overcome by the sleep of the just. Sleep, that is, that came upon her without anger or regret. Sleep that came after knowing you had done your very best that day.

I stayed with her, watching neurons fire through her dreams. I caught an image or two, but mostly I couldn't make sense of them. I didn't look at any of her thoughts about me. Instead, I stood like a sentry in the corner of her mind, waiting to welcome her back to consciousness.

In my cell, I did not sleep that night. It was more restful to stay awake within Ellen's brain as she slept in her bed with a duvet curled up around her, than to sleep in my own brain, on my thin cot, covered in a scratchy blanket.

And I was afraid to break the connection. What if I couldn't find her again? That had happened on Friday. I didn't want it to happen again.

Ellen woke early on Monday. I watched her go through her morning ablutions without speaking, sensing she needed time. Finally, after a cup of coffee, I tentatively said, *"Good morning."*

"You're here?" she said, and it was sort of like the sparkle of sun coming out from behind a cloud. I'd never experienced someone so happy to see me. Or at least communicate with me. Not that I knew, anyway.

After breakfast, she got her car and headed out to get Joe. She had a little trouble at the office, as they tried to put roadblocks in her way to prevent her from taking Joe on an outing, but she dealt with them patiently and firmly. Twenty minutes after reaching Wind Haven, we were back on the road with Joe.

"How are you today, Joe?" she asked.

"I hope he's compos mentis *today,"* I said to her.

He grunted. "Usual."

"We're going to the Boston Garden, today. For a tour," Ellen told him.

"Goddamn Garden. Waste of fucking space. What was wrong

with the old one, I want to know?"

"Yes. Jason said you told him there was a problem with the new Garden."

Getting Joe started was not the problem. Keeping him focused was. He was not in good shape today. His brain was caught in some ancient dispute with his wife over fixing the lawn mower, and whatever we did, he would circle back to that.

Ellen tried to describe to him the room I had seen in the mind of the person who placed the bomb, and he would get angry and start talking about the stupid Garden design. But before he could tell us anything useful, he would switch back to his wife.

"The mower's no good. It's not a matter of fixing. It's a gas leak. As soon as catch fire as cut the grass. We'd have to replace the whole damn engine. It's better to buy a new one."

Then he would eye Ellen suspiciously and say, "Don't look at me like that, Donna. It's not my fault you invited your sisters over today. They'll just have to have their tea in the long grass."

I suppose it was Ellen's idea first, but the answer was obvious. I had to leave Ellen and go into Joe, and see what answers I could salvage. I suggested to Ellen that she stop at St. Mary's before going to Toby's because I was pretty good at casting there.

Our diversion through St. Mary's was going to make us a little late to Toby's, so Ellen called in on her cell. As we arrived, the St. Mary's T stop was its usual sedate and empty self. Ellen helped Joe out of the car and had him sit in the little bus shelter next to the T line.

"Get him a little riled up about the mower. Then I'll have something to look for."

"I don't think that'll be hard," Ellen said.

I hesitated. I didn't want to leave. I had been hoping to stay in her mind all day, and maybe another night. It made sitting in my cell bearable.

"You've got to, Jason."

"I know."

"I'll miss you too, okay."

"Yeah."

We spent another few seconds in communion, then I said, *"I'm breaking off now."*

"Cool."

I was suddenly alone in my cell. I checked in the guard's mind. He was surprised at how calm and immobile I seemed to be. Most people in solitary got restless. But it was no skin off his nose. It was nice to be watching someone who wasn't any trouble.

I breathed deeply and cast back again to St. Mary's. I felt like I knew just where I was heading. Still, the first two times, I overshot. After that, I landed in the right place, but I couldn't find Joe.

Time passed and I figured Ellen would be getting nervous. I cast again and finally found a key phrase, *"the goddamn mower,"* floating through the air, and followed it in. I had found Joe.

It was worse than I expected. I still don't know what sort of diagnosis Joe may have had, but I've read up on Alzheimer's and other brain diseases of the elderly since then, and I know that some conditions can cause their brains to shrink noticeably in size. It's not like all the old connections are there but somehow inaccessible; rather, many of the connections are actually gone, like they'd crumbled into dust.

At any rate, Joe's brain was a poor thing. The thoughts were faint and sporadic. Instead of the synapses firing like the climax of a Fourth of July fireworks show, they went off like a couple of kids had found a box of soggy, leftover fireworks a couple of days later. Pop . . . wait . . . wait . . . wait . . . wait . . . wait . . . maybe they're done . . . wait . . . pop!

My subjective sensation was that Joe's thoughts were whispered and disjointed. I had to move carefully in his mind, like it was an old book whose pages might disintegrate with rough contact.

Moving around his brain was like swimming in molasses, and finding the answers I needed was like navigating a website without a search function.

Hank says I'm mixing metaphors now something terrible and I have to stop. But the point is, it was different and difficult. My presence in Joe's brain was less robust than my presence in Ellen's. And the hope I had that I could use my ESP to go into Joe's brain and cure whatever ailed him—reestablish his old synapses and re-organize things—was quickly disabused.

But, that said, I was in his mind and we could talk.

"Hi, Joe. It's Jason."

"Where the hell are you?"

"I'm in your mind. It's my new superpower. Reading minds. ESP."

"Well, I'll be damned," was all Joe said. There was no sense of violation or even surprise that I was there. Maybe being old and in a nursing home, he had little sense of privacy left. Also, with his brain dysfunction, maybe hearing voices was nothing new.

"Can you tell Ellen I'm here and that we can go to Toby's."

He did so, and Ellen got him back in the car and headed in toward Boston while I searched Joe's mind gingerly.

Because I was in Joe, and he took in what was going on around him only in fits and starts, often misunderstanding what was happening, I only have a disjointed view of the rest of the day. According to what people told me afterwards, the initial meeting went down something like this. Ellen organized everyone, figuring out roles and responsibilities. She decided that Sylvia would stay outside and be our contact if anything went wrong. Raffy set up a connection for Sylvia that would give her direct access into our phones' cameras and microphones. She would document our activities and, if anything went wrong, like we were arrested, she could send out the video feed to a dozen high-traffic social media sites at the press of a button.

Hank, meanwhile, was studying bomb disposal techniques based on a thousand pages of web research he had managed to print out since that morning, and some manuals from Iraq that Toby had managed to acquire from the son of one of his friends who had been one of the *Zero Dark Thirty* guys over there. The latter were useful because they were completely confidential. The publicly available stuff about disarming bombs ("render safe procedures" they were called, or "RSPs") was all for outdated technology.

I had seen Hank do this kind of thing before, that is, learn a new subject from scratch. It was a wonder to behold, if you could convince yourself he was not putting you on. He would sit glancing at and flipping pages as if he was absorbing them, which in fact he was. Raffy, for one, was dubious.

"Jason says it'll work," Ellen assured him. "I saw Hank do something similar when we hacked into the traffic cams."

It was hard looking at Hank through Joe's eyes. I should say that, in some ways, Joe was not a very nice person. He was quite a racist and had ideas about women and violence that were, at the very best, quite nineteenth century. I knew a lot of this just from talking to him. But getting in his mind made it just that much more obvious.

On the other hand, age had mellowed him, and you could tell there was confusion and guilt about a lot of his old beliefs. I even wondered whether his Alzheimer's or whatever it was might have a psychological, self-flagellating component—guilt about who he had been was slowly destroying his brain. (Ellen insists I add this disclaimer: My speculation here has no scientific basis and it is completely irresponsible for me to suggest that people suffering from dementia might be somehow at fault for their own sickness because of past sins. Here ends the disclaimer.)

Whatever. I do think some accumulated wisdom was trying

to poke its way through his beliefs. Ideas about how you couldn't judge people on appearances. About how much he owed to women and minority colleagues. About how he could have been kinder to his kids. I wasn't inclined to judge him too harshly. I'd been in a lot of people's minds by this point, and I was not sure how many of us could really withstand the pressures of having our innermost thoughts revealed to the world.

At one point, an almost obscene image flashed in Joe's mind of Hank being fanned by a girl who looked like Betty Boop. I had no how idea to interpret that until Ellen told me later that Toby had gone around the group expressing his admiration of Hank. "Not often you see a future Nobelist in action." I guess this had gotten enough of Penny's attention to cause her to sit and watch Hank flip through pages.

Raffy insisted on testing Hank, and was taken aback when Hank answered every question easy as pie, even unfair ones about foot-notes in 10-point type. Joe heard Raffy mutter, "Memorization is a trick, not intelligence." But, to give Raffy credit, he didn't seem to hold it against Hank, and they geek-bonded later by going out to Home Depot together to buy Hank a tool belt filled with pliers, screwdrivers, electrician's tape and other bomb-disposal necessities.

Not long after they returned, Ellen turned her attention to Joe. "Are you and Jason finding where we have to go?"

Joe said, "How about it, Jason, how are we doing in there?"

Joe could not subvocalize, but spoke out loud, hoping whatever he said would form a picture in his mind that I could see. It worked okay. And my being in his mind did allow me to keep him on track for the most part. He had stopped obsessing over the fight with his wife about the lawnmower and was following the action around him better. On the occasions where he might have lost the thread of a conversation, I was able to serve as something like a go-between, linking messages between synapses that were lost in the growing empty spaces of his brain.

I suspect that I had him functioning at a higher level than he had in years. And we were making progress. He was remembering more and more details about the TD Garden's infrastructure, and I was pretty sure that it was only a matter of time before we found what we were looking for. It looked like the bomb had been placed in the subbasement where the main generators were. And now all we had to do was figure out how to get there from whatever public spaces we saw during the tour.

"We're making progress," I said through Joe, "I think we're ready to roll."

After Joe repeated this to the group, Ellen announced a weapons check.

"I have my tool belt," Hank said.

"That's your utility belt. Like Batman!" Penny said.

"Yeah, like Batman," Hank said.

I was stunned. What the hell was Penny doing making a comics reference? What the hell was Hank doing acknowledging it like it was clever?

"You need your tools," Ellen said. "I mean real weapons. What do we have?"

Toby showed the knife that he had stuck me with, and Raffy produced a short sword from his Benedict Cumberbatch-like raincoat.

"Right," Ellen said, grabbing them and putting them on Toby's kitchen counter, "we're leaving those at home."

"What if we need to fight our way out?" Toby asked.

"Not in the plans," Ellen said. "No fighting. No violence. And definitely no stabbing."

What an unlikely tour we must have seemed. Sylvia had told her friend that we were some college buddies in town from Ohio or somewhere, and all we wanted was a tour of the Garden. But the only guy anywhere near Sylvia's age was Toby, who had a wicked Boston accent. And Raffy in his raincoat, Penny, more demure and gorgeous than ever, Hank clanking in his tool belt, imperfectly covered up by an XXL sweatshirt. Not to mention, Ellen starting right in on questions about security, and insisting that we (they, I guess) stop by the video-monitoring room and greet two women in private security uniforms watching television screens. It must have been insanely clear that none of us had the slightest interest in basketball or hockey.

But the tour guide, Brittney, was a perky young woman, utterly dedicated to giving her spiel in the most mechanical way possible, and paying no attention at all to her customers. Most of what happened, of course, I had to piece together talking with people afterwards, because all I saw of the Garden was what Joe was thinking about. And with me helping, he was very focused on finding his bearings vis-à-vis the subbasement housing the generator.

As the tour went on, though, he was getting more confident that he knew his way around. Then, near the end of the tour, back in a long corridor after having seen the visiting team's locker room, I realized Joe knew where we were and where we had to go. The funny thing was that Joe himself was hardly aware of the neurons firing. I think he would have missed it if I hadn't been there.

"That door," I practically shouted at him. *"That's the one, isn't it?"*

"Well . . . " Joe said out loud.

"I mean, it will lead where we need to go, right?"

"Yeah."

"Tell Ellen. Now."

Joe and I were behind the group now as the cheery tour leader was driving us relentlessly forward.

I saw Joe call out hoarsely. "Ellen!" She turned and he gestured to the door. "This is it."

As I heard the story later, Ellen had a whispered conversation with Raffy, who peeled off the group and made his way to the video-monitor room, while Ellen grabbed Brittney and turned her attention back to Joe.

"My uncle is not feeling well."

"Where is the other one going?"

"To get help." Then, politely but firmly, Ellen led Brittney back to Joe.

"What's wrong with him?" Brittney asked.

"Does this door open?" Ellen asked, indicating the door Joe had pointed out.

Penny tried it. It was locked.

"Do you have the key?"

"It's not on the tour."

"I really need a bathroom. There was one in the locker room we passed, right?" Ellen started to walk back.

"That's not for visitors," Brittney said, but Ellen had already disappeared into the locker room. "Oh, for heaven's sake."

"We should all go," Toby said. "She has a loose bladder. When she gets nervous for her uncle, she really needs to go." And Penny, Joe and Toby followed Ellen back to the locker room.

"What's wrong with your uncle anyway?" Brittney asked, hurrying to catch up with the wayward group.

"Nothing!" said Joe, losing the thread a little.

"See?" Toby said apologetically. "How many playoff games did you say that the Bruins won in this building?"

Gathered back in the visitor's locker room, Brittney talked, clearly annoyed, while waiting for Ellen. Once Ellen received a text from Raffy indicating that the video monitors were out of commission, she emerged.

Raffy was always vague about how he had put the screens out of commission. He would just insist that the women were seriously underemployed doing nothing but watching video screens.

He just helped them make the process more efficient, and showed them how to set up some Amazon reselling accounts so they could supplement their income from the Garden. A few months after the event, he boasted to Ellen, "I'm still in touch with them. They're doing well enough that they may quit their day jobs."

At any rate, Ellen nodded to Toby and Penny, who seemed to know, like magic, what was expected of them. They each took one of Brittney's arms and marched her over to Ellen. Ellen expertly searched the young woman, removing her radio, her keys and a can of mace.

"Toby, you'll watch her, right?"

"Yes."

Man, I wish I had been there for this. Instead, all I saw was Joe's inadequate rendering of the scene, from whose perspective there was almost no conflict or menace. It did, however, ignite in his memory scenes of an imperious Katherine Hepburn giving Humphrey Bogart orders in the *African Queen*.

"What's happening?" Brittney asked.

"Nothing bad, and we won't hurt you," Ellen said. "We're stopping an attack on the Garden."

Then Hank, Ellen, Joe, Penny and I hurried back to the door and tried Brittney's keys. One of them opened the door and we found ourselves in a narrow service corridor.

This is where Joe took over. With a little help from me, his synapses really began to sparkle. We turned left and right and left again, finding ourselves in another long corridor that ended at another door with a sign on it: "No unauthorized persons beyond this point."

"In there is the boiler," Joe said. "We get in there and there's a passage to the right that heads to a stairway. Down the stairs is the generator. It happens to be located directly between two load-bearing pillars. Stupid!"

"Okay," Ellen said, "but how do we get in there? None of Brittney's keys fit this door."

There was a moment of silence.

"Go on," I prompted Joe. He had nearly forgotten his key insight.

"Back a hundred feet or so there is a break room with a small kitchen. It's got a vent for one of the air ducts. If you can climb in there and go about 50 feet, it will tee. Take the right tee for about 50 feet. It slopes downward. You'll be at another vent above the generator. There should be plenty of crawl space in the duct."

"Okay," Ellen said. "Lead us to the kitchen."

Five minutes later, we were there. The vent, near the ceiling, had a grate in it. Hank and Penny pulled a table over to take a look. Using a pair of pliers, Hank removed the grate and handed it down to Ellen.

Penny boosted Ellen up and she climbed into the vent. Then Ellen put an arm down and helped Hank up from above while Penny lifted him from below.

"Hey, it's dark in here," Hank said.

"Oh, that's right. I have some flashlights," Penny said, handing up two flashlights to Hank and Ellen. "I have one more for myself."

"No," Ellen said, looking Penny and Joe over. "You guys stay here. We need to move quickly and it's a small space. You got us here. That's the main thing."

"Are you sure?"

"Take care of Joe. Go back and gather up Raffy and Toby. Any last thing we should know, Joe? Jason?"

I saw Joe think, his brain working better than I had seen it before.

"Nah," he said.

"I don't see anything either," I said to Joe. But he didn't repeat my thought.

With that, Ellen and Hank turned to leave, and any direct knowledge of the story would have been over if I hadn't had a sudden premonition that all was not well with Hank. I was thinking back over his behavior. When he was learning something new, he sometimes went into his shell in order to be able to concentrate. But he had been unusually noncommunicative. Of course, he was brilliant, but there was a lot of pressure on him. Was he up to what we were asking of him? I had a sudden conviction that he and Ellen might need me yet.

Like leaving Ellen before, though for entirely different reasons, it was somewhat of a wrench to leave Joe. He was functioning better with me in his brain to help him concentrate and to carry messages. That improvement would stop when I left, and I realized that the man I knew would slowly fade away, and, likely, disappear altogether within the year. For all his irascibility, I liked Joe and wished I could do more for him.

"*Goodbye, Joe,*" I said in his mind.

"You leaving?" he asked, and I saw fear and loss in his thoughts.

"*Yeah, but I'll be back.*"

"In my mind?"

"*To visit. In real life. If I ever get out of my cell.*"

"Okay then." By which I saw he meant, "I'll miss you."

"*Me too,*" I said. "*Tell Penny that I'm going with Ellen and Hank.*"

He did, and in his thoughts I saw a great happiness as Penny smiled at him.

"Take care of him, Penny," I thought. "He's going to be disoriented when I leave. Get him home safely." But I didn't know how to communicate that to her through Joe. I hoped she would figure it out herself.

I cut the connection with Joe and began to cast for Hank and Ellen. I was getting better at casting, and had discovered that if I had been in an area, it was easier to hit it again. There was some sort of "muscle memory" involved. I cast quickly before I lost the feel.

I heard the buzz of thoughts and dove in. My heart wanted to join Ellen's thoughts again, but it was Hank who really needed me. And it was his thoughts, madly reviewing "RSPs" to stave off incipient claustrophobia, that I connected with first.

I zoomed in and found a quiet little place in his brain to sit and watch the proceedings as he and Ellen crawled down the tunnel, trying to avoid hitting their heads. I didn't announce myself to Hank because I knew he had a horror of someone in his mind, and I didn't want to add to his worries. Instead, I sat quietly, limiting my ESP to the thoughts at the surface of his brain. I figured that, if I was going to read his mind contrary to his wishes, I could at least try to minimize the invasiveness of my presence.

At the tee, as Joe had described, the left vent led down to the subbasement. Negotiating this was tricky because it angled steeply down. In order not to just tumble down into the basement, Ellen and Hank had to brace themselves against the walls of the vent as they climbed down. For all their qualities, my friends were not athletes, and this exercise took a good deal of their concentration and strength.

Ellen went first, partly to prove to Hank, who was near hyperventilating, that it could be done. Hank followed tentatively, afraid of falling and pushing his legs and back into the sides of the duct with more force than he needed. I wondered if I could give him some sort of soothing message without revealing my presence. But I didn't know how. I just watched him suffer as he descended.

Finally, they managed to make it down to the subbasement. Ellen had already found the latch and opened the vent by the time Hank arrived, so all they had to do was turn around and drop down the few feet from the ceiling to the floor. They managed this without grace but also without injury.

"Now what?" Hank said.

"Find the bomb," Ellen said.

Actually, the first thing Ellen did was find the light switch so that they could put away their flashlights. I had a sudden panicked thought: what if I had been wrong? What if there was no bomb? I had just gotten my friends in an awful lot of trouble.

But that thought did not last long. As soon as Hank and Ellen turned around with the lights on, the bomb was obvious. A big ugly thing, draped around the generator, between the weight-bearing pillars, just as I had previously seen, and as Joe had predicted. And the whole thing connected to an electric clock silently ticking down the seconds to detonation. Lovely.

The truth is, however, that my first sight of it, through Hank's thoughts, probably made it look scarier and more complex than it was. What I saw was a monster and Hank thinking, "I don't know how to do this."

Which was quite possible if the bomb was really modern. Because, as I mentioned above, Hank had only had a chance to see those bits and pieces of classified material about disarming modern IEDs, the stuff Toby had managed to scrounge up. Nothing comprehensive.

And even if he had all the information, bomb-disposal units had equipment. They had protective suits. They had robots. They had tools. Hank had nothing but a knife, pliers, scissors, a screwdriver and a flashlight. What if the bomb was booby-trapped?

"I'm too young to die," Hank thought. And then, *"I have things to contribute to the world. Why are we fucking doing this at all? It's Jason's fault. He is so immature. I should have had the superpowers. Then maybe some good would have come from them . . ."*

Let's just say, things devolved from there. It was hard hearing all the awful thoughts Hank secretly harbored about me. I won't lie about that. But I didn't take offense as I might have. He was ranting. He was scared. I understood that. For all his brilliance and self-control, Hank wasn't used to dealing with life-and-death situations. He wasn't used to the potential for bodily harm. None of us were. He was panicking and he took his panic out on me.

In a way, I figured (or at least I tried to tell myself), it was a sign how much he cared about me. Like kids who blame their parents when things go wrong. It's not because they hate their parents, necessarily, but because they trusted their parents to make everything right.

Not that it didn't hurt, particularly because many of his accusations were true. I had been immature. I had gotten him and Ellen in trouble over and over again. I hadn't done anything useful.

But, and maybe this was just an advantage of being disembodied, I somehow maintained a calm within Hank's panicked brain.

"Hey, Hank," I said.

That stopped him.

"Yeah, I'm here."

Guilt piled on the panic.

"Don't worry about that," I said. *"The thing is the bomb."*

"I can't do it." The panic was still strong, and now it was being supplemented by the fear of having me inside of him.

"Sure you can, Hank. When has your brain let you down?" I was using my most soothing mental voice.

"That has absolutely fucking zero to do with it," he shouted out loud.

I had gone down the wrong path. I saw that at once. Everyone told him he was smart, but being smart wasn't what mattered. It was being calm. That's what he needed now. And the more he thought about how he was smart, and how much people were relying on brilliance, when his brains couldn't do anything about the problem in front of him, the more pressure and panic he felt.

"Fuck, you're right," I said. *"But, c'mon. It'll be fun."*

"Not if I fucking blow myself and Ellen to smithereens."

"Jesus, Hank! I wouldn't entrust the two people I love most in the world to you if I thought that was the case."

The use of the word "love" threw him off, but not for long.

"Right, like you have any idea."

"We'll do it together. Like we've done everything. Tell me about the

bomb. Describe it. Then we cut the red wire."

"*The blue wire, you mean.*"

It was an internet meme we sometimes laughed about. I guess there was some forgettable '70s action flick—I never knew the name—where the whole plot came down to a 50-50 chance to stop a bomb from exploding. The hero just had to guess which of two wires to cut.

"*So tell me what you see.*" I'd distracted him and broken his panic. Now if I could engage his analytical side, maybe he could stay focused.

He started describing the bomb to me.

"*The bomb consists of six barrels, wired together. If it's like a fertilizer bomb, one will be full of ignition material. Say nitroglycerin.*"

"*I wonder how the guy got that stuff down here,*" I said.

"*Irrelevant,*" Hank said. "*Anyway, the barrels are connected by two wires and surrounded by blast shields designed to direct the main impact into the pillars. A timer attaches to each of the wires, and will presumably provide the shock to detonate the nitroglycerin. I say we are talking about a half megaton explosion.*"

"*Sounds complicated,*" I said.

"*Oh, it's not,*" Hank said, forgetting his panic in his urge to correct me. "*It's among the most basic bombs imaginable. And there's no protection of the bomb casing. You can see that easily enough. It was meant not to be discovered so there was no need to hide or booby-trap the mechanism.*"

"*But can you defuse it?*"

"*I think so. I expect I could simply cut the wires between the timer and the bomb. But it would be safer to unscrew the timing canister and RSP that part of the bomb first.*"

"*Well, let's do it,*" I said.

"What's that?" Ellen said.

We turned.

"I heard something."

Listening, we heard it too. Footsteps down the corridor. Lots of them.

"Hurry," I said to Hank.

He did, moving with the confidence I had in him. He unscrewed the back of the timing canister and examined the triggering mechanism inside. I tamped down another wave of panic, just like spreading a blanket over open flames.

We heard a key in the lock of the door.

Hank followed the wires with his eyes, calculating what led where, what did what.

The door opened. Men in SWAT uniforms with machine guns burst in.

"There's a bomb!" Ellen yelled, moving to stand in front of Hank.

The men didn't shoot, instead moving quickly and silently to take positions around us.

I saw Hank start to lose concentration. Gently, I moved his focus back to the bomb. At the same time, I saw realization blossom in Hank's mind that he understood how the bomb worked. He knew what to do.

"Do it," I said. *"You know you're right."*

Tom followed the SWAT team in, and stood at the door surrounded by his men with guns.

Ellen moved between Hank and the police. "He's disarming it. Don't disturb him, and don't fucking shoot anything!"

No one said anything. They just watched Hank do his work. His fingers moved, disconnecting the trigger mechanism from the timer, eventually leaving the wires leading into the barrels hanging loose and disconnected. It took maybe another three minutes.

When he was done, he stood up from where he had been crouching over the timer. "Okay," he said. "It should be okay. We just have to open the barrels and remove the detonating materials without too much shock."

That's when the SWAT guys rushed up, manhandling Hank and Ellen down onto the floor. As they did so, Hank's last thought, before the police—accidentally on purpose, I'm sure—smashed his head into the floor and he blacked out, breaking our connection, was *"Go Professor X!"*

CHAPTER 33

Professor X

I looked up to find myself in my cell and stiff as hell. I'd been in Ellen's or Joe's or Hank's head for almost 24 hours straight, and my own head hurt like a motherfucker, and I desperately needed to pee.

I made a motion for the bedpan, thinking I would use it and then go back as quickly as I could to Ellen, or someone, so I didn't lose track of what was happening.

How could I have been so stupid? Of course, Tom and Gerry had put my friends back under surveillance. Why hadn't I checked on that while I was in Tom's mind? Now, they were in Tom and Gerry's hands.

And where was the fucking bedpan? I looked up and saw Gerry grinning at me from the little window onto my cell. I went right into his mind, which he was expecting. He wanted me to see how hopeless my situation was. How he had all the evidence he needed of my friends planting a bomb in the Boston Garden, and how they would be sent their separate ways to live out the rest of their lives in maximum-security facilities. He wanted me to read the glee and assuredness in his mind that I, meanwhile, would just be quietly disappeared offshore, never to be heard from again. It was all a done deal.

"*What the fuck?*" I said into his mind.

I saw him look up and around, surprised out of his smugness. He still didn't know I could send as well as receive.

"*I told you about the bomb. We were disarming it. Someone else planted it. Why can't you understand that?*"

I saw the answer before he said anything. It was the same stupid lack of logic that he had displayed ever since he learned I had ESP. Even if I was innocent, I was too dangerous, both to him and to the general security of the United States. I and my friends had to be taken down. For the good of the country.

Also, he suspected that we were behind the attack in the first place. We could have just gone to the police if we thought something was up.

"*I did fucking go to the police,*" I said. "*I went to you. And you somehow refused to listen. And then you set up a reporting network so none of my friends could talk to the police.*"

His thought, again before he said anything, was, "*How did you know about that?*"

"*Because I can read your mind wherever you are, idiot. It doesn't matter if there's a wall between us, or if you're in fucking Natick.*"

He was off-balance, confused by the revelation of my new ability, and by my responding to his thoughts before he even realized himself that he had had them. He was also angry that the point of his visit, to lord his total victory over me, had gotten so offtrack.

"*Okay, I get it.*" I thought to him. "*You're afraid of what I can do. But we don't have to be enemies. I won't say anything about your business. And you let me and my friends go. No harm, no foul.*"

He thought, "*But you'll keep quiet anyway. I'll keep you in solitary.*"

And then he realized he couldn't keep me quiet if I could project my thoughts into other people from a distance. And then we realized at the same time, that in fact he could. But it didn't involve me being in some jail somewhere.

His next thought was crystal clear: *"Gotta gas him."* He grabbed his radio to call up to the guard to tell him to hit the switch. That was when I suddenly realized what Hank meant by thinking, "Go Professor X." Marvel's Charles Xavier, played in the movies by the suave Patrick Stewart, could not only read minds and communicate, he could also control people. He could seize their brains and determine their actions and beliefs. At first I had thought I could only read minds, then I had learned I could also transmit my thoughts. Who's to say that I didn't have the ability to control people too?

I was already in Gerry's mind. Now, having no idea what I was doing, I reached out and imagined myself grabbing control of his primary motor cortex. Right! What does that even mean? Did Gerry pause briefly? Was there a brief hiccup in his movements? I imagined there was, but I couldn't say for sure. Whatever the case, it didn't stop him for long. He radioed his guard. There was a hissing sound and smoke started emerging from a small nozzle in the ceiling that looked like a sprinkler. I felt oddly at peace.

When I woke up, I was in a hospital room surrounded by Ellen, Toby, Sylvia, Raffy and Penny. And next to me, with a big bandage around his head, was Hank.

"Uh," I groaned. I felt like I had woken up from the best sleep I had ever had. But my thoughts were still fuzzy.

"Good morning, sleepy head," Ellen said.

"Where are we?"

"Brigham and Women's. It's Wednesday. Hank needed stitches, and they wanted to keep you under surveillance until the effects of the gas wore off."

"But . . . ." My head buzzed with questions that I couldn't quite formulate. It turned out that it didn't matter. My friends were eager to explain.

As Hank was learning bomb-defusing techniques, Ellen and Sylvia had discussed the danger that, rather than get credit for defusing the bomb, they would get blamed for placing it. Ellen told Sylvia all the dirt I had on Gerry, and how she had never trusted him. Sylvia said to leave it to her, and, while everyone else was headed to the Garden, she contacted a couple of former students. One was now an assistant to the mayor on neighborhood policing, and the other was a journalist on the crime desk for the *Boston Beacon*.

Sylvia told them a story about how a colleague had reported overhearing a conversation about a bomb in the Garden and had been ignored. She said her friends were taking matters into their own hands. Then she invited them to come and watch the video stream that Raffy had set up of their tour of the Garden. So they watched as Hank found and defused the bomb, and the police broke in and smashed his head open.

At that point, they called some friends, including a senior lawyer at the Civilian Review Board, basically a police oversight group, and a captain in the Massachusetts Standards and Training division. As it happened, both these guys had had previous run-ins with Gerry and were sympathetic to our story. (And were very interested to pick my brain about Gerry's relationship with Rory the Sparrow.) At any rate, they knew what precinct Tom would bring my friends to for processing after their arrest, and met them there.

After a whole lot of shouting, bluff and bluster about who had the biggest dicks, the lawyers won the day, getting my friends released and forcing Tom to take them to the safe house where I was being kept. They arrived shortly after I was gassed, and gave Gerry a dressing down about unlawful arrest and potential civil and criminal penalties if I was not released immediately.

So thanks to Sylvia, here I was, free and unharmed, while Gerry and Tom were facing a long investigation, not only into their response to my tip about the bombing, but also about other activity going back years.

I found that I had no real desire for them to be punished. I didn't like Tom, but I had spent enough time in his mind to catch a glimpse of some of the childhood trauma and daddy issues he was dealing with. As for Gerry . . . well, could I judge him any more harshly than I judged Joe? Both had worked hard to protect their city, Gerry as the head of Boston's antiterrorism unit, Joe as fire chief in Everett. Sure, Gerry had been compromised by old friendships and prejudices, but it was hardly any different with Joe. Maybe hardly different for any of us. In the end, Gerry would be an old man, burdened with unhappiness and regret, and then we would forgive him for his crimes, just as we forgave Joe for the cruelties of his youth.

My only worry, really, was that somehow the investigators would uncover information about my powers. And maybe, whatever compromising material Gerry had collected to keep me in line. But it turned out, with some prompting from Sylvia's contact in the mayor's office, that the investigators decided that, to avoid the potential of a messy lawsuit, and the spread of ridiculous stories about superpowered humans, it might be best if all Gerry's files about me were suppressed.

In the end, it only took a few days for the regular police to catch the guy who *had* planted the bomb in the TD Garden. It turned out that only so many people had the opportunity to bring four barrels of explosives down to the Garden subbasement.

So all was well, if very little of it thanks to me. Sure, I had overheard about the bomb, but that was about it. I just sat in a room, while my friends risked their lives finding and defusing it. And then I had lain peacefully anesthetized while Sylvia had organized my escape from Tom and Gerry's safe house.

"Go Professor X," Hank had told me, thinking I might have mental abilities I had not explored. But, like all my other powers, my ESP had limits. I couldn't control people like puppets. Honestly, it was a relief.

Yeah, people were sometimes annoying. Sometimes they were worse than annoying. They were evil. And I guess Professor X could change that. He could change Vladimir Putin into Mother Theresa. Kim Jong-un into Abraham Lincoln. But in the real world, was that really a good idea? At the beginning of this year, I might have given it a try. Now, I was wary about exercising that kind of power.

Was that wrong? Was I abdicating the great responsibility that came with great power? Or was I exercising it? Murderous dictators are not a sympathetic bunch. But would I make the world a better place if I comic-book-magicked them into Gandhi? Or would I cause nuclear war through some sort of butterfly effect? I mean, it's not like any of my other attempts to intervene had ever worked out. Maybe man—a single ordinary schlub of a man like me—was not meant to manipulate the fate of the universe. Or was that just cowardice talking? I didn't know, and I still don't.

CHAPTER 34
A Girlfriend

Hank and I didn't get discharged until late in the day. When, at last, we walked out of the hospital, our friends met us to take us out to the North End for a celebratory dinner.

"Can you manage that?" Penny asked Hank, whose head was still bandaged. "That was a pretty big knock you got." When Hank insisted he wanted to come, Penny went over and took his arm. I was amazed to find that I felt no jealousy.

But then, there wasn't much to be jealous of. I ended up sitting next to fucking Captain America. Well, Ellen, actually, but the way she had taken control of our bunch of ragtag talents and turned them into the Mission Impossible team, she might as well be the Captain.

We weren't quite ready to announce our couplehood, which made it all the nicer. We sat up straight, knees touching, and just occasionally allowed our hands to graze up to inappropriate places on each other's thighs. There was joy in the transgression.

At dessert, Toby read a short article that had appeared on the *Boston Beacon* website under the byline of Sylvia's former student, Raphaela Consuelo:

BOSTON TEACHERS HELP SAVE GARDEN: The Police Department expressed its extreme gratitude today to five teachers from Flynn High School, Toby Jones, Sylvia Reining, Raffy Sanso, Penelope Waters and Ellen Rinaldi, as well as an MIT graduate student, Hank Nichols, and a former Everett Fire Chief, Joe Butler, for their aid in foiling a plot to blow up the TD Garden during tonight's game between the Celtics and the Oklahoma Thunder. "The group not only uncovered the plot, but at great personal risk managed to defuse the bomb," said head of the Massachusetts Police Special Investigations unit, Gerald Spence. "The city owes a great debt of gratitude to these men and women." According to police sources, they have significant clues as to the perpetrators of the attempted crime and expect to announce arrests soon.

"You must remember Raphaela, Toby," Sylvia said. "Petite, very driven. Graduated 10 years ago. Played the part of Ariel in *The Tempest*?"

"Umm," Toby said, and I could not tell if he remembered her or not.

"But Jason, you weren't mentioned," Raffy said. "We should correct that."

"No, it's better like this," I said. "People would ask what I did. I wouldn't know how to answer. You guys were the real heroes."

"Another round?" Raffy asked. "My treat?"

We all looked surprised, but Toby turned him down first. "No, I missed school today. Need an early start tomorrow."

"Me too," Sylvia said.

"How about you guys?" Raffy asked Ellen, Hank, Penny and me.

"Hank should be in bed," Penny said.

"Yeah, I should take him," I said.

"Don't be foolish," Penny said. "What do you know about head wounds? I'll take care of him."

I was tempted to slip into her mind then. What were her intentions toward my friend? Were they honorable? I am sure the idea of dating a Nobel Prize winner was attractive, but would she love him and leave him? And what about Hank? Did he want her ministrations? He had never liked her. Had that changed? Maybe the bump on his head had done him some good.

But Hank was grinning, and honestly, how bad could it be for him to finally lose his virginity to a 10. And I was distracted by Ellen scraping her nails down my leg. Also, I was feeling lazy. I'd been in one person's mind or another for almost 24 hours straight, and now I was enjoying some me time.

Penny led Hank away, and Raffy was left with just Ellen and me.

"Beer or something stiffer?"

"Funny you should ask that," Ellen said, "I think Jason and I should head home too."

"Fine," Raffy said. "At least I've gotten out of buying a round. I'm heading to the bar."

We watched him go, find the most beautiful waitress in the restaurant, order what was likely the most expensive scotch on the menu and start a flirtation.

"I guess it's good night," I said.

"I thought you could read minds," Ellen replied.

"Yeah, but . . ."

"Or at least hear." She leaned over me and said, "I chose Raffy's second option."

CHAPTER 35
A Job

I woke up the next morning far too early. Ellen was still asleep, her brown hair spread across her pillow like silly string.

I could tell that I still had my ESP. Now that I was attuned, the whole world buzzed with inchoate thoughts calling to me to come and take a look. The buzzing itself wasn't too annoying, sort of like the white noise of a waterfall, but it could have been a temptation, like the smell of a grilled steak to a hungry person. But at that moment, lying next to Ellen's zonked-out form, I wasn't hungry.

I didn't even want to look into the mind of the girl beside me and finally check out her Jason files. I had a suspicion, now, what was in them, and that it might have made flattering reading. But they were hers and not mine. And I wanted it to stay that way.

What I wanted to do was get to school and teach a fucking good lesson on Anne Frank. And then read the junior papers on *The Great Gatsby*.

Which was a good thing, on the one hand, because when I finally tried, later that day, to slip into the mind of one of the freshmen who was having a full-blown emotional breakdown, I couldn't. Instead, I just had to sit with him and do things the old-fashioned way, with talking, patience and sympathy. Very inefficient.

And over the entire summer, no matter what Ellen, Hank and I tried, we never could find another superpower.

On the other hand, it was a bad thing, because that Tuesday afternoon, Principal Snowe called me to her office and said she was rescinding her offer of employment.

"You ran out of school on Friday without telling anyone where you were going," she said, "and then were absent without excuse again on Monday."

"I told the secretary on Friday," I said, feeling desperate. "And Monday, I was . . . I was . . . I couldn't call in."

"Jason, you told the secretary you'd be out for an hour. You were gone all afternoon. And there is no excuse for not being able to call in."

"Not even being arbitrarily arrested and imprisoned for no good reason?" I thought, and tried desperately to enter her mind to see if there was any way to save the situation.

"Jason, I like you. The kids like you. And you're a good teacher. But the most important thing in this profession is reliability. This last incident was the final straw. I just can't rely on you. I'm sorry."

I spent two days feeling sorry for myself before I finally explained to Ellen what had happened. She told me not to worry, she'd fix things. And she did.

The next day, Toby and Sylvia met with Principal Snowe and explained that I had been helping them save the Garden, and that she had to rehire me or they would quit.

And the day after that, I had another meeting and was reinstated. Principal Snowe, it must be said, was not particularly magnanimous about it.

"I'm being blackmailed, it seems," she said, "to give you another chance. I don't like it. Not one bit. But I have little choice. The school cannot afford to lose Toby and Sylvia at this time. So you have a job next year and next year only. But let me be clear, you will be under very close scrutiny. Very close indeed."

Not a ringing endorsement. But a job. The job I wanted, at least for next year.

CHAPTER 36

And a Future

There's more of course. There almost always is. But it doesn't involve superpowers, sadly. Or maybe not sadly. That was a chapter of my life, and the life of my friends, that ended at the end of my first year of teaching.

We never really found out what caused me to develop superpowers. Whether it was a mass delusion, as Ellen theorized, or something else. Hank and I spent a lot time talking about it. We really did. But we never came up with a better explanation.

My guess is that the origin story, if there is one at all, is literary. I mean, I was following a well-worn narrative, in which a young man has a chance to try out multiple paths in a journey of self-discovery.

So you could say there is no origin story and there never was. Or maybe the facts of the story originate in the narrative necessity of the story itself. This is circular, sure, but more a productive, hermeneutic circularity, than the vicious type.

Ellen and Hank roll their eyes when I talk like this. They think it is the highest order of bullshit. But, whatever the case, the events of these months changed us, or at least most of us.

Raffy probably would have followed the same course with or

without the bizarre interlude. He left Flynn the next year because, as I have mentioned, one of his many projects got major funding. A couple of years later it did an IPO, leaving him a multimillionaire. He's now calling himself an angel investor, handing out mediocre advice to younger versions of himself in exchange for usurious interests in their work. Rumor has it that he has also taken an uxorious interest in one of the entrepreneurs he is advising, and a big, tech-bro blowout wedding in the Maldives is in the works. But I won't be invited, and I couldn't afford to attend if I was.

Hank and Penny only dated for the summer because Hank had a grant to do some research at CERN and he wanted to be "free to play the field" in Switzerland.

Penny survived the breakup. She parlayed her "Hero" status into a weatherwoman gig on Channel 5. She had a schtick that became super popular. When the weather first got really cold, she'd introduce her weather reports singing Foreigner's *Cold as Ice*. When it got hot, she'd sing *Hot Blooded*. Her Boston-based minor celebrity status was cemented by marrying a Red Sox relief pitcher.

Hank's newfound sexual confidence won him a string of partners at MIT and beyond. He is still at MIT, now as an associate professor on a fast track to tenure. He is still studying subjects that are too esoteric for me to even know how to refer to them. But I am not sure he is happy. At dinner the other day, I suggested to him that he might get more out of his relationships if he allowed them to last a little longer. He rolled his eyes.

Joe died in October of the following year. He had lost most memory of who he was and who we were. But the events at the Garden had given him some status at Wind Haven, and Ellen and I made sure he was treated well until the end. Hank, Ellen and I were all there keeping a vigil when he died.

I never heard anything about Tom again, but I saw a short article in the paper about Gerry a few years after these events. He'd quit the police force and gone to seminary. Still later, I heard that he had become a popular priest in Dorchester.

Toby is still at Flynn and still going strong. In the past year, he not only led the track team to a Massachusetts state championship, but also somehow convinced 20 sophomores to sign up for introductory Latin. He has come out publicly, and Ellen and I have gotten to know his partner, Abe. Abe should be way out of Toby's league. Not only is he an extraordinarily handsome older gentleman, but he is a professional tabla player, a stained-glass artist, and vegan.

Sylvia has given up teaching at Flynn, but got a gig as a consultant to the Boston Public Schools. She works half the time and makes twice as much, but says she misses being in the classroom.

Ellen? Well, Ellen and I are still together, which she will admit is a very good thing, but not so often that it gives me a big head. In addition to teaching biology, she is dean of students at Flynn. She is still our Captain America, making sure the Flynn team works together. And sometimes we think that we are making a difference. For what it's worth, Flynn was the only Boston Public School to receive a grade of A in the recent federally mandated review of the New and Revised Common Core implementation.

Lastly me. I discovered that superpowers were pretty useless. That being a hero was overrated. That, like with children, sometimes you just had to let the world find its own way and solve its own problems. And that Ellen Rinaldi was a fox, both in and out of bed.

I discovered that I liked teaching, and that I wanted to do more of it, at least for the immediate future. Was I done with the more prestigious gigs? Well, for the moment. But I remember my James Bond: never say never again.

And every once in a while, no more than once a month or so, I jump off a curb, or stick a pin into my finger, or try to grab for a salt shaker a little out of my reach, just to test that my powers have not come back. Just the other day, I almost convinced myself that I had grown an unnatural inch or two. But Ellen said that was just because my cords had shrunk in the wash.

So there you are. Unheroic, but still trying.

Acknowledgments

Thank you to all of my friends and readers who provided comments and advice for this book. These include, at the very least: Dean Whitlock, Watt Alexander, Rick Greenwald, Mike Pepe, Stephanie Cabot, Neyla Downs, Jason Overdorf, Diana Burnham, Justin Albert, Corisande Albert, Kevin Mills and Emily Rhinelander. Thanks also to: Chris and Andrew for providing me with an important and distinctive name; Bri, Emily and TA for the use of their high jump mats; Ryan for his amazing leaps and patient modeling; and, of course, Chan, Linc, Julie and Hollie.

High-quality, professional copy-editing and advice was provided by Alan Berolzheimer. Beautiful text and cover designs were provided by Linnea Spelman. Of course, I am responsible for any of the errors that remain in the book.

All my love and gratitude go to my mother and father, my first readers and most long-suffering supporters.

And to my kids, Alex, Lily and Casey, who, among their many wonderful qualities, provided an excuse to buy lots and lots of comic books.

And to Katy, for everything.

Ted has worked as a lawyer, teacher, consultant, paralegal, receptionist and soccer coach in Hanover, Boston, New York, Ann Arbor, London, Philadelphia, Hamburg and Berlin. He and his wife live in Thetford, Vermont. In 2016, Ted published *The Blue Marauders*, a book about a travel soccer team.